Bonus Book!

For your enjoyment, we've added in this volume *Night Heat,* a favorite book by Brenda Jackson!

Selected praise for *New York Times* and *USA TODAY* bestselling author Brenda Jackson

"Brenda Jackson writes romance that sizzles and characters you fall in love with."
—*New York Times* and *USA TODAY* bestselling author Lori Foster

"Jackson's trademark ability to weave multiple characters and side stories together makes shocking truths all the more exciting."
—*Publishers Weekly*

"Jackson's characters are wonderful, strong, colorful and hot enough to burn the pages."
—*RT Book Reviews* on *Westmoreland's Way*

"The kind of sizzling, heart-tugging story Brenda Jackson is famous for."
—*RT Book Reviews* on *Spencer's Forbidden Passion*

"This is entertainment at its best."
—*RT Book Reviews* on *Star of His Heart*

BRENDA JACKSON

is a die "heart" romantic who married her childhood sweetheart and still proudly wears the "going steady" ring he gave her when she was fifteen. Because Brenda believes in the power of love, her stories always have happy endings. In her real-life love story, Brenda and her husband of thirty-eight years live in Jacksonville, Florida, and have two sons.

A *New York Times* bestselling author of more than seventy-five romance titles, Brenda is a recent retiree who now divides her time between family, writing and traveling with Gerald. You may write Brenda at P.O. Box 28267, Jacksonville, Florida 32226, by email at WriterBJackson@aol.com or visit her website at www.brendajackson.net.

BRENDA JACKSON

FEELING THE HEAT

&

NIGHT HEAT

Harlequin®

Desire

ISBN-13: 978-0-373-83776-2

FEELING THE HEAT & NIGHT HEAT

Copyright © 2012 by Harlequin Books S.A.

The publisher acknowledges the copyright holder
of the individual works as follows:

FEELING THE HEAT
Copyright © 2012 by Brenda Streater Jackson

NIGHT HEAT
Copyright © 2006 by Brenda Streater Jackson

Recycling programs
for this product may
not exist in your area.

Printed in U.S.A.

CONTENTS

Dear Reader,

Wow! It's time to savor another Westmoreland. I actually felt the heat between Micah and Kalina while writing their story.

Feeling the Heat is a story of misunderstanding and betrayal. Kalina thinks Micah is the one man who broke her heart. A man she could never love again. Micah believes if Kalina really knew him she would know he could never cause her pain. So he is determined that she get to know the real Micah Westmoreland. He also intends to prove that when a Westmoreland wants something—or someone—he will stop at nothing to get it, and Micah Westmoreland wants Kalina Daniels back in his life.

Relax and enjoy Micah and Kalina's story. And with every Brenda Jackson book it is suggested that you have a cold drink ready. Be prepared to feel the heat!

Happy reading!

Brenda Jackson

FEELING THE HEAT

* * *

To Gerald Jackson, Sr.
My one and only. My everything.

To all my readers who enjoy reading about the
Westmorelands, this book is especially for you!

To my Heavenly Father. How Great Thou Art.

For we walk by faith, not by sight.
—*II Corinthians* 5:7

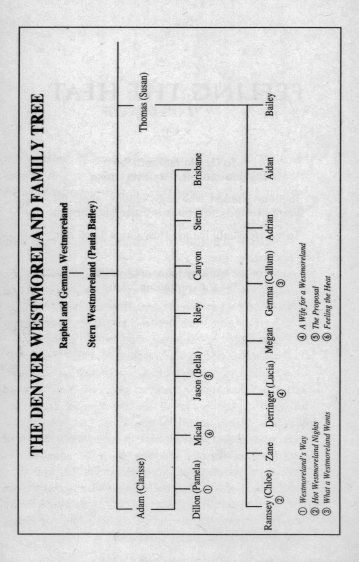

THE DENVER WESTMORELAND FAMILY TREE

Raphel and Gemma Westmoreland

Stern Westmoreland (Paula Bailey)

Thomas (Susan)

Adam (Clarisse)

Dillon (Pamela) ①   Micah ⑥   Jason (Bella) ⑤   Riley   Canyon   Stern   Brisbane

Ramsey (Chloe) ②   Zane   Derringer (Lucia) ④   Megan   Gemma (Callum) ③   Adrian   Aidan   Bailey

① *Westmoreland's Way*
② *Hot Westmoreland Nights*
③ *What a Westmoreland Wants*
④ *A Wife for a Westmoreland*
⑤ *The Proposal*
⑥ *Feeling the Heat*

CHAPTER ONE

MICAH WESTMORELAND glanced across the ballroom at the woman just arriving and immediately felt a tightening in his gut. Kalina Daniels was undeniably beautiful, sensuous in every sense of the word.

He desperately wanted her.

A shadow of a smile touched his lips as he took a sip of his champagne.

But if he knew Kalina, and he *did* know Kalina, she despised him and still hadn't forgiven him for what had torn them apart two years ago. It would be a freezing-cold day in hell before she let him get near her, which meant sharing her bed again was out of the question.

He inhaled deeply and could swear that even with the distance separating them he could pick up her scent, a memory he couldn't seem to let go of. Nor could he let go of the memories of the time they'd shared together while in Australia. And there had been many. Even now, it didn't take much to recall the whisper of her breath on him just seconds before her mouth—

"Haven't you learned your lesson yet, Micah?"

He frowned and shot the man standing across from him a narrowed look. Evidently his best friend, Beau Smallwood, was also aware of Kalina's entry, and Beau, more than anyone, knew their history.

Micah took a sip of his drink and sat back on his heels. "Should I have?"

Beau merely smiled. "Yes, if you haven't, then you should. Need I remind you that I was there that night when Kalina ended up telling you to go to hell and not to talk to her ever again?"

Micah flinched, remembering that night, as well. Beau was right. After Kalina had overheard what she'd assumed to be the truth, she'd told him to kiss off in several languages. She was fluent in so damn many. The words might have sounded foreign, but the meaning had been crystal clear. She didn't want to see him again. Ever. With the way she'd reacted, she could have made that point to a deaf person.

"No, you don't need to remind me of anything." He wondered what she would say when she saw him tonight. Had she actually thought he wouldn't come? After all, this ceremony was to honor all medical personnel who worked for the federal government. As epidemiologists working for the Centers for Disease Control, they both fell within that category.

Knowing how her mind worked, he suspected she probably figured he wouldn't come. That he would be reluctant to face her. She thought the worst about him and had believed what her father had told her. Initially, her believing such a thing had pissed him off—until he'd accepted that given the set of circumstances, not to mention how well her father had played them both for fools, there was no way she could not believe it.

A part of him wished he could claim that she should have known him better, but even now he couldn't make that assertion. From the beginning, he'd made it perfectly clear to her, as he'd done with all women, that he wasn't interested in a serious relationship. Since Kalina was as into her career as he'd been into his, his suggestion of a no-strings affair hadn't bothered her at all and she'd agreed to the affair knowing it wasn't long-term.

At the time, he'd had no way of knowing that she would eventually get under his skin in a way that, even now, he found hard to accept. He hadn't been prepared for the serious turn their affair had taken until it had been too late. By then her father had already deliberately lied to save his own skin.

"Well, she hasn't seen you yet, and I prefer not being around when she does. I do remember Kalina's hostility toward you even if you don't," Beau said, snagging a glass of champagne from the tray of a passing waiter. "And with that said, I'm out of here." He then quickly walked to the other side of the room.

Micah watched Beau's retreating back before turning his attention to his glass, staring down at the bubbly liquid. Moments later, he sighed in frustration and glanced up in time to see Kalina cross the room. He couldn't help noticing he wasn't the only man watching her. That didn't surprise him.

One thing he could say, no matter what function she attended, whether it was in the finest restaurant in England or in a little hole in the wall in South Africa, she carried herself with grace, dignity and style. That kind of presence wasn't a necessity for her profession. But she made it one.

It had been clear to him the first time he'd met her—

that night three years ago when her father, General Neil Daniels, had introduced them at a military function here in D.C.—that he and Kalina shared an intense attraction that had foretold a heated connection. What had surprised him was that she had captivated him without even trying.

She hadn't made things easy for him. In fact, to his way of thinking, she'd deliberately made things downright difficult. He'd figured he could handle just about anything. But when he'd later run into her in Sydney, she'd almost proven him wrong.

They'd been miles away from home, working together while trying to keep a deadly virus from spreading. He hadn't been ready to settle down. While he didn't consider himself a player in the same vein as some of his brothers and cousins, women had shifted in and out of his life with frequency once they saw he had no intention of putting a ring on anyone's finger. And he enjoyed traveling and seeing the world. He had a huge spread back in Denver just waiting for the day he was ready to retire, but he didn't see that happening for many years to come. His career as an epidemiologist was important to him.

But those two months he'd been involved with Kalina he had actually thought about settling down on his one hundred acres and doing nothing but enjoying a life with her. At one point, such thoughts would have scared the hell out of him, but with Kalina, he'd accepted that they couldn't be helped. Spending time with a woman like her would make any man think about tying his life with one woman and not sowing any more wild oats.

When he'd met the Daniels family, he'd known immediately that the father was controlling and the daughter was determined not to be controlled. Kalina was a woman who liked her independence. Wanted it. And she was determined to demand it—whether her father went along with it or not.

In a way, Micah understood. After all, he had come from a big family and although he didn't have any sisters, he did have three younger female cousins. Megan and Gemma hadn't been so bad. They'd made good decisions and stayed out of trouble while growing up. But the youngest female Westmoreland, Bailey, had been out of control while following around her younger hellion brothers, the twins Aidan and Adrian, as well as Micah's baby brother, Bane. The four of them had done a number of dumb things while in their teens, earning a not-so-nice reputation in Denver. That had been years ago. Now, thank God, the twins and Bailey were in college and Bane had graduated from the naval academy and was pursuing his dream of becoming a SEAL.

His thoughts shifted back to Kalina. She was a woman who refused to be pampered, although her father was determined to pamper her anyway. Micah could understand a man wanting to look out for his daughter, wanting to protect her. But sometimes a parent could go too far.

When General Daniels had approached Micah about doing something to keep Kalina out of China, he hadn't gone along with the man. What had happened between him and Kalina had happened on its own and hadn't been motivated by any request of her father's, although she now thought otherwise. Their affair had been one of those things that just happened. They had been attracted to each other from the first. So why she would assume he'd had ulterior motives to seek an affair was beyond him.

Kalina was smart, intelligent and beautiful. She possessed the most exquisite pair of whiskey-colored eyes, which made her honey-brown skin appear radiant. And the lights in the room seemed to highlight her shoulder-length brown hair and show its luxuriance. The overall picture she presented would make any male unashamedly aware of his sexuality. As he took another sip of his drink and glanced across the room, he thought she looked just as gorgeous as she had on their last date together, when they had returned to the States. It had been here in this very city, where they'd met, when their life together had ended after she discovered what she thought was the truth. To this day, he doubted he would ever forgive her father for distorting the facts and setting him up the way he had.

Micah sighed deeply and took the last sip of his drink, emptying his glass completely. It was time to step out of the shadows and right into the line of fire. And he hoped like hell that he survived it.

Micah was here.

The smile on Kalina's face froze as a shiver of awareness coursed through her and a piercing throb hit her right between the legs. She wasn't surprised at her body's familiar reaction where he was concerned, just annoyed. The man had that sort of effect on her and even after all this time the wow factor hadn't diminished.

It was hard to believe it had been two years since she had found out the truth, that their affair in Australia had been orchestrated by her father to keep her out of Beijing. Finding out had hurt—it still did—but what Micah had done had only reinforced her belief that men couldn't be trusted. Not her father, not Micah, not any of them.

And especially not the man standing in front of her with the glib tongue, weaving tales of his adventures in the Middle East and beyond. If Major Brian Rose thought he was impressing her, he was wrong. As a military brat, no one had traveled the globe as much as she had. But he was handsome enough, and looked so darn dashing in his formal military attire, he was keeping her a little bit interested.

Of course, she knew that wherever Micah was standing he would look even more breathtaking than Major Rose. The women in attendance had probably all held their breath when he'd walked into the room. As far as she was concerned, there wasn't any man alive who could hold a candle to him, in or out of clothes. That conclusion reminded her of when they'd met, almost three years ago, at a D.C. event similar to this one.

Her father had been honored that night as a commissioned officer. She'd had her own reason to celebrate in the nation's capital. She had finally finished medical school and accepted an assignment to work as a civilian for the federal government's infectious-disease research team.

It hadn't taken her long to hear the whispers about the drop-dead-gorgeous and handsome-as-sin Dr. Micah Westmoreland, who had graduated from Harvard Medical School before coming to work for the government as an infectious-disease specialist. But nothing could have prepared her for coming face-to-face with him.

She had been rendered speechless. Gathering the absolute last of her feminine dignity, she had picked up her jaw, which had fallen to the floor, and regained her common sense by the time her father had finished the introductions.

When Micah had acknowledged her presence, in a voice that had been too sexy to belong to a real man, she'd known she was a goner. And when he had taken her smaller hand in his in a handshake, it had been the most sensuous gesture she'd ever experienced. His touch alone had sent shivers up and down her spine and put her entire body in a tailspin. She had found it simply embarrassing to know any man could get her so aroused, and without even putting forth much effort.

"So, Dr. Daniels, where is your next assignment taking you?"

She was jerked out of her thoughts by the major's question. Was that mockery she'd heard in his voice? She was well aware of the rumor floating around that her father pretty much used his position to control her destinations and would do anything within his power to keep her out of harm's way. That meant she would never be able to go anyplace where there was some real action.

She'd been trying to get to Afghanistan for two years and her request was always denied, saying she was needed elsewhere. Although her father swore up and down he had nothing to do with it, she knew better. Losing her mother had been hard on him, and he was determined not to lose his only child, as well. Hadn't he proven just how far he would go when he'd gotten Micah to have that affair with her just to keep her out of Beijing during the bird-flu epidemic?

"I haven't been given an assignment yet. In fact, I've decided to take some time off, an entire month, starting tomorrow."

The man's smile widened. "Really, now, isn't that a coincidence. I've decided to take some time off, too, but I have only fourteen days. Anywhere in particular that you're going? Maybe we can go there together."

The man definitely didn't believe in wasting time, Kalina thought. She was just about to tell the major, in no uncertain terms, that they wouldn't be spending any time together, not even if her life depended on it, when Brian glanced beyond her shoulder and frowned. Suddenly, her heart kicked up several beats. She didn't have to imagine why. Other men saw Micah as a threat to their playerhood since women usually drooled when he was around. She had drooled the first time *she'd* seen him.

Kalina refused to turn around, but couldn't stop her body's response when Micah stepped into her line of

vision, all but capsizing it like a turbulent wave on a
blast of sensual air.

"Good evening, Major Rose," he said with a hard
edge to his voice, one that Kalina immediately picked
up on. The two men exchanged strained greetings, and
she watched how Micah eyed Major Rose with cool ap-
praisal before turning his full attention to her. The hard
lines on his face softened when he asked, "And how
have you been, Kalina?"

She doubted that he really cared. She wasn't surprised he was at this function, but she *was* surprised he
had deliberately sought her out, and there was no doubt
in her mind he'd done so. Any other man who'd done
what he had done would be avoiding her like the plague.
But not Dr. Micah Westmoreland. The man had courage
of steel, but in this case he had just used it foolishly. He
was depending on her cultured upbringing to stop her
from making a scene, and he was right about her. She
had too much pride and dignity to cause a commotion
tonight, although she'd gone off on him the last time
they had seen each other. She still intended to let him
know exactly how she felt by cutting him to the core,
letting it be obvious that he was the last person she
wanted to be around.

"I'm fine, and now if you gentlemen will excuse me,
I'll continue to make my rounds. I just arrived, and
there are a number of others I want to say hello to."

She needed to get away from Micah, and quick. He
looked stunning in his tux, which was probably why so
many women in the room were straining their necks to
get a glimpse of him. Even her legs were shaky from

being this close to him. She suddenly felt hot, and the cold champagne she'd taken a sip of wasn't relieving the slow burn gathering in her throat.

"I plan to mingle, myself," Micah said, reaching out and taking her arm. "I might as well join you since there's a matter we need to discuss."

She fought the urge to glare up at him and tell him they had nothing to discuss. She didn't want to snatch her arm away from him because they were already getting attention, probably from those who'd heard what happened between them two years ago. Unfortunately, the gossip mill was alive and well, especially when it came to Micah Westmoreland. She had heard about him long before she'd met him. It wasn't that he'd been the type of man who'd gone around hitting on women. The problem was that women just tended to place him on their wish list.

"Fine, let's talk," she said, deciding that if Micah thought he was up to such a thing with her, then she was ready.

Fighting her intense desire to smack that grin right off his face, she glanced over at Major Rose and smiled apologetically. "If you will excuse me, it seems Dr. Westmoreland and I have a few things to discuss. And I haven't decided just where I'll be going on vacation, but I'll let you know. I think it would be fun if you were to join me." She ignored the feel of Micah's hand tightening on her arm.

Major Rose nodded and gave her a rakish look. "Wonderful. I will await word on your plans, Kalina."

Before she could respond, Micah's hand tightened on her arm even more as he led her away.

"DON'T COUNT ON Major Rose joining you anywhere," Micah all but growled, leaning close to Kalina's ear while leading her across the ballroom floor toward an exit. He had checked earlier and the French doors opened onto the outside garden. It was massive and far away from the ball, so no one could hear the dressing-down he was certain Kalina was about to give him.

She glared at him. "And don't count on him doing otherwise. You don't own me, Micah. Last I looked, there's nothing of yours on my body."

"Then look again, sweetheart. Everything of mine is written all over that body of yours. I branded you. Nothing has changed."

They came to a stop in front of what was the hotel's replica of the White House's prized rose garden. He was glad no one was around. No prying eyes or over-eager ears. The last time she'd had her say he hadn't managed to get in a single word for dodging all the insults and accusations she'd been throwing at him. That wouldn't be the case this time. He had a lot to say and he intended for her to hear all of it.

"Nothing's changed? How dare you impose your presence on me after what you did," she snarled, transforming from a sophisticated lady to a roaring lioness. He liked seeing her shed all that formality and cultural adeptness and get downright nasty. He especially liked that alteration in the bedroom.

He crossed his arms over his chest. "And what exactly did I do, other than to spend two months of what I consider the best time of my life with you, Kalina?"

He watched her stiffen her spine when she said, "And I'm supposed to believe that? Are you going to stand here and lie to my face, Micah? Deny that you weren't in cahoots with my father to keep me away from Beijing, using any means necessary? I wasn't needed in Sydney."

"I don't deny that I fully agreed with your father that Beijing was the last place you needed to be, but I never agreed to keep you out of China."

He could tell she didn't want to hear the truth. She'd heard it all before but still refused to listen. Or to believe it. "And it wasn't that you weren't needed in Sydney," he added, remembering how they'd been sent there to combat the possible outbreak of a deadly virus. "You and I worked hard to keep the bird-flu epidemic from spreading to Australia, so it wasn't just sex, sex and more sex for us, Kalina. We worked our asses off, or have you forgotten?"

He knew his statement threw her for a second, made her remember. Yes, they might have shared a bed every night for those two months, but their daytime hours weren't all fun and games. No one except certain members of the Australian government had been aware that their presence in the country had been for anything other than pleasure.

And regardless of what she'd thought, she had been needed there. He had needed her. They had worked well together and had combated a contagious disease. He had already spent a year in Beijing and had needed to leave when his time was up. Depression had started to set in with the sight of people dying right before his eyes, mostly children. It had been so frustrating to work nonstop trying unsuccessfully to find a cure before things could get worse.

Kalina had wanted to go to Beijing and get right in the thick of things. He could just imagine how she would have operated. She was not only a great epidemiologist, she was also a compassionate one, especially when there was any type of outbreak. He could see her getting attached to the people—especially the children—to the point where she would have put their well-being before her own.

That, and that alone, was the reason he had agreed with her father, but at no time had he plotted to have an affair with her to keep her in Sydney. He was well aware that all her hostility was because she believed otherwise. And for two years he had let her think the worst, mainly because she had refused to listen to anything he had to say. It was apparent now that she was still refusing to listen.

"Have you finished talking, Micah?"

Her question brought his attention back to the present. "No, not by a long shot. But I can't say it all tonight. I need to see you tomorrow. I know you'll be in town for the next couple of days and so will I. Let's do lunch. Even better, let's spend that time together to clear things up between us."

"Clear things up between us?" Kalina sneered in an angry whisper as red-hot fury tore through her. She was convinced that Micah had lost his ever-loving mind. Did he honestly think she would want to spend a single minute in his presence? Even being here now with him was stretching her to the limit. Where was a good glass of champagne when she wanted it? Nothing would make her happier right now than to toss a whole freakin' glass full in his face.

"I think I need to explain a few things to you, Micah. There's really nothing to clear up. Evidently you think I'm a woman that a man can treat any kind of way. Well, I have news for you. I won't take it. I don't need you any more than you need me. I don't appreciate the way you and Dad manipulated things to satisfy your need to exert some kind of power over me. And I—"

"Power? Do you think that's what I was trying to do, Kalina? Exert some kind of *power* over you? Just what kind of person do you honestly think I am?"

She ignored the tinge of disappointment she heard in his voice. It was probably just an act anyway. At the end of those two months, she'd discovered just what a great actor Micah could be. When she'd found out the truth, she had dubbed him the great pretender.

Kalina lifted her chin and straightened her spine. "I think you are just like all the other men my father tried throwing at me. He says jump and you all say how high. I thought you were different and was proven wrong. You see Dad as some sort of military hero, a legend, and whatever he says is gospel. And although Micah is a book in the Bible, last time I checked, my father's name was not. I am twenty-seven and old enough to make my own decisions about what I want to do and where I want to go. And neither you nor my father have anything to say about it. Furthermore—"

The next thing she knew, she was swept off her feet and into Micah's arms. His mouth came down hard, snatching air from her lungs and whatever words she was about to say from her lips.

She struggled against him, but only for a minute. That was all the time it took for those blasted memories of how good he tasted and just how well he kissed to come crashing over her, destroying her last shred of resistance. And then she settled down and gave in to what she knew had to be pleasure of the most intense kind.

GOD, HE HAD missed this, Micah thought, pulling Kalina closer into his embrace while plundering her mouth with an intensity he felt in every part of his body. She had started shooting off her mouth, accusing him of things he hadn't done. Suddenly, he'd been filled with an overwhelming urge to kiss her mouth shut. So he had.

And with the kiss came memories of how things had been between them their last time together, before anger had set in and destroyed their happiness. Had it really been two years since he'd tasted this, the most delectable tongue any woman could possess? And the body pressed against his was like none other. A perfect fit. The way she was returning the kiss was telling him she had missed this intimate connection as much as he had.

Her accusations bothered him immensely because there was no truth to what she'd said. He, of all people, was not—and never would be—a yes-man to her father, or to anyone. Her allegations showed just how little she knew him, and he intended to remedy that. But for now, he just wanted to enjoy this.

He deepened the kiss and felt the simmer sear his flesh, heat his skin and sizzle through to his bones. Then there was that surge of desire that flashed through his veins and set off a rumble of need in his chest. He'd found this kind of effect from mouth-to-mouth contact with a woman only happened with Kalina. She was building an ache within him, one only she had the ability to soothe.

Over the past two years he'd thought he was immune to this and to her, but the moment she had walked into the ballroom tonight, he'd known that Kalina was in his blood in a way no other woman could or would ever be. Even now, his heart was knocking against his ribs and he was inwardly chanting her name.

Lulled by the gentle breeze as well as the sweetness of her mouth, he wrapped his arms around her waist as something akin to molten liquid flowed over his senses. Damn, he was feeling the heat, and it was causing his pulse to quicken and his body to become aroused in a way it hadn't in years. Two years, to be exact.

And now he wanted to make up for lost time. How could she think he had pretended the passion that always flowed through his veins whenever he held her, kissed her or made love to her? He couldn't help tunneling his fingers through her hair. He'd noticed she was wearing it differently and liked the style on her. But there was very little about Kalina Daniels that he didn't like. All of which he found hard to resist.

He deepened the kiss even more when it was obvious she was just as taken, just as aroused and just as needy as he was. She could deny some things, but she couldn't deny this. Oh, she was mad at him and that was apparent. But it was also evident that all her anger had transformed to passion so thick that the need to make love to her was clawing at him, deep.

Conversation between an approaching couple had Kalina quickly pulling out of his arms. All it took was one look in her eyes beneath the softly lit lanterns to see the kiss had fired her up.

He leaned in, bringing his lips close to hers. "You are wrong about me, Kal. I never sold out to your father. I'm my own man. No one tells me what to do. If you believe otherwise, then you don't really know me."

He saw something flicker in her eyes. He also felt the tension surrounding them, the charged atmosphere, the electrified tingle making its way up his spine. Now more than ever, he was fully aware of her. Her scent. Her looks.

She was breathtaking in the sexy, one-shoulder, black cocktail dress that hugged her curves better than any race car could hug the curves at Indy. There was a sensuality about her that would make any man's pulse rise. Other men had been leery of approaching her that night in D.C. when he'd first flirted with her. After all, she was General Daniels's daughter and it was a known fact the man had placed her on a pedestal. But unlike the other men, Micah wasn't military under her father's command. He was civilian personnel who didn't have to take orders from the general.

She surprised him out of his thoughts when she leaned forward. He reached out for her only to have his hands knocked out of the way. The eyes staring at him were again flaring in anger. "I'm only going to say this once more, Micah. Stay away from me. I don't want to have anything else to do with you," she hissed, her breath fanning across his lips.

He sighed heavily. "Obviously you weren't listening, Kalina. I didn't have an affair with you because your father ordered me to. I was with you because I wanted to be. And you're going to have a hard time convincing me that you can still be upset with me after having shared a kiss like that."

"Think what you want. It doesn't matter anymore, Micah."

He intended to make it matter. "Spend tomorrow with me. Give it some thought."

"There's nothing to think about. Go use someone else."

Anger flashed through him. "I didn't use you." And then in a low husky tone, he added, "You meant a lot to me, Kalina."

Kalina swallowed. There was a time when she would have given anything to hear him say that. Even now, she wished that she could believe him, but she could not forget the look of guilt on his face when she'd stumbled across him discussing her with her father. She had stood in the shadows and listened. It hadn't been hard to put two and two together. She had fled from the party, caught a cab and returned to the hotel where she quickly packed her stuff and checked out.

Her father had been the first one she'd confronted, and he'd told her everything. How he had talked Micah into doing whatever it took to keep her in Sydney and away from Beijing. Her father claimed he'd done it for her own good, but he hadn't thought Micah would go so far as to seduce her. An affair hadn't been in their plan.

"You don't believe you meant something to me," he said again when she stood there and said nothing.

She lifted her chin. "No, I don't believe you. How can I think I meant anything to you other than a good time in bed when you explicitly told me in the very beginning that what we were sharing was a no-strings affair? And other than in the bedroom, you'd never let me get close to you. There's so much about you I don't know. Like your family, for instance. So how can you expect me to believe that I meant anything to you, Micah?"

Then, without saying another word, she turned and walked back toward the ballroom. She hoped that would be the end of it. Micah had hurt her once, and she would not let him do so again.

CHAPTER TWO

BY THE TIME Micah got to his hotel room he was madder than hell. He slammed the door behind him. When he had returned to the ballroom, Kalina was nowhere to be found. Considering his present mood, that had been a good thing.

Now he moved across the room to toss his car keys on a table while grinding his teeth together. If she thought she'd seen the last of him then he had news for her. She was sadly mistaken. There was no way he would let her wash him off. No way and no how.

That kiss they'd shared had pretty much sealed things, whether she admitted it or not. He had not only felt her passion, he'd tasted it. She was still upset with him, but that hadn't stopped them from arousing each other. After the kiss, there had been fire in her eyes. However, the fire hadn't just come from her anger.

He stopped at a window and looked out, breathing heavily from the anger consuming him. Even at this hour the nation's capital was busy, if the number of cars on the road was anything to go by. But he didn't want to think about what anyone else was doing at the moment.

Micah rubbed his hand down his face. Okay, so Kalina had told the truth about him not letting her get too close. Thanks to an affair he'd had while in college, he'd been cautious. As a student, he'd fallen in love with a woman only to find out she'd been sleeping with one of her professors to get a better grade. The crazy thing about the situation was that she'd honestly thought he should understand and forgive her for what she'd done. He hadn't and had made up in his mind not to let another woman get close again. He hadn't shared himself emotionally with another woman since then.

But during his affair with Kalina, he had begun to let his guard down. How could she not know when their relationship had begun to change from a strictly no-strings affair to something more? Granted, there hadn't been any time for candlelight dinners, strolls in the park, flowers and such, but he had shared more with her than he had with any other woman…in the bedroom.

He drew in a deep breath and had to ask himself, "But what about outside the bedroom, man? Did you give her reason to think of anything beyond that?" He knew the answer immediately.

No, he hadn't. And she was right, he hadn't told her anything about his family and he knew why. He'd taken his college lover, Patrice, home and introduced her to the family as the woman he would one day marry. The woman who would one day have his children. She had gotten close to them. They had liked her and in the end she had betrayed them as much as she had betrayed him.

He lifted his head to stare up at the ceiling. Now he could see all his mistakes, and the first of many was letting two years go by without seeking out Kalina. He'd been well aware of what her father had told her. But he'd assumed she would eventually think things through and realize her dad hadn't been completely truthful with her. Instead, she had believed the worst. Mainly because she truly hadn't known Micah.

His BlackBerry suddenly went off. He pulled it out of his pocket and saw it was a call from home. His oldest brother, Dillon. There was only a two-year difference in their ages, and they'd always been close. Any other time he would have been excited about receiving a call from home, but not now and not tonight. However, Dillon was family, so Micah answered the call.

"Hello?"

"We haven't heard from you in a while, and I thought I would check in," Dillon said.

Micah leaned back against the wall. Because Dillon was the oldest, he had pretty much taken over things when their parents, aunt and uncle had died in a plane crash. There had been fifteen Westmorelands—nine of them under the age of sixteen—and Dillon had vowed to keep everyone together. And he had.

Micah had been in his second year of college and hadn't been around to give Dillon a hand. But Ramsey, their cousin, who was just months younger than Dillon, had pitched in to help manage things.

"I'm fine," Micah heard himself saying when in all honesty he was anything but. He drew in a deep breath and said, "I saw Kalina tonight."

Although Dillon had never met Kalina he knew who she was. One night while home, Micah had told

Dillon all about her and what had happened to tear them apart. Dillon had suggested that he contact Kalina and straighten things out, as well as admit how he felt about her. But a stubborn streak wouldn't let Micah do so. Now he wished he would have acted on his brother's advice.

"And how is she?"

Micah rubbed another hand down his face. "She still hates my guts, if that's what you want to know. Go ahead and say I told you so."

"I wouldn't do that."

No, he wouldn't. That wasn't Dillon's style, although saying so would have been justified.

"So what are you going to do, Micah?"

Micah figured the only reason Dillon was asking was because his brother knew how much Kalina meant to him…even if *she* didn't know it. And her not knowing was no one's fault but his.

"Not sure what I'm going to do because no matter what I say, she won't believe me. A part of me just wants to say forget it, I don't need the hassle, but I can't, Dil. I just can't walk away from her."

"Then don't. You've never been a quitter. The Micah Westmoreland I know goes after what he wants and has never let anyone or anything stand in his way. But if you don't want her enough to fight for her and make her see the truth, then I don't know what to tell you."

Then, as if the subject of Kalina was a closed one, Dillon promptly began talking about something else. He told Micah how their sister-in-law, Bella, was coming along in her pregnancy, and that the doctors had verified twins, both girls.

"They're the first on our side," he said. Their parents had had all boys. Seven of them.

"I know, and everyone is excited and ready for them to be born," Dillon replied. "But I don't think anyone is as ready as Jason," he said of their brother and the expectant father.

The rest of the conversation was spent with Dillon bringing Micah up to date on what was going down on the home front. His brother Jason had settled into wedded bliss and so had his cousin Derringer. Micah shook his head. He could see Jason with a wife, but for the life of him, considering how Derringer used to play the field and enjoy it immensely, the thought of him settled down with one woman was still taking some getting used to. Dillon also mentioned that Ramsey and Chloe's son would be born in a few months.

"Do you think you'll be able to be here for li'l Callum's christening?"

Micah shook his head. Now, that was another one it was hard to believe had settled down. His cousin Gemma had a husband. She used to be a real pistol where men were concerned, but it seemed that Callum Austell had changed all that. She was now living in Australia with him and their two-month-old son.

"I plan to be there," Micah heard himself saying. "In a few weeks, I'll have thirty days to kill. I leave for Bajadad the day after tomorrow and I will be there for two weeks. I'll fly home from there." Bajadad was a small and beautiful city in northern India near the Himalayan foothills.

"It will be good seeing you again."

Micah couldn't help chuckling. "You make it sound like I haven't been home in years, Dil. I was just there seven months ago for Jason's wedding reception."

"I know, but anytime you come home and we can get everyone together is good."

Micah nodded. He would agree to that, and for Gemma's baby's christening, all the Westmorelands would be there, including their cousins from Atlanta, Texas and Montana.

Moments later, Micah ended his phone conversation with Dillon. He headed for the bedroom to undress and take a shower. The question Dillon asked him rang through his head. What was he going to do about Kalina?

Just like that, he remembered the proposition she'd made to Major Rose. And as he'd told her, he had no intention of letting the man go anywhere with her.

And just how are you going to stop her? His mind taunted. *She doesn't want to have anything to do with you. Thanks to her daddy's lie, you lost her. Get over it.*

He drew in a deep breath, knowing that was the kicker. He couldn't get over it. Dillon was right. Micah was not a quitter, and it was about time he made Kalina aware of that very fact.

Micah was pulled from his thoughts when his cell phone rang again. Pulling it from his pants pocket, he saw it was an official call from the Department of Health and Human Services. "Yes, Major Harris?"

"Dr. Westmoreland, first I want to apologize for calling you so late. And secondly, I'm calling to report changes in the assignment to India."

"And what are the changes, Major?"

"You will leave tomorrow instead of Monday. And Dr. Moore's wife went into labor earlier today so he has to be pulled off the team. We're going to have to send in a replacement."

Micah headed the U.S. epidemic response team consisting of over thirty epidemiologists, so calling to let him know of any changes was the norm. "That's fine."

He was about to thank her for calling and hang up when she said, "Now I need to call Dr. Daniels. Unfortunately, her vacation has to be canceled so she can take Dr. Moore's place."

Micah's pulse rate shot up and there was a deep thumping in his chest, close to his heart. "What did you say?" he asked, to make sure he'd heard her correctly.

"I said Dr. Daniels will be Dr. Moore's replacement since she's next in line on the on-call list. Unfortunately, her vacation was supposed to start tomorrow."

"What a pity," he said, not really feeling such sympathy. What others would see as Kalina's misfortune, he saw as his blessing. This change couldn't be any better if he'd planned it himself, and he intended to make sure Kalina's canceled vacation worked to his advantage.

Of course, when she found out she would automatically think the worst. She would assume the schedule change was his idea and that he was responsible for ruining her vacation. But it wouldn't be the first time she'd falsely accused him of something.

"Good night, Dr. Westmoreland."

He couldn't help smiling, feeling as if he had a new lease on life. "Good night, Major Harris."

He clicked off the phone thinking someone upstairs had to like him, and he definitely appreciated it. Now he would have to come up with a plan to make sure he didn't screw things up with Kalina this time.

KALINA PACED HER hotel room. *What was she going to do about Micah?*

She came to a stop long enough to touch her lips. She'd known letting him kiss her had been a bad move, but she hadn't been able to resist the feel of his mouth on hers. She should have been prepared for it. She'd seen the telltale signs in his eyes. He hadn't taken her off to a secluded place to talk about the weather. She'd been prepared for them to face off, have it out. And they'd done that. Then they'd ended up kissing each other senseless.

As much as she would like to do so, she couldn't place the blame solely at his feet. She had gone after his mouth just as greedily as he'd gone after hers. A rush of heat had consumed her the moment he'd stuck his tongue inside her mouth. So, okay, they were still attracted to each other. No big deal.

Kalina frowned. It *was* a big deal, especially when, even now, whirling sensations had taken over her stomach. She knew with absolute certainty that she didn't want to be attracted to Micah Westmoreland. She didn't want to have anything to do with him, period.

She glanced over at the clock and saw it was just past midnight. She was still wearing her cocktail dress, since she hadn't changed out of her clothes. She had begun pacing the moment she'd returned to her hotel room. Why was she letting him do this to her? And why was he lying, claiming he had not been in cahoots with her father when she knew differently?

Moving to the sofa, she sat down, still not ready to get undressed, because once she got in bed all she would do was dream about Micah. She leaned back in her seat, remembering the first time they'd worked together. She had arrived in Sydney, and he had been the one to pick her up from the airport. They had met a year earlier and their attraction to each other had been hot and instantaneous. It had taken less than five minutes in his presence that day to see that the heat hadn't waned any.

She would give them both credit for trying to ignore it. After all, they'd had an important job to do. And they'd made it through the first week, managing to keep their hands off each other. But the beginning of the next week had been the end of that. It had happened when they'd worked late one night, sorting out samples, dissecting birds, trying to make sure the bird flu didn't spread to the continent of Australia.

Technically, he had been her boss, since he headed the government's epidemic response team. But he'd never exerted the power of that position over her or anyone. He had treated everyone as a vital and important part of the team. Micah was a born leader and everyone easily gave him the respect he deserved.

And on that particular night, she'd given him something else. He had walked her to her hotel room, and she had invited him in. It hadn't been a smart move, but she had gotten tired of playing games. Tired of lusting after him and trying to keep her distance. They were adults and that night she'd figured they deserved to finally let go and do what adults did when they had the hots for each other.

Until that night, she'd thought the whole sex act was overrated. Micah had proven her wrong so many times that first night that she still got a tingling sensation just remembering it. She'd assumed it was a one-night stand, but that hadn't been the case. He had invited her out to dinner the following night and provided her with the terms of a no-strings affair, if she was interested. She had been more than interested. She was dedicated to her career and hadn't wanted to get involved in a serious relationship any more than he did.

That night they had reached a mutual agreement, and from then on they'd been exclusively involved during the two months they'd remained in Sydney. She was so content with their affair that when her earlier request for an assignment to Beijing had been denied, it really hadn't bothered her.

That contentment had lasted until she'd returned to the States and discovered the truth. Not only had her father manipulated her orders, but he'd solicited Micah's help in doing whatever he had to do to make sure she was kept happy in Sydney. She had been the one left looking like a complete fool, and she doubted she would forgive either of them for what they'd done.

Thinking she'd had enough of strolling down memory lane where the hurt was too much to bear, Kalina got up from the sofa and was headed toward the bedroom to change and finally attempt to sleep, when her cell phone rang. She picked it up off the table and saw it was Major Sally Harris, the administrative coordinator responsible for Kalina's assignments. She wondered why the woman would be calling her so late at night.

Kalina flipped on the phone. "Yes, Major Harris?"

"Dr. Daniels, I regret calling you so late and I want to apologize, because I have to deliver bad news."

Kalina frowned. "And what bad news is that?"

"Dr. Moore's wife went into labor earlier today so he has to be pulled off the epidemic response team headed out for Bajadad. I know your vacation was to start tomorrow, but we need your assistance in India."

Kalina drew in a deep breath. Although she hadn't made any definite vacation plans, she had looked forward to taking time off. "How long will I be needed in Bajadad?"

"For two weeks, beginning tomorrow, and then you can resume your vacation."

She nodded. There was no need to ask if there was someone else they could call since she knew the answer to that already. The epidemic response team had thinned out over the past few years with a war going on. And since the enemy liked to engage in chemical warfare, a number of epidemiologists had been sent to work in Afghanistan and Iraq.

"Dr. Daniels?"

Resigned, she said, "Yes, of course." Not that she had a choice in the matter. She was civilian, but orders from her boss were still meant to be followed, and she couldn't rightly get mad at Jess Moore because his wife was having a baby. "I'll be ready to head out tomorrow."

"Thanks. I'll send your information to your email address," Major Harris said.

"That will be fine."

"And Dr. Westmoreland has been notified of the change in personnel."

Kalina almost dropped the phone. "Dr. Westmoreland?"

"Yes?"

She frowned. "Why was he notified?"

"Because he's the one heading up the team."

Kalina's head began spinning. No one would be so cruel as to make her work with Micah again. She drew in a deep breath when a suspicion flowed through her mind. "Was Dr. Westmoreland the one to suggest that I replace Dr. Moore?"

"No, the reason you were called is that you're the next doctor on the on-call list."

Lucky me. Kalina shook her head, feeling anything but lucky. The thought of spending two weeks around Micah had her fuming inside. And regardless of what Major Harris said, it was hard to believe it was merely a coincidence that she was next on the call list. Micah was well liked and she knew all about his numerous connections and contacts. If she found out he had something to do with this change then...

"Dr. Daniels?"

"Yes?"

"Is there anything else you'd like to know?"

"No, there's nothing else."

"Thank you, Dr. Daniels, and good night."

"Good night, Major Harris."

Kalina hung up the phone knowing she couldn't let her feelings for Micah interfere with her work. She had a job to do, and she intended to do it. She would just keep her distance from him. She went into the bedroom and began tugging off her clothes as she became lost in a mix of disturbing thoughts.

The first thing she would do would be to set ground rules between her and Micah. If he saw this as a golden opportunity to get back in her bed then he was sadly mistaken. She was not the type of woman to forgive easily. Just as she'd told him earlier tonight, there was nothing else they had to say to each other regarding what happened between them two years ago. It was over and done with.

But if that kiss was anything to go by, she would need to be on guard around him at all times. Because their relationship might be over and done with, but the attraction between them was still alive and well.

CHAPTER THREE

MICAH SAW THE fire in Kalina's eyes from ten feet away. She glared as she moved toward him, chin up and spine stiff. She meant business. He slid a hand into the pocket of his jeans, thinking that he was glad it was Sunday and there were few people around. It seemed they were about to have it out once again.

This morning, upon awakening, he had decided the best way to handle her was to let her assume he wasn't handling her at all, to make her think that he had accepted her decision about how things would be between them. And when he felt the time was right, he would seize every opportunity he could get and let her know in no uncertain terms that her decision hadn't been his.

His gaze swept over her now. She was dressed for travel, with her hair pulled back in a ponytail and a pair of comfortable shoes on her feet. She looked good in her jeans and tank top and lightweight jacket. But then, she looked better than any woman he knew, in clothes or out of them.

He continued to stare at her while remembering her body stretched out beneath his when he'd made love to her. Even now, he could recall how it felt to skim his hands down the front of her body, tangle his fingers in her womanly essence while kissing her with a degree of passion he hadn't been aware of until her.

His heart began racing, and he could feel the zipper of his pants getting tight. He withdrew his hand from his pocket. The last thing he needed was for her to take note of his aroused state, so he turned and entered the private office he used whenever he was in D.C. on business. Besides, he figured the best place to have the encounter he knew was coming was behind closed doors.

By the time she had entered the office, all but slamming the door behind her, he was standing behind the desk.

He met her gaze, and felt the anger she wasn't trying to hide. As much as he wanted to cross the room and pull her into his arms and kiss her, convince her how wrong she was about him, common sense dictated he stay put. He intended to do what he hadn't done two years ago. Give her the chance to get to know him. He was convinced if she'd truly known him, she would not have been so quick to believe the worst about him.

"Dr. Daniels, I take it you're ready to fly out to Bajadad."

Her gaze narrowed. "And you want me to believe you had nothing to do with those orders, Micah?"

He crossed his arms over his chest and met her stare head-on. "At this point, Kalina, you can believe whatever you like. For me to deny it wouldn't matter since you wouldn't believe me anyway."

"And why should I?" she snapped.

"Because I have no reason to lie," he said simply. "Have you ever considered the possibility that I could be telling the truth? Just in case you need to hear it from me—just like I had nothing to do with your father's plan to keep you out of Beijing, your orders to go to Bajadad were not my idea. Although I embrace the schedule change wholeheartedly. You're a good doctor, and I can't think of anyone I want more on my team. We're dealing with a suspicious virus. Five people have died already and the government suspects it might be part of something we need to nip in the bud as soon as possible. However, we won't know what we're dealing with until we get there."

He watched as her whole demeanor changed in the wake of the information he had just provided. Her stiffened spine relaxed and her features became alert. No matter what, she was a professional, and as he'd said, she was good at what she did.

"What's the point of entry?" she asked, moving to stand in front of the desk.

"So far, only by ingestion. It's been suspected that something was put in the water supply. If that's true, it will be up to us to find out what it is."

She nodded, and he knew she completely understood. The government's position was that if the enemy had developed some kind of deadly chemical then the United States needed to know about it. It was important to determine early on what they were up against and how they could protect U.S. military personnel.

"And how was it detected, Micah?" she was calm and relaxed as she questioned him. He moved to sit on the edge of his desk. Not far from where she stood. He wondered if she'd taken note of their proximity.

He wished she wasn't wearing his favorite perfume and that he didn't remember just how dark her eyes would become in the heat of passion. Kalina Daniels was an innately sensuous woman. There was no doubt about it.

"Five otherwise healthy adults over the age of fifty were found dead within the same week with no obvious signs of trauma," he heard himself saying. "However, their tongues had enlarged to twice the normal size. Other than that, there was nothing else, not even evidence of a foreign substance in their bloodstream."

He saw the look in her eyes while she was digesting what he'd said. Most terrorist groups experimented on a small number of people before unleashing anything in full force, just to make sure their chemical warfare weapon was effective. It was too early to make an assumption about what they would be facing, but the researcher who was already there waiting on them had stated his suspicions. Before 9/11 chemical weapons were considered a poor-man's atomic bomb. However, because of their ability to reach millions of people in so many different ways, these weapons were now considered the worst and most highly effective of all forms of warfare.

"Have you ever been to Bajadad?" she asked him.

He met her gaze. "Yes, several years ago, right after the first democratic elections were held. It was my first assignment after leaving college and coming to work for the federal government. We were sent there on a peace-finding mission when members of the king's household had become ill. Some suspected foul play.

However, it didn't take us long to determine it hadn't been all that serious, just a contaminated sack of wheat that should never have been used."

He could tell by the look in her eyes that she'd become intrigued. That's how it had always been with her. She would ask a lot of questions to quench that curiosity of hers. She thought he'd lived an adventurous life as an epidemiologist, while, thanks to her father, she'd been deliberately kept on the sidelines.

In a way, he was surprised she was going to Bajadad. Either the old man had finally learned his lesson or he was getting lax in keeping up with his daughter's whereabouts. He knew her father had worked behind the scenes, wielding power, influencing his contacts, to make sure Kalina had assignments only in the States or in first-world countries. He'd discovered, after the fact, that her time in Sydney had been orchestrated to keep her out of Beijing without giving her a reason to get suspicious.

Micah stood and decided to shift topics. He met Kalina's gaze when he said, "I think we need to talk about last night."

He watched her spine stiffen as she once again shifted into a defensive mode. "No, we don't."

"Yes, we do Kalina. We're going out on a mission together, and I think it's going to be important that we're comfortable around each other and put our personal differences aside. I'd be the first to admit I've made a lot of mistakes where you're concerned, and I regret making them. Now you believe the worst of me and nothing I can say or do will change that."

He paused a moment, knowing he had to chose his words carefully. "You don't have to worry about me mixing business with pleasure, because I refuse to become involved with a woman who doesn't trust me. So there can never be anything between us again."

There, he'd said it. He tasted the lie on his tongue, but knew his reasons for his concocted statement were justified. He had no intention of giving her up. Ever. But she had to learn to trust him. And he would do whatever he had to do to make that happen.

Although she tried to shelter her reaction, he'd seen how his words had jolted her body. There was no doubt in his mind she had felt the depth of what he'd said. A part of him wanted to believe that deep down she still cared for him.

She lifted her chin in a stubborn frown. "Good. I'm glad we got that out of the way and that we understand each other."

He glanced down at his watch. "Our flight leaves in a few hours. I would offer you a ride to the airport, but I'm catching a ride with someone myself."

She tilted her head back and looked at him. "No problem. I reserved a rental car."

Kalina looked at her own watch and slipped the straps of her purse onto her shoulders. "I need to be going."

"I'll walk out with you," he said, falling into step beside her. He had no problem offering her a ride if she needed one, but he hadn't wanted to appear too anxious to be in her company. "We're looking at a twelve-hour flight. I'd advise you to eat well before we fly out. The food we're going to be served on the plane won't be the best."

She chuckled and the sound did something to him. It felt good to be walking beside her. "Don't think I don't know about military-airplane food. I'm going to stop and grab me a sandwich from Po'Boys," she said.

He knew she regretted mentioning the restaurant when he glanced over and saw the blush on her face. Chances were, like him, she was remembering the last time they'd gone there together. It had been their first night back in the States after Australia. He might not recall what all they'd eaten that night, but he did re-member everything they'd done in the hotel room af-terward.

"Whatever you get, eat enough for the both of us," he said, breaking the silence between them.

She glanced over at him. "I will."

They were now outside, standing on the top steps of the Centers for Disease Control. "Well, I guess I'll be seeing you on the flight. Take care until then, Kal."

Then, without looking back, he moved to the car that pulled up to the curb at that very moment. He smiled, thinking the timing was perfect when he saw who was driving the car.

He glanced up at the sky. He had a feeling someone up there was definitely on his side. His cousin, Sena-tor Reggie Westmoreland, had called him that morn-ing, inviting him to lunch. Reggie, his wife, Olivia, and their one-year-old twin sons made Washington their home for part of the year. It was Olivia and not Reggie who'd come to pick him up to take him to their house in

Georgetown. She was a beautiful woman, and he could just imagine the thoughts going through Kalina's mind right now.

KALINA STOOD AND watched Micah stroll down the steps toward the waiting car. He looked good in a chambray shirt that showed the width of his broad shoulders and jeans that hugged his masculine thighs, making her appreciate what a fine specimen of a man he was.

He worked out regularly and it showed. No matter from what angle you saw him—front, back or side—one looked just as good as the other. And from the side-glances of several women who were climbing the steps and passing by him as he moved down, she was reminded again that she wasn't the only one who appreciated that fact.

Oh, why did he have to call her Kal? It was the nickname he'd given her during their affair. No one else called her that. Her father detested nicknames and always referred to her by her first and middle name. To her dad she was Kalina Marie.

She tried not to show any emotion as she watched a woman get out of the car, smiling brightly while moving toward Micah. She was almost in his face by the time his foot touched the last step, and he gave the woman a huge hug and a warm smile as if he was happy to see her, as well.

No wonder he's so quick to write you off, she thought in exasperated disgust, hating that seeing Micah with another woman bothered her. *He's already involved with someone else. Well, what did you expect? It's been*

*two years. Just because you haven't been in a serious
relationship since then doesn't mean he hasn't. And
besides, you're the one who called things off. Accused
him of being in league with your father…*

Kalina shook her head as the car, with Micah in it,
pulled off. Why was she trying to rehash anything? She
knew the truth, and no matter how strenuously Micah
claimed otherwise, she believed her father. Yes, he was
controlling, but he loved her. He had no reason to lie.
He had confessed his part and had admitted to his involvement in Micah's part, as well. So why couldn't
Micah just come clean and fess up? And why had she
felt a bout of jealousy when he'd hugged that woman?
Why did she care that the woman was jaw-droppingly
beautiful, simply gorgeous with not a hair on her head
out of place?

Tightening her hand on her purse, Kalina walked
down the steps toward the parking lot. She had to get a
grip on more than her purse. She needed to be in complete control of her senses while dealing with Micah.

"SORRY TO IMPOSE, but I think this is the only seat left
on the plane," Micah said as he slid into the empty seat
next to Kalina.

Her eyes had been closed as she waited for take-
off, but she immediately opened them, looking at him
strangely before lifting up slightly to glance around, as
if to make sure he was telling the truth.

He smiled as be buckled his seat belt. "You need to
stop doing that, you know."

She arched an eyebrow. "Doing what?"

"Acting like everything coming out of my mouth is a lie."

She shrugged what he knew were beautiful shoulders. "Well, once you tell one lie, people have a tendency not to believe you in the future. Sort of like the boy who cried wolf." She then closed her eyes again as if to dismiss him.

He didn't plan to let her response be the end of it. "What's going to happen when you find out you've been wrong about me?"

She opened her eyes and glanced over at him, looking as if the thought of her being wrong was not even a possibility. "Not that I think that will happen, but if it does then I'll owe you an apology."

"And when it does happen I might just be reluctant to accept your apology." He then leaned back in his seat and closed his eyes, this time dismissing her and leaving her with something to chew on.

The flight attendant prevented further conversation between them when she came on the intercom to provide flight rules and regulations. He kept his eyes closed. Kalina's insistence that he would conspire with her father grated on a raw nerve each and every time she said it.

Moments later, he felt the movement of the plane glide down the runway before tilting as it eased into the clouds. Over the years, he'd gotten used to air travel, but that didn't mean he particularly liked it. All he had to do was recall that he had lost four vital members of his family in a plane crash. And he couldn't help remembering that tragic and deep-felt loss each and every time he boarded a plane, even after all these years.

"She's pretty."

He opened his eyes and glanced over at Kalina. "Who is?"

"That woman who picked you up from the CDC today."

He nodded. "Thanks. I happen to think she's pretty, too," he said honestly. In fact, he thought all his cousins and brothers had married beautiful women. Not only were they beautiful, they were smart, intelligent and strong.

"Have the two of you been seeing each other long?"

It would be real simple to tell her that Olivia was a relative, but he decided to let her think whatever she wanted. "No, and we really aren't seeing each other now. We're just friends," he said.

"Close friends?"

He closed his eyes again. "Yes." He had been tempted to keep his eyes open just to see her expression, but knew closing them would make his nonchalance more effective.

"How long have the two of you known each other?"

He knew she was trying to figure out if Olivia had come before or after her. "Close to five years now."

"Oh."

So far everything he'd said had been the truth. He just wasn't elaborating. It was his choice and his right. Besides, he was giving her something to think about.

Deciding she'd asked enough questions about Olivia,

he said, "You might want to rest awhile. We have a long flight ahead of us."

And he intended on sharing every single hour of it with her. It wasn't a coincidence that the last seat on the military jet had been next to her and that he'd taken it. There hadn't been any assigned seats on this flight. Passengers could sit anywhere, and, with the help of the flight attendant, he'd made sure they had sat everywhere but next to Kalina. The woman just happened to know that *New York Times* bestselling author Rock Mason, aka Stone Westmoreland, was Micah's cousin. The woman was a huge fan and the promise of an autographed copy of Stone's next action thriller had gone a long way.

Micah kept his eyes closed but could still inhale Kalina's scent. He could envision her that morning, dabbing cologne all over her body, a body he'd had intimate knowledge of for two wonderful months. He was convinced he knew where every mole was located, and he was well acquainted with that star-shaped scar near her hip bone that had come as a result of her taking a tumble off a skateboard at the age of twelve.

He drew in a deep breath, taking in her scent one more time for good measure. For now, he needed to pretend he was ignoring her. Sitting here lusting after Kalina wasn't doing him any good and was just weakening his resolve to keep her at a distance while he let her get to know him. He couldn't let that happen. But he couldn't help it when he opened his eyes, turned to her and said, "Oh, by the way, Kalina. You still have the cutest dimples." He then turned to face straight ahead before closing his eyes once again.

Satisfied he might have soothed her somewhat, he stretched his long legs out in front of him, at least as far as they could go, and tilted his seat back. He might as well get as comfortable as he could for the long flight.

He'd been given a good hand to play and he planned on making the kind of win that the gambler in the family, his cousin Ian, would be proud of. The stakes were high, but Micah intended to be victorious.

So MICAH HAD known the woman during their affair. Did that mean he'd taken back up with her after their time together had ended? Kalina wondered. He said he and the woman were only friends, but she'd known men to claim only friendship even while sleeping with a woman every night. Men tended not to place the same importance on an affair as women did. She, of all people, should know that.

And how dare he compliment her on her dimples at a time like this and in the mood she was in. She had to work with him, but she was convinced she didn't even like him anymore. Yet in all fairness, she shouldn't be surprised by the comment about her dimples. He'd told her numerous times that her dimples were the first thing he'd noticed about her. They were permanent fixtures on her face, whether she smiled or not.

And then there was the way he'd looked at her when he'd said it. Out of the clear blue sky, he had turned those gorgeous bedroom-brown eyes on her and remarked on her dimples. Her stomach had clenched. It had been so unexpected it had sent her world tilting for a minute. And before she'd recovered, he'd turned back around and closed his eyes.

Now he was reclining comfortably beside her. All man. All sexy. All Westmoreland. And seemingly all bored...at least with her. She had a good mind to wake him up and engage in some conversation just for the hell of it, but then she thought better of it. Micah Westmoreland was a complex man and just thinking about how complex he could be had tension building at her temples.

She couldn't help thinking about all the things she didn't know about him. For some reason, he'd never shared much about himself or his family. She knew he had several brothers, but that fact was something she'd discovered by accident and not because he'd told her about them. She'd just so happened to overhear a conversation between him and his good friend Dr. Beau Smallwood. And she did know his parents had died in a plane crash when he was in college. He'd only told her that because she'd asked.

Her life with her military father was basically an open book. After her mother had died of cervical cancer when Kalina was ten, her father had pretty much clung to her like a vine. The only time they were separated was when he'd been called for active duty or another assignment where she wasn't allowed. Those were the days she spent on her grandparents' farm in Alabama. Joe and Claudia Daniels had passed away years ago, but Kalina still had fond memories of the time she'd spent with them.

Kalina glanced over at Micah again. It felt strange casually sitting next to a man who'd been inside her body…numerous times. A man whose tongue had licked her in places that made her blush to think about. Someone who had taken her probably in every position known to the average man and in some he'd probably created himself. He was the type of man a woman fantasized about. A shiver raced through her body just thinking about being naked with him.

Up to now, she had come to terms with the fact that she'd be working with Micah again, especially after what he'd said in his office earlier that morning. He didn't want to become involved with her, just as she didn't want to become involved with him. So why was she tempted to reach out and trace the line of his chin with her fingers or use the tip of her tongue to glisten his lips?

Oh, by the way, you still have the cutest dimples. If those words had been meant to get next to her, they had. And she wished they hadn't. She didn't want to remember anything about the last time they were together or what sharing those two months with him had meant to her.

And she especially did not want to remember what the man had meant to her.

Having no interest in the movie currently being shown and wanting to get her mind off the man next to her, she decided to follow Micah's lead. She tilted her seat back, closed her eyes and went to sleep.

CHAPTER FOUR

MICAH AWAKENED THE next morning and stretched as he glanced around his bedroom. He'd been too tired when he'd arrived at the private villa last night to take note of his surroundings, but now he couldn't help smiling. He would definitely like it here. Kalina's room was right next door to his.

He slid out of bed and headed for the bathroom, thinking the sooner he got downstairs the better. The government had set up a lab for them in the basement of the villa and, according to the report he'd read, it would be fully equipped for their needs.

Twelve hours on a plane hadn't been an ideal way to spend time with Kalina, but he had managed to retain his cool. He'd even gone so far as to engage in friendly conversation about work. Otherwise, like him, she'd slept most of the time. Once he'd found her watching some romantic movie. Another time she'd been reading a book on one of those eReaders.

A short while after waking, Micah had dressed and was headed downstairs for breakfast. The other doctor on the team had arrived last week and Micah was looking forward to seeing him again. Theodus Mitchell was a doctor he'd teamed with before, who did excellent work in the field of contagious diseases.

Micah opened his bedroom door and walked out into the hallway the same time Kalina did. He smiled when he saw her, although he could tell by her expression that she wasn't happy to see him. "Kalina. Good morning."

"Good morning, Micah. You're going down for breakfast?"

"Yes, what about you?" he asked, falling into step beside her.

"Yes, although I'm not all that hungry," she said.

He definitely was, and it wasn't all food that had him feeling hungry. She looked good. Well rested. Sexy as hell in a pair of brown slacks and a green blouse. And she'd gotten rid of the ponytail. She was wearing her hair down to her shoulders. The style made her features appear even more beautiful.

"Well, I'm starving," he said as they stepped onto the elevator. "And I'm also anxious to get to the lab to see what we're up against. Did you get a chance to read the report?"

She nodded as the elevator door shut behind them. "Yes, I read it before going to bed. I wasn't all that sleepy."

They were the only ones in the elevator and suddenly memories flooded his brain. The last time they had been in an elevator alone she had tempted him so much that he had ended up taking her against a wall in one hell of a quickie. Thoughts of that time fired his blood.

Now, she had moved to stand at the far side of the elevator. She was staring into space, looking as if she didn't have a care in the world. He wanted to fire her blood the way she was firing his.

The elevator stopped on the first floor and as soon as the doors swooshed open, she was out. He couldn't help chuckling to himself as he followed her, thinking she was trying to put distance between them. Evidently, although she'd pretended otherwise, she had remembered their last time in an elevator together, as well.

A buffet breakfast was set up on the patio, and the moment he walked out onto the terrace, his glance was caught by the panoramic view of the Himalayas, looming high toward a beautiful April sky.

"Theo!"

"Kalina, good seeing you again."

He turned and watched Theo and Kalina embrace, not feeling the least threatened since everyone knew just how devoted Theo was to his beautiful wife, Renee, who was an international model. Inhaling the richness of the mountain air, Micah strolled toward the pair. The last time the three of them had teamed up together on an assignment had been in Sydney. Beau had also been part of their team.

Theo released Kalina and turned to Micah and smiled. "Micah, it's good seeing you, as well. It's like old times," Theo said with a hearty handshake.

Micah wondered if Theo assumed the affair with Kalina was still ongoing since he'd been there with them in Australia when it had started. "Yes, and from what I understand we're going to be busy for the next two weeks."

Theo nodded and a serious expression appeared on

his face. "So far there haven't been any more deaths and that's a good thing."

Micah agreed. "The three of us can discuss it over breakfast."

KALINA SAT BESIDE Micah and tried to unravel her tangled thoughts. But there was nothing she could do with the heat that was rushing through her at that moment. There was no way she could put a lid on it. The desire flowing within her was too thick to confine. For some reason, even amidst the conversations going on— mostly between Micah and Theo—she couldn't stop her mind from drifting and grabbing hold of memories of what she and Micah had once shared.

"So what do you think, Kalina?"

She glanced over at Micah. Had he suspected her of daydreaming when she should have been paying attention? Both men had worked as epidemiologists for a lot longer than she had and had seen and done a lot more. She had enjoyed just sitting and listening to how they analyzed things, figuring she could learn a lot from them.

Micah, Theo and another epidemiologist by the name of Beau Smallwood had begun work for the federal government right out of medical school and were good friends; especially Beau and Micah who were the best of friends.

"I think, although we can't make assumptions until we have the data to support it, I agree that the deaths are suspicious."

Micah smiled, and she tried downplaying the effect

that smile had on her. She had to remind herself that smile or no smile, he was someone who couldn't be trusted. Someone who had betrayed her.

"Well, then, I think we'd better head over to the lab to find out what we're up against,' Micah said, standing.

He reached for her tray and she pulled it back. "Thanks, but I can dispense with my own trash."

He nodded. "Suit yourself."

She stood and turned to walk off, but not before hearing Theo whisper to Micah, "Um, my friend, it sounds like there's trouble in paradise."

She was tempted to turn and alert Theo to the fact that "paradise" for them ended two years ago. Shaking off the anger she felt when she thought about that time in her life and the hurt she'd felt, she continued walking toward the trash can. She'd known at the start of her affair with Micah that it would be a short-term affair. He'd made certain she understood there were no strings, and she had.

But what she couldn't accept was knowing the entire thing had been orchestrated by her controlling father. The only reason she was here in India now was because the general was probably too busy with the war in Afghanistan to check up on her whereabouts. He probably felt pretty confident she was on vacation or assigned to some cushy job in the States. Although he claimed otherwise, she knew he was the reason she hadn't been given any hard-hitting assignments. If it hadn't been for Dr. Moore's baby, chances are she wouldn't be here now.

She was about to turn, when Micah came up beside her to toss out his own trash. "Stop being so uptight with me, Kalina."

She glanced over at him and drew in a deep breath to keep from saying something that was totally rude. Instead, she met his gaze and said, "My being uptight, Micah, should be the least of your worries." She then walked off.

Micah watched her go, admiring the sway of her hips with every step she took. His feelings for Kalina were a lot more than sexual, but he was a man, and the woman had a body that any man would appreciate.

"I see she still doesn't know how you feel about her, Micah."

Micah glanced over and saw the humor in Theo's blue gaze. There was no reason to pretend he didn't know what the man was talking about. "No, she doesn't know."

"Then don't you think you ought to tell her?"

Micah chuckled. "With Kalina it won't be that easy. I need to show her rather than tell her because she doesn't believe anything I say."

"Ouch. Sounds like you have your work cut out for you then."

Micah nodded. "I do, but in the end it will be worth it."

KALINA WAS FULLY aware of the moment Micah entered the lab. With her eyes glued to the microscope, she hadn't looked up, but she knew without a doubt he was there and that he had looked her way. It was their first full day in Bajadad, and it had taken all her control to fight the attraction, the pull, the heat between them. She had played the part of the professional and had, hopefully, pulled it off. At least she believed Theo hadn't picked up on anything. He was too absorbed in the findings of today's lab reports to notice the air around them was charged.

But *she* had noticed. Not only had she picked up on the strong chemistry flowing between her and Micah, she had also picked up on his tough resistance. He would try to resist her as much as she would try to resist him, and she saw that as a good thing.

Even if they hadn't been involved two years ago, there was no way they would not be attracted to each other. He was a man and she was a woman, so quite naturally there would be a moment of awareness between them. Some things just couldn't be helped. But hopefully, by tomorrow, that awareness would have passed and they would be able to get down to the business they were sent here to carry out.

What if it didn't pass?

A funny feeling settled in her stomach at the thought of that happening. But all it took was the reminder of how he had betrayed her in the worst possible way to keep any attraction between them from igniting into full-blown passion.

However, she felt the need to remind herself that her best efforts hadn't drummed up any opposition to him when they'd been alone in the lab earlier that day. He had stood close while she'd gone over the reports, and she'd inhaled his scent while all kinds of conflicting emotions rammed through her. And every time she glanced up into his too-handsome face and stared into his turn-you-on brown eyes she could barely think straight.

Okay, she was faced with a challenge, but it wouldn't be the first time nor did she figure it would be the last. She'd never been a person who was quick to jump into bed with a man just for the sake of doing so, and she had surprised herself with how quickly she had agreed to an affair with Micah two years ago. She had dated in college and had slept with a couple of the guys. The sex between them hadn't been anything to write home about. She had eventually reached the conclusion that she and sex didn't work well together, which had always been just fine and dandy to her. So when she'd felt the sparks fly between her and Micah in a way she'd never felt before, she'd believed the attraction was something worth exploring.

Kalina nibbled on her bottom lip, thinking that was then, this was now. She had learned her lesson regarding Micah. They shared a chemistry that hadn't faded with time. If he thought she had the cutest dimples then she could say the same about his lips. She could imagine her tongue gliding over them for a taste, and it wouldn't be a quick one.

She shook her head. Her thoughts were really getting out of hand, and it was time to rein them back in. Today had been a busy day, filled with numerous activities and a conference call with Washington that had lasted a couple of hours. More than once, she had glanced up from her notes to find Micah staring at her. And each time their gazes connected, a wild swirl of desire would try overtaking her senses.

"Have you found anything unusual, Kalina?"

Micah's deep, husky voice broke into her thoughts, reminding her he had entered the room. Not that she'd totally forgotten. She lifted her gaze from the microscope and wished she hadn't. He looked yummy enough to eat. Literally.

He had come to stand beside her. Glancing up at him, she saw the intense concentration in his eyes seemed hot, near blazing. It only made her more aware of the deep physical chemistry radiating between them, which she was trying to ignore but finding almost impossible to do.

"I think you need to take a look at this," she said, moving aside so he could look through her microscope.

He moved in place and she studied him for a minute while he sat on the stool, absorbed in analyzing what she'd wanted him to see. Moments later, he glanced back up at her. "Granulated particles?"

"Yes, that's what they appear to be, and barely noticeable. I plan on separating them to see if I can pinpoint what they are. There's a possibility the substance entering the bloodstream wasn't a liquid like we first assumed."

He nodded, agreeing with her assumption. "Let me know what you find out."

"I will." God, she needed her head examined, but she couldn't shift her gaze away from his lips. Those oh-so-cute lips were making deep-seated feelings stir inside her and take center stage. His lips moved, and it was then she realized he had said something.

"Sorry, did you say something?" she asked, trying to regain her common sense, which seemed to have taken a tumble by the wayside.

"Yes, I said I dreamed about you last night."

She stared at him. Where had that come from? How on earth had they shifted from talking about the findings under her microscope to him having a dream about her?

"And in my dream, I touched you all over. I tasted you all over."

Her heart thudded painfully in her chest. His words left her momentarily speechless and breathless. And it didn't help matters that the tone he'd used was deep, husky and as masculine as any male voice could be. Instead of grating on her nerves, it was grating on other parts of her body. Stroking them into a sensual fever.

She drew in a deep breath and said, "I thought you were going to stay in your place, Micah."

He smiled that sexy, rich smile of his, and she felt something hot and achy take her over. Little pangs of sexual desire, and the need she'd tried ignoring for two years, expanded in full force.

"I *am* staying in my place, Kalina. But do you know what place I love most of all?"

Something told her not to ask but she did anyway. "What?"

"Deep inside you."

She wasn't sure how she remained standing. She was on wobbly legs with a heart rate that was higher than normal. She compressed her lips, shoving to the back of her mind all the things she'd like to do to his mouth. "You have no right to say something like that," she said, shaking off his words as if they were some unpleasant memory.

A crooked smile appeared on his face. "I have every right, especially since you've practically spoiled me for any other woman."

Yeah, right. Did he think she didn't remember the woman who'd picked him up yesterday at the CDC? "And what happened to your decision not to become involved with a woman who didn't trust you?"

He chuckled. "Nothing happened. I merely mentioned to you that I dreamed about you last night. No harm's done. No real involvement there."

She frowned. He was teasing her, and she didn't like it. A man didn't tell a woman he'd dreamed about her without there being a hint of his desire for an involvement. What kind of game was Micah playing?

"Theo has already made plans for dinner. What about you?"

She answered without thinking. "No, I haven't made any plans."

"Good, then have dinner with me."

She stared at him. He was smooth, but not smooth enough. "We agreed not to become involved."

He chuckled. "Eating is not an involvement, Kalina. It's a way to feed the urges of one's body."

She didn't say anything, but she knew too well about bodily urges. Food wasn't what her body was craving.

"Having dinner with me is not a prerequisite for an

affair. It's where two friends, past lovers, colleagues…
however you want to describe our relationship…sit
down and eat. I know this nice café not far from here.
It's one I used to frequent when I was here the last time.
I'd like to take you there."

Don't go, an inner voice warned. *All it will take is for
you to sit across from him at a table and watch him eat.*
The man had a way of moving his mouth that was so
downright sensual it was a crying shame. It had taken
all she had just to get through breakfast this morning.

"I don't think going out to dinner with you is a good
idea," she finally said.

"And why not?"

"Mainly because you forgot to add the word *enemy*
to the list to describe our relationship. I don't like you."

He simply grinned. "Well, I happen to like you a lot.
And I don't consider us enemies. Besides, you're not the
injured party here, I am. I'm an innocent man, falsely
accused of something he didn't do."

She turned back to the microscope as she spoke. "I
see things differently."

"I know you do, so why can't you go out to eat with
me since nothing I say or do will change your mind?
I merely invited you to dinner because I noticed you
worked through lunch. But if you're afraid to be with
me then I—"

"I'm not afraid to be with you."

"So you say," he said, turning to leave. Before reaching the door, he shot her a smile over his shoulder. "If
you change your mind about dinner, I'll be leaving here

around seven and you can meet me downstairs in the lobby."

Kalina watched him leave. She disliked him, so she wasn't sure why her hormones could respond to him the way they did. The depth of desire she felt around him was unreal. And dangerous. It only heightened the tension between them, and the thought that he wanted them to share dinner filled her with a heat she could very well do without.

The best thing for her to do was to stay in and order room service. That was the safest choice. But then, why should she be a coward? She, of all people, knew that Micah did not have a place in her life anymore. So, despite his mild flirtation—and that's what it was whether he admitted to it or not—she would not succumb. Nor would she lock herself in her room because she couldn't control her attraction to him. It was time that she learned to control her response to him. There would be other assignments when they would work together, and she needed to put their past involvement behind her once and for all.

She stood and checked her watch, deciding she would have dinner with Micah after all. But she would make sure that she was the one in control at all times.

CHAPTER FIVE

AT PRECISELY seven o'clock, Micah stepped out of the elevator hoping he hadn't overplayed his hand. When he glanced around the lobby and saw Kalina sitting on one of the sofas, he felt an incredible sense of relief. He had been prepared to dine alone if it had come to that, but he'd more than hoped that she was willing to dine with him.

He walked over to her. From the expression on her face, it was obvious she was apprehensive about them dining together, so he intended to make sure she enjoyed herself—even as he made sure she remembered what they'd once shared. A shiver of desire raced up his spine when she saw him and stood. She was wearing a dress that reminded him of what a nice pair of legs she had. And her curvy physique seemed made for that outfit.

He had gone over his strategy upstairs in case she joined him. He wouldn't make a big deal of her accompanying him. However, he would let her know he appreciated her being there.

He stopped when he reached her. "Kalina. You look nice tonight."

"Thanks. I think we need to get a couple of things straight."

He figured she would say that. "Let's wait until we get to the restaurant. Then you can let go all you want," he replied, taking her arm and placing it in the crux of his.

He felt her initial resistance before she relaxed. "Fine, but we will have that conversation. I don't have a problem joining you for dinner, but I don't want you getting any ideas."

Too late. He had gotten plenty already. He smiled. "You worry too much. There's no need for me to ask if you trust me because I know you don't. But can you cut me a little slack?"

Kalina held his gaze for a moment longer than he thought necessary, before she released an exasperated breath. "Does it matter to you that I don't particularly like you anymore?"

He took her hand in his to lead her out of the villa. "I'm sorry to hear that because I definitely like you. Always have. From the first."

She rolled her eyes. "So you say."

He chuckled. "So I know."

She pulled her hand from his when they stepped outside. The air was cool, and he thought it was a smart thing that she'd brought along a shawl. He could visualize her wrapped up in it and wearing nothing else.

She had done that once, and he could still remember her doing so. It had been a red one with fringes around the hem. He had shown up at the hotel where they were staying in Sydney with their take-out dinner, and she had emerged from the bedroom looking like a lush red morsel. She had ended up being his treat for the night.

"Micah?"

He glanced over when he realized she'd said something. "Yes?"

"Are we walking or taking a cab?"

"We'll take a cab and tell the driver not to hurry so we can enjoy the beautiful view. Unless, however, you prefer to walk. It's not far away, within walking distance."

"Makes no difference to me," she said, moving her gaze from his to glance around.

'In that case, we'll take the cab. I know how much you like a good ride."

KALINA'S FACE FLUSHED after she heard what Micah said. There was no way he could convince her he hadn't meant what she thought he'd meant. That innocent look on his face meant nothing. But then, he, of all people, knew how much she liked to be on top and he'd always accommodated her. She just loved the feel of being on top of a body so well built and fine it could make even an old woman weep in pleasure.

She decided that if he was waiting on a response to his comment, he would be disappointed because she didn't intend to give him one. She would say her piece at the restaurant.

"Here's our cab."

The bellman opened the door for her. Kalina slid in the back and Micah eased in right behind her. The cab was small but not small enough where they needed to be all but sitting in each other's lap. "You have plenty of space over there," she said, pointing to Micah's side.

Without any argument he slid over, but then he turned and flashed those pearly-white teeth as he smiled at her. Her gaze narrowed. "Any reason you find me amusing?"

He shrugged. "I don't. But I do find you sexy as hell."

That was a compliment she didn't need and opened her mouth to tell him so, then closed it, deciding to leave well enough alone. He would be getting an earful soon enough.

When he continued to sit there and stare at her, she found it annoying and asked, "I thought you said you were going to enjoy the view."

"I am."

God, how had she forgotten how much he considered seduction an art form? Of course, he should know that using that charm on her was a wasted effort. "Can I ask you something, Micah?"

"Baby, you can ask me anything."

She hated to admit that his term of endearment caused a whirling sensation in her stomach. "Why are you doing this? Saying those things? I'm sure you're well aware it's a waste of your time."

"Is it?"

"Yes."

He didn't say anything for a moment and then, "To answer your question, the reason I'm doing this and saying all these things is that I'm hoping you'll remember."

She didn't have to ask what he wanted her to remember. She knew. Things had been good between them.

Every night. Every morning. He'd been the best lover a woman could have and she had appreciated those nights spent in his arms. And speaking of those arms…they were hidden in a nice shirt that showed off the wide breadth of his shoulders. She knew those shoulders well and used to hold on to him while she rode him mercilessly. And then there were his hands. Beautiful. Strong. Capable of delivering mindless pleasure. And they were hands that would travel all over her body, touching her in places no man had touched her before and leaving a trail of heat in their wake.

Her gaze traveled upward past his throat to his mouth. It lingered there while recalling the ways he would use that mouth to make her scream. Oh, how she would scream while he took care of that wild, primal craving deep within her.

Gradually, her gaze left his mouth to move upward and stared into the depth of his bedroom-brown eyes. They were staring straight at her, pinning her in place and almost snatching the air from her lungs with their intensity. She wished she could dismiss that stare. Instead she was ensnarled by it in a way that increased her heart rate. An all-too-familiar ache settled right between her thighs. He was making her want something she hadn't had since he'd given it to her.

"Do you remember all the things we used to do behind closed doors, Kalina?"

Yes, she remembered and doubted she could ever forget. Sex between them had been good. The best. But it had all been a lie. That memory of his betrayal cut through her desire and forced a laugh from deep within her throat. "I've got to hand it to you, Micah. You're good."

He shrugged and then said in a low, husky tone, "You always said I was."

Yes, she had and it had been the truth. "Yes, but you're not good enough to get me into bed ever again. If you'll recall, I know the reason you slept with me." She was grateful for the glass partition that kept the cabby from hearing their conversation.

"I know the reason, as well. I wanted you. Pure and simple. From the moment you walked into that ballroom on your father's arm, I knew I wanted you. And being with you in Sydney afforded me the opportunity to have you. I wanted those legs wrapped around me, while I stroked you inside out. I wanted to bury my head between your thighs, to know the taste of you, and I wanted you to know the taste of me."

Her traitorous body began responding to his words. Myriad sensations were rolling around in her stomach. "It was all about sex, then," she said, trying to once again destroy the heated moment.

He nodded. "Yes, in the beginning. That's why I gave you my ground rules. But then…"

She shouldn't ask but couldn't help doing so. "But then what?" she asked breathlessly.

"And then the hunter got captured by the prey."

She opened her mouth and then closed it when the cabdriver told them via a speaker that they'd arrived. She glanced out the window. It was a beautiful restaurant—quaint and romantic.

He opened the door and reached for her hand. The

reaction to his touch instantly swept through her. The man could make her ache without even trying.

"You're going to like the food here," he said, helping her out of the cab and not releasing her hand. She wanted to pull it from his grasp, but the feel of that one lone finger stroking her palm kept her hand where it was.

"I'm sure I will."

They walked side by side into the restaurant and she couldn't recall the last time they'd done so. It had felt good, downright giddy, being the center of Micah Westmoreland's attention and he had lavished it on her abundantly.

She didn't know what game Micah was playing tonight or what he was trying to prove. The only thing she did know was that by the time they left this restaurant he would know where she stood, and he would discover that she didn't intend to be a part of his game playing.

"The food here is delicious, Micah."

He smiled. "Thanks. I was hoping you would join me since I knew you would love everything they had on the menu. The last time I was here, this was my favorite place to eat."

He recalled the last time he'd been in Bajadad. He'd felt guilty about being so far away from home, so far away from his family, especially when the younger Westmorelands, who'd taken his parents' and aunt's and uncle's deaths hard, had rebelled like hell. Getting a call from Dillon to let him know their youngest brother, Bane, had gotten into trouble again had become a common occurrence.

"We need to talk, Micah."

He glanced across the table at Kalina and saw the firm set of her jaw. He'd figured she would have a lot to say, so he'd asked that they be given a private room in the back. It was a nice room with a nice view, but nothing was nicer than looking at the woman he was with.

He now knew he had played right into her father's hands just as much as she had. The general had been certain that Micah would be so pissed that Kalina didn't believe him that he wouldn't waste his time trying to convince her of the truth. He hadn't. He had allowed two years to pass while the lie she believed festered.

But now he was back, seeking her forgiveness. Not for what he had done but for what he hadn't done, which was to fight for her and to prove his innocence. Dillon had urged him to do that as soon as Kalina had confronted him, but Micah had been too stubborn, too hurt that she could so easily believe the worst about him. Now he wished he had fought for her.

"Okay, you can talk and I'll listen," he said, pushing his plate aside and taking a sip of his wine.

She frowned and blew out a breath. "I want you to stop with the game playing."

"And that's what you think I'm doing?"

"Yes."

He had news for her, what he was doing was fighting for his survival the only way he knew how. He intended to make her trust him. He would lower his guard and include her in his world, which is something he hadn't done since Patrice. He would seduce her back into a relationship and then prove she was wrong. He would do things differently this time and show her he wasn't the man she believed him to be.

"What if I told you that you're wrong?"

"Then what do you call what you're doing?" she asked in a frustrated tone.

"Pursuing the woman I want," he said simply.

"To get me in your bed?"

"Or any other way I can get you. It's not all sexual."

She gave a ladylike snort. "And you expect me to believe that?"

He chuckled. "No, not really. You've told me numerous times that you don't believe a word I say."

"Then why are you doing this? Why would you want to run behind a woman who doesn't want you?"

"But you *do* want me."

She shook her head. "No, I don't."

He smiled. "Yes, you do. Even though you dislike me for what you think I did, there's a part of you that wants me as much as I want you. Should I prove it?"

She narrowed her gaze. "You can't prove anything."

He preferred to disagree but decided not to argue with her. "All right."

She lifted her brow. "So you agree with what I said?"

"No, but I'm not going to sit here and argue with you about it."

She inclined her head. "We are not arguing about it, we are discussing it. Things can't continue this way."

"So what do you suggest?"

"That you cease the flirtation and sexual innuendoes. I don't need them."

Micah was well acquainted with what she needed. It was the same thing he needed. A night together. But sharing one night would just be a start. Once he got her back in his bed he intended to keep her there. Forever. He drew in a deep breath. The thought of forever with any other woman was enough to send him into a panic. But not with her.

He placed his napkin on the table as he glanced over at her. "Since you've brought them up, let's take a moment to talk about needs, shall we?"

She nodded. That meant she would at least listen, although he knew in the end she wouldn't agree to what he was about to suggest. "Although our relationship two years ago got off on a good start, it ended on a bad note. I'm not going to sit here and rehash all that happened, everything you've falsely accused me of. At first I was pretty pissed off that you would think so low of me. Then I realized the same thing you said a couple of nights ago at that party—you didn't know me. I never gave you the chance to know the real me. If you'd known the real *me* then you would not have believed the lie your father told you."

She didn't say anything, but he knew that didn't necessarily mean she was agreeing with him. In her eyes, he was guilty until proven innocent. "I want you to get to know the real me, Kalina."

She took a sip of her wine and held his gaze. "And how am I supposed to do that?"

At least she had asked. "You and I both have a thirty-day leave coming up as soon as we fly out of India. I'd like to invite you to go home with me."

KALINA SAT UP straight in her chair. "Go home with you?"

"Yes."

She stared at him across the lit candle in the middle of the table. "And where exactly is home?"

"Denver. Not in the city limits, though. My family and I own land in Colorado."

"Your family?"

"Yes, and I would love for you to meet them. I have fourteen brothers and cousins, total, that live in Denver. And then there are those cousins living in Atlanta, Montana and Texas."

This was the first time he'd mentioned anything about his family to her, except for the day he had briefly spoken of his parents when she'd asked. "What a diverse family." She didn't have any siblings or cousins. He was blessed to have so many.

He leaned back in his chair with his gaze directly on her. "So, will you come?"

"No." She hadn't even needed to think about it. There was no reason for her to spend her vacation time with Micah and his family. What would it accomplish?

As if he had read her mind, he said, "It would help mend things between us."

She narrowed her gaze. "Why would I want them mended?"

"Because you are a fair person, and I believe deep down you want to know the truth as much as I want you to. For whatever reason—and I have my suspicions as to what they are—your father lied about me. I need to redeem myself."

"No, you don't."

"Yes, I do, Kalina. Whether there's ever anything between us again matters to me. Like I told you before, I truly did enjoy the time we spent together, and I think if you put aside that stubborn pride of yours, you'll admit that you did, too."

He was right, she had. But the pain of his betrayal was something she hadn't been able to get beyond. "What made you decide to invite me to your home, Micah?"

"I told you. I want you to get to know me."

She narrowed her gaze. "Could it be that you're also planning for us to sleep together again?"

His mouth eased into a smile, and he took another sip of his wine. "I won't lie to you. That thought had crossed my mind. But I have never forced myself on any woman and I don't ever plan to do so. I would love to share a bed with you, Kalina, but the purpose of this trip is for you to get to know me. And I also want you to meet my family."

She set down her glass. "Why do you want me to get to know your family now, Micah, when you didn't before?"

Kalina noted the serious expression that descended upon his features. Was she mistaken or had her question hit a raw nerve? Leaning back in her chair, she stared at him while waiting for an answer. Given that he'd invited her to his home to meet his family, she felt she deserved one.

He took another sip of wine and, for a moment, she thought he wasn't going to answer and then he said. "Her name was Patrice Nelson. I met her in my second year of college. I was nineteen at the time. We dated only a short while before I knew she was the one. I assumed she thought the same thing about me. We had been together a few months when a plane carrying my parents went down, killing everyone on board, including my father's brother and his wife."

She gasped, and a sharp pain hit her chest. She had known about his parents, but hadn't known other family members had been killed in that plane crash, as well. "You lost your parents and your aunt and uncle?"

"Yes. My father and his brother were close and so were my mother and my aunt. They did practically everything together, which was the reason they were on the same plane. They had gone away for the weekend. My parents had seven kids and my aunt and uncle had eight. That meant fifteen Westmorelands were left both motherless and fatherless. Nine of them were under the age of sixteen at the time."

"I'm sorry," she said, feeling a lump in her throat. She hadn't known him at the time, but she could still feel his pain. That had to have been an awful time for him.

"We all managed to stay together, though," he said, breaking into her thoughts.

"How?"

"The oldest of all the Westmorelands was my brother

Dillon. He was twenty-one and had just graduated from the university and had been set to begin a professional basketball career. He gave it all up to come home. Dillon, and my cousin Ramsey, who was twenty, worked hard to keep us together, even when people were encouraging him to put the younger four in foster homes. He refused. Dil, with Ramsey's help, kept us all together."

In his voice, she could hear the admiration he had for his brother and cousin. She then recalled the woman in his life at the time. "And I'm sure this Patrice was there for you during that time, right?"

"Yes, so it seemed. I took a semester off to help with things at home since I'm the third oldest in the family, although there's only a month separating me from my cousin Zane."

He took a sip of wine and then said, "Patrice came to visit me several times while I was out that semester, and she got to know my family. Everyone liked her... at least everyone but one. My cousin Bailey, who was the youngest of the Westmorelands, was barely seven, and she didn't take a liking to Patrice for reasons we couldn't understand."

He didn't say anything for a moment, as if getting his thoughts together, then he continued, "I returned to school that January, arriving a couple of days earlier than planned. I went straight to Patrice's apartment and..."

Kalina lifted a brow. "And what?"

"And I walked in on her in bed with one of her professors."

Of all the things Kalina had assumed he would say, that definitely wasn't one of them. She stared at him, and he stared back. She could see it, there, plain, right in his features—the strained look that came from remembered pain. He had been hurt deeply by the woman's deception.

"What happened after that?" she asked, curious.

"I left and went to my own apartment, and she followed me there. She told me how sorry she was. She said that she felt she needed to be honest with me, as well as with herself, so she also admitted it hadn't been the first time she'd done it with one of her professors, nor would it be the last. She said she needed her degree, wanted to graduate top of her class and saw nothing wrong with what she was doing. She said that if I loved her I would understand."

Kalina's mouth dropped. *The nerve of the hussy assuming something like that!* "And did you understand?"

"No." He didn't say anything for a moment. "Her actions not only hurt me, but they hurt my family. They had liked her and had become used to her being with me whenever I came home. It probably wouldn't have been so bad if Dillon's and Ramsey's girls hadn't betrayed them around the same time. We didn't set a good example for the others as far as knowing how to pick decent and honest women."

He paused a moment and then said in a low, disappointed voice, "I vowed then never to get involved with a woman to the extent that I'd bring her home to my family. And I've kept that promise...until now."

Kalina took a sip of her drink and held Micah's gaze,

not knowing what to say. Why was he breaking his vow now, for her? Did it matter that much to him that she got to know him better than she had in Sydney?

Granted, she realized he was right. Other than being familiar with how well he performed in bed, she didn't know the simplest things about him, like his favorite color, his political affiliation or his religious beliefs. Those things might not be important for a short-term affair, but they were essential for a long-term relationship.

But then they'd never committed to a relationship. They had been merely enjoying each other's company and companionship. She hadn't expected "forever" and frankly hadn't been looking for it, either. But that didn't mean the thought hadn't crossed her mind once or twice during their two-month affair.

And she was very much aware that the reason he wanted her to get to know him now still didn't have anything to do with "forever." He assumed if she got to know him then she would see that she'd been wrong to accuse him of manipulating her for her father.

The lump in her throat thickened. What if she was wrong about him and her father had lied? What if she had begun to mean something to Micah the way he claimed? She frowned, feeling a tension headache coming on when so many what-ifs flooded her brain. Her father had never lied to her before, but there was a first time for everything. Perhaps he hadn't outright lied, but she knew how manipulative he could be where she was concerned.

"You don't have to give me your answer tonight, Kal, but please think about it."

She broke eye contact with him to study her wineglass for a moment, twirling the dark liquid around. Then she lifted her gaze to meet his again and said, "Okay, I will think about it."

A smile touched his lips. "Good. That's all I'm asking." He then checked his watch. "Ready to leave?"

"Yes."

Moments later, as they stood outside while a cab was hailed for them, she couldn't help remembering everything Micah had told her. She couldn't imagine any woman being unfaithful to him, and she could tell from the sound of his voice while he'd relayed the story that the pain had gone deep. That had been well over ten years ago. Was he one of those men, like her father, who could and would love only one woman?

She was aware of how her mother's death had affected her father. Although she'd known him to have lady friends over the years, she also knew he hadn't gotten serious about any of them. Her mother, he said, would always have his heart. Kalina couldn't help wondering if this Patrice character still claimed Micah's heart.

When they were settled in the cab, she glanced over at him and said, "I'm sorry."

He lifted a brow. "For what?"

"Your loss. Your parents. Your uncle and aunt." She wouldn't apologize for Patrice because she didn't see her being out of the picture as a loss. Whether he real-

ized it or not, finding out how deceitful his girlfriend
was had been a blessing.

His gaze held hers intensely, unflinchingly, when he
said, "I didn't share my history with you for your pity
or sympathy."

She nodded. "I know." And she did know. He had
taken the first steps in allowing her to get beyond that
guard he'd put up. For some reason, she felt that he truly
wanted her to get to know him. The real Micah Westmoreland. Was he truly any different from the one she
already knew?

She had to decide just how much of him, if any, she
wanted to get to know. He had invited her to spend time
with him and his family in Denver, and she had to think
hard if that was something she really wanted to do.

A FEW HOURS later, back in his room at the villa, Micah
turned off the lamp beside his bed and stared up at
the ceiling in darkness. He had enjoyed sharing dinner
with Kalina, and doing so had brought back memories
of the time they'd spent together in Sydney. Tonight,
more than ever, he had been aware of her as a woman.
A woman he wanted. A woman he desired. A woman
he intended to have.

He'd never wanted to be attracted to Kalina, even in
the beginning. Mainly because he'd known she would
hold his interest too much and for way too long. But
there hadn't been any hope for him. The chemistry had
been too strong. The desire too thick. He had been attracted to her in a way he had never been attracted to
another woman.

And tonight she had been a good listener. She had asked the questions he had expected her to ask and hadn't asked ones that were irrelevant. The private room they'd been given had been perfect for such a conversation. But even the intense subject matter did nothing to lessen the heat that stirred in the air, or waylay the desire that simmered between them.

Very few people knew the real reason he and Patrice had ended things. He'd only told Dillon, Ramsey and Zane, the cousin he was closest to. Micah was certain the others probably assumed they knew the reason, but he knew their assumptions wouldn't even come close.

Walking in and finding the woman he loved in bed with another man had been traumatic for him, especially given that he'd been going through a very distressing time in his life already. The sad thing was that there hadn't been any remorse because Patrice had felt justified in doing what she'd done. She just hadn't been able to comprehend that normal men and women didn't share their partners.

He shifted in bed and thought about Kalina. He had enjoyed her company tonight and believed she'd enjoyed his. He'd even felt an emotional connection to her, something he hadn't felt with a woman in years. He didn't need to close his eyes to remember the stricken look on her face two years ago when she'd overheard words that had implicated him. And no matter how much he had proclaimed his innocence, she hadn't believed him.

For two years, they had gone their separate ways. At first, he'd been so angry he hadn't given a damn. But at night he would lie in bed awake. Wanting her and missing her. It was then that he'd realized just how much Kalina had worked her way into his bloodstream, how deeply she'd become embedded under his skin. He had traveled to several countries over the past two years. He had worked a ton of hours. But nothing had been able to eradicate Kalina from his mind.

Now she was back in his life, and he intended to use this opportunity to right a wrong. If only she would agree to go home to Denver with him. He wouldn't question why it was so important to him for her to do so, but it was. And although he hadn't told her, he wouldn't accept no for an answer.

So what are you going to do if she turns you down, Westmoreland? Kidnap her?

Kidnapping Kalina didn't sound like a bad idea, but he knew he wouldn't operate on the wrong side of the law. He hoped that she gave his invitation some serious consideration so it didn't come to that.

It had been hard being so close to her and having to keep his hands to himself when he'd wanted them all over her, touching her in places he'd been privy to before. But as he'd told her, it was important that they get to know each other, something they hadn't taken the time to do in Sydney.

On the cab ride back, he'd even discovered she knew how to ride a horse and that her grandparents had been farmers in Alabama. Her grandparents had even raised, among other things, sheep. His cousin Ramsey, who was the sheep rancher in the Westmoreland family, would appreciate knowing that. And Micah couldn't

CHAPTER SIX

THE NEXT DAY, Kalina's body tensed when she entered the lab and immediately remembered that she and Micah would be working alone together today. Theo was in another area analyzing the granules taken from the bodies of the five victims.

She eased the door closed behind her and stood leaning against it while she looked over at Micah. He was standing with his head tilted back as he studied the solution in the flask he was holding up to the light. She figured he wasn't aware she had entered, which was just as well for the time being.

His request from last night was still on her mind, and even after a good night's sleep, she hadn't made a decision about what she would do. She had weighed the pros and cons of accompanying him to Denver, but even that hadn't helped. It had been late when she had returned from dinner, but she'd tried reaching her father. The person she'd talked to at the Pentagon wouldn't even tell her his whereabouts, saying that, at the moment, the general's location was confidential. She had wanted to hear her father tell her again how Micah had played a role in keeping her out of China. A part of her resented the fact that Micah was back in her life, but another part of her felt she deserved to know the truth.

She wrapped her arms around herself, feeling a slight damp in the air. Everyone had awakened to find it raining that morning. And although the showers only lasted for all of ten minutes, it had been enough to drench the mountainside pretty darn good.

Micah's back was to her, and her gaze lowered to his backside, thinking it was one part of his body she'd always admired. He certainly had a nice-looking butt. She'd heard from Theo that Micah had gotten up before five this morning to go to the villa's gym to work out. She would have loved to have been a fly on the wall, to watch him flex those masculine biceps of his.

Her thoughts drifted to the night before. On the cab ride back to the villa he'd told her more about his brothers and cousins. She wasn't sure if he was feeding her curiosity or deliberately enticing her to want to meet them all for herself. And she would admit that she'd become intrigued. But was that enough to make her want to spend an entire month with him in Denver?

"Are you going to just stand there or get to work? There's plenty of it to be done."

She frowned, wondering if he had eyes in the back of his head, as he'd yet to turn around. "How did you know it was me?"

"Your scent gave you away, like it always does."

Since she usually wore the same cologne every day, she would let that one slide. She moved away from the door at the same time as he turned around, and she really wished he hadn't when he latched those dark, intense eyes onto her. Evidently, this was going to be one of her "drool over Micah" days. She'd had a number of them before. He was looking extremely handsome today. He probably looked the same yesterday, but today her hormones were out in full force, reminding her just how much of a woman she was and reminding her of all those sexual needs she had ignored for two years.

"Have most of the tissues been analyzed?" she asked, sliding onto her stool in front of a table that contained skin samples taken during autopsies of the five victims.

"No, I left that for you to do."

"No problem."

She glanced over at Micah, who was still studying the flask while jotting down notes. He was definitely engrossed in his work. Last night, he'd been engrossed in her. Was this the same man whose gaze had filled her with heated lust last night during the cab rides to the restaurant and back? The same man who'd sat across from her at dinner with a look that said he wanted to eat her alive? The same man whose flirtation and sexual innuendoes had stirred her with X-rated sensations? The same man who exuded a virility that said he was all man, totally and completely?

"Are you going to get some work done or sit there and waste time daydreaming?"

She scowled, not appreciating his comment. Evidently, he wasn't in a good mood. She wondered who had stolen his favorite toy. Now he was sitting on a stool at the counter and hadn't glanced up.

"For your information, I get paid for the work I do and not the time it takes me to do it."

She shook her head. And to think that this was the

same man who'd wanted her to spend thirty days with him and his family. She'd have thought he would be going out of his way to be nice to her.

"In other words…"

"In other words, Dr. Westmoreland," she said, placing her palms on the table and leaning forward. "I can handle my business."

He looked up at her and his mouth twitched in a grin. "Yes, Dr. Daniels, I know for a fact that you most certainly can."

She narrowed her eyes when it became obvious he'd been doing nothing more than teasing her. "I was beginning to wonder about you, Micah."

"In what respect?" he asked.

"Your sanity."

"Ouch."

"Hey, you had that coming," she said, and couldn't help the smile that touched her lips.

"I wish I had something else coming about now. My sanity as well as my body could definitely use it."

Her eyebrows lifted. The look in his eyes, the heated lust she saw in their dark depths told her they were discussing something that had no place in the lab. Deciding it was time to change the subject, she said, "How are things going? Found anything unusual?"

He shook his head. "Other than what you found yesterday, no, I could find nothing else. Theo's dissecting those tissue particles now. Maybe he'll come across something else in the breakdown."

She blew out a breath, feeling a degree of frustration. Granted, it was just the second day, but still, she was anxious about those samples Theo was analyzing. So far there hadn't been any more deaths and that was a good thing. But, at the same time, if they couldn't discover the cause, there was a chance the same type of deaths could occur again.

She glanced over at Micah at the exact moment that he raised his head from his microscope. "Come and take a look at this."

There was something in his voice that made her curious. Without thinking, she quickly moved across the room. When he slid off his stool, she slid onto it. She looked down into his microscope and frowned. She then looked up at him, confused. "I don't see anything."

"Then maybe you aren't looking in the right place."

Kalina wasn't sure exactly what she was expecting, but it wasn't Micah reaching out and gently pulling her from the stool to wrap his arms around her. His manly scent consumed her and his touch sent fire racing all through her body. She drew in a steadying breath and tilted her head back to look up at him. And when he brought her closer to his hard frame, she felt every inch of him against her.

Although her pulse was drumming erratically in response, she said, "I don't want this, Micah." She knew it was a lie the moment she said it and, from the heat of his gaze, he knew it was a lie, as well.

"Then maybe I need to convince you otherwise," he said, seconds before lowering his mouth to hers.

She had intended to shove him away…honestly she had, but the moment she parted her lips on an enraged sigh and he took the opportunity to slide his tongue in her mouth, she was a goner. Her stomach muscles quivered at the intensity and strength in the tongue that caught hold of hers and began sucking as if it had every right to do so. Sucking on her tongue as if it was the last female tongue on earth.

He was devouring her. Feasting on her. Driving her insane while tasting her with a sexual hunger she felt all the way to her toes. A strong concentration of that hunger settled in the juncture of her thighs.

And speaking of that spot, she felt his erection—right there—hard, rigid, pressing against her belly, making her remember a time when it had done more than nudge her, making her remember a time when it had actually slid inside her, between her legs, going all the way to the hilt, touching her womb. It had once triggered her inner muscles to give a possessive little squeeze, just seconds before they began milking his aroused body for everything they could get and forcing him to explode in an out-of-this-world orgasm. She remembered. She couldn't forget.

And then she began doing something she was driven to do because of the way he was making love to her mouth, as well as the memories overtaking her. Just like the last time he'd overstepped his boundaries in a kiss, she began kissing him back, taking the lead by escaping the captivity of his tongue and then capturing his tongue with hers. Ignoring the conflicting emotions swamping her, she kissed him in earnest, with a hunger only he could stir. She took possession of his mouth and he let her. He was allowing her to do whatever she wanted. Whatever pleased her. And when she heard a deep guttural moan, she wasn't sure if it had come from his throat or hers.

At the moment she really didn't care.

MICAH DEEPENED THE kiss, deciding it was time for him to take over. Or else he would have Kalina stretched across the nearest table with her legs spread so fast neither of them would have a chance to think about the consequences. He doubted he would ever get tired of kissing her and was surprised this was just the second time their tongues had mingled since seeing each other again. But then, staying away from each other had been her decision, not his. If he had his way, their mouths would be locked together 24/7.

As usual, she fit perfectly in his arms, and she felt as if she belonged there. There was nothing like kissing a beautiful woman, especially one who could fill a man's head with steamy dreams at night and heated reality during the day. He found it simply amazing, the power a woman could wield over a man. Case in point, the power that this particular woman had over him.

It didn't matter when he kissed her, or how often, he always wanted more of her. There was nothing quite like having her mouth beneath his. And he liked playing the tongue game with her. He would insert his tongue into her mouth and deepen the kiss before withdrawing and then going back in. He could tell from her moans that she was enjoying the game as much as he was.

His aroused body was straining hard against his zipper, begging for release, pleading for that part of her it had gotten to know so well in Australia. Her feminine scent was in the air, feeding his mind and body with a heated lust that had blood rushing through his body.

A door slamming somewhere had them quickly pulling apart, and he watched as she licked her lips as if she could still taste him there. His guts clenched at the thought. He'd concluded from the first that she had a very sexy mouth, and from their initial kiss he'd discovered that not only was it sexy, it was damn tasty as sin. She took a step back and crossed her arms over her chest, pulling in quick breaths. "I can't believe you did that. What if someone had walked in on us?"

He shrugged while trying to catch his own breath. His mouth was filled with her taste, yet he wanted more. "Then I would have been pretty upset about the interruption," he said.

She glared. "We should be working."

He smiled smoothly. "We are. However, we are entitled to breaks." He leaned against the table. "I think you need to loosen up a little."

"And I think you need to get a grip. You've gotten your kiss, Micah. That's two now. If I were you, I wouldn't try for a third."

He had news for her, he would try for a third, fourth, fifth and plenty more beyond that. There was no way his mouth wouldn't be locking with hers again. She had sat back down on the stool and had picked up one of the vials as if to dismiss not only him but also what they'd just shared. He had no intention of letting her do that. "Why can't we kiss again? I'm sure there's plenty more where those two came from."

She lifted her gaze to his. "I beg to differ."

He chuckled. "Oh, I plan to have you begging, all right."

Her eyes narrowed, and he thought she looked absolutely adorable. Hot, saucy and totally delectable. "If you're trying to impress me then—"

"I'm not. I want you to get to know me and the one thing you'll discover about me is that I love the unexpected. I like being unpredictable, and when it comes to you, I happen to be addicted."

"Thanks for letting me know. I will take all that into consideration while deciding if I'm going home with you in a couple of weeks. You might as well know none of it works in your favor."

"I never took you for a coward."

She frowned. "Being a coward has nothing to do with it. It's using logical thinking and not giving in to whims. Maybe you should do the same."

He couldn't help the grin that spread across his lips. Lips that still carried her taste. "Oh, sweetheart, I *am* using logical thinking. If I got any more sensible I would have stripped you naked by now instead of just imagining doing it. In fact, I'm doing more than imagining it, I'm anticipating it happening. And when it does, I promise to make it worth every moan I get out of you."

Ignoring her full-fledged glare, he glanced at his watch. "I think I'll go grab some lunch. I've finished logging my findings on today's report, but if you need help with what you have to do then—"

"Thanks for the offer, but I can handle things myself."

"No problem. And just so we have a clear under-standing… My invitation to go home with me to Denver has no bearing on my kissing you, touching you or wanting to make love to you. You have the last word."

She raised an eyebrow. "Do I really?"

"Absolutely. But I'd like to warn you not to say one thing while your body says another. I tend to listen more to body language."

"Thanks for the warning."

"And thanks for the kiss," he countered.

She frowned, and he smiled. If only she knew what he had in store for her… Hell, it was a good thing that she didn't know. His smile widened as he removed his lab jacket. "I'll be back later. Don't work too hard while I'm gone. You might want to start storing up your energy."

"Storing up my energy for what?"

He leaned in close, reached out, lightly stroked her cheek with his fingertips and whispered, "For when we make love again."

Seeing the immediate flash of fire in her gaze, he said, "Not that I plan on gloating, but when you find out the truth, that I've been falsely accused, I figure you'll want to be nice to me. And when you do, I'll be ready. I want you to be ready, as well. I can't wait to make love to you again, and I plan to make it worth the hell you've put me through, baby."

The heat in her gaze flared so hotly he had to strug-gle not to pull her back into his arms and go after that third kiss. He was definitely going to enjoy pushing her buttons.

As he moved to walk out of the lab, he thought that if that last kiss was anything to go by, he might as well start storing up some energy, as well. He turned back around before opening the door and his gaze traveled over her. He wanted her to feel the heat, feel his desire. He wanted her to want to make love to him as much as he wanted to make love to her.

She held his gaze with a defiant frown and said nothing. He smiled and gave her a wink before finally opening the door to leave.

"IT'S ALL HIS FAULT," Kalina muttered angrily as she tossed back her covers to ease out of bed. It had been almost a week since that kiss in the lab and she hadn't had a single good night's sleep since.

She was convinced he was deliberately trying to drive her loony. Although he hadn't taken any more liberties with her, he had his unique ways of making her privy to his lusty thoughts. His eye contact told her everything—regardless of whether it was his lazy perusal or his intense gaze—whenever she looked into his eyes there was no doubt about what was on his mind. More than once she'd looked up from her microscope to find those penetrating dark eyes trained directly on her.

It didn't take much to get her juices flowing, literally, and for the past week he'd been doing a pretty good job of it. She knew he enjoyed getting on her last nerve, and it seemed that particular nerve was a hot wire located right at the juncture of her thighs.

She had tried pouring her full concentration into her

work. All the test results on the tissues had come back negative. Although they suspected that some deadly virus had killed those five people, as of yet the team hadn't been able to pinpoint a cause, or come up with conclusive data to support their hypothesis. The granules were still a mystery, and so far they had not been able to trace the source. The Indian government was determined not to make a big to-do about what they considered nothing and wouldn't let them test any others who'd gotten sick but had recovered. The team had reported their findings to Washington. The only thing left was to wrap things up. She knew that Micah was still concerned and had expressed as much in his report. A contagious virus was bad enough, but one that could not be traced was even worse.

Although it had been over a week since he'd issued his invitation, she still hadn't given Micah an answer regarding going with him to Denver. With only three days before they left India, he had to be wondering about her decision. Unfortunately, she still didn't have a clue how she would answer him. The smart thing would be to head for Florida for a month, especially since Micah hadn't made the past week easy for her. He deliberately tested her sanity every chance he got. And although he hadn't tried kissing her again, more than once he had intentionally gotten close to her, brushed against her for no reason at all or set up a situation where he was alone with her. Those were the times he would do nothing but stare at her with a heated gaze as potent as any caress.

Kalina drew in a deep breath, suddenly feeling hot

and in need of cool air. After slipping into her robe, she crossed the room and pushed open the French doors to step out on the balcony. She appreciated the whisper of a breeze that swept across her face. The chill made her shiver but still didn't put out the fire raging inside her.

Over the past two years she'd gone each day without caring that she was denying her body's sexual needs. Now, being around Micah was reminding her of just what she'd gone without. Whenever she was around him, she was reminded of how it felt to have fingertips stroke her skin, hands touch her all over and arms pull her close to the warmth of a male body.

She missed the caress of a man's lips against hers, the graze of a male's knuckles across her breasts, the lick of a man's tongue and the soft stroke of masculine fingers between her legs.

There was nothing like the feel of a man's aroused body sliding inside, distended and engorged, ready to take her on one remarkable ride. Making her pleasure his own. And giving all of himself while she gave everything back to him.

Her breathing quickened and her pulse rate increased at what she could now admit she'd been missing. What she had given up. No other man had brought her abstinence more to the forefront of her thoughts than Micah. She felt hot, deliriously needy, and she stood there a moment in silence, fighting to get her bearings and control the turbulent, edgy desire thrumming through her.

Nothing like this had ever happened to her before. All it took was for her to close her eyes to recall how it felt for Micah's hands to glide over the curve of her backside, cup it in his large palms and bring her closer to his body and his throbbing erection.

The memories were scorching, hypnotic and almost more than she could handle. But she would handle them. She had no choice. She would not let Micah get the best of her. She had no qualms, however, about getting the best of him—in the area right below his belt.

She rubbed her hand down her face, not believing her thoughts. They had gotten downright racy lately, and she blamed Micah for it. She was just about to turn to go back inside when a movement below her balcony caught her attention. A man was out jogging and she couldn't help noticing what a fine specimen of a man he was.

The temperature outside had to be in the low thirties, yet he was wearing a T-shirt and a pair of shorts. In her opinion, he was pneumonia just waiting to happen. Who in their right mind would be out jogging at this hour of the night, half dressed?

She leaned against the railing and squinted her eyes in the moonlight. That's when she saw that the man who'd captured her attention was Micah. Evidently, she wasn't the only one who couldn't sleep. She found that interesting and couldn't help wondering if perhaps the same desire that was keeping her awake had him in its lusty clutches, as well.

Serves him right if it did. He had spent a lot of his time this week trying his best to tempt her into his bed, but apparently he was getting the backlash.

He was about to jog beneath her balcony, so she held

her breath to keep him from detecting her presence. Except for the glow of the half moon, it was dark, and there was no reason for him to glance up...or so she reasoned. But it didn't stop him from doing so. In fact, as if he'd sensed she was there, he slowed to a stop and stared straight up at her, locking in on her gaze.

And he kept right on staring at her while her heart rate increased tenfold. Suddenly there was more than a breeze stirring the air around her, and it seemed as if her surroundings got extremely quiet. The only thing that was coming in clear was the sound of her irregular breathing.

She stared right back at him and saw that his gaze was devouring her in a way she felt clear beneath her robe. In fact, if she didn't know for certain she was wearing clothes, she would think that she was naked. Oh, why were the sensual lines of his lips so well-defined in the moonlight? Knowing she could be headed for serious trouble if their gazes continued to connect, she broke eye contact, only to be drawn back to his gaze seconds later.

He had to be cold, she thought, yet he was standing in that one spot, beneath her balcony, staring up at her. She licked her lips and felt his gaze shift to her mouth.

Then he spoke in a deep, husky voice, "Meet me in the staircase, Kalina."

His request flowed through her, touching her already aroused body in places it shouldn't have. Turbulent emotions swept through her, and from the look in his eyes it was obvious that he expected her to act on his demand. Should she? Could she? Why would she?

She was bright enough to know that he didn't want her to meet him so they could discuss the weather. Nor would they discuss their inability to pinpoint the origin of the deadly virus. There was no doubt in her mind as to why he wanted to meet her on the stairs, and she would be crazy, completely insane, to do what he asked.

Breaking eye contact with him, she moved away from the balcony's railing and slid open the French doors to go back inside. She moved toward her bed, tossed off her robe and was about to slide between the sheets, when she paused. Okay, she didn't like him anymore, but why was she denying herself a chance to have a good night's sleep? She had needs that hadn't been met in more than two years, and she knew for a fact that he was good at that sort of thing. She didn't love him, and he didn't love her. It would be all about needs and wants being satisfied, nothing more.

She drew in a deep breath, thinking she might be jumping the gun here. All he'd asked her to do was to meet him at the stairs. For all she knew, he might just want to talk. Or maybe he merely wanted to kiss her. She gave herself a mental shake, knowing a kiss would only be the start. Any man who looked at her the way Micah had looked at her a few moments ago had more than kissing on his mind.

Deciding to take the guesswork out of it, she reached for the blouse and skirt she'd taken off earlier and quickly put them on. She knew what she wanted, and Micah better not be playing games with her, because she wasn't in the mood.

Heaven help her, but she was only in the mood for

one thing, and at the moment, she didn't care whether she liked him or not just as long as he eased that ache within her.

As she grabbed her room key off the nightstand and shoved it into the pocket of her skirt, she headed toward the door.

MICAH PACED THE stairway, trying to be optimistic. Kalina would come. Although he knew it would be a long shot if she did, he refused to give up hope. He had read that look in her eyes. It had been the same one he knew was in his. She wanted him as much as he wanted her. He had been playing cat-and-mouse games with her all week, to the point where Theo had finally pulled him aside and told him to do something about his attitude problem. He'd almost laughed in his friend's face. Nothing was wrong with his attitude; it was his body that had issues.

So here he was. Waiting. Hoping she wouldn't walk through the door just to tell him to go to hell. Well, he would have news for her. As far as he was concerned, he was already there. Going without a woman for two years hadn't been a picnic, but he hadn't wanted anyone except her and had denied himself because of it. It was unbelievable how a man's desire for one woman could rule his life, dictate his urges and serve as a thermostat for his constant craving. He was feeling the heat. It was flooding his insides and taking control of every part of his being.

Over the past several days, he'd thought about knocking on Kalina's door but had always talked himself out of it. He wouldn't have been so bold as to ask her to meet him on the staircase tonight if he hadn't seen that particular look in her eyes. He knew that look in a woman's eyes well enough: heated lust. He'd seen it in Kalina's eyes many times.

He turned when he heard footsteps. It was late. Most normal people were asleep. He should be asleep. Instead, he was up, wide awake, horny as hell and lusting after a woman. But not just any woman. He wanted Kalina. She still hadn't told him whether she'd made a decision about going home with him, and he hoped that no news was good news.

He heard the sound of the knob turning and his gaze stayed glued to the door. Most people used the elevator. He preferred the stairs when jogging, for the additional workout. He drew in a deep breath. Was it her? Had she really come after two years of separation and the misunderstanding that still existed between them?

The door slowly opened, and he gradually released his breath. It was Kalina, and at that moment, as his gaze held tight to hers, he couldn't stop looking at her. The more he looked at her, the more he wanted her. The more he needed to be with her.

Had to be with her.

But he needed her to want to be with him just as much. Deciding not to take her appearance here for granted, he slowly moved toward her, his steps unhurried yet precise. His breathing was coming out just as hard as the erection he felt pressing against his shorts.

Micah reached her and lifted his hand to push a lock of hair from her face. Knowing what she thought was the truth about him, he understood that it had taken a lot for her to come to him. He intended to make sure she didn't regret it.

He opened his mouth to say something, but she placed a finger to his lips. "Please don't say anything, Micah. Just do it. Take me now and take me hard."

Her words fired his blood, and his immediate thought was that, given the degree of his need, he would have no problem doing that. He tightened his hand on hers. "Come on, let's go up to my room."

She pulled back and shook her head. "No. Do it here. Now."

He met her gaze, stared deep into her eyes. "I wouldn't suggest that if I were you," he warned. "You just might get what you ask for."

"I'm hoping."

He heard the quiver in her voice and saw the degree of urgency in her expression. There was a momentous need within her that was hitting him right in the gut and stirring his own need. He drew in a deep breath. There was no doubt in his mind that he was about to lose focus, but he also knew he was about to gain something more rewarding.

He then thought of something. *Damn, damn and triple damn.* "I don't have a condom on me."

His words didn't seem to faze her. She merely nodded and said, "I'm still on the pill and still in good health."

"I'm still in good health, as well," he said and thought there was no need to admit that he hadn't made love to another woman since her.

"Then do it, Micah."

He heard the urgency and need in her voice. "Whatever you want, baby."

Reaching behind her, he locked the entry door before lifting her off her feet to place her back against the wall. Raising her skirt, he spread her legs so they could wrap around him. His shaft began twitching, hardening even more as he lowered his zipper to release it. He skimmed his hands between Kalina's legs and smiled when he saw there were no panties he needed to dispense with. She was hot, and ready.

So was he.

He lowered his head to take her mouth, and at the same moment he aimed his erection straight for her center and began sliding in. Her hands on his shoulders were used to draw him closer into the fit of her.

She took in several deep breaths as he became more entrenched in her body. She felt tight, and her inner muscles clenched him. He broke off the kiss, closed his eyes and threw his head back as he clutched her hips and bottom in his hands and went deeper and deeper. There was nothing like having your manhood gripped, pulled and squeezed by feminine muscles intent on milking you dry.

His lips returned to hers in a deep, openmouthed kiss as he began thrusting hard inside her, tilting her body so he could hit her G-spot. He wanted to drive her wild, over the edge.

"Micah. Oh, Micah, don't stop. Please don't stop. I missed this."

She wasn't alone. He had missed this, as well. At

that moment, something fierce and overpowering tore through him and like a jackhammer out of control, he thrust inside her hard, quick and deep. Being inside her this way was driving him over the edge, sending fire through his veins and rushing blood to all parts of his body, especially the part connected to her.

"Micah!"

Her orgasm triggered his as hard and hot desire raged through him. He plunged deeper into her body. The explosion mingled their juices as his release shot straight to her womb as if that's where it wanted to be, where it belonged. She shuddered uncontrollably, going over the edge. He followed her there.

Unable to resist, he used his free hand to push aside her blouse and bra and then latched his mouth to her nipple, sucking hard. At the same time, his body erupted into yet another orgasm and a second explosion rocketed him to heights he hadn't scaled in two years.

He now knew without a doubt what had been missing in his life. Kalina. Now more than ever he intended to make sure she never left him again.

CHAPTER SEVEN

KALINA SLOWLY OPENED her eyes. Immediately, she knew that although she was in her room at the villa, she was not in bed alone. Her backside was spooned against hard masculine muscles with an engorged erection against the center of her back.

She drew in a deep breath as memories of the night before consumed her. Micah had a way of making her feel feminine and womanly each and every time he kissed her, touched her or made love to her. And he had made love to her several times during the night. It was as if they were both trying to make up for the two years they'd been apart.

Considering the unfinished business between them, she wasn't sure their insatiable passion had been a good thing. But last night she hadn't cared. Her needs had overridden her common sense. Instead of concentrating on what he had done to betray her, she had been focused on what he could do to her body. What he had done last night had taken the edge off, and she had needed it as much as she'd needed to breathe. He had gone above and beyond the call of duty and had satisfied her more than she had imagined possible. Now all she wanted to do was stay in bed, be lazy and luxuriate in the afterglow.

"Hey, babe. You awake?" Micah asked while sliding a bare leg over her naked body.

If she hadn't been awake, she was now, she thought when the feel of his erection on her back stiffened even more. She drew in a deep breath, not sure she was ready to converse with him yet. With the sensation of him pressing against her, however, she had a feeling conversation was the last thing on Micah's mind.

"Kal?"

Knowing she had to answer him sometime, she slowly turned onto her back. "Yes, I'm awake."

He lifted up on his elbow to loom over her and smiled. "Good morning."

She opened her mouth to give him the same greeting, but that was as far as she got. He slid a hand up her hip just seconds before his lips swooped down and captured hers. The second his tongue entered her mouth she was a pathetic goner. No man kissed like Micah. He put everything he was into the kiss, and she could feel all kinds of sensations overtaking her and wrapping her in a sensual cocoon.

A part of her felt that maybe she should pull back. She didn't want to give him the wrong message, but another part of her was in a quandary as to what the wrong message could be, in light of what they'd shared the night before.

And as he kissed her, she remembered every moment of what they'd shared.

She recalled them making love on the stairwell twice before he'd carried her back to her room. Once inside, they had stripped off their clothes and showered together. They'd made out beneath the heated spray of water before lathering each other clean. He had dried her off, only to lick her all over and make her wet again.

Then they had made love in her bed several times. She had ridden him, and he had ridden her. Then they had ridden each other. The last thing she remembered was falling asleep totally exhausted in his arms.

It was Micah who finally pulled his mouth away, but not before using his tongue to lick her lips from corner to corner.

"You need to stop that," she said in a voice that lacked any real conviction.

"I will, when I'm finished with you," he said, nibbling at the corners of her mouth.

She knew that could very well be never. "You need to go to your room so I can get dressed for work, and you need to get dressed, too."

"Later."

And then he was kissing her again, more passionately than before. She tried to ignore the pleasure overtaking her, but she couldn't. So she became a willing recipient and took everything he was giving her. His kiss was so strong and potent that when he finally pulled his mouth away, she actually felt light-headed.

"I missed that," he murmured, close to her ear. "And I missed this, as well." He moved to slide his body over hers, lifted her hips and entered her in one smooth thrust.

He looked down at her and held her gaze in a breathless moment before moving his body in and out of her. "Being inside you feels so incredibly good, Kal," he whispered, and she thought a woman could get spoiled by this. She certainly had been spoiled during their time in Sydney. So much so that she had suffered through withdrawal for months afterward.

"Oh, baby, you're killing me," Micah growled out, increasing the intensity of his strokes. Kalina begged to differ. He was the one killing her. Her body was the one getting the workout of a lifetime. Blood was rushing through all parts of her, sending shock waves that escalated and touched her everywhere. Never had she been made love to so completely.

All further thought was forced from her mind when he hollered her name just seconds before his body bucked in a powerful orgasm. She felt the essence of his release shoot straight to her womb. The feel of it triggered a riot of sensations, which burst loose within her.

"Micah!"

"I'm here, baby. Let it go. Give yourself to me completely. Don't hold anything back."

She heard his words and tried closing her mind to them but found that she couldn't. She couldn't hold anything back, even if she tried. The strength of her need for him stunned her, but whether she wanted to admit it or not, she knew that what she and Micah were sharing was special. She wanted to believe it was meant just for them.

He continued to hold her, even when he eventually shifted his body off hers. He'd gotten quiet, and she wondered what he was thinking. As if he'd read her thoughts, he reached out and cupped her chin in his hand then tilted her head so she could look at him and he could look at her.

She felt the heat of his gaze in every part of her body. He brushed a kiss across her lips. "Have dinner with me tonight."

She quickly recalled that dinner after a night of passion was how their last affair had begun. They had slept together one night after work and the next evening he'd taken her out to eat. After dinner, they'd gone back to her place and had been intimately involved for two glorious months.

"We've done that already, Micah."

At his confused look, she added, "Dinner and all that goes with it. Remember Sydney? Different place. Same technique."

He frowned. "Are you trying to say I'm boring you?"

She couldn't help smiling. "Do I look bored? Have I acted bored?"

He laughed. "No to both."

"All right, then. All I meant was that I recall a casual dinner was how things started between us the last time."

"You have to eat."

"Yes, but you don't have to be the one who's always there to feed me. I'm a big girl. I can take care of myself."

"Okay, then," he said, leaning in close to run the tip of his tongue around her earlobe. "What do you want from me?"

She chuckled. "What I got last night and this morning was pretty darn good. I have no complaints."

He lifted his head and frowned down at her. "Shouldn't you want more?"

"Are you prepared to give me more?" she countered.

He seemed to sober with her question. He held her gaze a moment then said, "I want you to get to know the real me, Kal. You never did decide if you're willing to go home with me or not."

Mainly because she'd tried putting the invitation out of her mind. She hadn't wanted to talk about it or even think about it. "I need more time."

"You have only two days left," he reminded her.

Yes, she knew. And she wasn't any closer to making a decision than she had been a week ago. Sleeping together had only complicated things. But she had no regrets. She had needed a sexual release.

She had needed him.

"Well, that's it," Micah told Kalina and Theo several hours later, at the end of the workday. "There haven't been any more reported deaths, and with the case of the few survivors, the Indian government won't let us get close enough to do an examination since we have no proof it's linked and the people did survive."

"The initial symptoms were the same. They could have survived for a number of reasons," Kalina said in frustration.

The only way to assure the U.S. military had a preventative mechanism in place if the virus popped up again was to come up with a vaccine. Micah and his team hadn't been able to do that. The chemicals that had been used were not traceable in the human body after death. And the only sign of abnormality they'd been able to find was the enlargement of the tongue. Other than that, all they had was an unexplained virus that presented as death by natural causes.

She, Theo and Micah knew there was nothing natural about it, but there was nothing they could do in this instance except report their findings to Washington and hope this type of "mysterious illness" didn't pop up again. Before the Indian government had pulled the plug on any further examinations of the survivors, Kalina had managed to obtain blood samples, which she had shipped off to Washington for further study.

"I'm flying out tonight," Theo said, standing. "I'm meeting Renee in Paris for one of her shows. Where are you two headed now?"

"I'm headed home to Denver," Micah said. He then glanced over at Kalina expectantly.

Without looking at Micah, she said, "I'm not sure where I'm going yet."

"Well, you two take care of yourselves. I'm going up to my room to pack. It's been a lot of fun, but I'm ready to leave."

Micah was ready to leave as well and looked forward to going home to chill for a while. He glanced over at Kalina, deciding he wouldn't ask her about her decision again. He'd made it pretty clear he wanted her to spend her time off with him.

He glanced over at her while she stood to gather up her belongings. He couldn't stop his gaze from warming with pleasure as he watched her. Kalina Daniels had the ability to turn him on without even trying. His response to her had set off warning bells inside his head in Sydney, and those same bells were going off now. He hadn't taken heed then, and he wouldn't be taking heed now.

He wanted her. Yes, she had hurt him by believing the worst, but he was willing to overlook that hurt because he had been partially to blame. He hadn't given her the opportunity to really get to know him. Now, he was offering her that chance, but it was something she had to want to do. So far, she didn't appear to know if she wanted to make that effort.

"I'm glad I was able to draw that blood and have it shipped to Washington before the Indian government stepped in," he heard her say.

He nodded as he stood. "I'm glad, as well. Hopefully, they'll be able to find something we couldn't."

"I hope so."

He studied her for a moment. "So, what are your plans for the evening?" Because of what she'd said that morning, he didn't want to ask specifically about dinner.

She drew in a deep breath. "Not sure. I just might decide to stay in with a good book."

"All right."

He fought back the desire to suggest they stay in together. Regardless of what they'd shared last night and this morning, Kalina would have to invite him to share any more time with her. The decision had to be hers…but there was nothing wrong with making sure she made the right one.

"I'm renting a car and going for a drive later," he of-fered.

She glanced over at him. "Really? Where?"

"No place in particular. I just need to get away from the villa for a while." He felt that they both did. Although they would be leaving India in a couple of days, they had pretty much stayed on the premises during the entire investigation. "You're invited to come with me if you'd like."

He could tell by her expression that she wanted to but was hesitant to accept his invitation. He wouldn't push. "Well, I'll see you later."

He had almost made it to the door, when she called after him. "Micah, if you're sure you don't mind having company, I'll tag alone."

Inwardly, he released a sigh of relief. He slowly turned to her. "No, I wouldn't mind. I would love having you with me. And there's a club I plan to check out, so put on your dancing shoes." Then without saying anything else, he walked out of the room.

Dancing shoes?

She shook her head recalling Micah's suggestion as she moved around her room at the villa. She loved dancing, but she'd never known him to dance. At least he'd never danced with her during those two months they'd been together. Even the night they'd met, at the ball. Other guys had asked her to dance, but Micah had not.

Micah had a lean, muscular physique, and she could imagine his body moving around on anyone's dance floor. So far, that had been something she hadn't seen. But she had been more than satisfied with all his moves in the bedroom and couldn't have cared less if any of those moves ever made it to the dance floor.

She heard a knock at the door, and her breath caught. Even with the distance separating them, she could feel the impact of his presence. After making love that morning, he had left her room to go to his and dress. They had met downstairs for breakfast with Theo. Today had been their last day at the lab. Tomorrow was a free day to do whatever they wanted, and then on Friday they would be flying out.

Major Harris had already called twice, asking where she wanted to go after she returned to Washington, and Kalina still wasn't certain she wanted to join Micah in Denver.

She knew she'd have to decide soon.

She quickly moved toward the door and opened it. Micah's slow perusal of her outfit let her know she'd done the right thing in wearing this particular dress. She had purchased it sometime last year at a boutique in Atlanta while visiting a college friend.

"You look nice," he said, giving her an appreciative smile.

She let her gaze roam over him and chuckled. "So do you. Come in for a moment. You're a little early, and I haven't switched out purses."

"No problem. Take your time."

Micah followed her into a sitting area and took the wingback chair she offered. When she left the room, he glanced around at the pictures on the wall. They were

different from the ones in his room. His cousin Gemma
was an interior decorator, and while taking classes at
the university, she had decorated most of her family
members' homes for practice. He would be the first to
admit she'd done a good job. No one had been disappointed. He had been home for a short visit while she'd
decorated his place, and she had educated him about
what to look for in a painting when judging if it would
fit the decor.

He was sure these same paintings had been on the
wall when he'd carried Kalina through here in his arms
last night. But his mind had been so preoccupied with
getting her to bed, he hadn't paid any attention.

"I'm ready. Sorry to make you wait."

He glanced around, smiled and came to his feet. "No
problem."

For a moment, neither of them said anything, but
just stood there and stared at each other. Then finally
he said, "I'm not going to pretend last night and this
morning didn't happen, Kal."

She nodded slowly. "I don't recall asking you to."

She was right, she hadn't. "Good, then I guess it's
safe for me to do this, since I've been dying to all day."

He reached out, tugged her closer to him and lowered his mouth to hers.

The arms that encompassed Kalina in an embrace
were warm and protective. And the hand that rubbed
up and down her spine was gentle.

But nothing could compare to the mouth that was
taking her over with slow, deep, measured strokes. Already, desire was racing through her, and she couldn't

do anything but moan her pleasure. No other two tongues could mate like theirs could, and she enjoyed the feel of his tongue in her mouth.

He shifted his stance to bring them closer, and she felt his hard erection pressing into her. It wouldn't bother her in the least if he were to suggest they stay in for the evening.

Instead, he finally broke contact, but immediately placed a quick kiss on her lips. "I love your taste," he whispered hotly.

She smiled up at him. "And I love yours, too."

The grin he shot her was naughty. "I'm going to have to keep that in mind."

She chuckled as she saw the glint of mischief in his gaze. "Yes, you do that."

Kalina always thought she could handle just about anything or anyone, but an hour or so after they'd left her room, she wasn't sure. She was seeing a side of Micah she had never seen before. It had started with the drive around the countryside. There had been just enough daylight left to enjoy the beauty of the section of town they hadn't yet seen, especially the shops situated at the foot of the Himalayas.

They had dined at a restaurant in the shopping district, and the food had been delicious. Now they were at the nightclub the restaurant manager had recommended.

She was in Micah's arms on the dance floor. The music was slow, and he was holding her while their bodies moved together in perfect rhythm. She was vaguely aware of their surroundings. The inside of the club was dark and crowded. Evidently this was a popular hangout. The servers were moving at a hurried pace to fill mixed-drink orders. And the live band rotated periodically with a deejay.

"I like this place, Micah. Thanks for bringing me here."

"You're welcome."

"And this is our first dance," she added.

He glanced down at her, tightened his arms around her and smiled. "I hope it's not our last."

She hoped that, as well. She liked the feel of being held by him in a place other than the bedroom. It felt good. But she could tell he wanted her from the hard bulge pressing against her whenever their bodies moved together. She liked the feel of it. She liked knowing she was desired. She especially appreciated knowing she could do that to him—even here in a crowded nightclub in the middle of a dance floor.

"Excalibur."

She glanced up at him. "Excuse me."

"My middle name is Excalibur."

She blinked, wondering why he was telling her that. "Oh, okay."

He chuckled. "You didn't know that, did you?"

She shrugged. "Was I supposed to?"

"I wish you had. I should have told you. We were involved for two months."

Yes, they had been involved, but their affair had been more about sex than conversation. He interrupted her thoughts by saying, "I know more about you than you know about me, Kalina."

She tilted her head to the side and looked at him. "You think so?"

"Yes."

"Well, then, tell me what you know," she said.

He tightened his arms around her waist as they swayed their bodies in time with the music. "You're twenty-seven. Your middle name is Marie. Your birthday is June fifteenth. Your favorite color is red. You hate eating beets. Your mother's name was Yvonne, and she died of cancer when you were ten."

He grinned as if proud of himself. "So what does that tell you?"

She stared at him for a few moments as if collecting her thoughts and then said, "I did more pillow talk than you did."

He laughed at that. "Sort of. What it tells me is that you shared more of yourself with me than I did with you."

They had already concluded there were a lot of things they didn't know about each other. So, okay, he had a heads-up on her information. That was fine. What they'd shared for those two months was a bed and not much else.

"It should not have been just sex between us, Kalina. I can see that now."

Now, *that's* where she disagreed. Their affair was never intended to be about anything but sex. For those two months, they had gotten to know each other intimately but not intellectually, and that's the way they'd wanted it. "If what you say is true, Micah, nobody told me. I distinctively recall you laying down the rules for a no-strings affair. And I remember agreeing to those rules. Your career was your life, and so was mine."

Evidently, she'd given him something to think about, because he didn't say anything to that. The music stopped, and he led her back to their table. A server was there, ready to take their drink order. One thing she'd noticed, two years ago and today, was that Micah was always a gentleman. He was a man who held doors open for ladies, who stood when women entered the room and who pulled out chairs for his date...the way he was doing now. "Thanks."

"You're welcome."

She glanced across the table at him. "You have impeccable manners."

He chuckled. "I wouldn't go that far, but I do my best."

"Do your brothers and cousins all have good manners like you?"

He winked. "Come home to Denver with me and find out."

Kalina rolled her eyes in exasperation. "You won't give up, will you?"

"No. I think you owe me the chance to clear my name."

He didn't say anything for a moment, allowing the server to place their drinks in front of them. Then she took a sip of her wine and asked, "Is clearing your name important to you, Micah?"

Leaning back, he stared over at her before saying, "If you really knew me the way I want you to know me, you wouldn't be asking me that."

She didn't say anything for a while. A part of her wanted to believe him, to believe that he truly did want her to get to know him better, to believe that he hadn't done what her father had said. But what if she went home with him, got to know him and, in the end, still felt he was capable of doing what she had accused him of doing?

"Micah—"

"You owe me that, Kalina. I think I've been more than fair, considering I am innocent of everything you've accused me of. Some men wouldn't give a damn about what you believed, but I do. Like I said, you owe me the chance to prove your father lied."

She drew in a deep breath. Did she owe him? She didn't have much time to think about it. He reached across the table and captured her small hand in his bigger one. Just a touch from him did things to her, made her feel what she didn't want to feel.

"I hadn't wanted to make love to you again until we resolved things between us," he said in a low tone.

She gave a cynical laugh. "So now you're going to claim making love last night and this morning was my idea?"

"No. I wanted you, and I knew that you wanted me."

He was right, and there was no need to ask how he'd known that. She had wanted him, and she'd been fully aware that he had wanted her.

"Would it make you feel more comfortable about going home with me if I promise not to touch you while you're there?"

She narrowed her gaze. "No, because all you'll do

is find ways to tempt me to the point where I'll end up being the one seeking you out. I'm well aware of those games you play, Micah."

He didn't deny it. "Okay, then. We are adults," he said. "With needs. But the purpose of you going to Denver with me is not to continue our sexual interactions. I want to make that clear up front."

He had made that clear more times than she cared to count. Her stomach knotted, and she wondered when she would finally admit that the real reason she was reluctant to go to Denver was that she might end up getting too attached to him, to his family, to her surroundings...

Her heart hammered at the mere thought of that happening. For years, especially after her grandparents' deaths, she had felt like a loner. She'd had her father—whenever he managed to stay in one place long enough to be with her. But their relationship wasn't like most parent-child relationships. She believed deep down that he loved her, but she also knew that he expressed that love by trying to control her. As long as she followed his orders like one of his soldiers, she remained in his good graces. But if she rebelled, there was hell to pay. The only reason he had apologized for his actions regarding her canceled trip to Beijing was that, for the first time in his life, he saw that he could make her angry enough that he could lose her. She had been just that upset with him, and he knew it. Although he had never admitted it, her father was just as much of a maverick as she was.

She glanced down at the table and saw that Micah

was still holding her hand. It felt good. Too good. Too right. She thought about pulling her hand away, but decided to let it stay put since he seemed content holding it. Her breathing quickened when he began stroking her palm in a light caress. His touch was so stimulating it played on her nerve endings as if they were the strings of a well-tuned guitar.

She glanced up and met his gaze. He stopped stroking her skin and curved his hand over hers to entwine their fingers. "No matter what you believe, Kal, I would never intentionally hurt you."

She nodded and then he slowly withdrew his hand from hers. She instantly felt the loss of that contact.

He glanced around the club and then at the dance floor. The deejay was playing another slow song. "Come on, I want to hold you in my arms again," he said, reaching out and taking her hand one more time.

He led her to the dance floor, and she placed her head on his chest. He wrapped his arms around her, encompassing her in his embrace. His heart was beating fast against her cheek, and his erection pressed hard against her middle again. She smiled. Did he really think they could go to Denver together and not share a bed?

She chuckled. Now she was beginning to wonder if he really knew *her* that well.

He touched her chin and tipped her head back to meet his gaze. "You okay?"

She nodded, deciding not to tell him what she'd found so comical, especially since he was wearing such a serious expression on his face.

CHAPTER EIGHT

"WELCOME TO Micah's Manor, Kalina,"

Micah stood aside as Kalina entered his home and looked around. He saw both awe and admiration reflected in her features. He hadn't told her what to expect and now he was glad that he hadn't. This was the first official visit to his place by any woman other than one of his relatives. What Kalina thought mattered to him.

In his great-grandfather's will, it had been declared that every Westmoreland heir would receive one hundred acres of land at the age of twenty-five. As the oldest, Dillon got the family homestead, which included the huge family house that sat on over three hundred acres.

Micah had already established a career as an epidemiologist and was living in Washington by the time his twenty-fifth birthday came around. For years, he'd kept the land undeveloped and whenever he came home he would crash at Dillon's place. But when Dillon got married and had a family of his own, Micah felt it was time to build his own house.

He had taken off six months to supervise the project. That had been the six months following the end of his affair with the very woman now standing in his living room. He had needed something to occupy his time, and his thoughts, and having this house built seemed the perfect project.

He could count on one finger the number of times he had actually spent the night here, since he rarely came home. The last time had been when he'd come to Denver for his brother Jason's wedding reception in August. It had been nice to stay at his own place, and the logistics had worked out fine since he, his siblings and cousins all had houses in proximity to each other.

"So, what do you think?" he asked, placing Kalina's luggage by the front door.

"This place is for one person?"

He couldn't help laughing. He knew why she was asking. Located at the south end of the rural area that the locals referred to as Westmoreland Country, Micah's Manor sat on Gemma Lake, the huge body of water his great-grandfather had named in honor of his wife when he'd settled here all those years ago. Micah's huge ranch-style house was three stories high with over six thousand square feet of living space.

"Yes. I admit I let Gemma talk me into getting carried away, but—"

"Gemma?"

"One of my cousins. She's an interior designer. To take full advantage of the lake, she figured I needed the third floor, and as for the size, I figured when my time ended with the feds, I would want to settle down, marry and raise a family. It was easier to build that dream house now instead of adding on later."

"Good planning."

"I thought so at the time. I picked the plan I liked best, hired a builder and hung around for six months to make sure things got off to a good start," he added.

"Oh, I see."

He knew she really didn't. She had no idea that when he'd selected this particular floor plan he had envisioned her sharing it with him, even though the last thing she had uttered to him was that she hated his guts. For some reason, he hadn't been able to push away the fantasy that one day she would come here and see this place. He had even envisioned them making love in his bedroom while seeing the beauty of the lake. Having Kalina here now was a dream come true.

"I had to leave on assignment to Peru for a few months and when I returned, the house was nearly finished. I took more time off and was here when Gemma began decorating it."

"It is beautiful, Micah."

He was glad she liked it. "Thanks. I practically gave Gemma an open checkbook, and she did her thing. Of course, since it wasn't her money, she decided to splurge a little."

Kalina raised a dubious brow. "A little?"

He shrugged and grinned. "Okay, maybe a lot. Up until a year ago she used this place as a model home to showcase her work whenever she was trying to impress new clients. As you can see, her work speaks for itself."

Kalina glanced around. "Yes, it sure does. Your cousin is very gifted. Is she no longer in the business?"

"She's still in it."

"But she no longer needs your house as a model?" Kalina asked.

"No, mainly because she's living in Australia now that she and Callum are married. That's where he's from. They have a two-month-old son. You'll get to meet them some time next week. She's coming home for a visit."

He had given his family strict orders to stay away from his place to give him time to get settled in with his houseguest. Of course, everyone was anxious to meet the woman he'd brought home with him.

"This should be an interesting thirty days," she said, admiring a huge painting on the wall.

"Why do you say that?"

She shrugged. "Well, all those markers I saw getting here. Jason's Place. Zane's Hideout. Canyon's Bluff. Ramsey's Web. Derringer's Dungeon. Stern's Stronghold… Need I go on?"

He chuckled. "No, and you have my cousin Bailey to thank for that. We give her the honor of naming everyone's parcel of land, and she's come up with some doozies." He picked up her luggage. "Come on, I'll show you to your room. If you aren't in the mood to climb the stairs, I do have an elevator."

"No, the stairs are fine. Besides, it gives me the chance to work the kinks out of my body from our long flight."

She followed him to one of the guest rooms on the third floor. They hadn't slept together since that one night he'd spent with her after they'd met on the staircase. Even after he'd taken her dancing, he had returned her to her room at the villa, planted a kiss on her cheek and left. The next day had been extremely busy with them packing up the lab's equipment and finalizing reports.

They had been too busy to spend time getting naked on silken sheets. But that hadn't meant the thought hadn't run through his mind a few times. Yesterday they'd taken the plane here, and sat beside each other for the flight. The twelve hours from India to Washington, and then the six hours from Washington to Denver had given him time to reflect on what he hoped she would get from her thirty days with him and his family.

"Wow!" Kalina walked into Micah's guest bedroom and couldn't do anything but stare, turn around and stare some more.

The room was done in chocolate, white and lime green. Everything—from the four-poster, white, queen-size bed, to the curtains and throw pillows—was perfectly matched. The walls of the room were painted white, which made the space look light and airy. Outside her huge window was a panoramic view of the lake she'd seen when they arrived. There was a private bath that was triple the size of the one she had in her home in Virginia. It had both a Jacuzzi tub and a walk-in shower.

She wasn't surprised Micah had given her one of his guest rooms to use. He wanted to shift their relationship from the physical to the mental. She just wasn't so sure she agreed with his logic. She could still get to know him while they shared a bed, and she didn't understand why he assumed differently. She watched him place the luggage by her bed. He said nothing as she continued to check out other interesting aspects of the room.

"I can see why Gemma used your house as a model home," Kalina said, coming to stand in front of him. "Your house should be featured in one of those magazines."

He chuckled. "It was. Last year. I have a copy downstairs. You can read the article if you like."

"All right."

"I'll leave you to rest up and relax. I plan on preparing dinner later."

She raised a surprised brow. "You can cook?"

He laughed. "Of course I can cook. And I'm pretty good at it, you'll see." He reached out and softly kissed her on the lips. "Now, get some rest."

He turned to leave, but she stopped him. "Where's your room?"

He smiled down at her as if he had an idea why she was asking. "It's on the second floor. I'll give you a tour of my bedroom anytime you want it."

She nodded, fully aware that a tour of his bedroom wasn't what she was really interested in. She wanted to try out his bed.

A FEW HOURS later, Kalina closed her eyes as she savored the food in her mouth. "Mmm, this is delicious," she said, slowly opening her eyes and glancing across the dinner table at Micah.

After indulging in a bath in the Jacuzzi, she had taken a nap, only to awaken hours later to the smell of something good cooking in the kitchen downstairs. She had slipped into a T-shirt and a pair of capris, and, not bothering to put shoes on, she had headed downstairs to find Micah at the stove. In his bare feet, shirtless, with jeans riding low on his hips, he'd looked the epitome of sexy as he moved around his spacious kitchen. She had watched him and had seen for herself just how at home he was while making a meal. She couldn't help admiring him. Some men couldn't even boil water.

He had told her he could cook, but she hadn't taken him at his word. Now, after tasting what he'd prepared, she was forced to believe him. *Almost*. She glanced around the kitchen.

"What are you looking for?" he asked her.

She looked back at him and smiled. "Your chef."

Micah chuckled. "You won't find one here. I did all this myself. I don't particularly like cooking, but I won't starve if I have to do it for myself."

No, he wouldn't starve. In fact, he had enough cooking skills to keep himself well fed. He had prepared meat loaf, rice and gravy, green beans and iced tea. He'd explained that he'd called ahead and had gotten his cousin Megan to go grocery shopping for him. She'd picked up everything he'd asked her to get and a few things he hadn't asked her for…like the three flavors of ice cream now in the freezer.

"Do you ever get lonely out here, Micah?"

He glanced across the table at her and laughed. "Are you kidding? I have relatives all around me. I try to catch up on my rest whenever I'm home, but they don't make it easy. Although I'm not here the majority of the time, I'm involved in the family business. I have a share in my brother's and cousins' horse-breeding business, in my cousin Ramsey's sheep business and I'm on the board of Blue Ridge Land Management." He then told her how his father and uncle had founded the company years ago and how his brother Dillon was now CEO.

Kalina immediately recognized the name of the company. It had made the Forbes Top 50 just this year. She could only sit and stare at him. She'd had no idea he was one of *those* Westmorelands.

Not that having a lot of money was everything, but it told her more about his character than he realized. He worked because he wanted to work, not because he had to. Yet he always worked just as hard as any member of his team—sometimes even harder. She couldn't help wondering how he'd chosen his field of work and why he was so committed and dedicated to it.

Over dinner he told her more about his family, his brothers and cousins, especially the escapades of the younger Westmorelands. Although she tried not to laugh, she found some of their antics downright comical and could only imagine how his brother Dillon and cousin Ramsey had survived it all while still managing to keep the family together.

"And you say there are fifteen of you?" she asked, pushing her plate away.

"Yes, of the Denver clan. Everyone is here except Gemma, who now lives in Sydney, and the few who are still away at college. Needless to say, the holidays are fun times for us when everyone comes home."

Getting up to take their plates to the sink, he asked, "Do you feel like going horseback riding later? I thought I'd give you a tour of the rest of the house and then we can ride around my property."

Excitement spread through her. "I'd like that."

He returned to the seat next to her. "But first I think we need to have a talk."

She lifted an eyebrow. "About what?"

"About whose bed you'll be sleeping in while you're here."

And before she could respond, he had swept her out of her chair and into his arms. He carried her from the kitchen into the living room where he settled down on the sofa with her in his lap.

MICAH SMILED AT the confused look on Kalina's face. She brushed back a handful of hair and then pinned him with one of her famous glares. "I didn't know there was a question about where I'd be sleeping."

She wasn't fooling him one bit. "Isn't there? I put you in the guest room for a reason."

She waved off his words. "Then maybe we do need to talk about that foolishness regarding your no-sex policy again."

He'd figured she would want to discuss it, which was why he'd brought up the subject. "It will be less complicated if we don't share the same bed for a while."

"Until I really get to know you?"

"Yes."

"I disagree with your logic on taking that approach, especially since you want me. Do you deny it?"

How could he deny it when he had an erection he knew she could feel since she was practically sitting on it. "No, I don't deny it, but like I said when I invited you here, I want you to—"

"Get to know you," she muttered. "I heard you. More times than I care to. And I don't think us sharing a bed has anything to do with what we do outside the bedroom."

"Well, I do. Last time we had an affair it was strictly sexual. Now I want to change the way you think about me, about us."

Now she really looked confused. "To what?"

He wished he could tell her the truth, that she was the woman he wanted above all others. That he wanted to marry her. He wanted her to have his babies. He wanted her to wear his name. But all the things he wanted meant nothing until she could trust him. They would never come into existence until she could believe he was not the man her father had made him out to be. This time around, Micah refused to allow sex to push those wants to the side.

"I want you to think of things other than sex when it comes to us, Kalina," he said.

She frowned. "Why?"

He could come clean and tell her how he felt about her, but he didn't think she would believe him, just as she still didn't believe he had not betrayed her two years ago. "Because we've been there before. Even you said that our relationship was starting with the same technique. I want you to feel that it's different this time."

He could tell she still didn't know where he was coming from, but the important thing was that *he* knew. A dawning awareness suddenly appeared on her features, but he had a feeling, even before she opened her mouth, that whatever she was thinking was all wrong.

"Okay, I think I get it," she said, nodding.

He was afraid to ask, but knew he had to. "And just what do you get?"

"You're one of the older Westmorelands and you feel you should set an example for the others." She nodded her head as if her assumption made perfect sense.

"Set an example for them in what way?" he asked.

"By presenting me as a friend and not a lover. You did say your cousin Bailey was young and impressionable."

He had to keep a straight face. He forced his eyes to stay focused even though he was tempted to roll them. Once she met Bailey she would see how absurd her assumption was. First of all, although she was twenty-three years old, Bailey probably didn't have much of a love life, thanks to all her older, overbearing and protective brothers and male cousins. And she had gone past being impressionable. Bailey could curse worse than any sailor when she put her mind to it. He and his brothers and cousins had already decided that the man who fell for Bailey would have to be admired…as well as pitied.

"The key word where Bailey is concerned is *was*. Trust me. I don't have to hide my affairs from anyone. Everyone around here is an adult and understands what grown-ups do."

"In that case, what other reason could you have for not wanting us to sleep together? Unless…"

He stared at her for several long moments, and when

she didn't finish what she was about to say, he prompted her. "Unless what?"

She looked down at her hands in her lap. "Nothing."

He had a feeling that again, whatever was bothering her, she'd figured wrong. He reached out, lifted her chin up and brought his face closer to hers. "And I know good and well you aren't thinking what I think you're thinking, not when my desire for you is about to burst through my zipper. There's no way you can deny that you feel it."

She nodded slowly. "Yes, I can feel it," she said softly.

So could he, and he was aware, even more than he'd been before, of just how much he wanted her. Unfortunately, pointing out his body's reaction made her aware of how much he wanted her, as well.

She stuck her tongue out and slowly licked the corner of his lips. "Then why are you denying me what I want? Why are you denying yourself what you want?"

Good question. He had to think hard to recall the reason he was denying them both. He had a plan. A little sacrifice now would pay off plenty of dividends in the years to come. Remembering his goals wouldn't have been so hard if she hadn't decided at that very moment to play the vixen. She purposely twisted that little behind of hers in his lap, against his zipper, making him mindful of just how good his erection felt against her backside. And what the hell was she doing with her tongue, using the tip of it to lick his mouth? She was deliberately boggling his mind.

"Kalina?"

"Mmm?"

"Stop it," he said in a tone he knew was not really strong on persuasion. It wasn't helping matters that he'd once fantasized about them making love in this very room and on this very sofa.

"No, I don't want to stop and you can't make me," she said in that stubborn voice of hers.

Hell, okay, he silently agreed. *Maybe I can't make her stop.* And he figured that reasoning with her would be a waste of time....

At that moment she moved her tongue lower to lick the area around his jaw and he groaned.

"Oh, I so love the way you taste, Micah."

Those were the wrong words for her to say. Hearing them made him recall just how much he loved how she tasted, as well. He drew in a deep breath, hoping to find resistance. Instead, he inhaled her feminine scent, a telltale sign of how much she wanted him. He could just imagine the sweetness of her nectar.

He thought of everything...counting sheep, the pictures on the wall, the fact that he hadn't yet cleaned off the kitchen table...but nothing could clear his mind of her scent, or the way she was using her tongue. Now she had moved even lower to lick around his shoulder blades. Hell, why hadn't he put on a shirt?

"Baby, you've got to stop," he urged her in a strained voice.

She ignored him and kept right on doing what she was doing. He tried giving himself a mental shake and found it did not work. She was using her secret weapon, that blasted tongue of hers, to break him down. Hell, he would give anything for something—even a visit from one of his kin—to interrupt what she was doing, because he was losing the willpower to put a stop to it.

Hot, achy sensations swirled in his gut when she scooted off his lap. By the time he had figured out what she was about to do, it was too late. She had slid down his zipper and reached inside his jeans to get just what she wanted. He tightened his arms on her, planning to pull her up, but again he was too late. She lowered her head and took him into her mouth.

KALINA IGNORED THE tug on her hair and kept her mouth firmly planted on Micah. By the time she was finished with him, he would think twice about resisting her, not giving her what she wanted or acting on foolish thoughts like them not sharing a bed now that she'd come all the way to Denver with him. He had a lot of nerve.

And he had a lot of this, she thought, fitting her mouth firmly on him, barely able to do so because he was so large. He was the only man she'd ever done this to. The first time she hadn't been sure she had done it correctly. But he had assured her that she had, and he'd also assured her he had enjoyed it immensely. So she might as well provide him with more enjoyment, maybe then he would start thinking the way she wanted him to. Or, for the moment, stop thinking at all.

"Damn, Kalina, please stop."

She heard his plea, but thought it didn't sound all that convincing, so she continued doing what she was doing, and pretty soon the tug on her hair stopped. Now he was twirling her locks around his fingers to hold her mouth in place. No need. She didn't intend to go anywhere.

At least she thought she wouldn't be. Suddenly, he pulled her up and tossed her down on the sofa. The moment her back hit the cushions he was there, lifting her T-shirt over her head and sliding her capris and panties down her legs, leaving her totally naked.

The heat of his gaze raked over her, and she felt it everywhere, especially in her feminine core. "No need to let a good erection go to waste, Micah," she said saucily.

He evidently agreed with her. Tugging his jeans and briefs down over his muscular hips, he didn't waste any time slipping out of the clothes before moving to take his place between her open legs.

She lifted her arms to receive him and whispered, "Just think of this as giving me a much-deserved treat."

Kalina would have laughed at his snort if he hadn't captured her mouth in his the moment he slid inside her, not stopping until he went all the way to the hilt. And then he began moving inside her, stroking her desire to the point of raging out of control. She lifted her hips off the sofa to receive every hard thrust. The wall of his chest touched hers, brushing against her breasts in a rhythm that sent sensations rushing through her bloodstream.

Then he pulled away from her mouth, looked down at her and asked in a guttural voice, "Why?"

She knew what he was asking. "Because it makes no sense to deny us this pleasure."

He didn't say whether he agreed with her or not. Instead, he placed his hands against her backside and lifted her hips so they would be ready to meet his downward plunge. She figured he probably wasn't happy with her. He wouldn't appreciate how she had tempted him and pushed him over the edge. She figured he would stew for a while, but that was fine. Eventually he would get over it.

But apparently not before he put one sensuous whipping on her, she thought, loving the feel of how he was moving inside her. It was as if he wanted to use his body to give her a message, but she wasn't sure just what point he was trying to make. She reached up and cupped his face in her hands, forcing him to look at her. "What?" she asked breathlessly.

He started to move his lips in reply, but then, instead, leaned down and captured her mouth in his, leaving her wondering what he had been about to say. Probably just another scolding. All thoughts left her mind when she got caught up in his kiss and the way he was stroking inside her body.

She dropped her hands to his shoulders and then wrapped her arms around his neck as every sensation intensified. Then her body exploded, and simultaneously, so did his. They cried out each other's names.

This, she concluded, as a rush swept over her, was pleasure beyond anything they'd shared before. This was worth his irritation once everything was over. For now, she was fueled by this. She was stroked, claimed and overpowered by the most sensuous lovemaking she had ever known. By Micah's hands and his body.

This had been better than any fantasy, and she couldn't think of a better way to be welcomed to Micah's Manor.

CHAPTER NINE

OKAY, SO SHE hadn't held a gun to his head or forced him to make love to her, but he was still pissed. Not only at her but at himself, Micah concluded the next morning as he walked out of the house toward the barn.

After they'd made love yesterday, Kalina had passed out. He had gathered her in his arms and taken her up the stairs to the guest room. After placing her naked body beneath the covers, he had left, closing the door behind him. He'd even thought about locking it. The woman was dangerous. She had not been so rebellious the last time.

Cursing and calling himself all kinds of names—including whipped, weakling and fickle—he had cleaned up the kitchen, unpacked his luggage and done some laundry. By the time he'd finished all his chores, it had gotten dark outside. He'd then gone into his office and made calls to his family to let them know he'd returned. Most had figured as much when they'd seen lights burning over at his place. He had again warned them that he didn't want to be disturbed. He'd assured them that he and his houseguest would make an appearance when they got good and ready. He ended up agreeing to bring her to dinner tomorrow night at the big house.

By the time he'd hung up the phone after talking to everyone, it was close to nine o'clock and he was surprised that he hadn't heard a peep out of Kalina. He checked on her and found her still sleeping. He had left her that way, figuring that when she'd caught up on her rest she would wake up. Still angry with himself for giving in to temptation and momentarily forgetting his plan, he'd gone to bed.

He'd awakened around midnight to the sound of footsteps coming down the stairs. He was very much aware when the footsteps paused in front of his closed bedroom door before finally progressing to the first floor. He had flipped onto his back and listened to the sound of Kalina moving around downstairs, knowing she was raiding his refrigerator—probably getting into those three flavors of ice cream.

When he had woken up this morning he had checked on her again. Sometime during the night she had changed into a pair of pajamas and was now sleeping on top of the covers. It had taken everything within him not to shed his own clothes and slide into that bed beside her.

Then he'd gotten mad at himself for thinking he should not have let her sleep alone. He should have made love to her all through the night. He should have let her go to sleep in his arms. He should have woken her up with his lovemaking this morning.

He had quickly forced those thoughts from his mind, considering them foolish, and had gone into the kitchen. He had prepared breakfast and kept it warming on the stove for her while he headed to the barn. He preferred not to be around when she woke up. The woman was pure temptation and making love to her every chance he got was not what he had in mind for this trip.

He had thought about getting into his truck and going to visit his family, but knew it wouldn't be a good idea to be off the property when Kalina finally woke up. He glanced at his watch. It was nine o'clock already. Was she planning to sleep until noon? His family probably figured he was keeping them away because he didn't want them to invade his private time with her. Boy, were they wrong.

"Good morning, Micah. I'm ready to go riding now."

He spun around and stared straight into Kalina's face. "Where did you come from?"

She smiled and looked at him as if he'd asked a silly question. "From inside the house. Where else would I have been?"

He frowned. "I didn't hear you approach."

She used her hand to wave off his words. "Whatever. You promised to take me riding yesterday, but we didn't get around to it since we were indulging in other things. I'm ready now."

His frown deepened, knowing just what those "other things" were. She was dressed in a pair of well-worn jeans, boots and a button-down shirt. He tried not to stare so hard at how the jeans fit her body, making him want to caress each of her curves. She looked good, and it took everything he had to keep his eyes from popping out of their sockets.

"Are we going riding or not?"

He glanced up at her face and saw her chin had raised a fraction. She expected a fight and was evidently ready for one. Just as she had been ready for them to make love yesterday. Well, he had news for her. Unlike yesterday, he wouldn't be accommodating her.

"Fine," he said, grabbing his Stetson off a rack on the barn wall. "Let's ride."

KALINA COULDN'T BELIEVE Micah was in a bad mood just because she had tempted him into making love to her. But here they were, riding side by side, and he was all but ignoring her.

She glanced over at him when he brought the horses to a stop along a ridge so she could look down over the valley. His Stetson was pulled low on his brow, and the shadow on his chin denoted he hadn't shaved that morning. He wore a dark brooding look, but, in her opinion, he appeared so sexy, so devastatingly handsome, that it was a total turn-on. It had taken all she had not to suggest they return to his place and make love. With his present mood, she knew better than to push her luck.

"Any reason you're staring at me, Kal?"

She inwardly smiled. So…he'd known she was looking. "No reason. I was just thinking."

He glanced over at her, tipped his hat back and those bedroom-brown eyes sent sensations floating around in her stomach. "Thinking about what?"

"Your mood. Are you typically a moody person?"

He frowned and looked back at the valley. "I'm not moody," he muttered.

"Yes, you are. Sex puts most men in a good mood. I see it does the opposite for you. I find that pretty interesting."

He glanced back at her. A tremor coursed through her with the look he was giving her. It was hot, regardless of the reason. "You just don't get it, do you?"

She shrugged. "Evidently not, so how about enlightening me on what I just don't get."

He inhaled deeply and then muttered, "Nothing."

"Evidently there is something, Micah."

He looked away again and moments later looked back at her. "There is nothing."

He then glanced at his watch. "I promised everyone I would bring you to dinner at the big house. They can hardly wait to meet you."

"And I'm looking forward to meeting them, too."

He watched her for a long moment. Too long. "What?" she asked, wondering why he kept staring at her.

He shook his head. "Nothing. I promised you a tour of the place. Come on. Let's go back home."

It was only moments later, as they rode side by side, that it dawned on her what he'd said.

"Let's go back home..."

Although she knew Micah hadn't meant it the way it had sounded, he'd said it as if they were a married couple and Micah's Manor was theirs. Something pricked inside her. Why was she suddenly feeling disappointed at the thought that Micah's home would never be hers?

"I LIKE KALINA, Micah, and she's nothing like I expected."

Micah took a sip of his drink as he stood with Zane on the sidelines, watching how his female cousins and cousins-in-law had taken Kalina into their midst and were making her feel right at home. He could tell from the smile on Kalina's face that she was comfortable around them.

Micah glanced up at his cousin. "What were you expecting?"

Zane chuckled. "Another mad scientist like you. Someone who was going to bore us with all that scientific mumbo jumbo. I definitely wasn't expecting a sexy doctor. Hell, if she didn't belong to you, I would hit on her myself."

Micah couldn't help smiling. He, of all people, knew about his cousin's womanizing ways. "I'm sure you would, and I'm glad you're not. I appreciate the loyalty."

"No problem. But you might want to lay down the law to the twins when they arrive next week."

He thought about his twin cousins, Aidan and Adrian, and the trouble they used to get into—the trouble they could still get into at times although both were away at college and doing well. It was something about being in Westmoreland Country that made them want to revert to being hellions—especially when it came to women.

"You haven't brought a woman home for us to meet since Patrice. Does this mean anything?"

Micah took another sip of his drink before deciding to be completely honest. "I plan to marry Kalina one day."

A smooth smile touched Zane's features. "Figured as much. Does she know it?"

"Not yet. I'm trying to give her the chance to get to know me."

If Zane found that comment strange he didn't let on. Instead, he changed the subject and brought Micah up to date on how things were going in the community. Micah listened, knowing that if anyone knew what was going on it would be Zane.

Micah was well aware that Westmoreland Country would become a madhouse in a few weeks, when everyone began arriving for the christening of Gemma's baby. They were expecting all those other Westmorelands from Atlanta, Texas and Montana. And his brothers and cousins attending college had planned to return for the event, as well.

"I hadn't heard Dillon say whether Bane is coming home."

Zane shrugged. "Not sure since he might be in training someplace."

Micah nodded. Everyone knew of his baby brother's quest to become a Navy SEAL, as well as Bane's mission to one day find the woman he'd given up a few years ago. And knowing his brother as he did, Micah knew Brisbane would eventually succeed in doing both.

"I like Kalina, Micah."

Micah turned when his brother Jason walked up. The most recent member of the family to marry, Jason and his wife, Bella, were expecting twins. From the look of Bella, the babies would definitely arrive any day now.

"I'm glad you do since you might as well get used to seeing her around," Micah said.

"Does that mean you're thinking of retiring as the

Westmoreland mad scientist and returning home to start a family?" Jason asked.

Micah chuckled. "No, it doesn't mean any of that. I love my career, and Kalina loves hers. It just means we'll be working together more, and whenever I come home we'll come together."

He took a sip of his drink, thinking that what he'd just said sounded really good. Now all he had to do was convince Kalina. She had to get to know the real him, believe in him, trust him and then they could move on in their lives together.

He still wasn't happy about the stunt she'd pulled on him yesterday. He was determined to keep his distance until she realized the truth about him.

KALINA GLANCED ACROSS the room at Micah before turning her attention back to the women surrounding her. All of them had gone out of their way to make her feel at home. She hadn't known what to expect from this family dinner, but the one thing she hadn't expected was to find a group of women who were so warm and friendly.

Even Bailey, who Micah had said had been standoffish to Patrice, was more than friendly, and Kalina felt the warm hospitality was genuine. She readily accepted the women's invitation to go shopping with them later this week and to do other things like take in a couple of chick flicks, visit the spa and get their hair done. They wanted to have a "fun" week. Given Micah's present mood, she figured spending time away from him wouldn't be a bad idea.

After they'd returned to the ranch from riding, he had taken her on a quick tour of his home. Just like yesterday, she had been more than impressed with what she'd seen. His bedroom had left her speechless, and she couldn't imagine him sleeping in that huge bed alone. She planned to remedy that. It made no sense for them to be sleeping in separate beds. He wouldn't be happy about it, but he would just have to get over it.

"Um, I wonder what has Micah frowning," Pam Westmoreland, Dillon's wife, leaned over to whisper to her. "He keeps looking over this way, and I recognize that look. It's one of those Westmoreland 'you're not doing as I say' looks."

Kalina couldn't help smiling. The woman who was married to the oldest Westmoreland here had pegged her brother-in-law perfectly. "He's stewing over something I did, but he'll get over it."

Pam chuckled. "Yes, eventually he will. Once in a while they like to have their way but don't think we should have ours. There's nothing wrong with showing them that 'their way' isn't always the best way."

Hours later, while sitting beside Micah as he drove them back to Micah's Manor, Kalina recalled the conversation she'd had with Pam. Maybe continuing to defy his expectations—showing him that his way wasn't the best way—was how she should continue to handle Micah.

"Did you enjoy yourself, Kalina?"

She glanced over at him. He hadn't said much to her all evening, although the only time he'd left her side was when the women had come to claim her. If this was his way of letting her get to know him then he was way off the mark.

"Yes, I had a wonderful time. I enjoyed conversing with the women in your family. They're all nice. I like them."

"They like you, too. I could tell."

"What about you, Micah? Do you like me?"

He seemed surprised by her question. "Yes, of course. Why do you ask?"

"Um, no reason."

She looked straight ahead at the scenery flying by the car's windshield, and felt a warm sensation ignite within her every time she was aware that he was looking at her.

She surprised him when she caught him staring one of those times. Just so he wouldn't know she was on to what he was doing, she smiled and asked, "Was your grandfather Raphel really married to all those women? Bailey told me the story of how he became the black sheep of the family after running off in the early 1900s with the preacher's wife and about all the other wives he supposedly collected along the way."

Micah made a turn into Micah's Manor. "That's what everyone wants to find out. We need to know if there are any more Westmorelands out there that we don't know about. That's how we found out about our cousins living in Atlanta, Montana and Texas. Until a few years ago, we were unaware that Raphel had a twin by the name of Reginald Westmoreland. He's the great-grandfather for those other Westmorelands. Megan is hiring a private detective to help solve the puzzle about Raphel's other wives. We've eliminated two as having given birth to heirs, and now we have two more to check out."

He paused a moment and said, "The investigator, a guy by the name of Rico Claiborne, was to start work on the case months ago, but his involvement in another case has delayed things for a while. We're hoping he can start the search soon. Megan is determined to see how many more Westmorelands she can dig up."

Kalina chuckled. "There are so many of you now. I can't imagine there being others."

Micah smiled. "Well, there are, trust me. You'll get to meet them in a few weeks when they arrive for Gemma and Callum's son's christening."

"Must be nice," she said softly.

He glanced over at her. "What must be?"

"To be part of a big family where everyone is close and looks out for each other. I like that. I've never experienced anything like that before. Other than my grandparents, there has only been me and Dad…and well, you know how my relationship with him is most of the time."

Micah didn't say anything, and maybe it was just as well. It didn't take much for Kalina to recall what had kept them apart for the past two years. Although he was probably hoping otherwise, by getting to know him better, all she'd seen so far was his moody side.

When he brought the car to a stop, she said, "You like having your way, don't you, Micah?"

He didn't say anything at first and then he pushed his Stetson back out of his face. "Is that what you think?"

"Yes. But maybe you should consider something?"

"What?"

"Whatever it is you're trying to prove to me, there's a possibility that your way isn't the best way to prove it. You brought me here so I could get to know you better. It's day two and already we're at odds with each other, and only because I tempted you into doing something that I knew we both wanted to do anyway. But if you prefer that it not happen again, then it won't. In other words, I will give you just what you want...which is practically nothing."

Without saying anything else, she opened the door, got out of the truck and walked toward the house.

BE CAREFUL WHAT *you ask for*, Micah thought over his cup of coffee a few mornings later as he watched Kalina enter the kitchen. She'd been here for five days. Things between them weren't bad, but they could be better. It wasn't that they were mad at each other. In fact, they were always pleasant to each other. Too pleasant.

She had no idea that beneath all his pleasantry was a man who was horny as hell. A man whose body ached to make love to her, hold her at night. He wished she could sleep with him instead of sleeping alone in his guest bedroom. But his mind knew his decision that he and Kalina not make love for a while was the right one to make. It was his body wishing things could be different.

They would see each other in the mornings, and then usually, during the day, they went their separate ways. It wasn't uncommon for one of his female cousins or cousins-in-laws to come pick her up. On those days, he wouldn't see her till much later. So much for them spending time together.

"Good morning, Micah."

He put down his cup and pushed the newspaper aside. "Good morning, Kalina. Did you enjoy going shopping yesterday?"

She sat down at the table across from him and smiled. "I didn't go shopping yesterday. We did that two days ago. Yesterday, we went into town and watched a movie. One of those chick flicks."

He nodded. She could have asked him, and he would have taken her to the movies, chick flick or not. He got up to pour himself another cup of coffee, trying not to notice what she was wearing. Most days she would be wearing jeans and a top. Today she had put on a simple dress. Seeing her in it reminded him once again of what a nice pair of legs she owned.

"Are you and the ladies going someplace again today?" he decided to ask her.

She shook her head. "No. I plan to hang around here today. But I promise not to get in your way."

"You won't get in my way." He came back to the table and sat down. "Other than that day we went riding, I haven't shown you the rest of my property."

She lifted an eyebrow in surprise. "You mean there's more?"

He chuckled. "Yes, there's a part that I lease out to Ramsey for his sheep, and then another part I lease out to my brother Jason and my cousins Zane and Derringer for their horse-breeding business."

He took a sip of his coffee. "So how about us spending the day together?"

She smiled brightly. "I'd love to."

HOURS LATER WHEN Micah and Kalina returned to Micah's Manor, she dropped down in the first chair she came to, which was a leather recliner in the living room. When Micah had suggested they spend time together, she hadn't expected that they would be gone for most of the day.

First, after she had changed clothes, they had gone riding and he'd shown her the rest of his property. Then he had come back so they could change clothes, and they had taken the truck into town. He had driven to the nursing home to visit a man by the name of Henry Ryan. Henry, Micah had explained, had been the town's doctor for years and had delivered every Westmoreland born in Denver, including his parents. The old man, who was in his late nineties, was suffering from a severe case of Alzheimer's.

It had been obvious to Kalina from the first that the old man had been glad to see Micah and vice versa. Today, Henry's mind appeared sharp, and he had shared a lot with her, including some stories from Micah's childhood years. On the drive home, Micah had explained that things weren't always that way. There would be days when he visited Henry and the old man hadn't known who he was. Micah had credited Henry with being the one to influence him to go into the medical field.

Today, Kalina had seen another side of Micah. She'd known he was a dedicated doctor, but she'd seen him interact with people on a personal level. Not only had he visited with Henry, but he had dropped by the rooms of others at the nursing home that he'd gotten to know over the years. He remembered them, and they remembered him. Before arriving at the home, he had stopped by a market and purchased fresh fruit for everyone, which they all seemed to enjoy.

Seeing them, especially the older men, made her realize that her father would one day get old and she would be his caretaker. He was in the best of health now, but he wasn't getting any younger. It also made her realize, more so than ever, just what a caring person Micah was.

She turned to Micah, who'd come to sit on the sofa across from her. "I'll prepare dinner tonight."

He raised an eyebrow. "You can cook?"

Kalina laughed. "Yes. I lived on my grandparents' farm in Alabama for a while, remember. They were big cooks and taught me my way around any kitchen. I just don't usually have a lot of time to do it when I'm working."

She glanced at her watch. "I think I'll cook a pot of spaghetti with a salad. Mind if I borrow the truck and go to that Walmart we passed on the way back to get some fresh ingredients?"

"No, I don't mind," he said, standing and pulling the truck keys from his pocket. His cousins had stocked his kitchen, but only with non-perishables. "Although you might want to check with Chloe or Pam. They probably have what you'll need since they like to cook."

"I'm sure they do, but I need to get a prescription filled anyway. I didn't think about it earlier while we were out."

"No problem. Do you want me to drive you?"

"No, I'll be fine." She stood. "And I won't be gone long."

"GLAD TO SEE that you're out of your foul mood, Micah," Derringer Westmoreland said with a grin as he fed one of the horses he kept in Micah's barn.

Micah shot him a dirty look, which any other man would have known meant he should zip it, but Derringer wasn't worried. He knew his cousin was not the hostile type. "I don't know what brought it on, but you need to chill. Save your frown for those contagious diseases."

Micah folded his arms across his chest. "And when did you become an expert on domestic matters, Derringer?"

Derringer chuckled. "On the day I married Lucia. I tell you, my life hasn't been the same since. Being married is good. You ought to try it."

Micah dropped his hands to his sides and shrugged. "I plan on it. I just have to get Kalina to trust me. She's got to get to know me better."

Derringer frowned, which didn't surprise Micah. Whereas Zane hadn't seen anything strange by that comment, Derringer would. "Doesn't she know you already?"

"Not the way I want her to. She thinks I betrayed her a couple of years ago, and I believe that once she gets to know me she'll see I'm not capable of doing anything like that."

Now it was Derringer who crossed his arms over his chest. "Wouldn't it be easier just to tell her that you didn't do it?"

"I tried that. It's her father's word against mine, and she chose to believe her father."

Derringer rubbed his chin in a thoughtful way. "You can always confront her old man and beat the truth out of him." He then glanced around. "And speaking of Kalina, where is she? I know the ladies decided not to do anything today since both Lucia and Chloe had to take the babies in for their regular pediatric visits."

"She's preparing dinner and needed to pick up a few items from the store." Micah checked his watch. "She's been gone longer than I figured she would be."

Concern touched Derringer's features. "You think she's gotten lost?"

"She shouldn't be lost since she was only going to that Walmart a few miles away. If she's not back in a few more minutes, I'll call her on her cell phone to make sure she's okay."

The two men had walked out of the barn when Micah's phone rang. He didn't recognize the number. "Yes?"

"Mr. Westmoreland, this is Nurse Nelson at Denver Memorial. There was a car accident involving Kalina Daniels, and she was brought into the emergency room. Your number was listed in her phone directory as one of those to call in case of an emergency. Since you're local we thought we would call you first."

Micah's heart stopped beating. "She was in an accident?"

"Yes."

"How is she?" he asked in a frantic tone.

"Not sure. The doctor is checking her out now."

Absently, Micah ended the call and looked at Derringer. "Kalina was in an accident, and she's been taken to Denver Memorial."

Derringer quickly tied the horse to the nearest post. "Come on. Let's go."

"DO YOU KNOW an E.R. doctor's biggest nightmare?"

Kalina glanced over at the doctor who was checking out the bruise on her arm. "What?"

"Having to treat another doctor."

Kalina laughed. "Hey, I wasn't *that* bad, Dr. Parker."

"No." The older doctor nodded while grinning. "I understand you were worse. According to the paramedics, you wouldn't let them work on you until they'd checked out the person who was driving the other car. The one who ran the red light and caused the accident."

"Only because I knew I was fine. She's the one whose air bag deployed," Kalina said.

"Yes, but still, you deserved to be checked out as much as she did."

Kalina didn't say anything as she remembered the accident. She hadn't seen it coming. She had picked up all the things she needed from the store and was on her way back to Micah's Manor when out of nowhere, a car plowed into her from the side. She could only be thankful that she'd been driving Micah's heavy-duty truck and not a small car. Otherwise, her injuries would have been more severe.

"I don't like the look of this knot on your head. I should keep you overnight for observation."

Kalina shook her head. "Don't waste a bed. I'll be fine."

"Maybe. Maybe not. I don't have to tell you about head injuries, do I, Dr. Daniels?"

She rolled her eyes. "No, sir, you don't."

"Are you living alone?"

"No, I'm visiting someone in this area. I think your nurse has already called Micah."

The doctor looked at her. "Micah? Micah Westmoreland?"

Kalina smiled. "Yes. You know him?"

The doctor nodded. "Yes, I went to high school with his father. I know those Westmorelands well. It was tragic how they lost their parents, aunt and uncle in that plane crash."

"Yes, it was."

"The folks around here can't help admiring how they all stuck together in light of that devastation, and now all of them have made something of themselves, even Bane. God knows we'd almost given up on him, but now I understand that he's—"

Suddenly the privacy curtain was snatched aside, and Micah stood there with a terrified look on his face. "Kalina!"

And before she could draw her next breath, he had crossed the floor and pulled her into his arms.

CHAPTER TEN

BACK AT MICAH'S MANOR, Kalina, who was sitting comfortably on the sofa, rolled her eyes. "If you ask me one more time if I'm okay, I'm going to scream. Read my lips, Micah. I'm fine."

Micah drew in a deep breath. He knew he was being anal, but he couldn't help it. When he'd received a call from that nurse about Kalina's accident, he'd lost it. It was a good thing Derringer had been there. There was probably no way he could have driven to the hospital without causing his own accident. He'd been that much of a basket case.

"Don't fall asleep, Kalina. If you do, I'm only going to wake you up," he warned.

She shook her head. "Micah, have you forgotten I'm a doctor, as well. I'm familiar with the dos and don'ts following a head injury. But, like I told Dr. Parker at the hospital, I'm fine."

"And I intend to make sure you stay that way." Micah crossed the room to her, leaned down and placed a kiss on her lips.

He straightened and glanced down at her. "I don't think you know how I felt when I received that call, Kal. It reminded me so much of the call I got that day from Dillon, telling me about Mom, Dad, Uncle

Thomas and Aunt Susan. I was at the university, in between classes, and it seemed that everything went black."

She nodded slowly, hearing the pain in his voice. "I can imagine."

He shook his head. "No, honestly, you can't." He sat down beside her. "It was the kind of emotional pain and fear I'd hoped never to experience again. But I did today, when I got that call about you."

She stared at him for a few moments and then reached over and took his hand in hers. "Sorry. I didn't mean to do that to you."

He sighed deeply. "It wasn't your fault. Accidents happen. But if I didn't know before, I know now."

She lifted a brow. "You know what?"

"How much I care for you." He gently pulled her onto his lap. "I know you've been thinking that I've been acting moody and out of sorts for the past couple of days, but I wanted so much for you to believe I'm not the person you think I am."

She wrapped her arms around him, as well. "I know. And I also know that's why you didn't want to make love to me."

She twisted around in his arms to face him. "You were wasting both our time by doing that, you know. I realized even before leaving India that you hadn't lied to me about our affair in Sydney."

He pulled back, surprised. "You had?"

"Yes. I had accepted what you said as the truth before I agreed to come here to Denver with you."

She smiled. "I figured that you *had* to be telling the

truth, otherwise, you were taking a big risk in bringing me here to meet your family. But then I knew for a fact that you had been telling the truth once you got me here and wanted to put a hold on our lovemaking. You were willing to do without something I knew you really wanted just to prove yourself to me. You really didn't have to."

He covered her hand with his. "I felt that I did have to do it. Someone once told me that sacrifices today will result in dividends tomorrow, and I wanted you for my dividend. I love you, Kalina."

"And I love you, too. I realized that before coming here, as well. That night you took me dancing and I felt something in the way you held me, in the way you were talking to me. That night, I knew the truth in what you had been trying to tell me. And I knew the truth about what my feelings were for you."

She quieted for a moment and then said, "Although there's not an excuse for my father's actions, I believe I know why he did what he did. He's always been controlling, but I never thought he would go that far. I was wrong. And I was wrong for not believing you in the first place."

He shook his head. "No, like I said, you didn't know me. We had an affair that was purely sexual. The only commitment we'd made was to share a bed. It didn't take me long to figure out that I wanted more from you. That night you ended things was the night I had planned on telling you how I felt. Afterward, I was angry that you didn't believe in me, that you actually thought I didn't care, that I would go along with your father about something like that."

He paused. "When I came home, I told Dillon everything and he suggested that I straighten things out. But my pride wouldn't let me. I wasted two years being angry, but the night I saw you again I knew that no matter what, I would make you mine."

"No worries then," Kalina said, reaching up and cupping his chin. "I am yours."

He inhaled sharply when her fingers slid beneath his T-shirt to touch his naked skin over his heart. It seemed the moment she touched him that heat consumed him and spread to every part of his body. Although he tried playing it down, his desire for her was magnified to a level he hadn't thought possible.

All he could think about was that he'd almost lost her and the fear that had lodged in his throat had made it difficult to breathe. And now she was here, back at his manor, where she belonged. He knew then that he would always protect her. Not control her like her old man tended to do, but to protect her.

"Make love to me, Micah."

Her whispered request swept across his lips. "I need you inside me."

Micah studied her thoughtfully. He saw the heat in her eyes and felt the feverishness of her skin. Other than that one time on the sofa, he hadn't touched her since coming to Denver, wanting her to get to know the real him. Well, at that moment, the real him wanted her with a passion that he felt even in the tips of his fingers. She knew him, and she loved him, just as he loved her.

"What about your head?" he whispered, standing, sweeping her into his arms and moving toward the stairs.

She wrapped her arms around him and chuckled against his neck. "My head is fine, but there is another ache that's bothering me. To be quite honest with you, it was bothering me a long time before the accident. It's the way my body is aching to be touched by you. Loved by you. Needed by you."

Just how he made it up the stairs to his bedroom, he wasn't sure. All he knew was that he had placed her in the middle of his bed, stripped off her clothes and taken off his own clothes in no time at all. He stood at the foot of the bed, gazing at her. He let his eyes roam all over her and knew there was nothing subtle about how he was doing it.

This was the first time she had been in his bed, but he had fantasized about her being here plenty of times. Even during the last five days, when he'd known she was sleeping in the bedroom above his, he had wanted her here, with him. More than once, he had been tempted to get up during the night and go to her, to forget about the promise of not touching her until she had gotten to know him. It had been hard wanting her and vowing not to touch her.

And she hadn't made it easy. At times she had deliberately tried tempting him again. She would go shopping with his cousins and then parade around in some of the sexiest outfits a store could sell. But he had resisted temptation.

But not now. He didn't plan on resisting anything,

especially not the naked woman stretched out in the middle of his huge bed looking as if she belonged there. He intended to keep her there.

"I love you," he said in a low, gravelly voice filled with so much emotion he had to fight from getting choked. "I knew I did, but I didn't know just how much until I got that phone call, Kalina. You are my heart. My soul. My very reason for existing."

He slowly moved toward the bed. "I never knew how much I cherished this part of our relationship until it was gone. I can't go back and see it as 'just sex' anymore. Not when I can distinctively hear, in the back of my mind, all your moans of pleasure, the way you groan to let me know how much you want me. Not when I remember that little smile that lets me know just how much you are satisfied. No, we never had sex. We've always made love."

Kalina breathed in Micah's scent as he moved closer to her. Not wanting to wait any longer, she rose up in the bed and met him. When he placed his knee on the bed, they tumbled back into the bedcovers together. At that moment, everything ceased to exist except them.

As if she needed to make sure this moment was real, she reached out and touched his face, using her fingertips to caress the strong lines of his features. But she didn't stop there, she trailed her fingers down to his chest, feeling the hard muscles of his stomach. Her hands moved even lower, to the hardest part of him, cupping him. She thought, for someone to be so hard, there were certain parts of him that were smooth as a baby's behind.

"What are you doing to me?" he asked in a tortured groan when she continued to stroke him.

She met his gaze. "Staking my claim."

He chuckled softly. "Baby, trust me. You staked your claim two years ago. I haven't been able to make love to another woman since."

Micah knew the moment she realized the truth of what he'd said. The smile that touched her features warmed him all over, made him appreciate that he was a man, the man who had *this* woman.

Not being able to wait any longer, he leaned over and brushed a kiss against her lips. Then he moved his mouth lower to capture a nipple in his mouth and suck on it.

She arched against him, and he appreciated her doing so. He increased the suction of his mouth, relishing the taste of her while thinking of all the hours he'd lain in this bed awake and aroused, knowing she'd been only one floor away.

"Micah."

The tone of her voice alerted him that she needed him inside that part of her that was aching. Releasing her nipple, he eased her down in the bed. Before he moved in place between her legs, he had to taste her. He shifted his body to bury his head between her legs.

KALINA SCREAMED THE moment Micah's tongue swept inside her. The tip of it was hot and determined. And the way it swirled inside her had her senses swirling in unison. She was convinced that no other man could do things with their tongue the way he could. He was devouring her senseless, and she couldn't do anything but lie there and moan.

And then she felt it, an early sign that a quake was about to happen. The way her toes began tingling while her head crested with sensations that moved through every part of her.

She sucked in a deep breath, and it was then that she saw he had sensed what was about to happen and had moved in place over her. The hardness of him slid through her wetness, filling her and going beyond.

She was well aware of the moment when their bodies locked. He gazed down at her, and their eyes connected. He was about to give her the ride of her life, and she needed it. She wanted it.

He began moving, thrusting in and out of her while holding her gaze. She felt it. She felt him. There was nothing like the feeling of being made love to by the one man who had your heart. Your soul.

He kept moving, thrusting, pounding into her as if making up for lost time, for misunderstandings and disagreements. She wouldn't delude herself into thinking those things wouldn't happen again, but now they would have love to cushion the blows.

At that moment, he deliberately curved his body to hit her at an angle that made her G-spot weep. It triggered her scream, and she exploded at the same time as he did. They clung to each other, limbs entwined, bodies united. She sucked up air along with his scent. And moments later, when the last remnants of the blast flittered away from her, she collapsed against Micah, moaning his name and knowing she had finally christened his bed.

Their bed.

THE NEXT TWO weeks flowed smoothly, although they were busy ones for the Westmoreland family. Gemma and Callum were returning to christen their firstborn. Ramsey and Chloe had consented to be godparents.

All the out-of-towners were scheduled to arrive by Thursday. Most had made plans to stay at nearby hotels, but others were staying with family members. Jason and his wife, Bella, had turned what had been the home she'd inherited from her grandfather into a private inn just for family when they came to visit.

Pam had solicited Kalina's help in planning activities for everyone, and Kalina appreciated being included. Her days were kept busy, but her nights remained exclusively for Micah. They rode horses around the property every evening, cooked dinner together, took their shower, once in a while watched a movie. But every night they shared a bed. She thought there was nothing like waking up each morning in his arms.

Like this morning.

She glanced over at him and frowned. "Just look what you did to me. What if I wanted to wear a low-cut dress?"

Micah glanced over at the passion mark he'd left on Kalina. Right there on her breast. There was not even a hint of remorse in his voice when he said, "Then I guess you'd be changing outfits."

"Oh, you!" she said, snatching the pillow and throwing it at him. "You probably did it deliberately. You like branding me."

He couldn't deny her charge because it was true. But what he liked most of all was tasting her. Unfortunately, he had a tendency to leave a mark whenever he did. Hell, he couldn't help that she tasted so damn good.

He reached out and grabbed her before she could toss another pillow his way. "Come here, sweetheart. Let me kiss it away."

"All you're going to do is make another mark. Stay away from me."

He rolled his eyes. "Yeah. Right."

When she tried scooting away, he grabbed her foot to bring her back. He then lowered his mouth to lick her calf. When she moaned, he said, "See, you know you like it."

"Yes, but we don't have the time. Everyone starts arriving today."

"Let them. They can wait."

When he released his hold on her to grab her around the waist, she used that opportunity to scoot away from him and quickly made a move to get out of bed. But she wasn't quick enough. He grabbed her arm and pulled her back. "Did you think you would get away, Dr. Daniels?"

She couldn't help laughing, and she threw herself into his arms. "It's not like I'm ready to get out of bed anyway," she said, before pressing her lips to his. He kissed her the way she liked, in a way that sent sensations escalating all through her.

When he released her lips she felt a tug on her left hand and looked down. She sucked in a deep breath at the beautiful diamond ring Micah had just slid on her finger. She threw her hand to her chest to stop the rapid beating of her heart. "Oh, my God!

Micah chuckled as he brought her ringed hand to his lips and kissed it. "Will you, Kalina Marie Daniels, marry me? Will you live here with me at Micah's Manor? Have my babies? Make me the happiest man on earth?"

Tears streamed down her face, and she tried swiping them away, but more kept coming. "Oh, Micah, yes! Yes! I'll marry you, live here and have your babies."

Micah laughed and pulled her into his arms, sealing her promise with another kiss.

It was much later when they left Micah's Manor to head over to Dillon's place. Dillon had called to say the Atlanta Westmorelands had begun arriving already. Micah had put his brother on the speakerphone and Kalina could hear the excitement in Dillon's voice. It didn't take long, when around the Westmorelands, to know that family meant everything to them. They enjoyed the times they were able to get together.

Micah had explained that all the Westmorelands were making up for the years they hadn't shared when they hadn't known about each other. Their dedication to family was the reason it was important to make sure there weren't any other Westmorelands out there they didn't know about.

Kalina walked into Dillon and Pam's house with

Micah by her side and a ring on her finger. Several family members noticed her diamond and congratulated them and asked when the big day would be. She and Micah both wanted a June wedding, which was less than a couple of months away.

Once they walked into the living room, Kalina suddenly came to a stop. Several people were standing around talking. Micah's arm tightened around her shoulders and he glanced down at her. "What's wrong, baby?"

Instead of answering, she stared across the room and he followed her gaze. Immediately, he knew what was bothering her.

"That woman is here," was all Kalina would say.

Micah couldn't help fighting back a smile as he gazed over at Olivia. "Yes, she's here, and I think it's time for you to meet her."

Kalina began backing up slowly. "I'd rather not do that."

"And if you don't, my cousin Senator Reggie Westmoreland will wonder why you're deliberately being rude to his wife."

Kalina jerked her head up and looked at Micah. "His wife?"

Micah couldn't hold back his smile any longer. "Yes, his wife. That's Olivia Jeffries Westmoreland."

"But you had me thinking that—"

Micah reached out and quickly kissed the words from Kalina's lips. "Don't place the blame on me, sweetheart. You assumed Olivia and I had something going on. I never told you that. In fact, I recall telling you that there was nothing going on with us. Olivia and Reggie had invited me to lunch while I was in D.C., but it was Olivia who came to pick me up that day. I couldn't help that you got jealous."

She glared. "I didn't get jealous."

"Didn't you?"

He stared at her, and she stared back. Then a slow smile spread across her face, and she shrugged her shoulders. "Okay, maybe I did. But just a little."

He raised a dubious eyebrow. "Um, just a little."

"Don't press it, Micah."

He laughed and tightened his hand on hers. "Okay, I won't. Come on and meet Reggie, Olivia and their twin sons, as well as the rest of my cousins. And I think we should announce our good news."

THE CHRISTENING FOR Callum Austell II was a beautiful ceremony, and Kalina got to meet Micah's cousin Gemma. She couldn't wait to tell her just how gifted she was as an interior designer, which prompted Gemma to share how her husband had whisked her off to Australia in the first place.

It was obvious to anyone around them that Gemma and her husband were in love and that they shared a happy marriage. But then, Kalina thought, the same thing could be said for all of Micah's cousins' marriages. All the men favored each other, and the women they'd selected as their mates complemented them.

After the church service, dinner was served at the big house with all the women pitching in and cooking.

Kalina felt good knowing the games she had organized for everyone, especially the kids, had been a big hit.

It was late when she and Micah had finally made it back to Micah's Manor. After a full day of being around the Westmorelands, she should have been exhausted, ready to fall on her face, but she felt wired and had Micah telling her the story about Raphel all over again. She was even more fascinated with it the second time.

"That's how Dillon and Pam met," Micah said as they headed up the stairs. An hour or so later, he and Kalina had showered together and were settling down to watch a movie in bed, when the phone rang.

He glanced over at the clock. "I wonder who's calling this late," he said, reaching for the phone. "Probably Megan wanting to know if we still have any of that ice cream she bought."

He picked up the phone. "Hello."

"Are you watching television, Micah?"

He heard the urgency in Dillon's voice. "I just turned it on to watch a DVD, why?"

"I think you ought to switch to CNN. There's something going on in Oregon."

Micah raised a brow. "Oregon?"

"Yes. It's like people are falling dead in the streets for no reason."

Micah was out of the bed in a flash. He looked at Kalina, who had the remote in her hand. "Switch to CNN."

She did so, and Anderson Cooper's face flared to life on the screen as he said, "No one is sure what is happening here, but it's like a scene out of *Contagion*. So

CHAPTER ELEVEN

MICAH LOOKED AROUND the huge room. His team was reunited. Kalina, Theo and Beau. They had all read the report and knew what they were up against. The Centers for Disease Control had called in an international team and the three of them were just a part of it. But in his mind they were a major part. All the evidence collected pointed to a possible terrorist attack. If they didn't get a grip on what was happening and stop it, the effect could make 9/11 look small in comparison.

It didn't take long to see, from the tissue taken from some of the victims, that they were dealing with the same kind of virus that he, Kalina and Theo had investigated in India just weeks ago. How did it get to the States? And, more important, who was responsible for spreading it?

He felt his phone vibrating in his pocket and didn't have to pull it out to see who was calling. It was the same person who'd been blowing up his phone for the past two days. General Daniels. He was demanding that Kalina be sent home, out of harm's way. Like two years ago, a part of Micah understood the man's concern for his daughter's safety. He, of all people, didn't want a single hair on Kalina's head hurt in any way. But as much as he loved Kalina and wanted to keep her safe,

he also respected her profession and her choices in life.
That's how he and the old man differed.

But still…

"That's all for now. I'll give everyone an update
when I get one from Washington. Stay safe." Micah
then glanced over at Kalina. "Dr. Daniels, can you
remain a few moments, please? I'd like to talk to you."

He moved behind his desk as the others filed out.
Beau, being the last one, closed the door behind him.
But not before giving Micah the eye, communicating
to him, for his own benefit and safety, to move the vase
off the desk. Micah smiled. Beau knew of Kalina's need
to throw things when she was angry. He had tried telling his best friend that the vase throwing had been limited to that one episode. It hadn't happened again.

"Yes, Micah? What is it?"

He pulled his still-vibrating phone out of his pocket
and placed it in the middle of his desk. "Your father."

He then reached into his desk and pulled out a
sealed, official-looking envelope and handed it to her.
"Your father, as well."

She opened the envelope and began reading the documents. Moments later, she lifted her head and met
his gaze. "Orders for me to be reassigned to another
project?"

"Yes."

She held his gaze for a long time as she placed the
documents back in the envelope. He saw the defeated
shift of her shoulders. "So when do I leave?"

He leaned back in his chair. "I, of all people, don't
want anything to happen to you, Kalina," he said in a

low voice. "I love you more than life itself, and I know how dangerous it is for you to be here. The death toll has gone up to fifteen. Already a domestic terrorist group is claiming victory and vows more people will lose their lives here before it's over, before we can find a way to stop it. I don't want you in that number."

There was an intensity, a desperation, in his tone that even he heard. It was also one that he felt. He drew in a deep breath and continued, "You are the other half that makes me whole. The sunshine I wake up to each morning, and the rock I hold near me when I go to bed at night. I don't want to lose you. If anything happens to you, I die, as well."

He could see she was fighting the tears in her eyes, as if she already knew the verdict. She was getting used to it. She lifted her chin defiantly. "So, you're sending me away?"

He held his gaze as he shook his head. "No, I'm keeping you safe. Your father doesn't call the shots anymore in your personal or professional life. I'm denying his orders on the grounds that you're needed here. You worked on this virus just weeks ago. You're familiar with it. That alone should override his request at the CDC."

She released an appreciative sigh. "Thank you."

"Don't thank me. The next days are going to be rough. Whoever did this is out there and waiting around for their attack to be successful. There have been few survivors and those who have survived are quarantined and in critical condition."

She sat down on the edge of his desk. "We're working against time, Micah. People want to leave Portland, but everyone is being forced to stay because the virus is contagious."

Already the level of fear among citizens had been raised. People were naturally afraid of the unknown… and this was definitely an unknown. Each victim had presented the same symptoms they'd found in India.

"I wish the CDC hadn't just put that blood sample I sent to them on the shelf," she added. "It was the one thing I was able to get from the surviving—"

Micah sat up in his seat. "Hey, that might be it. We need someone to analyze the contents of those vials, immediately. I don't give a damn about how behind they are. This is urgent." He picked up the phone that was a direct line to Washington and the Department of Health and Human Services.

FOUR MORE PEOPLE died over a two-day period, but Micah put the fire under the CDC to study the contents of those vials that Kalina had sent to them weeks ago. He had assembled his team in the lab to apprise them of what was going on.

"And you think we might be able to come up with a serum that can stop the virus?" Beau asked.

"We hope so," Micah said, rubbing a hand down his face. "It might be a shot in the dark, but it's the only one we have."

At that moment, the phone—his direct line to the CDC—rang, and he quickly picked it up. "Dr. Westmoreland."

He nodded a few times and then he felt a relieved

expression touch his features. "Great! You get it here, and we'll dispense it."

He looked over at his team. "Based on what they analyzed in those vials, they think they've come up with an antidote. They're flying it here via military aircraft. We are to work with the local teams and make sure every man, woman and child is inoculated immediately." He stood. "Let's go!"

FIVE DAYS LATER, a military aircraft carrying Micah and his team arrived at Andrews Air Force Base. The antidote had worked, and millions of lives were saved. Homeland Security had arrested those involved.

Micah and every member of his team had worked nonstop to save lives and thanks to their hard work, and the work of all the others, there hadn't been any more deaths.

He drew in a deep breath as he glanced over at Kalina. He knew how exhausted she was, though she didn't show it. All of them had kept long hours, and he was looking forward to a hotel room with a big bed… and his woman. They would rest up, and then they would ease into much-needed lovemaking.

They had barely departed the plane when an official government vehicle pulled up. They paused, and Micah really wasn't surprised when Kalina's father got out of the car. General Daniels frowned at them. All military personnel there saluted and stood at attention as he moved toward them.

As much as Micah wanted to hate the man, he couldn't. After all, he was Kalina's father and without the man his daughter would not have been born. So Micah figured that he owed the older man something. That was all he could find to like about him. At the moment, he couldn't think of a single other thing.

General Daniels came to a stop in front of them. "Dr. Westmoreland. I need to congratulate you and your team for a job well done."

"Thank you, sir." Micah decided to give the man the respect he had earned. Considering the lie the man had told, whether he really deserved it was another matter.

The general's gaze shifted to Kalina, and Micah knew where she had gotten her stubbornness. She lifted her chin and glared at her father, general or not. Micah noticed something else, as well. It was there in the older man's eyes as he looked at Kalina. He loved his daughter and was scared to death of losing her. Kalina had told him how her mother had died when she was ten and how hard her father had taken her mother's death.

"Kalina Marie."

"General."

"You look well."

"Thank you."

The general spoke to all the others and then officially dismissed them to leave. He then said to Kalina when the three of them were alone, "I'm here to take you and Dr. Westmoreland to your hotel."

Kalina's glare deepened. "I'll walk first. Sir."

Micah saw the pain from Kalina's words settle in the old man's eyes. He decided to extend something to General Daniels that the old man would never extend to him: empathy.

He then turned to Kalina and said in a joking tone, "No, you aren't walking to the hotel because that means I'll have to walk with you. We're a team, remember? And if I take another step, I'm going to drop. I think we should take your father up on his offer. Besides, there're a couple things we need to talk to him about, don't you think? Like our wedding plans."

The general blinked. "The two of you are back together? And getting married?"

Kalina turned on her father. "Yes, with no thanks to you."

The man did have the decency to look chagrined. Micah had a feeling the man truly felt regret for his actions two years ago. "And there's something else I think you should tell your father, Kalina."

She glanced up at Micah. "What?"

Micah smiled. "That he's going to be a grandfather."

Both Kalina and her father gasped in shock, but for different reasons. Kalina turned to Micah. "You knew?"

He nodded as his smile widened. "Yes, I'm a doctor, remember."

"And you still let me stay on the team? You didn't send me away, knowing my condition?"

He reached out and gently caressed her cheek. "You were under my love and protection, but not my control."

He then looked over at her father when he added, "There is a difference, General, and one day I'll be happy to sit down and explain it to you."

The old man nodded appreciatively and held Micah's

gaze as a deep understanding and acceptance passed between them.

"But right now, I'd like to be taken to the nearest hotel. I plan on sleeping for the next five days," Micah said, moving toward the government car.

"With me right beside you," Kalina added as she walked with him. She figured she'd gotten pregnant during the time the doctor had placed her on antibiotics after the auto accident. Even as a medical professional, it hadn't crossed her mind that the prescribed medicine would have a negative effect on her birth control pills. There had been too much going on for her emotionally at the time. Since she'd found out, she had been waiting for the perfect time to tell Micah that he would be a father. And to think, he'd suspected all the time.

Micah took Kalina's hand in his, immediately feeling the heat that always seemed to generate between them. This was his woman, soon to be his wife and the mother of his child. Life couldn't be better.

EPILOGUE

Two months later, on a hot June day, Micah and Kalina stood before a minister on the grounds of Micah's Manor and listened when a minister proclaimed, "I now pronounce you man and wife."

All the Westmorelands had returned to help celebrate on their beautiful day.

"You may now kiss your bride."

Micah pulled Kalina into his arms and gave her a kiss she had come to know, love and expect. He released her from the kiss only when a couple of his brothers and cousins began clearing their throats.

With the help of Pam, Lucia, Bella, Megan, Bailey and Chloe, Kalina had found the perfect wedding dress. She'd also formed relationships with the women she now considered sisters. Kalina and Micah's honeymoon to Paris was a nice wedding gift—compliments of her father.

And Bella had taken time to give birth to beautiful identical twin daughters. And Ramsey and Chloe now had a son who was the spitting image of his father. Already, the fathers, uncles and cousins were spoiling them rotten. Kalina had to admit she was in that number, and couldn't wait to hold her own baby in her arms.

A short while later, at the reception, Kalina glanced

over at her husband. He was such a handsome man, dashing as ever in his tux. More than one person had said that they made a beautiful couple.

She had been pulled to the side and was talking to the ladies when suddenly the group got quiet. Everyone turned when an extremely handsome man got out of a car. The first thing Kalina thought, with his dashing good looks, was that perhaps he was some Hollywood celebrity who was a friend of one of Micah's cousins, especially since it seemed all the male Westmorelands knew who he was.

When Micah approached and touched her hand she glanced up at him and smiled. She hadn't been aware he had returned to her side. "Who's that?" she asked curiously.

He followed her gaze and chuckled. "That's Rico Claiborne. Savannah and Jessica's brother."

Kalina nodded. Savannah and Jessica were sisters who'd married the Westmoreland cousins Durango and Chase. "He's handsome," she couldn't help saying. Then she quickly looked up at her husband and added sheepishly, "But not as handsome as you, of course."

Micah laughed. "Of course. Here, I brought this for you," he said, placing a cold glass of ice water in her hand. "And although Megan is hiring Rico, they are meeting for the first time today," he added. "But from the expression on Megan's face, maybe she needs this cold drink of water instead of you."

Kalina understood exactly what Micah meant when she, like everyone else, watched as the man turned to stare over at Megan, who'd been pointed out to him by some of the Westmoreland cousins. If the look on Megan's face, and the look on the man's face when he saw Megan, was anything to go by, then everyone was feeling the heat.

Kalina took a sip of her seltzer water thinking that Micah was right. Megan should be the one drinking the cooling beverage instead of her.

"Are you ready for our honeymoon, sweetheart?"

Micah's question reclaimed her attention and she smiled up at him, Megan and the hottie private investigator forgotten already. "Yes, I'm ready."

And she was. She was more than ready to start sharing her life with the man she loved.

* * * * *

To Gerald Jackson, Sr.,
the man who showed me what true love was all about.

To all my readers who continue to enjoy my love stories.

To my Heavenly Father, who gave me the gift to write.

And God called the light Day,
and the darkness he called Night.
And the evening and the morning were the first day.
—*Genesis* 1:5

PROLOGUE

"WHAT DO YOU mean I need to take time off work for medical reasons?" Sebastian Steele asked, squirming uncomfortably under Dr. Joe Nelson's intense gaze. It was that time of year again—the company physical. An event he detested.

Last year Dr. Nelson—who to Sebastian's way of thinking should be staring retirement real close in the face—had told Sebastian that his blood pressure was too high and as a result he needed to adopt a healthier lifestyle, a lifestyle that included improving his eating habits, taking the medication he'd been prescribed, becoming more physically active and eliminating stress by reducing his hours at work.

Sebastian had done none of those things.

It wasn't that he hadn't taken the doctor seriously; it was just that he hadn't had the time to make the changes the man had requested. Sebastian, better known as Bas, was single and used to grabbing something to eat on the run. Asking him to give up fried chicken was simply un-American. As far as taking the medication the doctor had prescribed, well, he would take the damn things if he could remember to have the prescription filled.

Then there was this thing about becoming physically

active. He guessed having sex on a regular basis didn't count. And even if it did, that would be a moot point now, since he'd broken his engagement to Cassandra Tisdale eight months ago and hadn't had another bed partner since.

Last but not least was this nonsense about eliminating stress by cutting his work hours. Now that was really asking a lot. He lived to work and he worked to live. The term *workaholic* could definitely be used to describe him. The Steele Corporation was more than just a company to Sebastian; it was a lifeline. He thoroughly enjoyed his job in the family business as troubleshooter and problem solver.

"You heard me correctly, Bas. I recommend that you take a three-month medical leave of absence."

Sebastian shook his head. "You can't be serious."

"I'm as serious as a heart attack, which is what you're going to have if you don't make immediate changes."

The muscle in Sebastian's jaw twitched and his teeth began clenching. "Aren't you getting a little carried away about this? I'm thirty-five, not seventy-five."

"And at the rate you're going you won't make it to forty-five," Dr. Nelson said flatly.

Sebastian got to his feet, no longer able to sit for this conversation. "Fine, I'll take a week off."

"One week isn't good enough. You need at least three months away from here." Dr. Nelson leaned back in his chair and continued his speech. "I know you don't want to accept what I'm telling you, and of course you're free to get a second opinion, but my recommendation will stand. And I will take it to the board if I have to. If you don't make some major and immediate changes to your lifestyle then you're a stroke or a heart attack just waiting to happen. I'm going to make sure you get to live to the ripe old age of seventy, like me," Dr. Nelson ended, chuckling.

Bas rolled his eyes heavenward. "What if I take two weeks off?" he asked, deciding to try and work a deal.

"You need at least three months."

"What about a month, Doc? I promise to give KFC a break and lay off the fried chicken, and I promise—"

"Three months, Bas. You actually need at least six but I'm willing to settle for three. At the end of that time you'll thank me."

Bas snorted before walking out the door. He seriously doubted it.

"Your brothers are here to see you, Mr. Steele."

Bas frowned, wondering what they wanted. Just as he'd known they would, they had bought into Dr. Nelson's recommendation as though it had been the gospel according to St. John. He was thankful his brothers had given him a week to tie up loose ends around the office instead of the two days Dr. Nelson had suggested.

He stood, crossing his arms over his chest, when the three walked in. There was Chance, who at thirty-seven was the oldest Steele brother and CEO of the corporation. Then came Morgan who was thirty-three and the head of the Research and Development Department. Donovan, at thirty, was in charge of Product Administration. Of the three, Chance was the only one married.

"I take it that you're still not excited about taking time off?" Chance said, dipping his hands in his pockets and leaning against the closed door. "But even I knew you were becoming a workaholic, Bas. You need a life."

Bas glared. "When did you become an expert in my needs?"

"Calm down, Bas," Morgan said, sensing a heated argument brewing between his two older brothers. "Chance is right and you know it. You've been spending too much time here. Time away from this place is what you need."

"And I'm backing them up," Donovan said, crossing his arms over his own chest. "Hell, I wish someone would give me three months away from here. I'd haul ass in a second and not look back. Just think of the things you can do in three months, all the women you can—"

"I'm sure he has more productive things planned," Chance interrupted Donovan. Bas figured his eldest brother knew just where Donovan was about to go. But Chance's other assumption was dead wrong. Bas didn't have anything planned. Before he could voice that thought, there was a knock at the door.

"Sorry to interrupt, Mr. Steele, but this just arrived by way of a courier and it looks important," his secretary said.

Bas took the envelope she handed to him and frowned, noting the return address. An attorney in Newton Grove, Tennessee. Seeing the name of the city suddenly brought back memories of a summer he would never forget, and of the man who had turned the life of a troubled young man completely around.

He ripped into the letter and began reading. "Damn."

"Bas, what is it? What's wrong?"

Bas glanced up and met his brothers' worried, yet curious expressions. "Jim Mason has died."

Although his brothers had never met Jim, they recalled the name. They also knew what impact Jim Mason had had on Bas. While he was growing up, Bas's reputation for getting into trouble was legendary and he dropped out of college, deciding to go off and see the world. Sebastian had met Jim when he'd been around twenty-one. In fact, the older man had gotten Bas out of a tight jam when Bas had stopped at a tavern in some small Georgia town for a cold beer and ended up getting into a fight with a few roughnecks. Jim, who'd been passing through the same town after taking his two daughters to their aunt in Florida for the summer, had stopped the fight and had also saved Bas from going to jail after the owner of the tavern accused him of having started the brawl.

Jim had offered to pay for any damages and then advised Bas he could pay him back by working for his construction company over the summer. Having been raised to settle all his debts, Bas had agreed and had ended up in the small town of Newton Grove.

That summer Jim had taught Bas more than how to handle a hammer and nails. He'd taught him about self-respect, discipline and responsibility. Bas had returned home to Charlotte at the end of the summer a different person, ready to go back to college and work with his brothers alongside their father and uncle at the Steele Corporation.

"How did he die?"

"Who's the letter from?"

"What else does it say?"

Bas sighed. His brothers' questions were coming to him all at once. "Jim died of pancreatic cancer. The letter is from his attorney and it says that Jim left me part of his company."

"The construction company?"

"Yes. I have a fourth and his younger daughter has a fourth. His older daughter gets half."

Bas had never met Jim's two daughters, Jocelyn and Leah, since they had been in Florida visiting an aunt all that summer, but he knew that the man had loved his girls tremendously and that they had held Jim's life together after his wife had died.

Bas quickly read a note that was included in the attorney's letter. Afterwards, he met his brothers' curious stare and said warily, "Jim wrote me a note."

"What does he want you to do?" Chance asked.

"He was concerned that his older daughter, Jocelyn, would have a hard time managing the construction company by herself, but would be too proud to ask for help. He wants me to step in for a while and make sure things continue to run smoothly and be there for her if she runs into a bind or anything."

"That's a lot to ask of you, isn't it?" Donovan asked quietly.

Bas shook his head. "Not when I think about what Jim did for me that summer."

For a long moment the room was quiet and then Morgan said, "Talk about perfect timing. At least now you know what you'll be doing for the next three months."

Bas met the gazes of his three brothers. "Yes, it most certainly looks that way, doesn't it?"

CHAPTER ONE

"AND THERE'S ABSOLUTELY nothing that can be done to overturn Dad's request, Jason?"

Jason Kilgore wiped the sweat from his brow. Over the years his office had survived many things. There'd been that fist fight between a couple who'd been married less than five minutes, and that throwing match between two land owners who couldn't agree on the location of the boundary lines that separated their properties.

But nothing, Jason quickly concluded, would remotely compare if Jocelyn Mason took a mind to show how mad she was. Oh, she was pretty upset; there was no doubt about it. She had already worn a path in his carpet and the toe of her booted foot seemed to give the bottom of his wingback chair an unconscious kick each time she passed it.

"There isn't anything you can do other than to offer to buy out your sister and Mr. Steele," he finally said. "Have you spoken to Leah about it?"

"No."

Jason knew that in itself said it all. Jocelyn and Leah had always been as different as night and day. Jocelyn, at twenty-seven, was the oldest by four years and had always been considered a caregiver, someone who was quick to place everyone else's needs before her own. She also believed in taking time out and having fun, which was why her name always came up to spearhead different committees around town.

Responsible Jocelyn eventually became the son Jim Mason never had, although he had tried to balance that fact by sending her each summer to visit an aunt in Florida whose job was to train her how to comport herself like a lady. Jason had seen her dressed to the nines in satin and sequins at several social functions in town, and then on occasion, he would run into her in Home Depot wearing jeans and a flannel shirt with a construction work belt around her waist. Jocelyn had managed to play both roles—lady and builder—while working alongside her father in the family business, Mason Construction Company.

Then there was Leah.

Jason readily remembered Leah as being one rebellious teenager. After her mother had died when she'd turned thirteen, Leah had become a handful and had given Jim plenty of sleepless nights. She had hated living in Newton Grove and as soon as she turned eighteen, she couldn't wait to leave home and abandon what she perceived as a dominating father, an overprotective and bossy older sister, and a boyfriend who evidently had been too country to suit her taste. Her return visits over the years had been short and as infrequent as possible. But she had come for the funeral and it was a surprise to everyone that she hadn't left town yet.

"Do you know of Leah's plans? Do you think she's going to stay?"

Jocelyn shrugged her shoulders. "Who knows? She's welcome to stay as long as she wants. This is her home, too, although she's never liked it here. You know that. But Leah is the least of my worries now since I believe I can buy her out. What I want to know is why Dad thought this Sebastian Steele deserved a fourth of the company."

It was Jason's turn to shrug. "I told you what your father said to me, Jocelyn. One summer this guy Steele worked for him. They became close, and leaving him a part of the company was a way to let Steele know how much your father thought of him."

Jocelyn turned with fire in her eyes, placed her hands palm down on Jason's desk and stared at him. "Why this Steele guy and not Reese? If anyone deserved a part of the company it's Reese," she said, speaking up for her father's foreman.

Jason blew out a breath. Jocelyn had finally gone into a rant, and was definitely in fighting mode now. "He did leave Reese Singleton a substantial amount in his will," Jason reminded her.

"Yes, but it wasn't part of the company."

"Jim had his reasons. He thought a lot of Reese and hoped the money he left him would set him up in his own business."

Jocelyn knew her father's reasoning. Although twenty-six-year-old Reese had worked as the foreman for Mason Construction for years, everyone in town knew of Reese's gift with his hands. It was legendary what he could do with a block of wood, and her father always thought he was wasting his talent building houses instead of making furniture.

"Well, all your questions about Steele will be answered shortly," Jason said, breaking into Jocelyn's thoughts. "He's due to show up any minute."

Jocelyn sneered. "And I can't wait for the illustrious Sebastian Steele to arrive."

Jason loosened his tie a little. He didn't envy the man one bit.

"MR. KILGORE IS expecting you, Mr. Steele. Just go right on in," Jason Kilgore's secretary said in a friendly voice.

Bas returned the older woman's smile. "Thanks."

He opened the door and glanced first at the older man sitting behind the desk who stood when he entered. Then out of the corner of his eye he saw that someone else was in the room and his gaze automatically shifted.

It was a woman and she didn't look too happy. She was definitely a beauty, with a mass of shoulder-length dark-brown curls that framed an oval honey-brown face with chocolate-brown eyes. Then there was the tantalizing fragrance of her perfume that was drifting across the room to him.

"Mr. Steele, I'm glad you made it. Welcome to Newton Grove," Jason Kilgore was saying.

Bas switched his attention from the woman and back to the man. "Thank you."

"So you're Sebastian Steele?"

Bas turned and met the woman's frown. "Yes, I'm Sebastian Steele," he answered smoothly. "And who are you?" he asked, although he had an idea. He could see Jim's likeness in her features, especially in the eyes. They were dark, sharp and assessing.

She crossed the room to stand directly in front of him, in full view, and he thought that she looked even better up close. She tipped her head, angled it back as if to get a real good look at his six-foot-three-inch form. And when she finally got around to answering his question, her voice was as cool as a day on top of the Smoky Mountains, and as unfriendly as a black bear encountering trespassers in his den.

"I'm Jocelyn Mason, and I want to know how you talked my father into leaving you a fourth of Mason Construction."

JOCELYN FELT A tightness in her throat and couldn't help but stare at the man standing in front of her. No man should look this good, especially when he was someone she didn't want to like. And that darn sexy cleft in his chin really wasn't helping matters. Standing tall, he had thick brows that were slanted to perfection over dark-brown eyes that made you feel you were about to take a dive into a sea of scrumptious chocolate.

His cheeks were high with incredible dimples and his jaw was clearly defined in an angular shape. Then there was his hair—black, cut low and neatly trimmed around his head. And his lean masculine body had broad shoulders, the kind you would want to rest your head on.

Even with all those eye-catching qualities, there was just something captivating about him, something that showed signs of more than just a handsome face. His look—even the one studying her intently—had caught her off guard and she didn't like the way her heart was pounding wildly against her ribs or the immediate attraction she felt toward him.

Jocelyn took a quick reality check to put that attraction out of her mind and brought her thoughts back to the business at hand—Mason Construction Company.

"Well, aren't you going to answer, Mr. Steele?" she finally asked, her eyes narrowing fractionally. Inwardly she congratulated herself for getting the words past the tightness in her throat without choking on them.

He lifted a brow and said, "Yes, but first I must say that I'm very pleased to meet you, Jocelyn, and please call me Bas." He extended his hand. The moment she placed hers in his he liked the feel of it. How could a woman who worked in construction have such soft hands?

She pulled her hand away. "Now that we've dispensed with formalities, will you answer my question. Why did my father leave you part of Mason Construction?"

He held her gaze. "What if I told you that I had nothing to do with it? Jim's decision was as much a surprise to me as it was to you and your sister."

Jocelyn considered his words. Leah hadn't been surprised. Nor had she been concerned. To Leah's way of thinking it had made perfect sense since she couldn't imagine Jocelyn running the male-dominated company alone. And as for Leah's share of the company, she had no problem with Jocelyn buying her out. She had other plans for her inheritance.

"Now that introductions have been made, can we all take a seat and get down to business?" Jason Kilgore said, halting any further conversation between Jocelyn and Bas. "I'm sure Mr. Steele would like to check into Sadie's Bed and Breakfast in time to take advantage of whatever she's fixed for lunch today. You know what a wonderful cook Sadie is, Jocelyn."

If Jocelyn did know she wasn't saying, Bas noted as he took his seat next to her in front of Jason Kilgore's desk. Her mouth was set in a tight line and he could tell she wasn't happy with his presence. *Furious* would probably be a better word.

He continued to study her, her cute perky nose and beautifully shaped mouth. He'd always been a sucker for a woman with sensuously curved lips. They were kissable lips, the kind that could easily mold to his.

"I was explaining to Jocelyn before you arrived just what your function will be for the next couple of months, Mr. Steele." Jason Kilgore yanked Bas out of his reverie.

"And I was telling Jason that I thought Dad got you involved prematurely," Jocelyn quickly interjected.

"Do you?" Bas asked, noting just how dark her irises were.

"Yes. Dad taught me everything I know growing up and then he sent me to college to get a degree as a structural engineer. It was always meant for me to run the company."

"And you think I'm standing in the way of you doing that?"

"For a short while, yes, and as I said, it's all for nothing. When it comes to construction work, I can handle things."

A dimple appeared in the corner of Bas's mouth. For some reason he couldn't imagine her on a construction site, wearing a hard hat and jeans and wielding a hammer and saw while standing anywhere near a steel beam.

"And you find all this amusing, Bas?"

In a way he did, but he'd cut out his tongue before admitting it to her. There was no need to get her any more riled up than she already was. "No, Jocelyn, I don't."

"Good, then I hope you'll hear me out. I think it will save us a lot of time if you do."

Bas nodded. "All right. I'm interested in whatever you have to say."

"So, Bas, I hope you can see why you being here, keeping an eye on things, won't work."

Bas's lips curved into a smile. Although she had spent the last twenty minutes stating her case, trying to explain why his services weren't needed, he didn't see any such thing.

He glanced over at Jason Kilgore. The man had stopped fighting sleep—or boredom, whichever the case—and was leaning back in his chair and dozing quietly. Unlike Kilgore, Bas had given Jocelyn his full attention. It was hard to do otherwise.

First she had paced in front of him a few times, as if she'd needed to collect her thoughts. He, on the other hand, had needed to rein in his. The sunlight filtering through Kilgore's window had hit her at an angle that made her dark skin look creamier, her hair shinier and her lips even more tempting.

The woman had legs that seemed endless and the skirt she was wearing was perfect to show them off. Each time she paced the room, her hem would swish around those legs, making him appreciate his twenty-twenty vision. He loved what that skirt was doing for her small waist and curvy hips. And he couldn't help but notice the gracefulness of her walk. Her strides were a perfect display of good posture in motion and the fluid precision of a body that was faultlessly aligned.

"Bas, are you listening to what I'm saying?"

He heard the frustration in her voice and with a sigh he leaned back in his chair. "Yes, but it changes nothing. Your father asked me to return a favor. I owe Jim big-time and I believe in paying back any debts."

He knew his words weren't what she wanted to hear and her expression didn't hide that fact. "Mr. Steele, you are being difficult."

He lifted a brow. Since she hadn't gotten her way, it seemed he was Mr. Steele instead of Bas. "I'm sorry you feel that way, Jocelyn, but your father evidently felt the need for me to be here, otherwise he would not have added that stipulation in his will."

"And what about your ownership in the company?"

"What about it?"

"I'd like to buy you out."

That didn't surprise him. "I'll let you know my decision at the end of three months."

"Three months? But you only have to be here for six weeks."

He flicked a smile. "Your father's will indicated six weeks as the minimum period of time. If I recall, there was no maximum time given."

Anger shone in her features. "Surely you're not going to hang around here for three months?"

"Hey, keep it up, Jocelyn and I'll think you don't want me hanging around at all."

"I don't."

He shrugged. At least she was honest. "I'm sorry you feel that way."

"I see that our talk today didn't accomplish anything," she said.

Oh, he wouldn't go so far as to say that. Just watching her prance around Kilgore's office had accomplished a lot.

"What about your own company?"

She almost snapped the words at him, reclaiming his attention. Not that she'd ever fully lost it. "What about the Steele Corporation?" he countered.

"Shouldn't that be your main concern?"

He wished. "I left the company in good hands. My three brothers and my cousin know what they're doing," he said, thinking about Chance, Morgan and Donovan, as well as his cousin Vanessa, who handled public relations for the company. His other two cousins, Taylor and Cheyenne, pursued careers outside of the family business, although they served on Steele Corporation's board of directors.

"Besides," he decided to add, "it's time for me to take a vacation anyway." There was no need to elaborate on the fact that it was a forced one.

"By the time this is over, Mr. Steele, you're going to wish you had gone to Disney World instead."

"Possibly, but I'll take my chances. And what about your sister?" he decided to ask her. From her expression he knew immediately he'd hit a nerve.

She frowned. "What about her?"

"Are you buying her out?"

"Yes. She's never liked this town and I'm surprised she's still here. I expected her to return to California right after Dad's funeral."

He nodded. "After I get checked in at Sadie's Bed and Breakfast, I want to go over to the office and look around."

"I wish you'd consider my offer," she said.

"I can't do that."

Her eyes darkened. "In the end you're going to wish you had."

He stood, and when he took a couple of slow steps toward her, she had the good sense to take a couple of steps back. "I intend to carry out your father's request. That said, I think it will be in our best interest if we got along."

She glared at him. "I don't see that happening."

A tight smile spread across his face. "Maybe I should have told you that I like challenges, Jocelyn."

CHAPTER TWO

Bas parked his car in front of Sadie's Bed and Breakfast and glanced around. He certainly hadn't expected this, all the changes that had taken place in Newton Grove since he'd last been here fourteen years ago.

It was still one of most beautiful, quaint towns he'd ever traveled to, but it no longer had that Mayberry look. He'd passed a Walmart and Home Depot, certainly two things that hadn't been here before. And the library had been given a face lift. But the drive-in theater appeared to still be intact, as well as the Newton Rail Station that provided a memorable excursion up into the Smoky Mountains.

And from what he saw it was still a favorite place with tourists, which meant the souvenir shops that formed a tight circle in the town square were still thriving. The county fair, which was always held the third weekend in August, was a major event and always brought enough excitement to last the townspeople until the fall festival in the middle of November. He smiled, remembering all the stories Jim had told about both events. Boy, had he enjoyed hearing them.

Bas got out of the car and shoved his keys into the pocket of his jeans, appreciating Jason Kilgore for making arrangements for him to have a place to stay while in town.

Just being back in Newton Grove was stirring memories of how closely he had worked with Jim that summer, the bond they'd made and the special friendship that had been forged. He took a moment to lean against the fender of his rented car and glanced around, reflecting. In his mind he could actually see Jim loading lumber into his pickup truck while preaching to Bas in that strong, firm, yet caring voice. He'd told him the importance of a man being a man, about handling your responsibilities and taking advantage of every opportunity. The memory tugged at Bas's heart, and emotions swamped him. They were emotions that Jim had effectively shown him that it was okay to possess.

Bas suddenly blinked when the sound of a car's horn reclaimed his attention. Sighing deeply he went to the trunk to get out his luggage, thinking of his encounter with Jocelyn Mason. If the woman had her way he would be headed back to Charlotte by now. He could almost feel the daggers she had thrown in his back when he'd walked out of Kilgore's office.

He sighed again and glanced up toward the sky. "Jim, old friend, I hope you knew what you were doing because I don't think your daughter likes me very much."

"AREN'T YOU THAT same young man who used to give us trouble?"

Sebastian glanced up from signing his name in Sadie's Bed and Breakfast's registration book and met the old woman's eyes. Something hard and tight settled in the pit of his stomach. It was a reaction he got whenever anyone recalled his less-than-sterling past.

If she had been someone from Charlotte, he would have shamefully admitted to it. But he distinctly remembered being on good behavior that summer while living in Newton Grove. For that reason he stared at her and said, "No, ma'am, you must have me mistaken for someone else."

Evidently she thought otherwise and her blue eyes sparked as she said, "No, I don't think so. I might be old—I'm pushing seventy—but I have a fairly good memory about some things. You worked with Jim, as part of his construction business one summer, over thirteen or fourteen years ago."

Bas's stomach began feeling unsettled again. She certainly did have a good memory. "Yes, but I didn't get into any trouble," he said defensively.

The old woman laughed. "Not any of your own making, trust me. But whenever you worked outside at a construction site on those extremely hot days, you drew an audience every time you took off your shirt."

She barked out another laugh and continued. "Yeah, I do remember that summer. You had all the young women acting like silly fools whenever they could take a peek at you. And I remember Marcella all but salivating whenever she saw you."

She studied him for a moment then said, "I understand you're going to be helping out at Mason's Construction again."

He took his Visa card out of his wallet to hand to her. News traveled fast in small towns. "Yes, ma'am, I am."

"I'm glad you saw fit to come help Jocelyn for a while now that Jim's gone. Lord knows she wouldn't ask for it, even if she needed it," Sadie went on to say. "And I'm curious as to what Leah's going to do. I expected her to leave town right after the funeral."

Bas put his charge card back into his wallet after she returned it to him. "She lives in California, right?"

"So we hear. Leah left here at eighteen. She hated this place, claimed Newton Grove was too small town for her. She wanted to see the world and headed to California."

After a quick pause she added, "She broke Reese Singleton's heart when she left. They'd been sweethearts. He's a good man who didn't deserve what she did to him. You'll get to know Reese rather well over the coming months."

Bas leaned against the counter. "I will?"

"Yes, he's the foreman at Mason Construction. But he might not be there for too much longer."

Bas lifted a brow. "Why not?"

"Because he's better suited as a carpenter than a builder, and I heard that Jim left him a bunch of money to start his own business."

Bas turned to follow Sadie up the stairs to his room. Once he got settled he would check out what was happening over at Mason Construction.

THE NAIL WAS taking a beating as Jocelyn hammered it relentlessly into the wood. A part of her wished it was Sebastian Steele's head.

If there was one thing she didn't need it was aggravation, and the man had gotten next to her like nobody's business. The nerve of him, thinking he could just waltz in and take over. Mason Construction was now hers and she would run things the way she saw fit, regardless of what he had to say.

It wasn't as though she didn't know what she was doing. Heck, she'd been reading blueprints practically since she could walk. Growing up, she'd spent hours at every job site with her father, learning each aspect of a builder's trade, from the ordering of the supplies to the overseeing of each structural design. While many construction workers had their specialties, Jocelyn was truly a jack-of-all-trades. She handled a paintbrush just as expertly as any artist; she could fit a pipe together as well as any master plumber, and she worked with brick, stone, concrete block and structural tile with the skill of an accomplished mason. For years she had worked alongside her dad and his crew as a fill-in, doing whatever task was needed and learning just about everything she could, before school, after school, weekends, whenever. She practically lived at Mason Construction except for those summer months when Jim Mason would ship her and Leah off to Aunt Susan in Florida.

Their mother's sister was as refined and proper as the words could get, and had been determined to pass those characteristics on to her nieces no matter how much they'd balked at the idea. After a while, Jocelyn and Leah discovered it was easier to just go with the flow and accept all the lacy, frilly dresses, the tea parties and the countless hours of walking with a book on their heads to perfect that graceful walk.

Now that she was a grown woman, Jocelyn appreciated her aunt's teachings and guidance to a degree she'd never thought would be possible as a young girl. She was glad she'd had the chance to express her gratitude to Aunt Susan before she died a few years ago. Jocelyn thought about the deaths of the three people who'd meant a lot to her—her mother when she'd turned sixteen; her Aunt Susan around six years ago and now her dad.

"If you keep beating that nail to death you'll whack it all the way through and bust up that board. Who ruffled your feathers today?"

Expelling a deep breath and clutching the hammer more tightly in her hand, Jocelyn decided Reese was right. There was no reason to take out her anger and frustration on a piece of wood.

She glanced up at him and knew he was waiting for an answer. It hadn't taken much for the men who worked for her to tell she was in a relatively foul mood, which is the reason they had been avoiding her. Reese had been at lunch when she'd arrived. Evidently the guys hadn't wasted any time giving him fair warning. Too bad all those deeply ingrained proper manners and stiff rules Aunt Susan had taught her weren't working for her today, especially the one about a lady not letting a man get on her last nerve, at least not to the point of showing it. A lady kept her cool and handled a man with charm and diplomatic grace.

Today, thanks to Sebastian Steele, all she could say to that notion was hogwash!

After leaving Jason's office she had gone home long enough to change into her work clothes, then joined the men at this particular jobsite. The only reason she hadn't been here at the crack of dawn like they had was because the mayor had requested her presence at a meeting in his office at eight. He liked being kept abreast of the plans for the city's Founder's Day Celebration next month, and since she was this year's chairperson, she had brought him up to date over bagels and coffee. And then there had been that ten o'clock meeting in Jason's office, the one she wished she could delete from her mind.

Jocelyn put the hammer down, deciding at the moment it was rather dangerous in her hand. "If you must know, Sebastian Steele is the person who ruffled my feathers. He has to be the most infuriating man I've ever met."

Reese smirked at her. "In other words, he wouldn't let you have your way with anything."

Jocelyn picked up the hammer again and hit it a couple of times in the palm of her hand. "You like your face, Reese?"

He grinned. "Yeah, I like my face, considering it's the only one I got."

And Jocelyn knew all the local girls thought it was a rather good-looking face, making him the most sought-after bachelor in town. But he was also the most elusive. She'd known Reese for six years, ever since his family had moved to Tennessee from Alabama when Reese was nineteen. The first time he'd seen her and Leah together out at the county fair, he had decided the then seventeen-year-old Leah, who was about to become a senior in high school, would one day be his wife. He was convinced he could erase the thought from Leah's mind of ever moving away from Newton Grove.

He'd been wrong and had gotten a broken heart to prove it.

"Well, if you like it so much, then knock it off. I'm not in a teasing mood."

"So I gather. Hey, this Steele guy can't be all bad since Jim thought enough of him to leave him part of the company."

Jocelyn frowned, narrowed her eyes, preferring not to be reminded of that. "Just because Dad liked him doesn't mean that I have to like him, too."

"No, but still I'd think you'd respect your father's wishes and try to make things work."

Jocelyn started hitting the hammer in the palm of her hand again. "You're really making me mad. Don't you have something to do?"

Reese grinned. "Yeah, but I thought I'd come over here to make sure you'll be more help than a hindrance today. You know how I feel about going behind you and—"

Oh, that did it! He had really pushed her the wrong way, and just from the smile on his face she knew he was enjoying every single minute of getting her riled. She shot him a dark look. "Okay, just wait until you have to follow Steele's orders and see how much you like it."

Reese leaned against a window casement. "I don't mind following orders as long as they're solid and sound. And like I said Jim evidently trusted this man's judgment or he wouldn't be here."

"And it doesn't bother you that Dad didn't leave you a part of the company?"

The smile on Reese's face suddenly disappeared and he said in a quiet tone. "The only thing I ever wanted from your father was his baby girl. But that's history. Some days I wish I had never laid eyes on Leah."

Jocelyn nodded, understanding his feelings completely. Because of the four-year gap in their ages and the differences in their personalities, she and Leah hadn't been particularly close while growing up and she could never understand how her sister could walk away from a man who loved her as much as Reese had.

She waited, knowing Reese had more to say. For years he had kept his battered feelings locked inside, refusing to talk to anyone, even her father, about Leah and the hurt she'd caused him. But they'd known and accepted that the main reason Reese had joined the army within months of Leah's departure was to get away for a while. And he'd stayed away for two years.

"And why is she still hanging around? When is she returning to California?" he asked, with deep bitterness in his voice.

Jocelyn asked herself those same questions every morning when she awoke to find her sister still there. It wouldn't surprise her if Leah left during the night without saying goodbye. That was how she'd done it the first time. Her father had been devastated, Reese heartbroken and Jocelyn left wondering if she could have done something, anything, to improve their relationship while growing up, if she should have been less overprotective and smothering as Leah had claimed.

"I don't know why she's still here, Reese. A part of me would like to think she's finally decided to come home to stay, but I won't get my hopes up wishing for that one."

"And I'm hoping for just the opposite. I wish she would leave and go back to wherever the hell she's been for the past five years."

Jocelyn felt Reese's pain and a part of her knew that even after all these years, he hadn't gotten over what Leah had done to him.

"Hope I'm not interrupting anything."

Jocelyn swirled around and her gaze collided with Sebastian Steele. She was surprised to see him, but should have known he would show up sooner or later. Her eyes narrowed. "Yes, your very presence is interrupting everything."

And with nothing else to say, she walked off.

No WOMAN, BAS quickly decided as he watched Jocelyn cross the floor into what would be a master bedroom, should look that good in a pair of jeans. He scrubbed one hand across his jaw, pondering that phenomenon, as he continued to stare at her. He had found her utterly attractive earlier that day in a skirt and blouse, but seeing her dressed in work wear was having a more potent effect on him.

Well-worn jeans clung to her body like another

layer of skin, but then gave a little with each step she took, providing a comfortable fit. Then there was her T-shirt, the one that boldly advertised Mason Construction across her chest, that made him appreciate, as he always did, a woman with a nice set of breasts.

The work boots and the bandana she wore around her head did nothing to detract from her femininity, and he had to concede that no matter what kind of clothes Jocelyn Mason wore, she was one of the sexiest-looking women he'd ever seen.

"I gather you're Sebastian Steele."

The man's words pulled Bas's attention back into focus and he shot him a curious glance. He had seen Jocelyn talking to him when he'd arrived, and the conversation had seemed pretty tense. Did the two of them have something going on more personal than business? "Yes, I'm Sebastian Steele."

The man studied him a moment and then said, "And I'm Reese Singleton, Mason Construction's foreman."

Bas remembered the name and everything Sadie had scooped him on earlier that day. This was the man who had gotten his heart broken by the other Mason female. He offered his hand. "Nice meeting you."

"The same here. I heard a lot about you from Jim."

"All good I hope," Bas said, returning his gaze to Jocelyn. He could tell from her body language that she was mad, from the way she was slapping the paintbrush against that wall as if she was brandishing a sword instead.

"She'll be fine. Jocelyn has a tendency not to stay mad for long."

Bas switched his gaze off Jocelyn and back to the man standing beside him—someone whose presence he had momentarily forgotten. Reese was grinning, his dark eyes flashing amusement behind the lenses of his safety glasses. "Is that right?" Bas asked, not liking the fact that Reese thought he knew Jocelyn so well.

"Yes, that's right," Reese said, hooking a thumb beneath his tool belt and leaning back against a solid wall. "I've known Jocelyn for almost six years now and her bark is worse than her bite. She's upset that her dad left you in charge of things for a while, and also that you got part of a company she felt was rightfully hers. But like I said, she'll get over it."

He studied the younger man and suddenly felt something he usually didn't experience with men other than his brothers—trust. For some reason, though, Bas knew that Reese Singleton was a man who could be trusted.

"I hope she gets over it because I have a job to do, one Jim left for me, and whether I want it or not, I plan to see it through. I owe him that much and more."

"Me, too," Reese said, following Bas's gaze as it moved to Jocelyn once more. "My family moved to the area when I was nineteen. I worked for Jim in the day and took college classes at the university at night. He replaced the father I lost at sixteen. He was my voice of reason when I didn't have one, my mentor and a good friend. At one point he stopped me from making a grave mistake, one that could have cost me my life."

Bas nodded. It sounded as if at one point he and Reese had been tortured by similar inner demons and in both situations it had been Jim who had helped to take them out of the dark and lead them into the light.

"How about if I introduce you to everyone?" Reese said, breaking into Bas's thoughts. "The sooner you know what's going on, the better. Right now everything's running smoothly but we can't expect things to stay that way since this is Marcella Jones's house we're presently working on and she's known to change her mind a lot. This is the third house we've built for her and her husband, and with this place she decided almost at the last minute that she wanted to add a huge lanai off her living room and bedroom. If nothing else changes, we'll be wrapping up things here in about three weeks."

"Thanks and yes, I'd like to meet everyone."

Bas glanced around as they made their way over to a group of men who were working on the cooking island that was part of the summer kitchen. Marcella Jones wasn't just getting a glass-enclosed lanai; she was getting a huge area that would be well suited for any and all her entertainment needs. He had to admit he liked the layout of the house and had admired each and every detail while passing through earlier.

The open-beam cathedral ceilings and the floor-to-ceiling windows would make the home light and airy, and provide a full mountain view no matter where you looked. In his mind he could see the finished product decorated with the finest of furnishings and beautiful art work.

Bas glanced over at Jocelyn and caught her staring at him. In that quick instance, something passed between them, and he felt it all the way to his gut. He frowned and told himself silently that the last thing he needed was to get interested in any woman, especially Jim's oldest daughter, no matter how tempting she was.

He had a job to do and he needed to get his mind on doing it and not on doing Jocelyn Mason.

JOCELYN SWALLOWED BACK the knot that threatened to block her throat. Why did Sebastian Steele have to look so damn good? And those jeans he had on weren't helping matters one bit.

She gritted her teeth, wondering why she found him so attractive, then quickly decided his good looks and well-built body definitely had something to do with it. She jumped when she felt the mobile phone in her back pocket vibrate. Putting aside the paintbrush, she pulled the phone out. A quick check of the caller ID indicated it was Leah.

For the past five days, ever since the funeral, her sister had mostly spent her time going through their father's belongings and packing things up to give away. At first they had started doing the task together and then the memories had gotten too much for Jocelyn and she'd asked Leah to finish without her. Her sister had agreed. That was the one thing Jocelyn noticed about Leah since she'd been back. She was a lot more agreeable and less argumentative these days. There was a time when the two of them would disagree about almost anything, including the weather.

"Yes, Leah?"

"Just wanted you to know I cooked dinner and I thought it would be nice if we invited a guest."

Jocelyn moved her shoulders in a nonchalant shrug. She definitely didn't have a problem with Leah preparing dinner since her sister was a pretty good cook, but she did have a problem with the suggestion of a guest. She couldn't help wondering if Leah was finally going to come out of hiding and face Reese by inviting him to dinner. She had done a pretty good job of avoiding him the few times she'd returned home over the past five years.

"And just who will this dinner guest be?" she asked, curious as to how many languages Reese would say the words *hell no* in when he got the invitation from Leah.

"Jason called for you a short while ago and happened to mention that Mr. Steele arrived in town today."

"And what of it?" Jocelyn asked, leaning back against a wall she hadn't started painting yet.

"I think it would be a good idea to invite him to dinner. After all, he was Dad's friend."

"But that doesn't make him ours," she snapped, looking down at the hammer she had placed at her feet. She then glanced across the room at Bas. It was a tempting thought but she quickly decided that nothing and no one was worth going to jail.

"But I want to meet him. Aren't you curious?"

Jocelyn rolled her eyes. "I've met him and prefer not spending unnecessary time in his company."

"You've met him?"

"Yes."

"When?"

"Earlier today at Jason's office."

"Well, what do you think of him?"

Jocelyn glanced back across the room. Bas was staring at her and it annoyed her that she felt a quick tightening in her stomach. She wished she could blame it on something like indigestion but knew she couldn't. "There's no way I could sum up what I think of him in twenty-five words or less."

"I didn't ask you to."

Jocelyn couldn't help but smile. Now this was the Leah she was used to, someone always ready for a fight, and not the mousy person Jocelyn had picked up from the airport a couple of days before the funeral.

"Well, then," Jocelyn decided to say, "how about infuriating, maddening, annoying, irritating, exasperating, galling—"

"Okay, okay, I get the picture, at least yours. I'd rather take my own snapshot and form my own opinion."

"Fine, then count me out."

"Aren't you being a little immature?"

That did it. Taking a slow, steadying breath, Jocelyn walked around the wall into a bathroom whose fixtures had yet to arrive. What she had to say to her sister needed to be said in private.

Closing the door behind her, she braced herself against the area where the pedestal sink would be and said rather heatedly, "How can *you* of all people fix your mouth to call anyone immature, Leah? I'm not the one who acted like a spoiled, immature brat by up and leaving home without as much as a goodbye, leaving her family worried for over a week before we finally heard from her."

Jocelyn knew now was not the time and place to unload feelings she'd held inside for years, but she'd done it and there was no way she could take back her words. Nor did she want to.

There was silence on the other end, and then Leah said in a somewhat quiet and unsteady voice, "There was a reason I left the way I did, Jocelyn, and maybe it's time I tell you why. At least that's what I've been told I should do."

Jocelyn felt an uncomfortable feeling in the center of her stomach. "Told by whom?"

"Look, I'll tell you everything when I'm able to talk about it, okay? Now getting back to Sebastian Steele, be forewarned. I do intend to invite him to dinner before I leave, Jocelyn."

"Leave? When are you leaving?" That uncomfortable feeling about being deserted by those she cared about was becoming unnerving. She lifted a hand to her chest, feeling a tug at her heart at the thought that she was losing her sister again, so soon after losing her father.

"I don't know, but I won't leave without telling you. I promise."

Before she could say anything, Jocelyn heard the gentle click in her ear. She took a deep breath. Her palms suddenly felt sweaty and she rubbed them against her jeans after returning the mobile phone to her back pocket. She had a feeling something was going on with Leah. But what?

She swung around when she heard the bathroom door swing open and her gaze collided with that of Sebastian Steele. She narrowed her eyes, madder than hell. "Don't you believe in knocking?"

He shrugged his broad shoulders as he leaned in the doorway. "I figured you couldn't be doing anything too private in here without any fixtures."

He was right, of course, but still. "Any closed door is an indication that a knock is warranted before entering," she retorted.

He shook his head. "Save your rules for another time. We need to talk."

"We have nothing to discuss."

She made a move to walk past him when he said, "Reese just let Manuel go on my recommendation."

She stopped and swung around to him, nearly all in his face. "What?" she almost shouted at the top of her lungs, not caring that her high-pitched voice didn't at all sound professional. "Manuel's the best and most dependable worker I have."

"Sorry, but you're going to have to find someone to replace him."

Jocelyn suddenly saw red, blood-red, and she fought the urge to go find her hammer and start knocking a few heads. First Bas's and then Reese's. She couldn't believe Reese had meekly followed Bas's orders without first consulting her. "How dare you think you can come in here and—"

"He's an illegal immigrant."

Jocelyn's mouth snapped shut and her gaze widened as if she'd been slapped by Bas's words. *Impossible* was the first word that came into her mind. Manuel had worked for her father for almost a year. There was no way Jim Mason would have broken the law by hiring an illegal immigrant. "I don't believe you. We have his citizenship papers on file at the office."

Bas then said easily, "Any papers you have are bogus. When I asked to see his green card, which is the same thing an inspector would have done had he shown up here, he got nervous and confessed the truth."

Jocelyn couldn't believe it. She didn't want to believe it. She shuddered at the thought of what would have happened if Duran Law had shown up. He was still plenty pissed about her continued refusal to go out with him. It seemed each time she'd turned him down his pride had gotten crushed. He would just love to hit her with a stiff fine and make her life miserable.

"And how did you know? I'm sure Manuel wasn't wearing a painted sign on his forehead," she all but snapped. A part of her was grateful Bas had saved her from possible misery under Duran's hands, but another part of her resented that he had discovered something she hadn't.

"I picked up on his nervousness when Reese introduced us. Trust me, in my line of work at the Steele Corporation, I'm faced with this fairly often enough. I wished there was a way around it but the law is the law."

She glared at him. "I know the law, Bas, and I don't have to trust you. But still, I appreciate you finding out about Manuel before I was faced with repercussions that I don't want or need. Thank you."

"No need to thank me. I was merely doing one of the things Jim brought me here to do."

And that was what bothered Jocelyn the most, knowing her father actually *had* brought him here and hadn't bothered to tell her. Jim Mason had been talking and in his right mind up to forty-eight hours before he'd died. Her father of all people knew that she didn't like surprises and should have told her about Bas.

"Fine," she said and began walking, annoyed when he automatically fell in place beside her. "That's a point for you. Now if you don't mind, I'd like to speak with my crew."

"They aren't here."

She stopped and stared at him as though he'd lost his mind. She quickly rounded the wall and looked around. "Where are they? It's only three o'clock. There's another hour of work time left."

Bas leaned back against an unpainted wall and crossed his arms over his chest. "I gave them the rest of the day off."

Jocelyn's mouth dropped. She wondered why it hadn't just fallen to the floor with his statement. "What do you mean you gave them the rest of the day off?"

"You would have done the same thing. Manuel has worked with these guys for almost a year. They're like family. All of them were shocked that he's in this country illegally, but they still felt bad that he won't be working with them any longer. They like him."

Jocelyn inhaled deeply. Bas was right. Now that she thought about it, she *would* have done the exact same thing. "What's going to happen to Manuel? He has a family. A wife and child."

"Yes, and he also admitted to receiving public assistance benefits, public education for his son, public housing and other taxpayer-funded benefits over the past year without being detected."

Jocelyn glared. "You make him sound like a criminal," she snapped.

"Just stating the facts, ma'am. And something else you need to remember is that illegal immigration in this country is a crime that extends to anyone giving them a job."

"I know that, and I'm sure Dad didn't know he was an illegal. Like I said, Manuel's papers looked legit."

"I'm sure Jim didn't know. As for what will happen to Manuel, I have a feeling he'll be moving his family again. I agreed not to turn him in to the authorities."

Despite herself, she appreciated him for that. "Thank you."

"You're welcome."

For a long moment neither said anything else, but Jocelyn felt it just as clearly as if it was something tangible that she could reach out and touch. It was there, that same damn attraction she had felt from the first moment when her gaze had collided with his in Jason's office. It was the same attraction that was there each time she'd stopped pacing on Jason's carpeted floor and found him staring at her with those intense dark eyes of his.

And it was there now as he leaned against the wall with his arms crossed over his chest, his head cocked to the side as if taking in the full view of her. A little more than a few feet separated them and whether she wanted to or not, she could feel his heat, and even at the distance she stood she could actually feel the warmth of his breath on her lips, coaxing her own to draw in his heat, mingle in his taste.

She inhaled deeply, thinking she must be losing her mind. She didn't want to be attracted to the man who owned a fourth of her company. The man who would be a pain in the butt for the next few months.

A man who had her stomach sizzling and intense heat gathering between her legs.

Drawing in another deep breath, she took a step back, started to move past him and stopped when he reached out and grabbed her wrist, gently pulling her closer, bringing her toe to toe, body to body.

"And another thing," he said huskily, before reaching out and lifting his hand to the knot in the scarf on her head. "I understand that on occasion you'll wear a hard hat or a scarf like this when there might be a lot of dust in the air. But just so you'll know, I really like seeing your head uncovered." And with that, he expertly took off her scarf, which made her curly locks tumble to her shoulders. And, as if he was satisfied with what he'd done, he then handed the scarf to her.

She balled it in her hand, crushed it while wishing it was his neck. Tilting her head, she glared at him. "I don't care what you like."

"Then maybe you should," he said, leaning in close, bringing his lips within a breathless inch. He smiled.

"You have some temper and whenever I see you mad it makes me want to taste your anger."

Taste her anger? What he said didn't make sense because she didn't have a temper...at least not normally. Typically, it took a lot to make her mad. But she had to admit that for some reason he seemed to bring out the worst in her. When she opened her mouth to state that fact, he inched even closer and was within a heartbeat of closing his mouth over hers when the sound of a car door slamming had them quickly moving apart.

Jocelyn was grateful for the timely interruption before anything could happen. Something they would both regret.

"That's probably Marcella coming to check on today's work...as well as to make more changes. Goodbye, Bas," she said, moving swiftly past him and walking as fast as her legs could carry her.

CHAPTER THREE

AN ENTIRE WEEK later, Jocelyn was still thinking about how close her and Bas's lips had come to touching. It would only have been a kiss, she'd tried telling herself over and over again. No big deal, she'd locked lips with other men before, although she could count on one hand the times she had done so.

Still, it annoyed her to no end that even after a week she could feel every muscle of Bas's body that had been pressed against hers. Then there had been his mouth, close, hot, ready. She could only imagine the taste of it. Her heart beat wildly in her chest at the mere thought. If Marcella hadn't shown up when she had, there was no doubt in Jocelyn's mind that they would have kissed.

Bas's face had been close to hers, breathing in her scent the same way she'd been breathing in his. Never had any man gotten absorbed in her senses so quickly the way Sebastian Steele had. And then it seemed that once Marcella arrived he had vanished into thin air, leaving the job site by way of the back entrance, making her wonder if the entire thing had been real.

She had tried to avoid him, knowing he was spending time at the office going through files and records. She had no idea what he was looking for, but as long as he stayed out of her way that was fine. Twice she had seen him when she had stopped by the office to sign some papers. He had been so wrapped up in what he'd been reading that he'd barely acknowledged her presence, and she'd barely acknowledged his.

"That pork chop is already dead, Jocelyn. There's no need to keep stabbing it to death."

Jocelyn snatched up her head and met Leah's gaze. Jocelyn had been so wrapped up in her thoughts that she had completely forgotten her sister was sitting across from her. They hadn't exchanged a lot of conversation during dinner and eventually their dialogue had drifted to a dead end.

Leah was nervous, Jocelyn could tell. If she had been stabbing at her pork chop for the past few minutes, then Leah had been guilty of nervously nipping at her lips, an old habit when she knew she was about to get into trouble. Evidently Leah had something on her mind, something serious. Jocelyn wondered if her sister was ready to explain why she'd left home so abruptly. The explanation was five years too late, but then, better late than never.

She decided to go ahead and get the conversation started. "Last week you said you wanted to tell me something when you felt you could talk about it. Can you talk about it now?" Jocelyn asked, after taking a bite of her pork chop and savoring the taste. Evidently Leah had kept up her cooking skills during the five years she'd been away.

Whenever she'd come home—which had only been twice in five years—she'd only stayed for a couple days, as if passing through, and she never talked about why she had left Newton Grove or what she was doing in California. The only thing she would say was that she was fine and making it; she refused any money they offered her.

"Yes, I can talk about it now, but first tell me about Sebastian Steele. You haven't mentioned him at all this week."

Leah's request caught Jocelyn off guard and she had to fight not to choke on the piece of pork she was chewing. She quickly picked up a glass of water to wash it down. She had to be careful, very careful, not to give anything away, like the fact she found him so damn attractive and that they had almost kissed.

"I haven't had any reason to talk about him. He spends his days over at the office and I spend my time over at the job site. I haven't seen him much and that's the way I like it," she said.

At the lifting of Leah's brow it occurred to Jocelyn she really hadn't answered her sister's question. "All right, what is it that you want to know?"

"Well, when you talked about him he didn't seem like a nice person, which makes me wonder about his relationship with Dad. Why would Dad strike up a friendship with such a man as Sebastian Steele?"

Jocelyn could understand Leah's concern. She also knew it wasn't fair for her to portray Bas as a totally awful person. His handling of the Manuel situation had proven him quite the contrary, and had certainly earned him Reese's and the men's respect. He could have easily called the authorities and had Manuel arrested but he hadn't, and according to what she'd heard after talking to Reese later, Bas had even gone so far as to suggest that Mason Construction advance Manuel a full month's salary in recognition of his hard work and dependability.

Although it would be a lot of effort on her part, considering her dislike of Bas, she needed to convince Leah that even though she didn't know the full story, Bas was probably just the type of person her father would hook up with.

She leaned back in her chair and smiled. "I might have gone a little overboard in my description of him earlier," she finally said. "I was upset about the situation Dad placed me in with Mr. Steele and I immediately formed my own opinions of him. In the first few hours of our meeting I refused to consider that I might like him."

"And do you like him?" Leah asked, taking a sip of her tea and watching her sister closely.

Jocelyn reached for another dinner roll. "To say I like him would be stretching it a bit since I don't really know the man," she said honestly. "Let's just say I can tolerate him."

"How long does he have to hang around and supervise?"

"Dad's will indicated a minimum of six weeks. But Bas mentioned he would be around for at least three months."

"Bas?"

Jocelyn glanced up and saw the curious light shining in Leah's eyes and decided to put it out. She didn't want her sister getting any ideas about her relationship with Sebastian Steele. "Yes, Bas is what he prefers to be called. It's short for Sebastian."

"Oh, I see." After a few moments Leah added, "I'm glad you'll be able to work with him, Jocelyn. And like I told you, I don't want my share of the business, so the sooner you can buy me out the better. I have plans for what I'm going to do with my money."

Although Jocelyn knew she didn't have any right asking, she couldn't help herself. "And what *do* you plan to do with it?"

To her surprise, Leah smiled and Jocelyn could see excitement shining in her dark-brown eyes. "I plan to open my own restaurant. For the past five years, I've been working as a cook while taking classes at a culinary school in San Diego to perfect the basics."

Jocelyn opened her mouth in astonishment. Leah had been working as a cook all this time? She didn't want to admit some of the things she'd wondered about what her sister was doing to stay alive. It had always been Leah's dream to hit California by storm and become a model. Jocelyn had heard just how unscrupulous some modeling agencies could be and had hoped and prayed that Leah hadn't gotten mixed up with one of them.

"What happened with your dream to become a model?" Everyone knew it had been Leah's aspiration. Everyone except for Reese. Oh, sure he'd known it, but he had counted on his love for her and her love for him changing her mind.

Jocelyn watched as Leah began nervously nipping at her lips again. "I'd changed my mind about that before I even left here."

Jocelyn frowned. Now she was confused. "Then why did you leave the way you did? If you wanted to become a cook you could have moved somewhere close by. There are a lot of good restaurants in Memphis and I'm sure Reese would have understood. Hell, considering how much he loved you, he probably would have moved there with you. The two of you could have made things work, Leah."

Jocelyn studied her sister, saw the tears that suddenly sprang into her eyes and knew she'd hit a sensitive nerve. "Yes, and believe it or not I had decided on doing just that and was going to suggest it to Reese, but…"

When Leah's voice drifted off and the tears began pouring more freely, more abundantly, Jocelyn immediately got up and went to her sister, leaned down and hugged her. "But what, Leah?" she inquired softly. "If you had planned to hang around, why did you leave the way you did and without telling anyone you were leaving? Especially Reese?"

Leah shook her head, trying to regain her composure before she could speak. "Something happened, Jocelyn, and I couldn't tell anyone. Especially not Dad or Reese. Not even you."

Jocelyn heard the trembling in her sister's voice and the strong conviction, as well. Whatever had happened was something Leah actually thought she could not have shared with anyone. She pulled back and met her sister's intense, tear-filled eyes. "What happened, Leah?"

Leah hung her head for a moment, then when she

lifted her gaze, Jocelyn saw in it tortured memories, recollections Leah didn't want to relive but was being forced to. Jocelyn felt a warning chill slowly work its way up her spine and thought that nothing could have been bad enough to make her sister flee into the night the way she'd done.

Jocelyn's hold on her sister tightened and she hoped she was giving Leah the strength to get out whatever it was she needed to say. When she felt Leah respond by holding tightly to her hand, she knew that she was. For the first time Leah was accepting all the smothering, the babying, the overprotectiveness she had refused from her for so many years.

"What happened, Leah?" Jocelyn inquired again, in an even softer tone of voice than before. "What happened to make you leave when you did?"

Leah opened her mouth to speak. Then paused. She slowly opened it again as she met her sister's intense stare. "I was raped, Jocelyn. Neil Grunthall raped me."

IF JOCELYN HAD been standing upright instead of leaning over with her arms around Leah, she would have fallen to her knees. If not the words her sister had just spoken, then the pain and suffering she saw lining Leah's face would have definitely knocked her there. For a moment she began trembling, or was it Leah? No, she was certain it was her and she was trembling in anger.

"Neil raped you?" As she heard herself saying the words, she was stunned that the no-good drifter their father had hired on that spring had gone so far.

"Yes," Leah answered softly, "and please sit down. It's time I tell you about that time."

Jocelyn moved around the table, still clutching Leah's hand in hers, not wanting to lose the connection, the closeness, the need to exchange strength. When Jocelyn returned to her seat, she braced herself against the chair, needing support. "All right, tell me everything."

Leah lowered her head and whispered, "I doubt if I can, but I will tell you what you need to know, okay?"

At Jocelyn's nod of understanding, Leah began talking. "You know Reese and Neil never got along. Everyone wondered why Dad even hired Neil because he was nothing but a drifter and he was always causing trouble. Well, Dad finally fired him but I didn't know it. Late that same afternoon I went to the construction site looking for Reese. I wanted to tell him that I had decided to accept his marriage proposal and would go to a cooking school around here and wouldn't be moving to California after all."

A tear fell down Leah's cheek, joining the others. "I arrived at the job site, thinking the work crew was supposed to be there, working on Alyssa Calhoun's home. Instead I found Neil there, gathering up his stuff. I didn't know Dad had fired him just a few hours earlier. Neil claimed Reese was downstairs in the basement, finishing up something and stupid me, I went looking for him."

Jocelyn felt her sister's palms getting sweaty, but she held them tighter, refusing to let them escape her grasp. "And when he got me alone in the basement, he raped me and dared me to tell Dad or Reese. He said if

I did he would deny it and convince Reese I went along with it."

"Reese would never have believed him, Leah, you know that."

"Yes, but nothing could erase the shame I felt after being taken like an animal on that floor. I felt humiliated, disgraced and dishonored. Reese had been the only man ever to touch me and I felt dirty and unworthy of him."

"So instead of telling anyone what happened, you left town," Jocelyn said, knowing that was exactly what her sister had done.

"Yes. If Reese had found out the truth, he would have killed Neil, if Dad didn't get to him first. And I couldn't let that happen. Neither could I stand the thought of going to the police, pressing charges and facing the humiliation of Neil claiming it wasn't rape. You remembered what happened to Connie Miller when she claimed that one of the Banks boys raped her. She became the town's spectacle and eventually she and her family left disgraced."

Yes, Jocelyn remembered. Everyone had known that Ronnie Banks had done it, but the Bankses had had enough money to make Ronnie the victim instead of Connie.

"But it didn't necessarily have to turn out that way for you, Leah," Jocelyn said, though she clearly understood why her sister would have thought otherwise. Although Neil had been a drifter with no family ties to the area, it still would have been his word against hers. And with him being the troublemaker that he'd been, and with his intense dislike of Reese, he would have loved to make it seem that Leah had practically begged for it.

It was through sheer will that Jocelyn didn't curse the ground the man was buried under. "If he weren't already dead I would find him and kill him."

Leah's trembling hands went still at the same moment she sucked in a deep breath. "Neil Grunthall is dead?" she asked in a shocked voice.

Jocelyn lifted a brow. "Yes, didn't you know? But then there was no way that you would have since you left town that same night. He left town drunk and drove to that tavern on the outskirts of town and got even drunker. It's my understanding that he was speeding, hit a tree and was killed instantly."

Leah hung her head and said softly, "I never knew that. The few times I came home I could never fix my lips to say his name to ever ask about him. It took me years just trying to deal with being a rape victim before admitting I needed help. I finally went to a victim assistance program and I discovered what I felt wasn't unusual. A rape victim feels ashamed, weak and wounded, and unless they get help they will continue to feel that way. The program I got into has helped me to come to terms with what Neil did, but I have some ways to go before fully recovering. Even to this day I haven't been able to let another man touch me intimately."

"Oh, Leah," Jocelyn said, tightening her hand around Leah's. "You shouldn't have gone through that alone. Even if you didn't want to confide in Reese and Dad, then what about me? You could have come to me."

Leah shook her head. "No, I couldn't have, Jocelyn. You were the one who always did the right thing. You would have gone straight to Dad and told him what happened and I couldn't risk you doing that. Neil was crazy and there was no way I was going to tell Dad or Reese what he'd done."

For a long moment neither of them said anything, and then Jocelyn quietly asked the question she needed to know. "Are you going to tell Reese?"

Leah met her sister's intense stare and shook her head. "No. I still can't stand the thought of Reese ever finding out what happened, Jocelyn, and I don't want his pity. This is something I have to overcome in my own way and time. Like I told you earlier, I can't stand the thought of a man touching me that way. I can barely tolerate the times I have to visit the doctor for my physicals. Besides, I hurt Reese in a way he would never forgive me for."

"Yes, but if knew the truth about why you left, then he—"

"No, Jocelyn, I won't tell him. It doesn't matter now because I can't ever be that way with a man again even if he did understand. So it doesn't matter. I won't tell him and I want you to promise me that you won't ever tell him, either."

Jocelyn turned her head and gazed out the window. She knew how much Leah leaving without a word had hurt Reese, so much, in fact, that he had left town for a couple of years to get over it. Once he had served time in the army he had returned, and barely ever mentioned Leah's name. Jocelyn had been nervous as to what his reaction would be upon seeing Leah again at their father's funeral. She had watched him, had studied his expression the exact moment Leah had walked into the church. Jocelyn had seen the pain and the hurt that was still there, that five years hadn't fully erased.

"Jocelyn, you have to promise me."

Jocelyn turned and met her sister's pleading gaze. Then she remembered the reason Leah hadn't come to her the night she'd been raped was that she'd known that no matter what, Jocelyn would have done the right thing and told her father anyway. There was no way she would have let Neil get away with hurting her sister.

And although she didn't agree with what Leah was asking her to do, it was her sister's decision to make, and she would do as she asked. "I promise. I won't tell Reese, but I'm hoping that one day you will."

THERE WEREN'T TOO many places to go in Newton Grove when you wanted to get away for a spell, but Jocelyn was determined to find one.

When she came to a traffic light she stopped and rubbed the bridge of her nose with her fingertips, recalling what Leah had shared with her at dinner. Each time she thought of her sister being powerless under the hands of Neil Grunthall, she literally felt sick to her stomach. And to think Leah had endured alone the humiliation of being raped.

She sighed, feeling tears sting her eyes. Now everything made sense and she felt angry with herself for not having known something hadn't been right. Before she'd disappeared, Leah had stopped talking about leaving Newton Grove. In fact her relationship with Reese had grown that much more serious. But Leah hadn't shared with Jocelyn her decision to marry Reese. If she had, then Jocelyn would have known for certain that something was wrong when she just up and left town.

After dinner she and Leah had tidied up the kitchen together, then, as if she'd needed to be alone, Leah had taken a shower and gone to bed early. Jocelyn had needed to go somewhere and take out her anger and frustration on someone, anyone, and for the past hour had been riding around town trying to cool down.

It was times like this that she missed her dad something awful. He would have known just what to say to Leah. Then there was the issue of Leah not telling Reese. Jocelyn thought Leah was making a big mistake by not doing so.

Not having any particular place to go, but knowing she wasn't ready to return home yet, she turned the corner toward the office where Mason Construction was located.

Jocelyn's hands tightened on the steering wheel when she pulled into the yard and slipped into the space right next to a car already there. She recognized the dark-blue sedan and immediately the anger she had tried cooling for the past hour rushed back in full force. What was Sebastian Steele doing at the Mason Construction office at nine o'clock at night?

Barely waiting for her car to come to a complete stop, she quickly unsnapped her seatbelt and then yanked open the car door. There couldn't be that many files that he had to go over to be practically spending the night here. Angrily, she grabbed her purse before slamming the car door shut. Just what was he looking for in those files anyway?

When she reached the top step, she could see through the glass door his profile as he sat at the conference table, and without even thinking of surprising him, she snatched open the door and then slammed it shut.

He turned from the papers he'd been reading and looked at her. And at that moment she wished he hadn't. There was just something about those dark eyes whenever they lit on her that prompted an overpowering sensation to slide all the way up her spine. Of course she was imagining things but for a moment she thought she felt the floor move. Still, to retain her balance, in case she hadn't imagined it at all, she tightened her fingers on the strap of her purse and placed pressure on the soles of her feet when he stood up.

He was wearing jeans and a black T-shirt. She hated admitting it, but he looked good in black. It did something to the darkness of his eyes and the tone of his complexion. Just looking at him was such a mind-boggling experience that for a moment she forgot what she was upset about. Until a half smile curved his lips.

Then she quickly remembered.

"What are you doing here, Bas?"

Instead of answering her, he said, "I'm curious about something, Jocelyn."

At the moment she didn't give a flip what he was curious about and was hoping her expression told him so.

Evidently not, since he then added, "Are you always in such a pleasant mood?"

She gave him a stony look, one that could probably solidify cement in an instant. "You're going to see just how pleasant I can be if you don't answer my question. What are you doing here? This office closes at five o'clock."

His smile widened. "My work hours aren't dictated by a clock. And as to what I'm doing, I'm still working."

She glanced at the papers spread out on the table and the stack of files on one of the chairs. She then looked back at him. "Why?"

He lifted a brow. "Why what?"

"Why are you here working this time of night? And not only that, why do you feel the need to? You just got here a week ago."

"Let's just say I'm an eager beaver. I believe in getting the job done."

Angrily, she shook her head and said, "But there isn't a job here to do. You can go through whatever you want, but you'll find everything is in order. Like I've said, there is no reason for you to be here."

"And my response to that is still the same," he said, taking his seat back at the table. "Evidently your father thought otherwise."

That statement, as usual, triggered Jocelyn's anger to the boiling point. She crossed the room and slapped her hands, palms down, on the table and leaned in toward him. Their lips were within inches of touching.

She opened her mouth to speak, but he beat her to it.

"Be careful about getting too close, Jocelyn. I'm liable to bite." And then in an even lower voice, he added, "I'm also known to lick, nibble, taste, sample. Should I go on?"

Bas watched as a deep color rose in her cheeks when she got the picture he'd painted. Unfortunately for her she didn't pull back quick enough and when she unconsciously tilted her head at an angle that brought her mouth even closer, Bas decided to carry out his threat. She was mad anyway, and a little more anger wouldn't make or break their already fiery relationship.

He locked his mouth to hers before either of them could take their next breath. And he felt her fingers reach out and curl into his shirt the exact moment his tongue entered her mouth. He heard her moan, not in protest but in surrender, and the sound spurred him on.

He had never indulged in a kiss that had made him forget his senses so quickly and so easily. He might have initiated it, but she was certainly adding a delicious topping.

From the taste of things it seemed that he was way over his head and sinking fast without any thoughts of a rescue. But there was only so much of Jocelyn Mason's passion he could take, and, after giving her tongue one final, passionate suck, he hesitantly pulled back. His gaze stayed glued to her features, and he saw she was dazed and for the moment speechless. But not for long.

"How dare you," she murmured angrily between moist lips.

"How dare I what? Kiss you or stop kissing you?" he

asked, leaning in a little closer. When she didn't speak up quickly enough for him, he clamped his mouth onto hers again, intent on showing her that he did dare, because from her response it was obvious that she was enjoying the exchange as much as he was. This time he savored her taste at a slow pace, licking, nibbling and tasting. He soon discovered that kissing her slowly wasn't a good thing because he didn't want to stop. There was something deeper, different, in her taste this time around. It was more succulent, heated, and it had him devouring her leisurely, at an unhurried pace, yet greedily, as if once the taste was gone, that would be it. It was either now or never.

He heard her protesting moan when he finally pulled back again. "Got enough or do you want more?" he whispered, finishing her off by taking his tongue and lining the outside of her lips.

"Enough," Jocelyn said softly, shaking her head as if to clear any lingering passion that had gotten lodged in her brain. His kiss was everything she'd somehow known it would be and then some. She could only stare at him in amazement and wonder. How many practice sessions had he endured to become a fantastic kisser?

Deciding she was better off not knowing, she leaned back and took a step away from the table. She would certainly think twice before she ever got in his face again. Although the kiss had whopped her senses, all it took was seeing the files and folders he'd been going through to make her recall that she was still angry at him for being here.

She crossed her arms over her chest. It was either

that or be tempted to reached out and grab him for another kiss. Jeez, what was happening to her? She might not have asked for his kiss but she had wanted it, and would shamefully go so far as to admit that she had anticipated his taste since meeting him.

"I need to know something," Jocelyn said slowly, struggling to understand why her father had thought Sebastian Steele was needed here.

He glanced up at her. "What?"

"Is there anything in particular you're looking for here? Did Dad give you any indication that something is wrong with the business? Something that I don't know about? Something that he didn't want me to know?"

Bas shrugged his broad shoulders and his gaze was level and calm when he responded, "No."

She lifted a brow. "Then explain the reason you're here, because until I understand it, I will continue to fight you at every turn. Dad hadn't been able to run the company for the past eight months. The chemo treatments took a toll on him. I've been in charge of things practically since the first of the year when the cancer was diagnosed, so why did he bring you in? Didn't he think I could handle things here?"

Bas leaned back in his chair. Evidently she didn't understand what he did for a living and the way he could benefit Mason Construction during the short time he'd be here. He held up his hand when she started talking again.

"First of all, let me assure you that my being here has nothing do to with your father's lack of confidence in your abilities, Jocelyn. Over the years, whenever I spoke to Jim he was always singing your praises and telling me what a great job you were doing."

What he had just told her was the truth and for some reason it was important to him that she believed what he said. He then decided to lean in closer to make sure she was taking in his every word. "I'm a troubleshooter, Jocelyn. Some corporations refer to us as consultants. After I dropped out of college I did a lot of odd jobs, working various places, so I had an in-depth knowledge of organization and customer support services. Your dad convinced me to return home, go back to school and become a part of my family business. When I did return to college, I concentrated on those areas I needed to polish and then went to work full-time with my dad and brothers at our company. My job is to avert trouble before it can cripple a corporation, whether it's in employee relations or customer services." Giving her a confident smile he said, "And at the risk of sounding cocky, I'm pretty damn good at what I do."

He motioned to the files he had spread out around him. "Already I can see several areas within Mason Construction that are red flags."

He knew she wouldn't like his observation. He saw the slow flaring of her nostrils, the way her eyebrows lifted ever so slightly, the way her lips turned down faintly. Maybe he was a sicko or something, but seeing the heat rise in her cheeks was actually turning him on. Was that crazy?

"What red flags?"

He studied her features and saw the fire in her eyes and the pout of annoyance around her mouth. He wanted to reach out and skim his fingers across those lips he had kissed just moments ago. Damn, but he really liked her mouth, the shape, texture and taste.

"Bas, I asked you, what red flags?"

His focus returned to her question with the sound of her impatient foot tapping against the hardwood floor. Not to get her dander up any more, he decided to answer. "Like this job for Marcella Jones, for instance."

The name of the woman who had that very afternoon given her even more changes to make caused Jocelyn to flinch involuntarily. "What about the Marcella Jones project?"

"All those changes are costing the company money and you didn't allow for them."

She absently rubbed the back of her wrist as her eyes narrowed. "There's no way you can allow for them. Marcella makes changes. A builder gets to live with it. Everyone knows it and accepts it."

"But why should you?"

Jocelyn breathed deeply. Unfortunately she was finding Bas's voice sexy, which was something she didn't like. She needed to stay focused on what they were discussing. "Because the contract pays big bucks. I've padded for some anticipated changes but there's no way I can cover all of them. Everyone knows Marcella is a builder's nightmare."

"I suggest you handle it differently."

Jocelyn's eyes narrowed again. "And just how do you suggest I handle it?"

"Let her know that with changes come surcharges

because they're costing you time and money. Once you hit her with enough surcharges, she'll lighten up."

Jocelyn laughed. "What she'll do is drop us like a hot potato."

"I don't think so."

The only thing he had in his favor in making that statement, Jocelyn thought, was that he didn't know Marcella. "And why wouldn't she?"

"Because she would want the best outfit building her home, someone she knows will do it right. You said this isn't the first home you've built for her, right?"

"Yes, it's the third."

"Then there's a reason she keeps coming back."

"Yes, to get on everyone's last nerve."

"But at some point it has to stop. I suggest we try it. The next time she makes changes tell her Mason Construction has implemented a new policy and then explain the surcharges to her."

Jocelyn hated admitting that what he was suggesting sounded reasonable, but as she'd told him earlier, Marcella would never go along with it. Her family had money, the man she'd married had money, and she liked to flaunt that fact. She was used to getting anything she wanted, no matter whom she inconvenienced.

"Like I said, it won't work."

"Try it. What do you have to lose?"

"Her business."

Bas chuckled. "I doubt if she would do anything that drastic this late in the building phase."

Jocelyn sighed deeply. She didn't relish the thought of Bas meeting up with Marcella, given her reputation as a married woman with a roving eye. But Jocelyn quickly decided that Bas was old enough to handle his own business and he deserved a confrontation with someone like Marcella. It would be the first real test he'd fail.

"Fine, if you want to tangle with Marcella then go right ahead, but don't say I didn't warn you," she tossed over her shoulder as she moved down the hall.

When she got to her office, she closed the door behind her, immediately dismissing Marcella from her thoughts. Instead she thought about the kiss she'd shared with Bas. Okay, they had kissed and it was out of her system. She licked her lips still moist with his taste. Out of her system? Not by a long shot.

CHAPTER FOUR

BAS TOSSED ASIDE another folder before looking at his watch. It was close to midnight. He'd accomplished a lot in his first week and felt pretty good about it. As he'd told Jocelyn, already he'd come across several red flags. Luckily, none of them were major and all could be taken care of before they reached problem status.

And speaking of Jocelyn...

He frowned at the stillness, the silence, the complete lack of sound. At one point during the night he had heard the keys of a computer clicking, the opening and closing of file cabinets and the soft hum of a song from a feminine voice. But now he heard nothing and since she would have had to pass him to leave, he could only assume she was still here. And if she was, just what the heck was she doing?

Curiosity had him standing and making his way down the narrow hallway. The door to her office was ajar and he could see that the room was crammed with a desk, a computer and several file cabinets, not to mention a number of healthy-looking green plants. He knocked.

"Come in."

He pushed the door open the rest of the way and stepped inside, glancing around. Jocelyn was stretched out on a sofa, flat on her stomach, in a comfortable position. And she was...coloring. He blinked, certain he was seeing things, but he wasn't. She had a thick coloring book and a huge box of crayons in front of her and was diligently at work. Instead of a twenty-seven-year-old woman, she reminded him of a ten-year-old.

All it took was a look at those serious curves outlined beneath her jeans and blouse to know she was definitely no kid; however, there was something about her gliding that crayon across the page that gave her an air of innocence. At that moment some unknown force crept into him and he was touched by a degree of tenderness he experienced only on very good days and then solely for certain people. Unable to help himself, he crossed the room and stared down at her for a moment. "What are you doing?"

She glanced up as if annoyed at the interruption. "What does it look like? I'm coloring." She then turned her attention back to her paper.

"Okay," he said, as if the reason made perfect sense. He decided to press further by asking, "Why?"

She didn't bother to look up when she responded. "Why what?"

Now he was getting annoyed. "Why are you coloring in a book at midnight? In fact, why are you coloring at all?"

She pushed the coloring book aside and pulled herself up to a sitting position. "I'm coloring because it's something I like doing. Always have. It relaxes me."

She studied him for a moment then asked, "Isn't

there something you used to do as a kid that you've carried into your adult life?"

Bas thought long and hard then answered. "Yes, now that I think about it, there is something."

"What?"

"Basketball. My brothers and I grew up playing basketball together, and we still do every Saturday morning, although now we do it for a different reason. It's no longer just for fun."

Jocelyn lifted a brow. "What is it for now?"

He smiled. "To leave our egos on the court." At the confused expression that crossed her features, he decided to explain.

"I have three brothers and all of us work at the Steele Corporation. We're different in personality and temperament, and it's not easy for us to work together because of our strong differences of opinions. Playing a game of basketball every Saturday morning helps get rid of any competitive frustrations we might have before the start of a new week. I'm really going to miss not being there to do that," he said, chuckling. "It will give Morgan a chance to elbow someone else in the ribs for a while."

"Um, sorry you'll be missing the game each week, but if you're nice I'll let you borrow my crayons," she said teasingly.

"Thanks, but I'll pass."

"Hey, coloring is fun, so don't knock it," she said, placing a playful pout on her lips.

Looking at her mouth Bas couldn't help but think about the kiss they had shared earlier. Now *that* had been fun. Kissing her had been such a delicious, intimate contact and had proven him right. She did have kissable lips. The moment he had coaxed her tongue into his mouth and latched on to it for all it was worth, he'd thought he'd actually felt the ground shake. The softness of her tongue had made him want to continue kissing her, the taste of her had tempted him to do more. Self-control eventually made him end the kiss. And that same self-control was keeping him from leaning in close and reclaiming her mouth now.

"And you probably don't watch cartoons either, do you?"

Her question intruded into his thoughts and he figured that was a good thing, since what he'd been thinking was liable to get him in trouble. "No, I don't do cartoons, either."

"Not even *Finding Nemo?*"

"Didn't know he was lost, so no, not even *Finding Nemo.*"

He watched her shudder as if the very thought of anyone not having seen that particular movie was incredible. Pretty much the same way he felt about anyone not eating Kentucky Fried Chicken.

"So tell me, Sebastian Steele, just what do you do for fun?" she asked, regaining his attention.

"Fun?"

"Yes, fun. You know, the activity that you're supposed to do when work ends."

"Work for me doesn't end. I enjoy what I do."

"I enjoy what I do too, but not 24/7. Come on, get with it. Everyone is entitled to some fun time to just unwind, regroup and relieve stress. Don't you believe in work/life balance?"

Bas chuckled. Work/life balance? Was there really such a thing? She was beginning to sound like his brothers, who thought too much work with no play-time was a deadly sin. If that was the case, then he was looking hell straight in the face, since he was used to working into the wee hours of the morning. As long as he could grab a few hours of sleep and wake up the next morning to a decent-tasting cup of coffee, then he was good to go.

Knowing that she was waiting for a response, he said, "I get my work/life balance when I go to sleep."

"Oh. And how many hours do you sleep each night?"

He was beginning to dislike her questions. "I get enough sleep. And speaking of sleep, it's late and I was about to leave."

"Okay. Good night."

He raised a brow and shoved his hands deep into the pockets of his jeans. "Aren't you leaving, too?"

"No, I plan to hang around awhile and color a few more pages," she said, brushing aside a curl that had fallen on her cheek.

He frowned, not liking her answer and not liking the fact that he was tempted to reach out and curl that lock of hair around his finger and tilt her mouth to his and…

Damn. He quickly sucked in a deep breath, determined to bring his heated thoughts back on track. He then forced himself to concentrate on what she had said about not leaving yet. There was no way he was going to leave her here alone at this time of night. "What's your day like tomorrow?"

"Since we can't do anything at the Jones place until the inspector gets there to check things out, which probably won't be until after lunch, I'm going to be at school in the morning."

He cocked his head to one side, trying to figure out what she was talking about. "School? Are you taking a class or something? "

"No. I offer my assistance to several schools where they need more help in the classrooms. Budget cuts have made smaller class sizes impossible, so I do what I can to help out. It's something I enjoy doing. For me it's another fun activity. And then at noon I have a business meeting." She raised her hand over her head as if to stretch the kinks from her upper body.

He tried not to notice how the stretching made her blouse tighten over her firm breasts. He cleared his throat. "Sounds like you have a rather full schedule tomorrow, which is all the more reason you should go home and get a good night's sleep. Let's go."

When she didn't move and sat there glaring at him, he lifted a brow. "Is there a problem?"

"Yes, there's a problem," she said, standing and placing her hands on her hips. "First of all, let's get a few things straight right now. You are not my keeper so don't tell me when to go or when to stay. Secondly, I don't like interruptions during what I consider my fun time, and thirdly, why should you care about how much sleep I get? Your concern should be with Mason Construction, and I hope you'll do what you came here to do then leave before getting too underfoot."

"Too underfoot?" he growled, not liking what she'd just said. In record speed he crossed the room and before she could blink, he had her backed up against a wall, his body pressed intimately to hers. "You wouldn't know underfoot if it bit you, Jocelyn. *This* is underfoot," he said heatedly, roughly, with more than a tinge of anger. "And yet this isn't as close as it can get."

He leaned in closer and whispered across her lips. "Don't push me," he warned huskily. "Especially for all the wrong reasons."

She frowned, refusing to back down. "With you there won't be any right reasons. And if I didn't make myself clear the first time then I'll repeat myself. You don't tell me what to do."

Bas inhaled deeply. For some reason she was itching for a fight, but he wasn't in a mood to accommodate her tonight. And she had no idea how close she was to being thoroughly kissed again. However, with her temper flaring, he knew better than to try it, although he couldn't stop the images flashing through his mind of all the other things he would love doing to her. Since he hadn't slept with a woman in over eight months he was horny as hell and it wouldn't take much to tumble her back on that damn sofa and seduce the hell out of her. But he had to remember the key element he'd learned and one he hadn't grasped during his teen years—discipline. He knew how to pull back and behave properly when he needed to, and this was one of those times.

His eyes met hers and he gazed into their angry depths. But he was experienced enough to see beyond the anger and notice something else, something she was trying like hell to fight—deep longing, need and heated desire. Those were the last things a man in his predicament needed to see in a woman's eyes.

Mustering his self-control and discipline, he took a step back. "Look, it's been a long and tiring day. How about if we call a truce tonight and go get some sleep, okay?"

Jocelyn sighed. Although she didn't like admitting it, Bas was right. It *had* been a long and tiring day, and having to deal with what Leah had told her had definitely taken a toll. Besides, she heard the weariness in his voice and if sleeping was the only way he got his work/life balance, then she definitely didn't want to stand in his way.

"Okay, I'll leave but only because I want to and not because you told me to," she said, putting away her coloring book and crayons.

"Here, take this. The temperature has dropped quite a bit since you got here," he said, taking off his jacket and placing it around her shoulders before she had time to protest. But he saw the stubborn set of her chin and the indecision that lit her eyes, and for a moment he wondered if she would snatch his jacket off. He was a little surprised when she said, "Thanks."

"You're welcome."

After locking up, they walked to their cars together, neither saying anything. After opening her car door and sliding behind the steering wheel, she was about to remove his jacket when he said, "No, you can keep it. I have another one."

When she opened her mouth to say something, he held up his hands and chuckled. "A truce, remember? And it's too late to argue."

She nodded. "Fine, but I'll give it back to you tomorrow."

"Do whatever you want and drive carefully tonight."

Jocelyn watched while he walked to his own car, trying not to notice the way his jeans covered firm, muscular thighs and a too-fine butt. The tingle that suddenly spread through her was so strong that her grip tightened on the steering wheel and her breath whooshed out from her lungs.

She pulled herself together, and as she switched on the ignition she inhaled deeply to get her breathing back right again. Moments later she noted that he had no intentions of pulling away until she did. Glancing down at the black leather jacket, the one with the strong scent of man, she breathed in deeply once again. She'd had every intention of giving back his jacket when he had first placed it around her shoulders, but then the alluring aroma was absorbed into her nostrils at the same time her body was flooded with soothing warmth, and she'd decided to keep it on. The man could certainly be a gentlemen when he wanted to be.

"Okay, he's nice, but I still don't like him," she muttered out loud.

And as she backed out of the parking space and headed toward home, she had to reaffirm her dislike for him several more times.

"ARE YOU TAKING your medicine like you're supposed to, Bas? What about getting an adequate amount of rest? Are you eating right?"

Bas shook his head as he wandered out of the bathroom, where he had just finished taking a shower, and into the bedroom. After awakening this morning and downing his first cup of coffee, he'd figured he would have a pretty good day...at least he'd thought so until the phone rang. Before he could say hello, his sister-in-law was bombarding him with questions.

"Did Chance put you up to calling me, Kylie?" he asked, sitting on the edge of the bed. The sunlight was pouring in through the window and in the far distance he could see the Smoky Mountains.

"No, I'm just concerned about you."

"I've only been gone a week."

"Yes, but you know what a worrywart I am. Besides, Chance and I want to tell you our news."

Bas lifted a brow. "What news?"

He could hear her throaty laugh. "Here's Chance. I'll let him tell you." He heard her handing over the phone to his brother.

"Bas?"

Bas leaned back against the headboard. "Okay, Chance, what's going on? What's this news you and Kylie have to tell me?"

"Nothing major. Just the fact that you're going to be an uncle...again."

A huge smile spread across Bas's face. His brother had remarried eight months ago after being a widower for seven years. "Hey, that's wonderful. Congratulations. How do the kids feel about the upcoming addition to your household?" By kids he meant Kylie's fifteen-year-old daughter, Tiffany, and Chance's sixteen-year-old son, Marcus.

"They're thrilled and already fighting over baby-sitting rights." Chance laughed. "I'll see how eager they are for the job when the baby arrives and they find out what changing diapers is all about."

Bas talked to his brother for another ten minutes, filling him in on how things were going. "So, Jocelyn Mason wasn't glad to see you, huh?" Chance asked.

"Nope, not that I figured she would be."

"She sounds like a handful."

Bas smiled. Yes, she was a handful all right, but at the moment he thought of her being a mouthful. At three in the morning he'd been wide awake remembering just how good that sassy mouth of hers had tasted. Even now the memory shot his pulse up a notch or two. And then there was the luscious scent of her perfume that he was convinced had gotten absorbed into his skin, since he could still smell her.

"Yes, she's a handful for now, only because she sees me as a threat. Once she sees that I'm only here to help, she'll be okay," he said with more confidence than he really felt.

"I hope you're right. The last thing you need is to get stressed about anything."

"Trust me, Chance. The last thing I'd do is let any woman stress me out. You should know that about me."

After a few more minutes of small talk with his brother and sister-in-law, who reminded him of the surprise party next month for his brother Donovan's birthday, Bas hung up the phone then stood and walked over to the window and looked out. What he'd told Chance was the truth. He didn't plan on letting any woman stress him out. If Cassandra Tisdale hadn't done it during the six months of their engagement then such a thing wasn't possible.

He smiled as he checked his watch. It was time for his workday to begin.

JOCELYN GLANCED OVER at the man sitting across from her and smiled. "I'm flattered by your interest in Mason Construction but it's not for sale, Mr. Cody," she said, sipping a glass of lemonade.

What she had told him was the truth. She was truly flattered. She had read enough articles in *Black Enterprises* to know that if Cameron Cody was looking at any company to add to his portfolio then there was a good reason for it, because he was fast becoming a powerhouse. He was a high-school dropout who had eventually gotten his act together to later graduate cum laude from Harvard Business School, and now, at thirty-four, he was one of the most success African-American men in the country.

Cameron Cody was a self-made millionaire who had a knack for investing in all kinds of profitable ventures. His latest was construction, after he, along with other noted celebrities, had combined their funds and formed a construction company to help rebuild communities in New Orleans destroyed by Hurricane Katrina. The success of that venture had given him the idea to purchase a number of construction companies in various parts of the country to build low-income housing. Jocelyn thought his idea was good as well as needed. But as she'd told him, Mason Construction was not for sale.

"If you change your mind," Cody said, going into his pocket to pull out a business card, "please let me know. The offer will stand. The task force I put together was thorough in providing me with the names of construction companies around the country that have good, solid reputations. You should be proud that your company is one of them. That speaks highly of your leadership."

Jocelyn smiled, placing her glass of lemonade back on the table. "Since I'm sure your task force did a good job of investigating Mason Construction, then you're well aware that my father is the one who ran things up until eight months ago, so he's the one who should receive all the credit. And yes, you're right, the success of Mason Construction speaks highly of his leadership skills. Dad was well liked and highly respected in this community."

Cameron Cody leaned back in his chair and Jocelyn thought that in addition to being successful, he was also extremely good looking, although she hadn't experienced any of the sizzle she'd felt when she first met Bas. And she hadn't felt that same jolt of current that had gone through her when their hands had made contact in a handshake as she'd felt with Bas. There had been no crackle or pop. She was a little daunted that it seemed her hyper-awareness of Bas was somewhat unique and at the moment unexplainable. Evidently there was some ingrained reason why Sebastian Steele could send heat shimmering through her with just a mere look or touch. She was clueless as to what it was.

She and Cameron were enjoying lunch at Kabuki, a popular Newton Grove restaurant that had a reputation for fine dining. Any time of any day, one would find it crowded with locals as well as tourists.

"You're not giving yourself enough credit, Ms. Mason," Cameron said smoothly, interrupting her thoughts. "But from all accounts, you've been doing a pretty good job since taking over things. The men who work for you respect you as well as admire your abilities and your knowledge of construction. To me that says a lot."

"Thank you." Once again she accepted his compliment, since from what she'd heard he didn't give them often. As she took another sip of her lemonade she got the feeling he didn't seem bothered that she had turned down his offer—an offer that had been rather generous. He had even gone so far as to assure her that the men who worked for her would remain employed with his corporation. She wondered if what she heard was true and that he had a telepathic sense when it came to good business deals. Did he think she would eventually change her mind?

Half an hour later she was walking through the front door of her home, hightailing it up the stairs to her bedroom to change clothes. She wanted to put in at least a few hours at the job site. After kicking off her shoes she wiggled out of her panty hose. While shimmying her skirt down her hips she noticed the red light blinking on the phone beside her bed. She quickly walked over to play the message.

"Jocelyn, this is Bas. I met with Marcella Jones this morning and explained the company's new policy regarding changes with her. She understood our position and has agreed to be surcharged for any additional changes she makes."

Jocelyn's mouth dropped open. Was he talking about the same Marcella Jones that everyone in Newton Grove knew? There's no way, she thought, quickly unbuttoning her blouse. If Bas had been able to get Marcella to cooperate, she couldn't help but wonder how. Then a thought hit her as she slipped into her jeans. No doubt Bas's good looks and perfect body had something to do with it; it was a known fact that even married, Marcella appreciated a nice piece of male flesh and had been involved in more than one extramarital affair. For some reason that thought didn't sit too well with Jocelyn.

She quickly pulled a T-shirt over her head and before taking off down the stairs, she grabbed Bas's jacket off the chair by her bedroom door, fully intending to return it to him today. As soon as she picked it up the scent of him enslaved her, subduing her with memories of the night before. For the rest of her life she would remember that kiss, the way his tongue had captured hers, sucked on it greedily, licked the moisture from her mouth with a need that had nearly pushed her over the edge and had sent intense desire pounding in her head. Never in her life had she been kissed that way.

The very air surrounding them had crackled with an intimacy she hadn't thought possible.

Just remembering the kiss, she felt overtaken by something so erotic, so lustful and so plain feverish that she had to hold her head down for a moment to catch her breath and get her bearings. How could one man have such a profound and sensuous impact on a woman?

She didn't want to think what would have happened if he had done more than kiss her. What if he had gone beyond the kiss and had touched her intimately? What if his fingers had gotten involved and had sneaked under her blouse to caress her breasts, eased down to her stomach and beneath the waistband of her jeans to slip inside her panties to stroke the area between her legs, and then—

"Jocelyn, are you okay?"

Jocelyn jumped at the sound of her sister's voice and fought the urge to moan in total embarrassment. Leah was standing in the hallway looking at her with concern in her eyes. Barely able to breathe, Jocelyn made herself move quickly to the stairs. "Of course I'm all right. I was just thinking about something."

"Must have been something intense. For a moment you seemed to be in another world."

If only you knew, Jocelyn thought, taking the stairs two at a time. "I probably won't make it back in time for dinner tonight," she threw over her shoulder. "I want to use the computer at the office to check the web for some arcade games we can lease for Founder's Day."

"No problem. I can always bring dinner to you."

Jocelyn turned, surprised by Leah's offer. Her sister had barely left the house since the funeral. Now, not only was she willing to venture out, but to the office, a place where she could very likely run into Reese. "Thanks. Are you sure you're up to doing that?"

Leah shrugged. "Yes. I still have no intention of ever telling Reese what happened, but I can't hide forever."

Jocelyn walked over to her sister to give her the hug she felt she needed. "No, you can't and I'm glad you finally realize that. But you know my feelings. I think that Reese deserves to know what happened."

Leah pulled back. "No, and you promised."

Jocelyn nodded. "And I plan to keep that promise, but I think it's something you need to think about, Leah. After you left, Reese was in a bad way. Do you know he hasn't seriously been involved with anyone since you?"

Leah's eyes widened in surprise. "No, I didn't know that."

Jocelyn smiled faintly. "And it wasn't from lack of interest on the women's parts, trust me. He refuses to let another woman get close enough to break his heart all over again."

Jocelyn watched a lone tear escape from Leah's eyes. She regretted having been so blunt but it wouldn't be fair for Leah not to know the depth of Reese's anger and pain.

Leah hung her head and said softly, "I never meant to hurt him, Jocelyn."

"Yes, I know, and now since you've told me everything, I understand. I just want you to be prepared for his attitude toward you if your paths ever cross. He's still hurt and rather bitter."

Leah tilted her head up and met Jocelyn's gaze. "Thanks for the warning."

"No problem," Jocelyn said, reaching out and touching Leah's arm. "And as far as dinner goes, don't worry about me. I ate a big lunch today."

She turned to leave but decided she needed to say something more to her sister. She turned back around. "I'm glad you're home, Leah, and more than anything, I don't want you hurting anymore."

She watched another tear fall from Leah's eyes. "Thanks, Jocelyn. That means a lot."

"Good."

Finally, Jocelyn left, and by the time she made it to her truck she felt good that she and Leah had crossed another hurdle together.

CHAPTER FIVE

"Why didn't you tell me about your meeting with Cameron Cody?"

Jocelyn turned and lifted the safety glasses from her eyes. All around was the loud noise of men busy at work. Drills and saws were buzzing and hammers and lumber were clashing, yet she'd been able to hear Bas's question as if he'd been right on top of her shouting in her ear when in fact he hadn't even raised his voice. However, she could tell from the expression on his face that he wasn't a happy camper.

He leaned against a post with his hands shoved into his pockets, his feet crossed at the ankles, wearing faded jeans and a Carolina Panthers T-shirt. She wondered if the man had a patent on sexuality because whenever she saw him, no matter what he was wearing, he looked too damn good.

She swallowed back the bated breath that filled her throat. Having such a fierce attraction to a man was something she wasn't used to. He was beginning to be a pain in the butt in more ways than one.

"You know," she said, flipping her safety glasses back in place, "you've got a lot of nerve coming up behind a woman with a screwdriver in her hand."

Her gaze then traveled down the length of his body

and deliberately froze on the area just below the belt. "Especially a woman who wouldn't mind giving new meaning to the term 'tightening up nuts' if she got angry enough."

He glared down at her. "Just answer my question, Jocelyn."

She glared back, not liking his attitude or his question. "I don't have to tell you everything that goes on with Mason Construction."

His step was quick and in two seconds, screwdriver or no screwdriver, he was standing directly in front of her. "Now that's where you're wrong. And since I prefer that the men didn't see us at odds with each other, I suggest we take this discussion elsewhere."

"Not interested," she said, already turning back around.

"Get interested. Let's go."

Before she could utter the next word, he grabbed her forearm and began tugging her along with him. She was grateful the men were too busy installing Marcella's granite countertops to give her or Bas the time of day. But still...

"Turn me loose," she warned him through clenched teeth. "Or you'll find out just how it feels to really get screwed."

That statement did the trick and he immediately dropped his hand from her arm. She was too ashamed to admit that her arm felt warm and tingly in the spot his fingers had been.

"We can use my car to go somewhere quiet."

His words reclaimed her attention and she stopped

dead in her tracks. "Excuse me, but I'm not going anywhere with you. I have work to do."

His dark gaze clashed with hers. "Your work can wait. You owe me an explanation and I intend to get one. Have you forgotten that I'm also an owner in this company?" he asked tightly.

"A mere technicality. I'm buying you out just like I'm buying Leah out."

His lips twitched and it was hard to tell if it was due to anger or amusement. She got her answer when he said, "I never agreed to sell my part of this company to you. In fact I'm giving serious thought to keeping it. I just might go so far as to talk to your sister about purchasing her share and be willing to match generously any offer you make. Then, just think, Jocelyn, if that happens, we'll become equal partners."

Jocelyn tipped her head. She could feel the steam coming out of her ears. Her hand, still holding the screwdriver, itched. She'd never been a violent person but Bas was putting some mighty mean thoughts into her head right now. If he planned to become an equal partner with her, then he had another thought coming.

"Now that I have your attention," he said, looking down at her, "I think we need to go someplace and talk."

Irritated, annoyed and angered beyond belief, Jocelyn expelled a deep breath. "Fine," she snapped. "We'll go somewhere to talk. But we'll take my truck."

Without giving him a chance to say anything, she turned and walked to where her truck was parked. And just as sure as she heard his footsteps right behind her, she knew that she had underestimated Sebastian Steele. It would never happen again.

"Just where the hell are you taking me?"

When Jocelyn brought the car to a traffic light, she tilted her head to one side and stared at Bas. Glared at him was more like it. "Not where I really want to take you, trust me."

Bas frowned. He'd never like smart-mouthed women.

"You wanted to talk so I'm taking you someplace where we can talk." She gave him a smile. It was polite and phony all rolled into one.

Bas's eyes narrowed. Not only did he not like smart-mouthed women, he liked even less women who thought they had the upper hand. "We don't have to go anywhere in particular," he decided to say, especially when he saw that damn screwdriver beside her on the seat. "We can talk just fine right now."

"Not while I'm driving, we can't," she said, rounding a corner on two wheels. And if that wasn't bad enough, she stepped on the gas to pass a speeding truck.

Bas had the good sense to reach out and spread his hands palms down against the dash. "Slow down. Are you trying to get us killed?"

She let out a short laugh that let him know she was still pretty pissed. "Now why would I want to do that?"

Yes, why indeed, Bas thought as he tested the shoulder harness of his seat belt. Okay, so maybe he should not have threatened to buy her sister's share—not that he had any intention of doing it anyway. There was one thing he and his brothers would not tolerate and that was anyone trying to come between them, whether it involved a business deal or otherwise. And there was no way he would have caused problems between Jocelyn and Leah by doing that same thing.

But he had wanted to make a point. When it came to him, she had better not assume anything. The right to sell or not to sell Mason Construction would have been her decision and he would not have taken it away from her. However, she needed to understand that there was such a thing as business respect.

"Okay, we're here."

He snapped out of his musings when the truck came to a stop. He swore as he hissed out a breath. Where in the world was he? When she nodded her head to the left, he saw the house through the clearing. It was a two-story brick structure with a double garage set in a bevy of tall oak trees that provided a lot of shade. And he could see the clear blue waters of a lake in the back.

"You know the people who live here?" he asked, admiring the structure and the land, which had to be at least ten acres.

"I'm the one who lives here," she muttered, opening the truck door and getting out.

He frowned as he watched her cross in front of the truck to get the mail out of a brick mailbox. She lived here? When she got back in the truck and thumbed through the letters, he stared at her for a moment then said, "I thought you lived in the house with Jim."

She glanced up at him. "I moved back home when Dad got sick, but I've been out on my own since I turned twenty-one. I lived in town in an apartment for a few years. I bought this place a year and half ago to stop Reese from burning it down."

Surprise glinted in the depths of Bas's eyes. "Reese was going to burn it down? Why?"

Jocelyn blew out a breath before tossing the envelopes on top of the dashboard. "This was Singleton land. At least this is the parcel that once belonged to Reese. He had always envisioned him and Leah living here together as man and wife, and without letting her know, he began building this house and was going to surprise her with it on her birthday. She left town before that. Afterward, Reese didn't have the heart to finish it."

Jocelyn paused a moment as if remembering that time. It was moments later before she continued. "At one point he hated this place, swore he would never finish it and even threatened to burn it to the ground. Dad and I talked him out of it. Told him if he didn't want it he should finish the work on it and sell it. And he did, to me."

Bas rolled down the window, suddenly needing air. Since he had never allowed a woman to cause him any pain, he could only imagine Reese's heartbreak. Hell, there wasn't a woman alive who could drive him to burn anything, not even a hot dog.

"Does your sister know about this house?" He had yet to meet Leah Mason but already from all accounts she sounded like a selfish person to turn her back on the love of a good man.

"No, she doesn't know *everything*."

Bas lifted a brow. "What doesn't she know?"

"She knows I bought the house from the Singletons but she doesn't know it had been meant for her." And now, after finding out the real reason Leah had left Newton Grove, in a way Jocelyn wished she wouldn't find out. That would only add to the guilt her sister was already carrying around.

Starting up the truck again, she said, "We didn't come here to talk about Reese and Leah."

"No, we didn't," he said, as she parked her truck in the driveway.

"I come here at least twice a week to get the mail and check on things." She tossed the words over her shoulder as she got out.

"When will you be moving back?" he asked, getting out the truck, as well.

"I hope in another week or so. I had planned to be back by now, but there's still a lot of Dad's stuff that Leah and I need to go through and I hadn't counted on Leah staying this long past the funeral, although I'm glad she has. And with the cost of gas, living in town has been convenient for me, although I miss the seclusion."

"You don't mind living this far from town alone?"

"Nope. I'm surrounded by so many people during the day that a secluded lifestyle pretty much suits me in the evenings and at night. Besides, Reese's brother and his wife live on the other side of the lake."

Bas didn't relish the thought of her living up here alone. His cousin Vanessa had bought a house in a rural section of Charlotte and it was awhile before he or his brothers got used to the idea. They still took turns checking on her every so often.

"Come on inside. I'll fix a pot of coffee and we can talk. I need to get clothes for the rest of the week anyway," she said as she started up the walkway.

Watching her stride toward the door was giving him a generous view of some very serious curves in her jeans, just like he'd gotten last night. But this time those curves were in motion and he could only stand and appreciate the sway of her hips. The sight was definitely holding him captive and he couldn't help but take the time to admire her. Not for the first time he thought that Jocelyn Mason was a very beautiful woman. Beautiful and tempting. And he quickly reminded himself that she was feisty. Too feisty for her own good…as well as for his.

Evidently noticing that he wasn't following meekly behind her, she stopped and turned around. "You got a problem?"

He recalled that was the same question he had tossed out at her last night. "No, I don't have a problem."

She nodded and began walking again. It was only then that he decided to follow. At least she had left that damn screwdriver in the car. For some reason he believed that if she got mad enough, she was a woman who made good on her threats.

INSIDE, BAS NOTED that the house was spacious, allowing a view of most of the rooms from the foyer, including a massive eat-in kitchen.

All the ceilings were vaulted and in the living room a

brick fireplace was flanked by built-in bookcases. The furnishings were elegant, traditional, with the leather sofa, love seat, wingback chair and table lamps strategically placed facing the window to get a good view of the mountains. Every item in the room seemed to have a place and the beautiful splashes of earth-tone colors blended well with everything else, including the two oil paintings on the wall.

The dignified furnishings in this house, he noted, reflected a side of Jocelyn he hadn't seen a lot of yet— her prim and proper side. It showed a woman who had good taste and who liked beautiful things. Even the polished wood floors had character.

He reached out and traced a finger along a mahogany curio, noting the intricate detail and the fine craftsmanship. "Nice place and super-nice furniture," Bas said, glancing beyond the foyer and living room to the dining room where the furnishings there was just as elegant, traditional, sturdy.

"Thanks. Reese built all the furniture," Jocelyn said as she shoved her hands into the pockets of her jeans and leaned back against the wet bar that separated the dining room from the kitchen.

Bas's gaze shifted back to her, surprised. "He did?"

"Yes. He has a gift when it comes to using his hands on wood."

That, Bas thought, was an understatement. The man was definitely gifted. No wonder Jim had left him a tidy sum to start up his own business. He was wasting his talent at Mason Construction.

"This place was really too big for what I had in mind

but like I said, I didn't want Reese to get rid of it," Jocelyn said, reclaiming Bas's attention.

The late-afternoon sunlight was shining through the huge kitchen window and the view of the lake from where they were standing was wonderful. But he thought the picture of Jocelyn standing in front of that window was even more so. She was a picture of refined elegance, just like her home.

"I can make us some coffee if—"

"No, I don't want anything," he said, interrupting what she was about to say. He thought it was safe to remember why they were there and not let other thoughts filter through his mind.

"I just want my question answered, Jocelyn. Why didn't you tell me about your meeting with Cody?" he asked, deciding to get down to business.

Jocelyn sighed as she stared at him. "The reason I didn't tell you was not because of some sinister plot on my part to keep you out of the loop about anything. I had honestly assumed you would accept my offer of a buy-out like Leah's doing. Why wouldn't I assume that? You and your brothers own a major corporation, the largest minority-owned one in North Carolina. You employ over a thousand people so I'm sure you're busy most of the time. To be quite frank with you, I'm surprised you're even here now. Not too many people would just up and drop everything and leave the running of a corporation even on a temporary basis to spend six to eight weeks supervising a construction company."

Bas nodded and shoved his own hands into the pockets of his jeans. "They would if the man who'd made the request was Jim Mason. Fourteen years ago I had left home with a chip on my shoulder and mad at the entire world. Your father helped me to turn my life around that summer and see things as they really were. If it hadn't been for him, no telling where I'd be today. I owe him a lot."

He decided it wasn't any of her business to know his other reason for coming—his health.

"Well, because I assumed what I did, I didn't think twice about not including you in the meeting since I had every intention of telling Cody that the company wasn't for sale. He made me a good offer but I wasn't interested."

A question came into her head. "How did you know about my meeting with Cameron Cody?" She hadn't mentioned it to anyone, not even to Reese.

"Cameron told me, and yes, I know him. He was interested in one of my cousins a few years back. I was surprised when I ran into him in town. Because he's always on top of things, he was well aware I was one of the owners, but figured you were speaking in my and your sister's behalf when you turned down his offer."

Deliberately, Bas moved in front of her. "Okay, I'll accept the way you were thinking, but in the future don't assume anything, especially when it comes to me. I want to know about anything that involves this construction company, no matter how minor the detail. It's a matter of respecting me as one of the owners. Understood?"

Jocelyn frowned. She didn't like anyone talking to

her as though she was a child, although he was right. She should have included him in her meeting with Cody. "Yes, I understand. Now it's time for you to understand something, as well."

"And just what might that be?"

"I'm not used to taking orders from any man except my father. In the future if you have a request, it will pay you to make it nicely."

He lifted a brow. "Or else?"

"Or else it won't happen. I tried to explain to you that with this outfit everyone can't be a leader. Reese is the foreman and I respect his position, but when all is said and done, I'm still the boss."

"Um, sounds like you have an ego issue."

Annoyance rattled her at his words. "Sometimes in a man-dominated world women have to have one. But I don't think I have an ego issue. I just refuse to let anyone push me around." She stepped past him to walk over to the window. To Jocelyn's way of thinking Bas was standing too close. She could feel his heat. She could breathe in his scent. And both were doing crazy things to her mind as well as to her body. She was experiencing that tingling sensation in the pit of her stomach again.

"If you were one of my brothers I would challenge you to a game of basketball. Working off your frustrations can help."

She tipped her head to the side and looked at him. "I take it that whatever game you're involved in, you play to win."

"Yes, just about."

She couldn't help wondering how often he played any games. From what she'd seen in the past two days the man spent most of his time working. She was dying to know how he relieved stress.

"Okay, since you think I need to work off my frustrations, I have the perfect game."

He lifted his brow. "What?"

"Follow me."

She led him through the kitchen to the basement, and when he reached the bottom stair he stopped, grinned and let out a long whistle. The place resembled a sports bar, with a huge plasma television screen on the wall, a wraparound bar with wooden stools as well as several pinball machines, a huge dartboard and a card table. And you couldn't miss the bold neon sign that read Jim's Place.

She must have read the question in his eyes because she said, "You know what a sports fanatic dad was, especially when it came to football. When I bought this house I decided to turn this room into a place where he and his cronies could hang out and enjoy whatever game they were into."

She chuckled. "On the weekends it became a regular hangout for him because there was always some game or another to watch on that huge television over there. It was nice seeing him and his friends have so much fun, and it felt good having him underfoot."

She swiped at the tears that suddenly appeared in her eyes and swore. "Damn, but I'm going to miss him."

Bas was across the room in a flash and gently pulled Jocelyn into his arms. "Hey, it's going to be okay. And it's all right to miss him. He was a good man and from what I can tell you were a good daughter. He had to have been proud of this place that you provided here for him, his own entertainment spot. That was pretty nice of you considering I bet Jim and his buddies could get rather loud at times," he said flicking her a teasing smile.

She chuckled. "If only you knew. I would be upstairs in bed reading with my ear plugs in. Still, it felt good knowing he was having a good time. They will be memories I will cherish forever, Bas."

"And you should. My parents retired a few years ago to move to Florida and left me and my brothers in charge. My first thought was good riddance, we wouldn't have to put up with Dad constantly checking our decisions or Mom forcing us to Sunday dinner. But they hadn't been gone two weeks and we were all missing them like crazy. We even thought about calling and telling them to move back. But then we decided it would have been selfish on our part. It was their time to enjoy life."

He squeezed her hand in assurance. "And from what I can see, you did that, Jocelyn. You gave Jim a chance to enjoy life."

"Everyone should," she said, moving around him to cross the room when she began feeling hot and tingly again. She stopped when she came to one of the pinball machines and turned around.

Her breath caught in her throat. He was looking at her the same way he'd been looking at her right before he had kissed her last night...and that wasn't good. She tried getting her bearings and said, "So, are you ready to play a game?"

He leaned against the bar and she watched his eyes darken. "And just what sort of game do you have in mind?"

Evidently not the one you're thinking about, she wanted to say. She might not have a lot of experience with men but she definitely could recognize one with heat in his eyes. "How about a game of pinball?"

He chuckled. "Pinball?"

"Yes. Don't you know how to play?"

"Sure, I do."

"Okay then, but I understand if you think you're not up to holding your own against me and—"

"Not up to holding my own?"

"Yes."

Still smiling, Bas crossed the room to where she stood. He'd planned to spend most of the evening at Mason Construction, going through some more files and working way past midnight again. But he refused to let Jocelyn think she could best him at a pinball machine. And this particular baby just happened to be a Stern Nascar. "Ms. Mason, you're about to meet the king of pinball."

She looked at him and grinned. "You think so?"

"I know so."

Jocelyn figured now was not the time to let him know that last year she had won the local pinball competition. She began rolling up her sleeve and grinned at him. "Okay, Steele, you're on."

"I'm not."

"You are, too. Admit it."

"Okay, I like to win."

"So do I."

"You know I'm going to want a rematch."

"We'll see." And with that said, she disappeared inside her bedroom.

Bas couldn't stop the chuckle that escaped his lips. Damn, he had spent the last two hours racking up over a billion points and still had lost to a female hotshot. The number of bonus points she'd gotten was downright sickening.

He shook his head, not believing he had actually taken time away from work to play a damn game of pinball. It had been the weirdest thing how his adrenaline had gotten pumped up, practically the same way it did whenever he played basketball against his brothers. He hadn't even thought about the files he had planned to go over at the office. The only thing he had thought about was whipping Jocelyn's butt big-time.

And what a butt it was. It didn't take much to remember her in front of the pinball machine, her stance sexy and stimulating as hell, and her display of excitement each and every time she deployed a ball. Just being able to ogle her undetected had been worth the loss. Once again he couldn't help but think about the too-serious curves on her body and what they did to a pair of jeans and a top. Each time her butt had moved, he'd found it almost impossible to sit still, stand still or to stop a certain part of him from getting hard.

He had played enough pinball to know it was a

mental game and if you weren't focused there was no chance in hell you could win. Of course he hadn't been focused. He hadn't even used a lot of the skilled flipper work he often used when he played against his brothers.

It was difficult to concentrate when you were playing against a woman whose perfume smelled of seduction and whose body made you think of a different kind of scoring. He'd known that whenever her tongue licked her lips she was setting up her shots to score big. And he had wanted to capture that same tongue with his.

"I'm all set."

He turned at the sound of her voice and crossed the room to relieve her of the load of clothes she carried.

Their hands touched and an electric current quickly flowed through their bodies. Silence hung between them for a long moment until she finally said, "Thanks."

"Don't mention it."

"We'd better go."

He sighed deeply. "Yes, I think we'd better."

By the time Jocelyn had locked up and they had walked back out to her truck, Bas wanted to punch something. The desire to kiss her had been so strong he'd felt his self-control slipping, and for the first time in a long time he hadn't wanted to do anything to regain it.

He didn't have to be a rocket scientist to know that if he didn't pull himself together he was headed for big trouble.

"So, WHAT'RE YOUR plans for dinner?"

The truck had come to a stop at a traffic light and Jocelyn glanced over at Bas. "I don't have any. Why?"

"After playing that game with you, I've worked up an appetite and thought we could stop and grab something to eat."

Jocelyn laughed. "I couldn't help noticing how much you got into the game. You're a good player."

"Yet you won."

"Yeah, but to give you credit I have to admit you played well. One of the keys to winning pinball is to concentrate on what shots are going to give you the biggest points."

He decided not to tell her the real reason he'd lost was because he'd been concentrating on her more than the game. "I was serious when I said I wanted a rematch," he said.

"I'm sure you were, and I don't mind accommodating you if you can handle another loss."

He laughed. "Kind of confident, aren't you?"

She smiled. "When playing pinball one has to be."

The sun had gone down and dusk was settling in, but even with the dim light in the truck's cab, Bas could see Jocelyn's features clearly, and a funny feeling flowed all through him. He turned to look out the window, thinking it was safer to do so. His attraction to her wasn't good at all. In fact it was bad news.

"So what are your plans?"

Jocelyn's question intruded into his thoughts and he glanced over at her. "Not sure, but I need something to eat." And nothing fried, he further thought, remembering Dr. Nelson's words as well as the promise he'd made to his sister-in-law. He'd gone a week without any fried chicken and it was about to kill him. Each time he passed a KFC he had to keep his control in check and not go in and order the dark-meat special.

"That place up there serves good food," she said, pointing to a restaurant just ahead.

"They have chicken?"

"Yes."

"Baked?"

"Yes, and it's pretty good. It's nice to meet a man who doesn't have to eat fried chicken. All that grease isn't good for you."

He decided not to tell her that all that grease was what he wanted, but he'd been sentenced to a life without it for a while. "Will you stop and have dinner with me?"

When she came to another traffic light, she settled her gaze on his, and he knew she was trying to make her mind up about whether she would join him for dinner. "Come on, you've got to eat sometime," he coaxed.

Another smile touched her lips. "I had a big lunch, but I do know for a fact that restaurant makes a dynamite salad."

He couldn't imagine anyone just having a salad for a meal, but he said anyway, "Okay, then what are we waiting for?"

She eased the truck into the turning lane and laughed. "Not one single thing. Besides, I'm curious as to how you got Marcella Jones to go along with those surcharges."

FOR A TUESDAY night the place was crowded, but fortunately, enough waitresses were working the tables and within a few minutes Jocelyn and Bas had been seated.

"Um, I can just smell the fried chicken," Bas said, inhaling the air and licking his lips.

Jocelyn raised a brow. "I thought you were getting baked."

"I am." He took a sip of coffee before picking up his menu.

"So how did you do it?" Jocelyn asked, glancing over her own menu. She wondered why she was bothering to look at it since she knew exactly what she wanted. But then looking at the menu meant she didn't have to look at Bas, because looking at Bas made her insides sizzle. Something about the restaurant's lighting made him that much more eye-droppingly handsome. She couldn't help noticing that the waitresses were definitely checking him out.

"How did I do what?"

His question reeled in her thoughts. "Get Marcella to cooperate."

Blowing out a breath he said, "Trust me, it wasn't easy."

"So how did you do it?" she asked again.

Bas decided it was best Jocelyn didn't know all the gory details. Just like Sadie, Marcella had remembered him from those summers long ago. She was brazen as hell and had actually told him how turned on she used to get seeing him shirtless, and she more than hinted that she would like to see him without his shirt again, or his pants.

He had remained professional and had told her in a nice way he wasn't interested in undressing for her and that their only business was the building of her house. She hadn't appreciated her sexual advances being turned down and had tried being difficult. He had refused to let her get on his last nerve, and had finally said since the two of them couldn't see eye to eye he would deal with her husband. Evidently, she'd gotten concerned that Bas would mention her less than estimable behavior to Mr. Jones, and decided to cooperate.

"At first she wasn't having any of what I said, so I told her I would discuss the situation with her husband. In the end, let's just say Marcella Jones and I decided it was best to keep her husband out of it."

Jocelyn's lips quirked. "She came on to you, didn't she?"

He lifted a brow. "Why would you think that?"

Jocelyn chuckled. "Because I know Marcella. Over the years I've heard the rumors. She came on to Reese when we were building her first house and he had to put her in her place. Unfortunately for her it was during the time Reese had sworn off all women. We were surprised she came to us to build another house for her. Rumor has it that she likes them young."

Bas took another sip of coffee. "She can't be that old."

"Try forty-five."

Bas blinked at her. "You're kidding."

"Nope. I admit she wears her age well. Most people take her to be ten years younger at least."

At that moment the waitress, who was all but drooling while looking at Bas, came back to take their orders. "I'll have a chef's salad," Jocelyn said, closing the menu.

The young woman nodded. She then turned her complete attention to Bas. Jocelyn couldn't help noticing that the waitress had undone the top button of her uniform and was now showing a lot of cleavage. And it was plain to see she was wearing a push-up bra.

"And what will you have?" the waitress asked Bas, all but purring the words.

Jocelyn had always thought that jealousy was a complete waste of time and energy, but watching the woman in action was almost too much. She glanced over at Bas while he gave his order. He either didn't see how the waitress was coming on to him or he was choosing to ignore it.

Feeling a little agitated, Jocelyn was about to excuse herself to go to the ladies' room when Bas reached over, squeezed her hand and said, after looking at the waitress's name tag, "And if you don't mind, Stacy, my fiancée and I would like to be served as soon as the cook can get it ready. We're in a hurry to get home."

Jocelyn saw the disappointment in the woman's eyes before she nodded and left. Jocelyn shook her head and slowly pulled her hand from Bas's. She didn't want to think how good his hand felt encompassing hers.

"That woman had some nerve coming on to you that way with me sitting here. For all she knew I could have been your wife."

Bas smiled. "She probably thought you weren't since you aren't wearing a ring."

Jocelyn frowned. "That shouldn't mean anything. The mere fact that I'm here with you should have garnered respect."

"Yes, it should have."

"You should not have had to pretend anything was going on between us."

"No, I should not have."

Jocelyn glared. The way he was agreeing with everything she said irked her. "I'm not amused, Bas."

His expression turned genuinely serious. "Neither am I, Jocelyn. We can always leave if she offended you. And if you want to stay we can request another waitress."

She shook her head. Another waitress would only drool like the last one had. In the woman's defense, though, she had to admit that cleft in Bas's chin was patently masculine and completed the total sexy package. Not that she'd say it aloud. "No, I'm fine. It just bothers me how brazen some women are. I would never be that bold."

And a part of Bas appreciated that she wouldn't. He couldn't imagine Jocelyn ever handling herself inappropriately. However, on the other hand, she could put you in your place if she felt the need.

"I think you're going to enjoy your baked chicken," she said a few minutes later.

Bas glanced over at the table next to theirs where a man had ordered fried chicken and seemed to be enjoying it. Bas felt his stomach whine. Sighing deeply, he said, "I really hope so."

BAS HAD TO admit his food was delicious. He had been careful while ordering to stay away from the items on the menu that Kylie had told him were a no-no. He couldn't help but smile, thinking about how his sister-in-law had encased herself in his and his brothers' lives.

Once she had found out that he needed to make a change in his eating habits, she had taken it upon herself to educate him on the proper food choices. It was a good thing he was here in Newton Grove. Had he remained in Charlotte he would be starving on some strict menu Kylie thought best for him.

"You're smiling. Does that mean you think the food tastes good?" Jocelyn asked.

He glanced up and the smile on his lips widened. "Yes, it tastes good, but that's not why I'm smiling. I was thinking about my sister-in-law."

"Your sister-in-law?"

"Yes. Kylie," he said, tossing his napkin down and leaning back in his chair. "She's a very nice person and the best thing to ever happen to my brother in a long time. They've only been married eight months."

"Which brother is this? You mentioned you had three." From Bas's smile Jocelyn could tell that he and his brothers shared a close relationship.

"Kylie's married to Chance, the oldest at thirty-seven. Then there are Morgan and Donovan. Chance is the only one of us who's ever been married. He was a widower for seven years and has a sixteen-year-old son named Marcus."

Bas chuckled. "In fact, Marcus and Kylie's daughter, Tiffany, who is fifteen, are the reason Chance and Kylie are together."

Jocelyn wiped her mouth with a napkin before asking. "How is that?"

"By playing cupid."

For the next twenty minutes Bas told Jocelyn how Marcus and Tiffany had felt that neither of their strict parents had a life and had decided to do something about it by orchestrating a plan to shift their parents' attention off them and onto each other.

Instead of using the napkin to wipe at her mouth, Jocelyn began dabbing at her eyes while laughing. She'd found the teens' escapades totally hilarious. "Well, evidently their plan worked."

Bas chuckled. "Yes, it did. Quite successfully." He took advantage of the break in conversation to question why he was here, sharing dinner with Jocelyn, instead of back at the office going through files. Although he wanted to think that this entire afternoon had been a total waste of good time, he couldn't. He had to admit that he enjoyed the time he had spent with Jocelyn, although it had started out pretty damn rocky.

He'd gotten a kick out of playing pinball with her even when she was slaughtering him in points, and dinner had been rather nice, as well. He felt comfortable talking to her, sharing tidbits about his family. The last woman he'd taken out had been Cassandra and they'd gone to an exclusive restaurant. She had spent the entire evening criticizing the outfits other women were wearing. To hear her talk, she was the only fashion plate in the place.

"You mentioned that Cameron Cody was interested in one of your cousins."

Bas studied the dark liquid in his glass and grinned. After dinner they had ordered scrumptious cheesecake and a glass of delicious dessert wine to go along with it. "Yes, and I have a feeling he still is. I met Cameron a few years ago when he tried to take over the Steele Corporation."

Jocelyn lifted a brow, not sure she had heard him correctly. "Cody tried forcing a takeover of your company?"

"Yes, and he would have been successful if my brothers and three cousins and I hadn't stuck together, which proved what a unified force we were. The Steele Corporation was formed over twenty-five years ago by my father and my Uncle Harold. It was always understood that I and my three brothers, as well as Uncle Harold's three daughters—Vanessa, Taylor and Cheyenne—would one day inherit the company. All of us are working there except for Taylor and Cheyenne. They decided to pursue careers outside of the corporation, although they sit on the board. Uncle Harold passed away ten years ago and my father retired five years after that, leaving Chance as CEO."

He took another sip of his wine before continuing. "As soon as word got out about my father's retirement, several corporate marauders tried to force a takeover. Cameron's company was just one of them."

Jocelyn took a sip of her own wine. "But when you mentioned him earlier I got the impression the two of you are friends."

Bas smiled and Jocelyn noticed each time he did so his dimples appeared and the cleft in his chin seemed even more profound. "We are. My brothers and I couldn't help but admire Cameron's accomplishments and give him the respect he's due. He earned everything he has, and he's built his empire by working hard. Anything he got he deserved. He is a hard man but fair. Once he saw that his attempt to take us over was futile, he pulled out and set his sights on another Steele—my cousin Vanessa. She heads our PR department. My brothers and I got over what Cameron tried to do and eventually became friends with him. However, Vanessa never could and as much as Cameron tried, he couldn't break through the barriers she had erected."

A half hour later, Jocelyn was returning Bas to the job site so he could get his car. It was almost ten o'clock. "You aren't thinking about going over to the office, are you?" she asked when she brought her truck to a stop next to his parked car.

He shook his head and chuckled. "No, not tonight. I think I'll go home and come up with a game plan to beat you at pinball the next go-round."

She returned his chuckle. "Come up with any game plan you want. The outcome will still be the same."

"We'll see."

She looked at him and said smartly, "Yes, we *will* see."

More than anything Bas wanted to kiss her. He still had memories of their last kiss, but he wanted to replace them with new memories. "Maybe," he said, leaning a little closer to her across the truck's bench seats, "we should consider a wager."

"A wager?" she asked, her voice soft, low.

"Yes."

"Sorry, but I don't make bets."

"But what if it's for something you might like?" he asked, lifting his hand to cup her cheek and feeling glad that she didn't pull back.

"Like what?"

"You tell me. What is it you want?" he asked, leaning even closer and hearing her suck in a deep breath.

"How about letting me buy you out so you can leave here by the weekend?"

He shook his head and released an easy chuckle. "Sorry, can't do that. Think of something else."

"What if I don't want anything else?"

"Then you need to think harder." His hand left her cheek and moved to the back of her neck.

"Can't think harder."

"Why not?"

"Because when you're this close to me, you make it impossible to think at all."

"Aw hell, Jocelyn." The words slipped from between Bas's lips just seconds before he captured her mouth with his. The moment their lips touched he remembered how good she had tasted the last time and was getting his fill of how good she was tasting now. That intangible chemistry they had been dealing with from the first day was back full force. If truth be known, it had never left. It was even more potent, compelling and intoxicating. That passionate moan she was making wasn't helping matters one bit. But what really made him lose it was when she laid a hand on his thigh to keep her balance. Whether she realized it or not—and he believed she didn't—her hand was too damn close to a part of him that was aching for her.

He deepened the kiss, their tongues mating, and he thought she was better than the dessert he'd had at dinner. They continued to kiss and for a while he thought he could spend the rest of the night doing just this. But he knew the last thing they should be doing was sitting in a parked truck at a vacant job site kissing, so he fought to regain control and slowly, with all the reluctance in the world, pulled back.

In the semi-darkened cab he saw her moist lips tremble, and he was tempted to lean forward and take them with his again. But he couldn't do that. He needed to go somewhere to clear his head and figure out what there was about Jocelyn Mason that made him want to take her somewhere and make love to her. All night and all day.

And that wasn't a good thought.

He sighed deeply. "I'd better go."

"All right," she said brushing her hair from her face and resnapping her seat belt. "I had fun with you today, Bas. You're not such a bad guy."

He smiled over at her. "Friends, then?"

She chuckled. "I wouldn't go that far. I'm not Cameron Cody. I don't make friends easily with the enemy."

He lifted a brow. "And you see me as the enemy?"

His question hung over them for a few minutes before she said, "I don't know how I see you," she said honestly. "I don't want you here and now you're beginning to complicate things."

"Why? Because of a few kisses?"

"Yes, because of a few kisses." *Not to mention all that heat that is surging between my thighs right now.*

CHAPTER SEVEN

JOCELYN FELT THE tap on her shoulder and slowly turned around to find Leah smiling at her. "Here. You look like you need this."

"I do and thanks." Jocelyn smiled and accepted the cup of steaming coffee and took a sip. Yes, she really did need it and nobody could make coffee like Leah. That was another thing she had missed when her sister had left. Sighing deeply, she turned back to look out the kitchen window.

"I heard you pacing the floor last night."

Jocelyn turned again and met Leah's gaze. "You did?"

"Yes." Leah walked across the kitchen to lean against the counter. "I know I agreed to sell you my part of Mason Construction, but is something going on that I should know about?"

Jocelyn frowned. "Something like what?"

Leah shrugged. "Um, I don't know. Anything. You paced the floor for a good thirty minutes or more."

Jocelyn knew it was more, although she hadn't been keeping time. "No, nothing is going on," she said, and then shifted from Leah's curious gaze to glance back out the window again.

She hadn't been able to sleep because thoughts of Sebastian Steele kept invading her mind. For the second time she had allowed him to kiss her, and there were things about him that she didn't know.

Last night at dinner he had talked freely about his brothers and cousins, but he hadn't mentioned anything about himself. In fact, he seemed very careful not to do so. She was pretty convinced he wasn't married and never had been, since he'd mentioned his brother Chance had been the only sibling who'd ever tied the knot. But what about a girlfriend or even worse, a fiancée? Men who looked like Bas usually weren't unattached, at least not for long.

"Well, I'm going to take your word that everything is fine," Leah said, glancing down at her watch. "I need to leave or I'm going to be late."

Jocelyn quickly turned around. "You're going somewhere?" she asked, noticing for the first time her sister was wearing slacks and a blouse and had her purse strapped to her shoulder.

Leah smiled. "Yes, don't you remember? I told you last night when you came in that I made an appointment at Kate's Beauty Salon."

Jocelyn nodded. Oh, yes, she remembered now. Leah *had* mentioned it but at the time Jocelyn's mind had been overtaken with memories of Bas's kiss. "That's right you did. How are you getting it styled?"

Leah chuckled. "I told you that, too. I even showed you the model in the picture I tore out of a magazine. You must have really been out of it last night." She tipped her head to the side to study Jocelyn. "Is Marcella Jones still driving all of you nuts?"

"No, it's not Marcella."

"Then it must be Sebastian Steele."

Hearing her sister say Bas's name had Jocelyn's heart pounding. "Why would you think that?"

"Because I got the impression a few days ago that he was getting on your nerves and you hadn't accepted him being here, not to mention his role with Mason Construction. I know how much you detest anyone looking over your shoulder. Just remember he's here for a good reason and when he leaves you probably won't ever hear from him again."

Jocelyn noted that Leah was smiling brightly, as if what she'd said should cheer Jocelyn up, yet it didn't. For some reason the thought of Bas leaving anytime soon was something Jocelyn didn't want to think about, although she had asked him to do that very thing last night.

"Maybe you're right."

"More than likely I am," Leah said as if to assure her. "I checked out the Steele Corporation on the internet yesterday. Sebastian Steele is a pretty wealthy guy who is used to a big city like Charlotte. There's nothing to keep him here. He's probably itching to get back to the lifestyle he left behind."

A half hour later, after Leah had left, Jocelyn was in her room getting dressed. Instead of reporting to the job site, she had a meeting scheduled with her Founder's Day Celebration committee, especially those members working closely with her on the ball. The governor had accepted an invitation and Jocelyn wanted to make sure all their plans were on target.

She shifted her thoughts to the conversation she'd had earlier with Leah. Jocelyn herself had checked out that same Web site and Leah was right. A man of Bas's status would have no reason to hang around Newton Grove any longer than necessary, not that she wanted him to hang around, mind you. But there had been something about them sharing dinner that wouldn't leave her alone.

Maybe it was the way he tipped his head whenever she was talking to let her know she had his absolute attention. Or it might have been the slow and methodical way he sipped his wine that had heat thrumming through her body each time she watched the liquid pass down his throat. Or maybe, just maybe, it had been the toe-curling kiss she couldn't seem to forget. Each time his tongue got hold of hers it was as if he was branding it while she went soaring into mind-blowing passion.

Jocelyn groaned. She'd never let any man get to her the way Bas was doing. But then she had to reconcile herself to the fact that there was a first time for everything.

Across town someone was having a similar rough morning. Bas frowned when he looked down at the bowl Ms. Sadie had placed in front of him. Oatmeal?

He had been deprived of a good night's sleep and he'd be damned if he'd be deprived of a good breakfast, as well. Where were the bacon, sausage, grits, eggs and toast whose aroma had awakened him that morning?

He glanced up and found Sadie Robinson looking at him with a smug smile. She had the nerve to say, "And if you drop by for lunch I'll prepare you a luscious fruit salad."

His frown deepened. When he thought of fruit he didn't think of luscious. When he thought of Jocelyn he thought of luscious, which was one of the reasons he hadn't slept well.

But that didn't explain why he was only getting oatmeal for breakfast and fruit for lunch. He was more than certain Ms. Sadie hadn't run out of food, since yesterday he'd noticed on his way out that she tended to cook a rather large quantity of everything. So what was going on?

Not taking his gaze off her, he asked in as calm a voice as he could, "Is there something going on that I should know about?"

Sadie never took her eyes off Bas either when she responded in a not-so-innocent voice, "Why would you think that?"

Ordinarily, Bas might let the matter go, eat the damn oatmeal and be merry about it. But not this morning, after having had dream after dream of a woman he'd best leave alone. He might never make love to her in reality but in his fantasies he could still see the heated look in the depths of her dark-brown eyes each and every time he—

"Besides, oatmeal is good for you."

Sadie's words interrupted his thoughts. A frustrated gush of air shot from his lungs and he leaned back in his chair and stared at the older woman with a look that usually told his brothers and cousins to back off. Evidently she didn't get the message because she continued talking.

"It's a good thing I noticed your medication while cleaning your room yesterday or I would never have known you were on a restricted diet. And now that I know I—"

"You were in my room yesterday?" he interrupted her, leaning forward in the chair and piercing her with an even deeper look.

"How else do you think it got clean?"

Bas's scowl deepened but it didn't seem to affect Sadie Robinson any. "So you snooped into my things?" he asked incredulously.

She waved her hand in the air. "Of course not. The pill bottle was right there on the counter in the bathroom. I had to pick it up and move it to clean off the area. Of course, when I did I couldn't help but notice you're taking the same medication my Albert used to take."

Her Albert? Bas hadn't realized she was married. "And where is *your Albert*?"

"Dead."

Out of respect, he bit back the word *damn* as he rubbed a hand down his face. That was all he needed to know. Her Albert who used to take the same medication he took was dead. Although Bas wished he could move on without asking the next question, something inside him made him inquire anyway.

"And how did he die?"

"He had high blood pressure and although the medication helped, he refused to give up some of his favorite foods that were killing him. And knowing what happened to Albert, I can't in good conscience allow the same thing to happen to you."

Bas lifted a brow, sure he'd heard her wrong. "Excuse me?"

She crossed her arms over her chest. "I said I won't allow the same thing to happen to you. My Albert only thought of himself. He should have cared enough to want to live longer so he could be here with me while we spent our retirement years together. But he didn't take care of himself and now he's gone. We were married almost fifty years and had four beautiful children and he didn't live long enough to be around for the first great-grand. I tried to tell him to eat healthy. I even offered to prepare him all the foods that were better for him. But he refused to give up that steak twice a week, as well as the potatoes, the bread and let's not talk about the desserts."

No, Bas didn't want to talk about the desserts. He didn't want to talk about food period. "But I'm not your husband, Ms. Sadie," he decided it was time to point out.

"No, but someday you'll be somebody's husband if you live long enough. You're young, too young to be worried about some nasty ailment like high blood pressure, which can lead to other problems like heart disease. It's best that you get a handle on things now before it's too late. And while you're living here I intend to help you. I owe it to my Albert and your mother to do so."

Bas shook his head in frustration. "But you don't know my mother."

"Doesn't matter. We're all members of the 'Mothers Club' and I know wherever she is, she'll thank me for trying to save her son from an early grave."

Bas sighed deeply, recognizing the stubborn glint in the woman's eyes. It was the same glint he'd seen in his own mother's eyes several times, and the one he had seen in Kylie's the day she had confronted him after finding out about his medical issues. Ms. Sadie was right. Once a mother, always a mother. All mothers shared a bond to make their kids' lives miserable.

Bas decided to use another approach. "Ms. Sadie, don't you think getting involved in my medical business is carrying things a little too far? I'm just a resident here for a while. I'm a grown man—thirty-five. Shouldn't my eating habits be my decision to make?"

"Yes."

Bas nodded, glad they were finally getting somewhere. "And don't you think you've crossed the line by serving me oatmeal instead of the breakfast you gave to everyone else this morning?"

He watched as the older woman pushed a curly lock of gray hair away from her face and in that instant he saw it—the look of stark worry in her eyes. She actually thought his fate could be sealed like her Albert's if he didn't eat differently. Aw hell. All he needed was the old woman worrying to death about him. And although she had agreed that what he ate was his business, he knew as far as she was concerned, to feed him the high-calorie foods he liked would be like signing his death warrant.

Bas knew there was only one thing he could do and that would be to find another place to stay as soon as he could. He refused to hang around Newton Grove for the next three months and live under the same roof with an older version of Kylie Hagan Steele.

It just so happened he had run across a place for sale the day he'd been out riding around with Reese. It was a quaint little cabin just outside of town on a small lake in the mountains. If nothing else it would be a nice piece of investment property. He would see a realtor about it first thing tomorrow.

He met Ms. Sadie's gaze. "Fine," he said. "I'll eat the oatmeal every morning if it makes you happy." *Just until I get that cabin,* he decided not to add.

Her worried look brightened into a smile. "Thank you and it will. And when you live to your late seventies with kids, grands and great-grands like me, you'll be grateful that someone cared enough about you to make sure you stuck to a proper diet."

"Not a chance," Bas muttered under his breath as he scooted back to the table to eat his oatmeal.

LEAH SMILED AS she looked at herself in the oval mirror she held in her hand. "I think even after all these years no one can take care of a woman's head like you can, Kate."

The older woman chuckled and waved her hand as if refusing to accept the flattering comment. "Doing your hair has always been easy. I'm glad you didn't put all that crazy dye in it while living out in Los Angeles. That would have damaged it for sure. Your hair is just as thick and healthy as it's always been."

Leah smiled at the compliment. "Thanks." Kate had been doing her hair ever since Leah was a teenager and her dad had agreed to let her get a perm. Kate was right, Leah's hair had always been thick and healthy, but what Kate had been too nice to add was that it had also been unmanageable. While Jocelyn could get by with going to the hair salon every two weeks, Kate was sentenced to see Leah on a weekly basis.

Leah couldn't help but remember those times. Jocelyn had been close to their father and she had been close to their mother. She'd died when Leah had been only twelve, and all Leah could remember was how empty she'd felt. Jocelyn had always been Daddy's girl and hadn't experienced the same sense of loss as Leah had. From the day they'd placed her mother in the ground, Leah couldn't wait to move away from a town filled with loneliness for her without the mother she had adored.

"I was sorry to hear about your dad, Leah. Everyone around here was. He was a good man."

Leah nodded. She hadn't realized just what a good man he was until she'd found herself alone, hurt and out in California on her own. More than once she'd come close to picking up the phone and telling him what had happened to her and why she'd left the way she had. But shame had kept her from doing so.

Her only saving grace was actually someone with the name of Grace. How she had ended up on the woman's doorstep one night, she still wasn't sure. All she knew was that she was convinced she'd heard footsteps behind her while walking home alone from the restaurant where she'd worked. Remembering what had happened to her before, she had gone almost stone-crazy and had run to the first house she'd come to and begged for help.

Help had come in the way of an older woman, no bigger than a mite, who had offered her safety. Grace Thorpe had been a godsend. After making sure Leah was safe, she'd offered her food to eat and a place to stay, much better than the dump where she'd been living.

Grace's two sons had threatened to move their mother in with them and their wives on a rotating basis, not wanting the old woman to live alone anymore. What Grace had needed was a companion, someone to be there with her during the day and to do the grocery shopping and drive Grace to church on Sundays. Since Leah worked at the restaurant at night, she grabbed the opportunity.

Half an hour later after leaving the hair salon, Leah was strolling through downtown Newton Grove, checking out the various shops and noticing what changes the town had made over the years. After living in the hustle and bustle of L.A. for five years, she appreciated the solitude and quiet a place like Newton Grove offered. She'd never realized how much she missed living in this town until now.

Tossing her hair out of her eyes, she kept walking, remembering a place close by that used to sell breakfast and wondering if it was still open. She had gotten up early and had started a pot of coffee but hadn't made breakfast for herself, or her sister, who rarely took the time for breakfast.

Jocelyn.

Leah couldn't help but wonder what was going on with her sister. There was never a time she didn't think her older sister was in control and made things happen just the way she wanted. But now, at twenty-three, Leah was seeing things through different eyes, more appreciative and caring eyes, and she hoped that whatever had caused Jocelyn to walk the floor last night would go away.

Leah passed in front of a store window and stopped. Then she noticed what had grabbed her attention. It was a baby store with a number of items on display. She pulled her jacket closer around her and not for the first time she remembered the dream she'd had to let go of years ago.

She would never have the baby she always wanted. A little one she could bounce on her knee, sing lullabies to and sprinkle with the scent of baby powder. She had dreamed about this child of hers for so long and how he would look up at her with dark-brown eyes and the same smile that had gone straight to her heart—like his father's had done six years ago. There was nothing that could even make her think of staying in Newton Grove until she had met Reese the summer before her senior year of high school.

Love and caring hadn't meant a damn thing to her until then. The only thing she wanted to do was hurry up and graduate and haul ass, go as far west and away from Tennessee as a plane ticket could take her.

Then, in a slow, methodical process Reese had broken down her defenses. He had done something no one else had been able to do—he'd understood her loss. He had listened when she had wanted to talk about her mother. He had understood her pain and sense of loss because he had experienced those same things himself when he'd lost his father at sixteen. With patience, care and understanding, he had made her fall in love with him in a way that was so complete that she hadn't thought of leaving town. The only thing she had wanted to do was to hang around, marry him and have his babies.

But now that was a dream that would never come true. Although there was no physical reason why she couldn't have a child, she would never be able to let a man touch her that way. At one point she had thought about artificial insemination, but a lot of things prevented that. First, she didn't have the money and her insurance would not cover such a procedure. Second, she would still have to take off her clothes for the procedure, and she couldn't do that in front of anyone. Third, the thought of carrying a baby from someone she didn't know was a turn-off for her. The only man's baby she'd ever dreamed of having was Reese's.

Feeling a knot settling in her throat, she wiped a hand across her face, swiping at the tears that she couldn't stop from flowing down her cheeks. Life was cruel, but considering all the hard times she had given her father while growing up, maybe in the end she had gotten everything she deserved. With that thought more tears began to fall.

REESE HAD JUST walked out of the café holding a steaming cup of coffee. It was early and the air was brisk, but nothing smelled better than fresh roasted brew in the morning. He headed for his parked truck, determined to be at the construction site before the men got there this morning. He needed to go over yet another change Marcella Jones had made, but at least thanks to Sebastian Steele, it was a change she would be paying for.

He liked Steele, although he knew Jocelyn hadn't yet gotten used to the guy hanging around. But he felt fairly certain that once she saw he wasn't one of the bad guys she would be okay. His handling of Manuel's situation had proven that he did have a heart.

Reese was about to unlock his truck door and get in when something made him look to the right. He blinked, thinking he was seeing things. Standing a few doors from the café was a woman whose profile so closely resembled Leah's that it was startling. And the more he stared at her, the more he began to realize that it was Leah.

He would know her anywhere, the woman who years ago had stolen his heart, just like he would always remember the one night he had made her his in a way no other man had. It had been special for the two of them and—

He immediately forced the thoughts from his mind. That night had been special for him, but evidently not for her, because less than a month later she had left town without looking back. He would never forget the pain he had felt when she'd left. It was pain that still lived in a place deep in his heart, although he wished it would get out of there and leave him alone. He knew that until he was able to let go he would never be worth a damn to any other woman. The thought that Leah had done that to him left a bitter taste in his mouth.

A part of him just wanted to get in the truck and drive away and pretend he hadn't seen her. But for some reason he couldn't do that. The only way he could eradicate Leah from his mind and heart forever finally was to come face to face with her again. He no longer wanted to know why she'd left the way she had, since nothing she said now would matter. He just had to be convinced that he could look her in the face and then turn and walk away.

He took slow steps toward her, and the closer he got the harder his heart began pounding. And when he finally came to stand behind her, he stood without moving since she hadn't noticed his presence. She was too busy studying the items in the store's window. He glanced beyond her to see what had her absolute attention and frowned. It was a baby shop and she was looking at baby clothes. Why would she be doing that?

The next question that skated through his mind was who was pregnant? He didn't like the answer he suddenly came up with. Could the reason Leah wasn't in a hurry to return to California be because she was pregnant?

A blade, sharper than any knife he'd ever handled, sliced through his insides at the thought that she could possibly be carrying a child that wasn't his. He hung his head as pain clouded his thoughts, and he knew he had to get away from there. But something held him transfixed and he knew he had to do this. He had to confront a part of his past that he wished at that moment had never taken place.

Sighing deeply, he took a step closer and noticed Leah was trembling and her shoulders were shaking. Evidently, she was a lot colder than he was.

Deciding not to prolong things, he forced her name from his lips. "Leah?"

LEAH'S BODY WENT stiff, and she hoped more than anything she had imagined the sound of the deep masculine voice. The last thing she needed at that particular moment was to come face to face with the one man who still had a clamp on her heart. The one man she had never stopped loving. The one man she had hurt deeply. And the one man she would never deserve to have again.

"Leah?"

When he said her name a second time, she knew fate was being more than cruel to her today. It was being outright merciless. Pulling in a deep breath, as deep as she could inhale, taking one final swipe at her tears and bracing herself, she slowly turned around while asking God to give her the strength to endure what she knew was going to be one of the hardest moments of her life.

CHAPTER EIGHT

NOTHING COULD HAVE prepared Reese for the impact of looking into the face of the woman who had shattered his heart into a thousand tiny pieces. Bitterness, anger, hurt and the pain he hadn't been able to let go of suddenly hit him full force, and he almost crushed the hot cup of coffee he held in his hand.

All he could think was that standing before him was the woman who'd once told him she loved him. The woman he had thought he would forever share his life with. The woman destined to be the mother of his children, and the one woman who even now had the love he hadn't been able to share with any other.

The thought that he still loved her, hadn't gotten over her, although he had tried, left a bitter taste in his mouth, left his joints achy with humiliation and made everything within him want to strike out and hurt her as much as she had hurt him. But something was keeping him from doing that. He frowned, seeing the wetness of her eyes and the single tear she'd tried to quickly swipe away. Leah was crying. Why? And why was he even giving a damn?

Then he remembered. She was standing in front of the display window at a baby store. Something about babies had her upset. He quickly jumped back to his earlier suspicion. Was Leah pregnant, and was that the reason she was hanging around?

"Reese, it's good seeing you."

Her words cut into him. The sound of her voice used to send excitement buzzing through every cell in his body. Now it hit a brick wall of resentment. How could she fix her mouth to say it was good seeing him when this was the first time they had come face to face in five years?

He sighed deeply. "I wish I could say the same thing, Leah," he said, his voice low while he fought to keep it steady. "But at the moment, it's not good seeing you again."

Although his words hurt, Leah knew they were what she deserved, and she stood still, feeling the intense anger radiating from him. Jocelyn had warned her, but nothing could have prepared her for this degree of anger. Not from the man who had taught her how to love. The man who had shown her it wasn't always about her but the people she cared about and who cared for her. She'd never got a chance to let him know she'd learned the lessons he had so lovingly taught. The night she was going to commit her heart and soul to him was the same night Neil had assaulted her.

She felt a tear she couldn't fight back slide down her cheek as she met his hostile gaze and said, "I'm sorry you feel that way, Reese."

She watched the frown that formed between his thick eyebrows and saw the narrowing of his eyes. "Why haven't you left yet? There's nothing here for you anymore. You made that decision five years ago, didn't you? That none of us were worthy of your time, consideration…and love."

Her heart clutched as a sharp pain ripped through it. He would think that, wouldn't he? And since he would continue to think that, there was nothing she could say or do to ease the pain or soothe his anger. The best thing to do was to leave.

"I think I'd better go now," she said, not wanting to argue with him. Besides, seeing the fury in his eyes was too much. Reese had always been one of the most easy-going, gentle and loving people she knew. To know he had become a ball of anger because of her was more than she could handle.

"Yeah, go, Leah. Walk away. Leave and don't look back. You're good at that, aren't you?"

She felt more tears well up in her eyes, tears she refused to stand before him and shed. "Yeah, I guess I am. Goodbye, Reese." And as quickly as her legs could carry her, she turned and began walking away. And although it broke her heart, she didn't look back.

"WHAT DO YOU mean we got the wrong tile?"

"Because it's not what we ordered," Harry Henderson answered Jocelyn in disgust. "The box says it's what we ordered but the color is off a shade. See for yourself."

Shaking her head in frustration, Jocelyn put down the saw and went to inspect the box in question. Mason Construction had used Harry exclusively for all their tile work for as long as she could remember. Over the years the older man had brought his son and his grandsons into the business; however, he refused to give up the work and retire.

She often wondered how, at seventy-one, he was able to get on his knees to lay tile. But she had to admit he was still good at what he did and could be depended on more than a lot of the younger workers.

She opened the box and looked in. He was right. These marble tiles had the wrong accent color.

She glanced back up at Harry. "How much of the wrong tile did we get?"

Harry rubbed his bald head, reluctant to tell her. "All thirty boxes, which was supposed to cover over three-hundred square feet."

The entire foyer. Jocelyn breathed in deeply. It was either that or scream. "Let's get the store on the phone."

"I did that already. They apologized for their mistake but said when they called the distributor they were told it's a popular shade that wouldn't be available for six weeks."

"Six weeks! But it was their mistake."

"I told them that. But six weeks was the best they could do."

"That's not good enough," Jocelyn said, seeing red. And it didn't help matters that she hadn't gotten a good night's sleep. "Marcella wants to move into this place in two weeks. Let's skip the distributor and go straight to the manufacturer."

"I did that, too. It's their policy to deal only with the distributor."

"I don't give a hoot about their policy. Give me the number," she said, snatching the cell phone out of her back pocket and punching in the numbers Harry was calling out to her. This was definitely not her morning. They'd had to cancel the committee meeting because three of the members had called at the last minute to say they couldn't make it. And then the traffic light on the corner of Rondell and Marlborough had been out, which had backed traffic up for almost an hour.

Jocelyn sighed when she encountered an auto prompter and had to punch in some more numbers. She glanced up and saw that Harry had had the good sense to get lost for a while after sensing she was getting hotter than fire. Reese would normally handle discrepancies such as this, but the guys told her he'd left to pick up supplies. They'd further told her that he was in a bad mood. She couldn't help but wonder what had Reese's dander up.

A half hour later, her head was spinning and she'd gotten nowhere. The six-week delay still stood.

Jocelyn snapped the phone shut. Didn't businesses believe in providing good customer service anymore?

"So, what's going on?"

She looked up and her eyes collided with those of Bas. For some reason, seeing him made more anger spike through her. He was the reason for her not getting the proper rest last night, and seeing him reminded her of it.

And to make matters even worse, the midday sunlight that was streaming through those windows they'd installed a couple of weeks ago was hitting him at an angle that made an uncomfortable quiver pass through her stomach, not to mention the flush of heat that spread through her body. As usual, he was wearing a pair of jeans and a T-shirt. This time the shirt was rooting for the Pittsburgh Steelers. She frowned, wondering if he had a real allegiance to any team. To any woman.

She shook her head, getting even angrier that she would wonder about such a thing; his love life was no concern of hers.

"Bas to Jocelyn," he said, waving a hand back and forth in front of her face. "Can you read me? You seemed to have zoned out."

Even angrier than before, she folded her arms over her chest. "And where have you been?"

He leaned back against the fireplace mantel and smiled slowly. "I didn't know you wanted me."

What he said and the way he said it sent her pulse into overdrive. It wasn't fair. The man had a sexy physique, he was handsome as all outdoors, and on top of everything else he had a sexy voice that could rival Barry White's any day.

"Did you want me, Jocelyn?"

Sighing deeply, she set her jaw, determined not to say anything. She thought better of it and opened her mouth to tell him a thing or two, but he was quick and placed a finger to her lips. "Remember our truce."

She glared. She didn't care one iota about their so-called truce. Her main concern was tile, namely marble. If Marcella got wind that she would have to wait six weeks for her foyer to be completed, all hell would break loose. A thought suddenly came into Jocelyn's head. Bas was supposed to be the expert troubleshooter, the fixer-upper, the problem solver. So let him deal with it and see if he made more progress than she did.

"We got the wrong tile," she snapped.

He gave her a carefree look. "Then return it."

As if she hadn't been trying to do that for the past half hour. "It'll be another six weeks before the distributor can replace it."

"Tough. We'll go to the manufacturer."

Did he think she hadn't tried that already, too? "I did that," she all but spat out. "And I got nowhere."

"What's the name of the distributor?"

Jocelyn blew out a sharp breath. "Arnett Distributors."

"Arnett Distributors?" He almost laughed. "Then there shouldn't be a problem."

He sounded so convinced she couldn't help but ask, "And why shouldn't there be a problem?"

He smiled again as he met her gaze while pulling out his cell phone and punching in numbers he evidently knew by heart. "Because the Steele Corporation is one of their biggest clients."

Jocelyn nervously chewed the insides of her cheeks. Could it be possible that Bas had enough clout with Arnett to rectify a major screw-up? She couldn't help remembering the last house they'd done for Marcella Jones and how she claimed the kitchen fixtures hadn't been the ones she'd ordered. She'd pitched such a fit that Jim had taken the six-hour drive to Birmingham and back to pick up the ones Marcella claimed she was supposed to have. Jocelyn didn't relish the thought of having to tell her about the tile.

"Mark Arnett, please."

Bas's words intruded into her thoughts and she wondered how he'd gotten past the auto prompts. She wondered too if he'd gotten any more sleep last night than she had. He didn't seem tired and grouchy this morning. Evidently he hadn't had a restless night remembering how they had indulged in such a mind-blowing kiss. Maybe it had been mind-blowing just to her. Maybe for him it was just so-so.

"Mark? How are you? This is Sebastian Steele. Yes, I'm fine." Then cutting to the chase he said, "Look, I need your help and I want you to put it to the top of your list." He nodded. "Good. There's been a mix-up with a supplier of one of our subsidiary companies and I need it straightened out. I need a particular style of marble tile sent to me right away." There was a pause. "How soon? Overnight if you can." Another pause. "Here's the style number," he said and began reading the information off the invoice.

"Think you can handle that?" he asked without missing a beat. "Great. Here's the address I want it sent to."

Five minutes later Bas was hanging up the phone, smiling. "Any other fires you want me to put out?"

Not unless he wanted to drop a gallon of water on her head, Jocelyn thought as intense heat ran through every part of her body. While he'd been on the phone with Mark Arnett, trying to save her company from Marcella Jones's wrath, she'd been studying him like a teenager in lust. Every time he moved his body, she got the full effect of seeing him in his tight-fitting jeans and saw how they contoured to his muscular thighs. And if that wasn't bad enough, that Pittsburgh Steelers T-shirt was clearly emphasizing muscular arms, a firm flat chest and nice wide shoulders. Display Bas on a poster and she would buy whatever he was advertising.

"Jocelyn?"

Snatched out of her reverie, she lifted her chin and straightened her shoulders. "No, there aren't any more fires you need to put out. Thanks."

"Don't mention it." He glanced around. "Where's Reese?"

"Doing a pickup."

He blew out a breath and frowned. "When do you expect him back?"

She lifted a brow. "Not sure. Is anything wrong?"

"No, just have him call the office when he returns."

For some reason Jocelyn felt he wasn't telling her everything. Why did he want to talk to Reese? He was just the foreman. She was the one in charge of things. Maybe she needed to remind him of that.

"Look," she said, leaning closer and looking intently at him.

"Yes?" he said, and she felt the force of his own gaze back.

"You do remember who's in charge, don't you?"

He smiled. "Yeah, I think so, but do you want to remind me again?"

She frowned, and suddenly wanted to find the hammer and clobber him. "I'm trying to be nice."

"You shouldn't have to try so hard. It should come naturally," he said and reached out and tweaked her nose. "I'll see you later."

She was ready to throw out an angry retort when she saw that Harry had reappeared and the two of them were talking with obvious familiarity. Evidently they remembered each other from that summer Bas had worked with her father. Jocelyn decided what she had to say to Bas could wait. There was no need to put him in his place in front of Harry. She would have enough time to read him later.

She was pulled away from those thoughts when her cell phone rang. "Yes?"

"Is Reese there?"

She recognized Leah's voice immediately. "No. Why?"

"Because I saw him this morning."

She could tell from the tone of her sister's voice that there was more. "And?"

"And we had words."

Jocelyn felt her throat tighten. "Not so nice ones, I gather."

"You gathered right."

Jocelyn nodded. No wonder Reese was in a bad mood. Now she understood why the men thought he was angry about something. "Are you okay?" she asked, concerned.

"Yes, but barely. And you were right. He hates me."

"I never said he hated you. I said he was still hurting."

"Same difference, since I'm the one who hurt him."

There was a pause because Jocelyn didn't know what to say. No, that wasn't true. She did know what to say, but she also knew Leah wouldn't want to hear it. She trailed a finger along the fine craftsmanship of the wooden banister Reese had completed last week. "I still think you should tell him the truth."

"I can't."

She decided not to press when she heard the trembling in Leah's voice. She didn't have to see her sister's face to know she'd been crying and probably still was. "Hey, how about the two of us doing something tonight?"

"Like what?"

"Going to a movie."

"A movie?"

"Yes, a movie. When was the last time we went to a movie together?" She could just imagine Leah bunching up her forehead trying to remember.

"Um, I think it was when Aunt Susan took us to see *Titanic*."

"Hey, you're right," Jocelyn said smiling as she remembered. "She really liked that picture, didn't she?"

"Yes, she did. We sat through it twice. After that I didn't care if I ever saw the ocean again."

"I felt the same way." Jocelyn laughed.

"You know," Leah then said in a quiet voice, "I wish she had been around five years ago. I would have gone to Florida instead of California. For all her proper ways, Aunt Susan was pretty special, wasn't she?"

Jocelyn nodded. "Yes, she was." After a brief pause she said, "So how about it? Do you want to do a movie?"

She heard Leah chuckle and liked the sound. "Will

going to a movie help you sleep better tonight?" Leah asked with a hint of teasing in her voice.

Jocelyn glanced across the room to Bas. He was still talking to Harry. And as if he felt her eyes on him, he tilted his head and looked at her. The deep intensity of his dark gaze was pinning her to the spot, heating her even more.

It was hard for Jocelyn to keep her voice steady when she replied, "No guarantees there, but it's worth a try."

BAS THREW THE file aside and glanced at his watch. It was almost four in the afternoon. He had a ton of files he still needed to review so there was no reason for Jocelyn Mason to be on his mind.

But she was.

Muttering a curse he leaned back in the chair and picked up a file he had placed to the side. He had done the accounting three times and still the figures weren't right, but before he jumped to any conclusions, he would do as Jim had instructed him in another letter that Kilgore had dropped off a few days ago. All the note had said was: Talk to Reese first about any discrepancies you may find in the bookkeeping records.

Then, just that quickly, he dismissed the note from his mind as his thoughts wandered to Jocelyn again. He had known she was troubled by something the moment he'd seen her. It was there in her face. She'd had that worried look. And ridiculous as it seemed, something deep within him had wanted to get rid of whatever was causing her stress.

Luckily all it had taken was a phone call and the use

of his connections to make things right and to remove her troubled frown. But as usual, they had almost gotten into another argument, something he hadn't been up to. After talking with Harry he had quickly left, eager to be gone from Jocelyn's presence before she found another bone to pick. After a sleepless night and dealing with Sadie that morning, he hadn't been in the best of moods, either. The last thing they needed was to be at each other's throats…or lips.

Damn, but he couldn't get their kiss out of his mind! He shook his head remembering. Whoever said 'out of sight, out of mind' didn't know what the hell they were talking about, he thought, reaching for an apple from the basket of fresh fruit Sadie Robinson had dropped off a few moments ago. The woman had stayed only long enough to lecture him on how much better fruit was than some of the other snacks she'd noticed him gobbling up. He hadn't found her spiel amusing but Noreen, Mason Construction's secretary, had.

Noreen Telfair.

The woman's name suddenly made him recall the accounting issue and why he needed to talk to Reese. The one thing he'd noticed about the attractive woman was that she appeared to be a good worker who didn't have much to say. He knew that she was in her late forties, a divorcée with a teenage daughter, and that she had moved to town three or four years ago from Atlanta. He'd discovered that bit of info from reading her employee records, which was something he had taken the time to do on everyone who worked at Mason's.

"The guys said you were looking for me."

Bas glanced up when Reese walked into what used to be Jim's office. Bas took one look at Reese, saw his tense expression and immediately knew something was bothering him. "Hey, man, you okay?"

"Yeah, I'm fine," he said, closing the door behind him and crossing the room to sit in a leather chair. "Today's been a rough one."

Bas chuckled. "Tell me about it." He was pretty good at reading people, and although Reese had said things were fine, Bas knew that something wasn't. But he was a person who made it a point not to get involved in anyone else's business unless he was asked.

He leaned forward, remembering why he needed to see Reese. "I was going through the accounting records and found several discrepancies. Kilgore delivered a letter to me a couple of days ago that Jim left. In it were instructions that I talk to you first if I found problems with the books."

Reese sat up straighter in his chair as a confused expression covered his face. "Jim said that?"

"Yes."

"I wonder why. As far as I know I'm not privy to any information regarding Mason Construction's accounting records. What's the discrepancy?"

"Several deposits of large amounts were placed in an account for Noreen. The last one was a couple of months before Jim died. I verified the signature and he signed off on all of them, but he doesn't note in the records what they were for."

"Oh," Reese said and then sat back and smoothed

his hands along the arms of the chair. "I don't know exactly what they were for, but I have an idea."

"All right," Bas said, sensing Reese's hesitancy in discussing the matter. "Was it a loan? Blackmail? Help me to understand, Reese. We're talking about a total of over a hundred thousand dollars here."

Reese shifted nervously in his chair and met the intensity in Bas's gaze. "No one was supposed to know and I only found out by accident."

Bas lifted a brow. "You found out what by accident?"

Reese shifted in his chair again and lowered his eyes when he spoke. "That Jim and Noreen were lovers."

Bas didn't so much as blink since that had been one of his suspicions. "Why did they keep it a secret? Jim was a widower and Noreen is divorced."

Reese shrugged and met Bas's eyes. "Yes, but there's the issue of the difference in their ages. We're talking about fifteen years. And besides that, this is a small town that sometimes feeds on gossip, and Noreen has a teenage daughter they wanted to protect. They were very discreet and most of the time they planned out-of-town trips. They had been together a couple of years before I found out. I happened to be visiting a cousin in Atlanta when I ran into the two of them in a hotel there. Needless to say, it was a very uncomfortable moment because it was the last thing I'd suspected."

Bas nodded. "Did Jocelyn know?"

"I doubt it. At least Jim and Noreen assumed she didn't know. I really don't think she would have had a problem with it had she known. But like I said, Jim was uncomfortable about the difference in their ages. Noreen didn't have a problem with it."

"And they were lovers until he died?"

"Yes, and I really thought things would come out then, but Jim made Noreen promise not to say or do anything to give them away. That part was pretty hard on her."

"I'm sure it was."

"And he didn't want to leave her a big chunk in his will like he did for me, to give everyone a reason to speculate why. That's why he set up a special account for her in this bank in Memphis. She didn't know he was doing it until right before he died."

"I see."

"That's probably why he wanted you to come in and check out things before Jocelyn got a mind to call in an independent accountant to audit the records."

Bas leaned back in his chair. "Thanks for sharing that with me. That clears up a lot."

"Well, Noreen and Jim cared a lot for each other and although their affair wasn't made public, they made each other happy, and to me that's all that mattered. For some people happiness is a rare commodity these days."

Bas said nothing for a moment after hearing the rancor in Reese's voice. He remembered having to deal with his brother Morgan's bitterness a few months ago when a woman he was interested in refused even to discuss the possibility of them pursuing a relationship.

Bas quickly made a decision about something. He might as well call it a day since he wasn't thinking about work much anyway. "So, what are your plans for the rest of the day, Reese?"

Reese stood. "I'm going over to the gym to work out awhile. I feel like hitting something and I prefer it to be a punching bag than a human being."

Bas nodded. He knew the feeling. He remembered passing the gym when he arrived in town. It seemed like a pretty new facility. He couldn't remember the last time he gave his body a good workout. "Mind if I join you?"

Reese smiled. "No, not at all."

"Good. I'll run by Sadie's and get my gear and then meet you there in about thirty minutes." Bas locked the files in the drawer for the night.

Beating up on a punching bag wasn't such a bad idea.

CHAPTER NINE

THIS WAS THE part of construction she loved the best. The finish. Or in this case, the part that was pretty close to being finished, because with Marcella Jones you never knew for sure. But since Bas had explained their pay-if-you-make-any-changes policy, she had kept the changes to a minimum. In fact she had made barely any at all.

Jocelyn glanced around with her hand on her hips. This was indeed a beautiful home and she could imagine how grand it would look furnished. Marcella wasn't known to skimp when it came to getting what she wanted so there was no doubt in Jocelyn's mind that this house would be the talk of the town for a while... at least until Marcella saw another design for a home that suited her fancy in one of those magazines of hers. Then there would be house number four.

"It looks nice, doesn't it?"

Jocelyn turned and smiled at Reese. "Yes, it does, and from the look of things, we'll finish on time. That marble tile came this morning and Harry and his crew have already put it down. They'll be back tomorrow to grout it."

She then studied Reese with concern in her eyes. She hadn't seen him yesterday and wondered if he was okay. "And how are you, Reese? Leah told me you saw each other yesterday."

Jocelyn watched as bitterness lined his lips. "Yes, we did. I should have been prepared but I wasn't," he said quietly.

"And I don't think she was prepared, either."

Reese's dark eyes flashed. "Then that's tough for her, isn't it?" He inhaled deeply and said, "Look, Jocelyn, I'd rather not discuss Leah, but there is something I need to know. If you can't tell me, then I'll understand."

"What?"

Reese hung his head and studied the gleaming wood floor for a second then met Jocelyn's gaze again. "Is Leah pregnant? Is that the reason she's not in a hurry to leave here?"

Of all the questions she had expected him to ask that sure wasn't one. "What gave you an idea like that? She definitely doesn't look pregnant."

"No, but yesterday morning I walked up on her staring into the display window of that baby store in town…and she was crying."

"Oh." Jocelyn pressed a hand to her chest as if she could feel her sister's pain. Poor Leah. She hadn't been crying for what she had, but for what she thought she could never have—Reese's child.

"Well, is she pregnant?"

She heard the anger in his voice and the pain. The thought that Leah might be pregnant with another man's child had to be hurting him deeply. At least that was one pain Jocelyn could take away. "No, she's not pregnant."

"How do you know for sure? She might be and just hasn't told you."

"Because I know," she snapped, feeling the need to come to Leah's defense, considering everything. "She can't be pregnant."

Reese frowned deeply. "You don't know that."

"I do know that," she said, rounding on him angrily. "She hasn't been involved with anyone since you and—" Jocelyn stopped abruptly, fearing she might have said too much.

"What the hell do you mean she hasn't been involved with anyone since me? Do you actually believe that lie?" he asked incredulously. "I never thought you of all people would be that gullible."

Jocelyn's eyes flashed fire. "Yes, I believe it because…"

He lifted a brow. "Because what?"

Disgusted with herself and the entire situation and knowing if Neil Grunthall wasn't dead already he would have been by the end of the day, she released a frustrated sigh. "Look, Reese, forget I said anything."

"What are you not telling me, Jocelyn?" he asked, grabbing her arm.

She snatched it back, although it cost her to do so. She would love for him to know what she wasn't telling him. "Look, let it be, okay? All you need to know is that Leah isn't pregnant." She turned to leave but Reese called out to her and she turned back around. "What?"

"Just in case I don't see you in the morning, I'm cutting out a little early tomorrow. Two of Bas's broth-

ers are coming in and I plan to take them up to Cedar
Springs for the weekend to do a little fishing."

"Fine," she said, shoving both hands into the pockets of her jeans. "Enjoy yourselves."

Then she turned back around and continued walking.

"THANKS FOR A great weekend, Reese," Bas said on
Sunday afternoon as he got out of Reese's truck and
gathered his belongings. "There were good lodgings,
good company, good fishing and damn good beer. What
more can a man ask for?"

"Nothing's wrong with a good woman every now
and then," Reese answered, grinning.

"Hell, but not on a fishing trip. They get too squea-
mish and want you to have pity and throw your catch
back. Women and fishing don't mix."

Reese gave a smooth laugh. "You must have never
gone fishing with the right woman. Leah could handle
just—" He stopped suddenly, then said. "Oh, hell,
dammit to three degrees. I promised myself that I
wouldn't mention her name, much less think about her
this weekend. She's not worth the effort."

Bas shook his head. "Evidently she is. What has it
been? Five years? And you're still carrying a torch?
That was some kind of love."

Reese's hand tightened on the steering wheel. It
would be useless to deny he was still carrying a torch.
"Yeah, and she didn't deserve any of it."

"Seems you haven't convinced your heart of that yet.
See you around, buddy."

Moments later Bas entered the cabin he had purchased with his brothers' blessings as investment property for the Steele Corporation. Reese, Morgan and Donovan had helped him to move in Friday afternoon then they had left to go fishing Saturday morning.

He couldn't help but ponder the fact that Reese was still in love with a woman who had torn out his heart and stomped on it. Bas was damn grateful he had never been in love. Even when he was engaged to Cassandra, he'd liked her, been fond of her, but not once did he think he loved her. Their marriage would have been a sort of business arrangement. With thirty staring her in the face, she wanted a husband who could keep her in the lifestyle she was accustomed to, and he'd wanted a proper lady who was refined as well as beautiful. What he hadn't been looking for but what he'd found in Cassandra had also been snobbery to a degree he just couldn't tolerate.

A half hour later, after taking a very relaxing shower, Bas walked out of the bathroom. Wrapped in a towel, not yet ready to put on any clothes, he crossed the room to look out the window, liking the view. Mountains in the distance and a small stream out back provided a picturesque scene. This could be a place he, his brothers or cousins could use when they just wanted to get away. Privacy was golden sometimes, and everybody needed it on occasion.

When he'd told Ms. Sadie that he had purchased the cabin and would be moving, she had smiled and made him promise to eat properly. But he had a feeling she would continue to show up at the office at lunch time with a fruit basket for him. In a way he looked forward to her visits, even realizing he actually enjoyed eating fruit.

After a few moments, Bas suddenly felt antsy and considered driving to the office to work on more files, but he quickly decided against it. This had been a relaxing weekend, and he didn't want to spoil it. He couldn't help the smile that touched his lips at that moment. He had been glad to see Morgan and Donovan, although he would never admit it to them. And Reese had been the perfect host. The four of them had fished to their hearts' content, drunk as much beer as their bellies could hold and talked about anything and everything… except women. They hadn't had much time to think of women, either.

But now, back in the privacy of his little place, Bas's mind was once again filled with thoughts of Jocelyn. He couldn't help wondering what she was doing. Had she thought of him any this weekend? Was the kiss they'd shared a few nights ago still seared on her brain the same way it was on his?

His lips quirked. There was only one way to find out. He wanted to see her. He needed to see her. Damn, he needed to kiss her again. He grinned. This was the first time he'd ever gotten addicted to a woman's taste and he wasn't sure what he was going to do about it other than feed his habit.

"So you're Sebastian Steele."

Bas nodded. If the woman who'd opened the door to him was Leah Mason, then he could understand why after five years Reese hadn't been able to eradicate her from his heart. She was a woman a man wouldn't be able to forget easily. But then so was her sister.

"Yes, I'm Sebastian and you're Leah, right?"

"Yes, I'm Leah. I'm glad I finally got to meet you. I've heard a lot about you."

Bas refused to throw out the cliché "all good I hope," since he knew if it came from Jocelyn that would not have been the case. "And I'm glad I finally got to meet you," he said slipping his hands into his pockets. "I was wondering if Jocelyn is home."

Leah smiled. "Yes, she's home but not here. She's at her place right outside of town. Do you know where that is?"

"Yes, I think I do." In all honesty, the day she had taken him there he had been too busy trying to survive the truck ride to care about the direction in which she'd been driving.

"It's real easy to find," she said, giving him instructions.

"Thanks."

"You're welcome. I'd like to invite you over for dinner one night when you're free. Dad thought a lot of you and I'd like to get to know you better."

"Thanks, and the same here. Good night."

"Good night."

When she closed the door, Bas turned and quickly walked back to his car. More than anything he wanted to see Jocelyn.

LEAH SMILED, WONDERING if she should give Jocelyn a call to prepare her for Sebastian Steele's visit, then decided not to. Whether her sister admitted it or not she knew something was going on between those two. She smiled and went to the sofa to settle back down with her book.

She'd never known Jocelyn to have a boyfriend. Oh, she had gone out on dates but had never gotten serious about anyone. Now it looked like that history was about to change.

JOCELYN TAPPED A finger to her lips as she glanced around the room. She had gone shopping yesterday and purchased this beautiful hand-carved vase, and she wasn't quite certain of the best spot for it.

The coffee table or the bookcase?

She was leaning toward the coffee table when her doorbell sounded. She automatically assumed it was Rita, Reese's brother's wife from across the lake.

Instead of asking who it was, she snatched open the door, only to find Sebastian Steele. His tall, broad-shouldered frame lounged against her porch rail, a dark silhouette, barely distinguishable in the faint light spilling out from her foyer.

Caught completely by surprise, she needed a moment before she could say anything. When she found her voice she said, "I usually don't open the door before finding out who it is first. I assumed you were my neighbor."

His lips twitched briefly. "I thought we had a serious discussion about the dangers of assuming anything."

She tipped her head and stared at him. Emotions she didn't need or want began clogging her throat. "What are you doing here, Bas?" she asked tightly. She hadn't seen him in three days and she wished to God she hadn't been counting. But she had.

Bas pushed away from the rail and took a couple of steps forward. He figured if he were to tell her the real reason for his visit—that he wanted to devour her mouth—the door would get slammed in his face, so instead he said, "It's early. I didn't want to go to the office, and I wasn't ready to go to bed yet. We had a great weekend down at Cedar Springs and I could only think of one way to end it."

"And what way is that?" Jocelyn's fingers tightened around the doorknob. Her mind was suddenly filled with forbidden yet romantic thoughts. Bas's gaze was locked on hers and she was beginning to feel this luscious, hot sensation flow all through her. She even felt the floor beneath her feet give way a little. A small smile tugged at the corner of his mouth, and in response she felt something tug deep in the pit of her stomach. Her world began to rock and she waited with bated breath for his reply.

"A rematch. I want to play another game of pinball with you."

CHAPTER TEN

JOCELYN DREW A breath, leaned in the doorway and stared at Bas. She guessed she should have been grateful that a game of pinball was all he had in mind but still… It wasn't helping matters that since meeting him and sharing two kisses, her body had become somewhat treacherous whenever he was around.

Her system automatically went on overload and it took everything she could muster to retain the common sense she was born with and had kept intact over the years. But another part of her being reminded her that she'd been celibate for a very long time…ever since senior year in college over six years ago. Why let the explosive spontaneous combustion she felt with Bas go to waste?

Because you're too sensible and dignified to play the games men want to play, she assured herself immediately. Although she was single, mature and unattached, with basic human urges like the next person, that didn't mean she was into casual sex. When the time came for a man to touch her again, by golly it would mean something and not be an appeasement of curiosity like the last time, which had left her totally disappointed.

"So you want to play pinball?" she finally asked,

cocking her brow. "Didn't you learn anything from our last game?"

He flashed a quick grin. "Oh yeah, I learned a lot. I know not to let my guard down again."

"Is that what happened?"

"Yes. I concentrated more on you than the game."

She hadn't expected him to admit that. "So what's your game plan this time?"

"Do you really expect me to tell you?"

She chuckled. "No, but I thought it wouldn't hurt to ask." She stepped aside. "Come on in and let the game begin."

AN HOUR OR so later Jocelyn glanced over at Bas and narrowed her eyes. He was leading by over one hundred thousand points and she was the one who was finding it hard to concentrate on the game. Frustration began to surface. It wasn't that she didn't like losing; she just didn't like the reason she was losing—her inability to focus.

"Winning this rematch means a lot to you, doesn't it?" she finally asked when he scored once again.

He grinned over at her. "Worried about losing?"

"No. But it does seem like you're deliberately dragging this game out."

"While staying ahead in points."

"For the moment, yes."

"Um, I'm just consolidating my shots and economizing my ball time," he said. "A strategy that works best for me."

"You're working too hard as usual," she said coming

to stand close to him, but not close enough to mess with his concentration. "All I do is focus on the shots I can hit consistently and patiently repeat them. In a game of pinball you can never lose control."

"Or concentration, so please step back, Jocelyn. Your perfume is getting to me."

"Is it?"

"Yes."

"In what way?"

His eyes flashed to hers. "I don't think you really want to know."

Jocelyn raised an arched brow. Did she or didn't she? She was pulled out of her thoughts by his muttered curse. He hadn't used his flippers fast enough and it was now her turn.

"Move over Steele. Time for me to recoup."

Deciding not to crowd her, Bas took the chair a few feet away and watched her in action. He liked seeing the way her eyes sparkled with the feel of victory and the way she licked her lips each time she deployed a ball. Then there was that simple turn of her head, the smile that tilted her lips whenever she hit a shot that made the machine flash.

And last but definitely not least was the way she leaned her body just so to the machine, breasts perked, hips aligned at an angle that had heat drumming through him. Even with her trying to best him at this game, he detected a gracefulness in the ease in which she was attempting to do so. The woman had style, something he noted even when she was holding a hammer, saw or a drill.

She had taste. And she tasted good.

He rubbed a hand over his face wishing he hadn't thought about her taste.

When the machine flashed that the game was over, he barely heard her unladylike curse, which let him know he had won this go-round.

"Want to do another game?"

He smiled. "No, we agreed on five and I won four of the five, which means I'm on top of you this time."

Although Jocelyn knew what he meant by those words, her mind suddenly conjured up something else and heat clawed viciously at the lower part of her stomach. She could just imagine him naked and on top of her beneath silken sheets. "Okay, so now I want a rematch," she said, needing to get her mind back on track and wondering how she had allowed it to veer into such an outlandish fantasy in the first place.

"I'll think about it."

Her eyes flamed. "What do you mean you'll think about it?"

He stood and slowly walked in front of her. "Just what I said." He smiled. "Now who's the sore loser?"

"I'm not a sore loser," she denied.

"Then why are you mad?"

"I'm not mad."

"If not, you're awfully close," he said in a husky tone.

He reached out and took her hand in his, letting his fingers run across her wrist to feel her pulse. "Those are anger beats."

"They're not," she said, refusing to let the feel of

his finger on her wrist unnerve her, stoke a desire she didn't want to acknowledge.

"And why are your eyes getting so dark if you aren't mad?" he asked in an even deeper tone of voice.

"They aren't getting dark."

"Yes, they are and getting even darker as we speak." The hand that wasn't stroking her wrist reached up and framed her face. "And why are your lips trembling if you aren't mad?"

She frowned. "You're seeing things."

He leaned in a little closer and let a single fingertip trace a path down to the base of her throat. "No, Jocelyn. I'm feeling things and I think it's time you felt them, too."

Suddenly, the air around them seemed to thicken as he leaned closer and lowered his mouth to hers. The moment their lips touched, lust of an intensity Jocelyn had never known flamed to life, and everything inside her, every cell, every pore, quivered with totally unique and unexpected pleasure.

When his tongue plundered her mouth, she felt her knees slipping and her nipples tingling against her blouse. Just as before, his tongue was in control, taking, giving and sharing. It was the most conducive pleasure mechanism she had ever felt, and with each and every stroke it was hitting its mark. She was beginning to feel drunk, intoxicated, just plain loose. He smelled good. The scent of him was going straight to her head and the taste of him was getting absorbed in areas she'd rather not think about. This kiss was different from the others, though. It was slow, deep, provoking. And overwhelming. Each time he mated his tongue with hers, captured it, sucked on it, she heard herself moan.

Reluctantly Bas broke the kiss, inhaled deeply before drawing her closer to him. He needed that. He needed her. He wanted to touch her a little while longer, let his hands skim slowly across her back. Apparently she felt at ease in letting him do so because she stood still, wrapped in his arms, in his heat.

Moments later, she pulled back, angled her head and gazed up at him and smiled slowly. Her eyes were still dark, her lips moist from his kiss. "If you're trying to make me forget that I want a rematch, forget it."

He released a soft chuckle and leaned down to let his lips brush against hers again, needing the taste, the feel, the touch. "Then I'm going to have to perfect my technique."

She doubted he could perfect it any more, but she wouldn't tell him that. "You can try."

"And I will." Bas smiled. He liked the art of seduction as much as the next guy, although he hadn't had to contemplate a plan in quite a while. They weren't talking about pinball anymore but something else, and they both knew it.

"Don't consider it, Bas," she warned, as if reading his thoughts. "We'll drive each other crazy. I like enjoying life, having fun. You're determined to work yourself to death."

He shook his head. "Hey, I've loosened up some."

She chuckled. "So I see, but you need to do it even more. Just think of all the fun you're missing."

He gazed at her for a moment. He had enjoyed the

workout at the gym with Reese the other day. He had definitely relieved a lot of stress. And going fishing this past weekend had been great, and playing pinball tonight had been just what he'd needed. But nothing could compare to kissing her. That had been like putting the icing on the cake. An idea suddenly popped into his mind.

"You want to show me how to have fun?"

He could tell his question surprised her, and he watched as she lifted a brow. "Not sure that I can."

He leaned closer to her and let his lips brush against her moist ones again. "Don't you want to try?" he asked, nibbling on her neck. "Unless you don't think you can handle me." He knew that would be a challenge she couldn't let slide.

"Oh, I can handle you, Sebastian Steele."

"Prove it," he whispered in her ear. "Teach me how to have fun, Jocelyn."

A deep, gentle trembling in the pit of her stomach answered before her lips could. "Be careful what you ask for Bas...but since you *did* ask, I'm going to take you on." She took a step back. "The first thing you have to do is stop work every day at five o' clock."

He looked at her as though she had lost her mind. "Five o'clock?"

"Yes."

He thought again about the time he'd spent at the gym. He could do that a couple of days a week in the afternoons. No big deal. "All right."

A frown drew Jocelyn's brows together. He was

being too agreeable and she was wondering what was going through his mind. "And you can't arrive at the office before nine in the morning," she decided to add just to cover all her bases.

She saw the defiance that sparked his eyes and grinned in spite of herself. He had only agreed to quit work at five because he'd intended to arrive at some ungodly hour every morning. She could tell he didn't like that she was one step ahead of him.

"And next weekend, there's a jazz festival in Memphis. You want to go have fun?" she asked, deciding to make him see that she meant business.

He shrugged. "Sure." And then he asked, "When do I get to come up with some of our fun activities?" A gleam shone in the depths of his eyes. "I think we should take turns coming up with stuff."

She nodded, thinking that would be only fair, but of course she would monitor the stuff he came up with. She knew men had a tendency to take advantage of what they perceived as a golden opportunity. "I don't have a problem with that. Do you have something in mind?"

He smiled as he grabbed his jacket off the back of the chair and slipped his arms in the sleeves. His gaze held hers when he said, "Yes, I have a few ideas."

She lifted a brow. "Should I be worried?"

He chuckled. "Of course not. You're going to have to trust me like I'm going to trust you." He leaned over and kissed her again, slow, thorough, and as if he desperately needed the memory.

"Come walk me to the door," he whispered and she

shivered when his tongue snaked out and trailed a wet path from her lips to an area beneath her ear.

Jocelyn could barely walk up the steps on unsteady legs and knew that after Bas left it would take the rest of the night to recover from his visit.

"So, I TAKE it Sebastian Steele found you last night."

Jocelyn lifted her eyebrows and gazed across the breakfast table at her sister. Jocelyn had arrived at her father's home a little more than thirty minutes ago to find Leah preparing breakfast. "What made you think he was looking for me?"

Leah smiled. "Because he came here first and then I directed him to your place. He's a cutie."

"Yes, he is," Jocelyn muttered and went back to eating her meal.

Amused, Leah watched her sister. She knew Jocelyn wouldn't volunteer any information so she decided to go ahead and pick it out of her. "So, are the two of you an item?"

The thought of that made Jocelyn choke on her toast and she quickly grabbed her glass of juice and took a gulp. "Whatever gave you that idea?"

Leah shrugged. "The obvious. He's good-looking and so are you. He's unattached and so are you. He's—"

"What makes you think he's unattached?" Jocelyn asked, setting down her juice glass.

Leah waved her left hand. "No ring. That's a sure sign."

"But not a concrete one."

Leah's eyes lifted. "You think he's married?"

"No, I don't think he's married."

"Then you think he has a girlfriend?"

"There's that possibility."

"Have you asked him about it?"

"No."

"Then I most certainly will."

"Why would you want to know?"

Leah rolled her eyes. "I don't want to know for myself. I want to know for you."

Jocelyn pushed her plate aside and leaned forward. "And why would you want to know for me?"

"Because you're interested in him. I can tell."

Jocelyn narrowed her eyes. "I hate to tell you that you're wrong, but you are. I admit Bas is handsome, but he's not my type."

"If you say so."

"I do, so let's change the subject."

"All right."

Jocelyn didn't miss how her sister's lips curved in a smile. "So, did you decide whether you want to go to the jazz festival in Memphis this coming weekend? I invited Bas along."

"You want me to make it a threesome?"

Jocelyn shook her head. "I told him it's nothing like that. In fact I'm supposed to show him how to have fun."

"Sounds interesting."

"It is, so do you want to go?"

"No, I'll pass. Besides, I need to start packing."

Surprise showed on Jocelyn's face. "You're leaving?"

"Eventually, Jocelyn. I need to start looking for an-other place to stay in California. I already told you that the lady whom I used to be a companion to died a couple of months ago. Her sons have been more than kind by letting me remain in the house for a while, but I can't take advantage of their generosity forever."

"You can come back and live here, you know," Jocelyn said, and gestured to encompass the house they were in. "If you don't, I'll eventually have to rent it out or sell it. I don't relish the thought of people I don't know living here."

Leah sighed deeply. "I wish I could move back home, but I can't."

Jocelyn didn't need to ask her why. "Leah, if you were to tell him what—"

"No. And I don't want to talk about it, Jocelyn," Leah said in a clear and distinct voice.

Jocelyn drew in a deep breath. She wanted so much for Leah, more than her sister was willing to accept as a way of life. If only she would tell Reese the truth.

"To hang around here any longer will be a mistake, Jocelyn."

"So you're planning to leave?"

"Yes, in a few weeks. I'm going to start checking out airline tickets later today."

"I really do wish you'd consider staying."

"And I really wish that you'll understand that I can't." That said, Leah rose gracefully, proving all of their Aunt Susan's teachings were still intact, and left the room.

"YOU'RE GOING TO Memphis this weekend with Jocelyn?" Reese asked, tipping his head to one side to stare at Bas.

Bas pushed aside the stack of files. It was four-thirty and if he intended to keep his word to Jocelyn, he had thirty minutes left before calling it a day. "Yes. And if it wasn't for that, I'd love going to the horse races this weekend with you and your brother."

Reese's lips twitched in amusement. "I can't wait until Duran Law hears about you and Jocelyn's weekend plans. He's been trying to get her to go to that jazz festival with him in Memphis for years and she's always turned him down. Now, just like that," he said, snapping his fingers for effect, "you breeze into town and talk her into going." Reese chuckled. "Yeah, old Duran is going to be pretty pissed."

Bas leaned back in his chair. "Actually the trip was her idea. She thinks I need to incorporate more fun into my life." Then, without missing a beat he asked, "And who's this Duran Law anyway? An old boyfriend?"

Reese snorted. "He wished. Duran's been a pain in Jocelyn's ass since high school. I guess he figures sooner or later he'll wear down her defenses, and he's too into himself to see that something like that won't happen."

Bas frowned, not liking the man already. "How are things going over at the Jones place?"

"Great. We hope to have our walk-through next week. But keep your fingers crossed. We're yet to have one on time for Marcella. She likes finding things for us to correct or change at the eleventh hour."

"Yeah, we'll all keep our fingers crossed." Bas then glanced at his watch.

"Ready to head over to the gym?" Reese asked.

"In a few seconds. I need to touch base with my brother about something."

"Okay, I'll meet you over there."

"Will do."

Bas pulled out his cell phone, pressed one number and within seconds he heard his brother Chance's deep voice. "Bas? What's going on?"

Before Bas could answer, Chance said, "Hey, hold on and let me take this other call." And then he clicked off.

Bas knew what a busy schedule his brother had as CEO of the corporation, but he smiled, thinking that time restraints hadn't gotten in the way of him pursuing Kylie once he'd become interested. To kill time while waiting for Chance, Bas glanced around Jim's office. There were numerous trophies proclaiming him to be Builder of the Year and several plaques awarded for his community service and involvement in such worthwhile organizations such as the Boy Scouts, Big Dads of America, the Newton Grove Mission and others. Apparently Jim hadn't had any qualms about occasionally putting his work aside to become involved in things he felt were important to him, activities that gave him enjoyment and the chance to do something other than work. *Fun* things.

"Sorry about that, Bas. That was a call I was waiting on from the Evans Group."

Bas lifted a brow. The Evans Group was currently in a bitter labor dispute with the Teamsters Union regarding a number of their employees who had been laid off. "Something going on I need to know about?"

"No, not now, but I'll keep you posted."

"Yeah, you do that. I know you're busy so I won't hold you. I just want to know if things are still on for Donovan's birthday party."

"Yes, Vanessa and Kylie are taking care of all the arrangements, but as far as I know they're on track. I talked to Taylor and Cheyenne and they're both flying in. Should be nice. You are coming home for it, aren't you?"

"Yes, and I might be bringing somebody with me."

"Oh, who?"

"Jocelyn Mason. I haven't asked her yet, but it'll be my turn to come up with some fun activity for us to do."

"Fun activity? Bas, what are you talking about?"

Bas chuckled, knowing his brother was confused. "I'll explain things the next time we talk. Just let Kylie and Vanessa know that I might be bringing a guest. I'll know for certain after this weekend."

"Okay, I'll pass on the word. Take care, Bas."

"You do the same."

After putting his cell phone away, Bas glanced at his watch. It was five o'clock on the dot. He bade Noreen a good afternoon when he passed her office, and walked out of the building while it was still daylight. Amazing.

The September evening was rather chilly and he pulled his leather jacket tighter around his body. He hadn't seen Jocelyn that day and had avoided dropping by the job site. It would be hard seeing her and not wanting a repeat performance of the kiss they'd shared last night. The art of kissing had always interested him, and depending on his partner, he usually varied his technique. Cassandra had gotten put off by the use of too much tongue. She liked her kisses the same way she wanted everything else they did that was connected to sex—in moderation. According to her, a true lady didn't get carried away with passion, especially with a kiss. It was just unthinkable.

He chuckled, glad not *all* true ladies thought that way. And Jocelyn was a true lady, hard hat, jeans, work boots and all. There was that gracefulness about her even when she was wielding a hammer. She was soft but not mushy. Regal but not overly so and she definitely wasn't a snob. But what he enjoyed most was how much she liked kissing—just as much as he did. And because she did, he'd never enjoyed kissing any woman as much as he enjoyed kissing her. One aspect of that realization disturbed him, while another kept constant heat drumming through his body.

Smiling, he couldn't help but look forward to the coming weekend.

CHAPTER ELEVEN

"IF I DIDN'T know better I'd think you were trying to avoid me this week."

A slow smile curved Jocelyn's lips as she snapped her seat belt in place. She glanced over at Bas and squinted her eyes against the glare of the sun peeking over the mountains. "Now why would you think that?"

Bas stared out of the windshield of his car for a second before tilting his head to meet her gaze. "Because this is the first time I've seen you since Sunday night."

"But we talked on the phone Wednesday," she reminded him.

"Yes, all of five minutes," he murmured, backing the car out of her driveway. "And that was to tell me this would be an overnight trip and you had made reservations for us at a hotel. With *separate* sleeping arrangements."

Jocelyn grinned and leaned over and tweaked his cheek. "Didn't want you to get any ideas, Steele."

An innocent look flashed across Bas's face before he gave her a warm smile. "You think I'd do something like that?"

"I'm not sure and I decided not to take any chances.

This is supposed to be a fun weekend. Our definitions of fun might be vastly different."

His smile widened as he recalled the kisses that had flooded his mind all week. He just couldn't shake the memory of how her lips had felt beneath his, the taste of her, how their tongues had mingled, chased each other back and forth. "Oh, I think our definitions might be the same."

"You think so? Then how about telling me what you have planned for us next?"

Bas glanced over at her when he came to a stop sign. "I want to take you home with me."

She lifted a brow. "Excuse me?"

He smiled. "My family is giving my youngest brother Donovan a party for his thirty-first birthday next month and I'd like you to go with me."

"To your family's function?"

"Yes, as my guest."

A tiny flush warmed her cheeks. In the good old days when a man took a woman home to meet his family it meant something, but she knew that in this day and age of modern dating, the rules had changed and so had the expectations. You no longer needed a formal date to become romantically involved. The two of you could just meet somewhere and get it on. She'd even heard of the concept of video mobile dating. It seemed "try before you buy" was the way to go now.

"How will your family handle something like that?" she couldn't help but ask.

He grinned over at her before easing the car onto the interstate. "Seeing you will raise a few brows, I'm sure.

I haven't seriously dated since I ended my engagement eight months ago."

She was about to tell him that he wasn't seriously dating now when the last part of his sentence stopped her. "You were engaged?" she asked, trying to stop her head from reeling and her eyes from spinning.

"Yes. You sound shocked. Don't you think I'm marriage material?"

She shrugged her shoulders. "For some reason I can't see you sitting by the fireplace with a pipe in your mouth while reading to the kiddies."

"Get rid of the pipe and go with the scene. I love kids and want a couple of them one day, and when I do settle down and marry, I plan to give my wife and children my absolute attention."

"Really. Then, what happened?"

"Let's just say Cassandra and I determined we weren't compatible after all," he said easily. Too easily for Jocelyn's way of thinking.

"How long were the two of you engaged?"

"Six months."

"And how long did the two of you date before becoming engaged?"

"Almost a year."

"Jeez, it took you that long to discover the two of you didn't fit? You don't come across to me as slow, Bas."

He didn't know whether to take her comment as a compliment or an insult. He chose the latter. "I'm not slow and there were reasons I hung in there for as long as I did."

Jocelyn sighed softly, wondering if love had been the

reason. Had he loved this Cassandra person so much that he'd been determined to make things work between them? Did he still love her? "Do you think the two of you will ever work things out and get back together?"

"Excuse my French, but hell no. There's no way I'd consider such a thing."

Brushing her hair back from her eyes, Jocelyn glanced over at him. He certainly didn't sound like a man who was still in love. But then she was comparing him with Reese. Although Reese was bitter and angry with Leah, Jocelyn could still detect the deep love in his voice whenever he spoke about her sister. With Bas just now, all she heard was disgust.

"So, will you go home with me to Donovan's party, Jocelyn?"

She wasn't ready to give him her answer yet. "I'll let you know. And thanks for offering to do the driving," she added, feeling the need to change the subject.

"No problem. Just put your head back and relax. I'll have you in Memphis before you know it."

She smiled and tilted her seat back. "Just stay within the speed limit. I'm not sharing the cost of a ticket with you."

Bas chuckled. "You are the last person to give someone advice about speeding."

A small giggle slipped from Jocelyn's lips as she closed her eyes.

THE HOTEL JOCELYN had chosen was right in the thick of things and as soon as they dropped their overnight bags off at their respective rooms, they met downstairs in the lobby, ready to explore, enjoy and have fun.

Memphis was known for its food, entertainment and hot spots. But this particular weekend it was all about jazz. What had begun a few years ago as an outdoor concert was now a full weekend of numerous blues and jazz events.

As if it was the most natural thing to do, Bas and Jocelyn wandered the streets holding hands as they shared meals and listened to music from jazz greats as well as students from the University of Memphis music department. One concert displayed a variety of cultures with the native music of the Caribbean, the Middle East and the rich musical heritage of the African-American culture blended together in a way that was soul-stirring at its best.

With vendors on each side the streets were narrow, and more than once Bas had to pull Jocelyn closer to his side to let others pass. Each time his hand touched her waist she would gaze up into the depths of his chocolate eyes and could only smile as an unnerving degree of heat slithered down her spine. Whenever she looked at him her thoughts wandered into forbidden territory and her mind was actually whirling with possibilities of how their night would end.

She clutched the bag filled with the purchases they had made, determined not to go there. Tonight she would go to her room and Bas would go to his; it was that simple. But a warm blush crept into her cheeks when she admitted that that likely wouldn't be the outcome at all. Something was happening to her. With very little effort Bas was doing something no other man had done—awakening her deepest desires. He was connecting to a part of her she had long denied existed. She inhaled deeply. Where was all that poise, self-control and composure she'd always prided herself on?

It was past midnight when they called it a day and began walking back toward their hotel, still holding hands. She recalled they'd even held hands throughout all the concerts they had attended.

"Did you have fun today?" she asked as they walked lazily through the streets. The crowd on the sidewalks had thinned out a lot. It was evident the people passing them by were party animals, still in a festive mood on their way to some nightclub or other.

Bas smiled at her. "Yes. This is the most fun I've had in a long time."

She grinned and leaned in closer to him. "Even more fun than the fishing trip last weekend?"

He chuckled. "This was a different sort of fun. I hadn't realized how much I've missed by not going to a jazz concert. CDs are nice but there's nothing like being right there in the audience, having the strings of a guitar and the melodic tune of a piano slowly hum through you. The vitality of it was awesome. Thanks for suggesting that we come."

She smiled, pleased. "You're welcome. I'm glad you enjoyed yourself."

When they reached the entrance to the hotel he suddenly stopped, turned toward her and slid his arms loosely around her neck. He leaned in closer, his mouth barely an inch from hers. "In fact, I may have had too much fun. I'm not ready for the night to end. Feel it?"

"Feel what?" The only thing she felt at that moment was the slow sizzle in her blood from the way he was looking at her. He was so close she could see the dark rings around his pupils, and that look made a deep-rooted longing uncurl inside her.

"Night heat."

She swallowed against the thickness that suddenly settled in her throat. "Night heat?"

"Yes. Maybe it's the sound of all that jazz, being surrounded by it while it works inexplicable sensations all through you. But I honestly think it's something else."

"What?"

"You. Me. Here. The night. The heat. The connection," he breathed against her lips. "Close your eyes and feel it."

Jocelyn closed her eyes and she began to feel it. She mentally savored the sounds around her, the conversations in the distance, the jazzy music that wasn't ready to end and the breathy sigh that escaped from between her own lips.

A sultry breeze made her sniff the air and she took in the smell of Cajun food, spicy barbecue ribs, the steamy aroma of blue crabs. Then there was the scent of man, at least of the man standing in front of her. Of all the things she had taken in, he was the one thing that made the night steamy. Hot. He was everything she imagined night heat was about—a male rich in sensuality, masculinity and irresistible charm. A man who could make her heart pound from just one heated look.

A man who gazed at you as though he was a predator and you were the object of his intent. "Yes, I can feel it," she murmured truthfully, before opening her eyes.

Her senses were jolted with the sudden feel of his mouth on hers. Hot and quick. His tongue captured hers before she could take her next breath and then just as quickly, he pulled away.

"There's a nightclub in the hotel. Do you want to go dancing?"

Jocelyn suddenly felt light-headed, dazed. The air surrounding them flickered softly across her skin, adding to the odd feeling she was experiencing. And at that moment she knew she too wasn't ready for the night to end. Trembling with a mixture of sensuality and excitement, she met his gaze, smiled and whispered, "Yes, I want to go dancing."

A DEEP TREMOR passed through Bas the moment he took Jocelyn into his arms on the dance floor. The air surrounding them was thick. The jazzy music encircling them was rich and smooth, and she was soft.

If she had been any other woman he would have suggested that they go up to his room instead of going dancing. Holding her against him, moving his body with hers to the sway of the music only intensified the temptation he was trying like hell to fight. He had been feeling something practically all day, but it had become more prevalent when night had set in. He wanted her to feel it, as well. He wanted her to acknowledge its existence as he had. From the first, this heat between them had been there. That was the reason he couldn't forget her kisses and the reason he wanted to hold her here now, sliding his body intimately against hers, wanting her to feel his desire, his longing, his want. He wanted to touch her all over and had to steady his hands, force them to remain at her back, stroking, caressing, although they were desperate to do more.

But he couldn't stop his lips from wanting to taste her, so he brushed them against hers, lightly, building passion one degree at a time. He doubted that he would ever get tired of kissing her, whether the kisses were light and breezy or deep and demanding. As he continued to delight her mouth with slow, easy kisses, he felt her body become almost weightless in his arms. He wanted to sweep her off her feet, into his embrace and take her to his room or hers to give her pleasure so intense she would remember this night for the rest of her life.

Damn. Something was happening to him. Emotions he was known to keep bottled up inside of him were fighting to seep out. In the past he'd been too busy plowing himself with work, but lately he'd had a lot of undemanding time to think and appreciate, to begin to enjoy life. And he was beginning to like having free time on his hands. He was enjoying having fun, leaving work on time and going to the gym and going fishing with Reese and his brothers. He couldn't recall the last time he had allowed himself the time to indulge in such simple pleasures.

After that summer with Jim, when he had returned home to finish college and work in the family business, he had placed himself on a rigid schedule that he'd gotten addicted to over the years. But now it seemed that Jocelyn Mason intended him to incorporate some fun into his life, and he was actually looking forward to it. He was even eager to settle down and start working on that paint-by-number kit she had talked him into purchasing today from one of the sidewalk vendors. It was a picture of a woodland chalet with snowcapped mountains in the background, a scene that reminded him of Newton Grove. He was excited to get started on it. More than anything, he'd enjoyed taking the time off this weekend to spend with Jocelyn.

The breath rushed out of him when he realized he was beginning to feel something for the woman he held so close to him. She had the ability to fire a need within him that he hadn't felt in years, if ever. And it wasn't all sexual, although he did have this vivid mental image in his mind of how wonderful it would be to have her in his bed to play out all those fantasies and dreams he'd had of her lately. Thinking about them only made him want her more. Being here with her, dancing with her, holding her in his arms while her cheek rested on his chest, seemed as natural as breathing, and a satisfying sensation skittered all the way down his belly.

"Bas?"

He barely heard her whisper his name. "Yes?"

"Can we go somewhere else?"

Her request heated the desire he felt through his entire body. "Where do you want to go?"

"You decide."

And with a low growl, he did. He took her hand in

his and led her off the dance floor and out of the night-club to a place where they could finish what they had started.

"YOU'RE BEAUTIFUL."

Bas whispered the words the moment he stepped into Jocelyn's hotel room and swept her into his arms. The heat that had been simmering within her all day had escalated during the ride in the elevator and what seemed like a long, endless walk down the hall to her room.

"If I'm beautiful, then you are, too," she said truthfully. There was just something about him that stirred her blood, awakened desires within her and sent rushes of heat thrumming all through her.

Jocelyn had stopped fighting the feeling and was willing to surrender to the inevitable. Since that day in Jason's office the attraction had been great, bigger, it seemed, than both of them. She hadn't planned for anything to happen between them this weekend; it was to be fun on her terms. She had gone through life without intimacy with a man, and she assumed she could certainly go on in the same way a while longer. But hadn't Bas warned her about assuming anything?

"Let's dispense with all the compliments," he said, moving toward the sofa instead of the bed. He saw her confused look and gave her a sexy smile that touched her all the way to her toes. After he'd sat down with her cuddled in his arms he said, "I won't go that far until I'm certain our definitions are the same, Jocelyn."

She frowned. "They are," she said, her voice raw and thick.

"I've got to be sure it's not just the night."

Her frown deepened. It *was* the night but that wasn't all it was. "I don't understand."

"When you wake up in the morning I don't want you to have any regrets."

"And you think I will?"

"Not sure. All I know is that when you left Newton Grove this morning you had no intentions of sleeping with me."

"Can't a girl change her mind?"

"Yes, but I have to know it's for the right reason. I won't assume anything."

He saw the flicker of disappointment in her eyes and his lips curved into a seductive smile. "If only you knew how much I want you, how much I want to be inside you, take you with every breath in my body, while replaying every dream I've had of you since the first day I laid eyes on you, you'd know how much not making love to you is killing me."

"It doesn't look like you're dying to me," she said with a bit of sting in her voice as she broke eye contact with him. She just couldn't figure men out. They wanted you when you weren't willing and didn't want you when you were.

As if he read her thoughts he reached out and placed a finger at her chin to lift her gaze back to his. "This is not a game I'm playing, Jocelyn. I want you so much I hurt, and to show you just how much, I'm going to leave you with something to remember me by tonight."

And then he kissed her with a demand that had her body shuddering all at once. He entered her mouth with a force that claimed it as his, totally, irrevocably. She felt him shift her body in his lap and ease the jacket from her shoulders while not breaking contact with her lips. And then his hands were on her, caressing her through her blouse, and then slipping his fingers beneath it to cup her breasts. He slowly stroked his thumb in the center, across her bra-clad nipple and captured in his mouth the ragged sigh that escaped from deep within her throat.

He eased his mouth from hers. "I want to taste you all over," he murmured. "I've been fantasizing about doing it since the first time I kissed you. You have a unique taste that drives me wild. It makes me want to savor every single inch of you."

Before Jocelyn could pull in her next breath Bas brought her to her feet to face him and in seconds he was pulling her blouse over her head, then tossing it aside to join her jacket. He released her long enough to slide the jacket off his shoulders and throw it aside, as well.

He took one look at her, standing in front of him in her black lace bra, before leaning over and covering his mouth with hers once again. Sexual sparks crackled, tore into her when she felt his fingers release the clasp of her bra, and then he broke the kiss long enough to strip it off her.

"I've got to taste you here," he whispered, seconds before capturing her around the waist and lowering his face to her chest. His mouth immediately latched on her breasts, kissed them until her nipples ached. He knew exactly how to flicker the tip of his tongue across them, lave them in a circle motion that drove her wild, made her panties wet. She was grateful for the strong, solid arms holding her upright or else she would have crumpled to the floor from the shockwaves that were tearing through her.

He slowly pulled back, got down on his knees and began working at the snap of her jeans. He glanced up, held her gaze while he eased the denim down her hips, pausing to help her step out of her shoes before taking the jeans completely off her and tossing them aside, leaving her standing in front of him in just a pair of black lacy boxer-style undies.

He leaned back on his haunches, and she wondered if he had changed his mind after all. Seconds later she knew he hadn't when he reached out and slowly eased her panties down her hips, inhaling deeply while doing so.

"You smell good," he said in a tone filled with so much desire it made her body tremble. He leaned forward, held her gaze and whispered, "I need to taste you. Now."

He trailed hot, wet kisses across her belly before moving lower, and with the palms of his hands he gently eased her legs apart. Jocelyn stopped breathing, anticipating his next move. He didn't disappoint her. He leaned closer and gripped her hips, then buried his face in her. When he slipped that same hot, wet tongue inside her, she released a moan that came from so deep in her throat she actually felt her knees buckle beneath her.

But his solid grip held her in place while his mouth made love to her, tasting, devouring, feasting. He was unashamedly greedy, intent on getting his fill, making her dig her nails into his shoulders. Unable to control the shudders racking her, she threw her head back and forced air through her lungs before screaming out his name.

"Bas!"

Her entire body shook, came apart with the force of the climax. Never had she encountered such a fierce, powerful reaction, an earth-shattering explosion. She held his shoulders tight and writhed helplessly against him, while his tongue did things to her no other man had ever done.

And as she continued to soar to a place she had never been before, she knew that Sebastian Steele was more than a troubleshooter and a problem solver. He was the epitome of what female fantasies were made of. He was temptation at its finest, a man who delivered with action, a man with one incredible mouth, a man who knew just how to pleasure a woman.

And at that moment, while aftershocks slithered down her spine, she was blinded by the staggering realization that if she didn't stop herself, she could fall deliriously and passionately in love with him.

"Umm." With a deep, satisfying moan Jocelyn shifted her body in bed as delicious dreams continued to filter through her sleep-induced mind. Strong, firm hands parted her thighs, and the urgency that filled her with profound emotions made her body brace for a joining she needed, one she craved and one that had every inch of her braced in anticipation for—

The sharp ringing of the phone had her bolting upright. She rubbed her hand across her face and snatched up the phone then hung it back up. It had merely been the hotel's wake-up call.

She settled back in bed and remembered her dream. Some of it had been a dream and some of it reality. She closed her eyes, remembering the part that had been real, and the memory wrenched a serious moan through her lips. Bas had kissed her all over, devoured her, made her come, then he'd picked her up, carried her over to the bed and tucked her in. Before leaving, he had kissed her, sending shudders through her body long after he'd left. And then she had drifted off to sleep, only to finalize in her dreams what he had refused to do during her wakeful moments.

Still, she felt wonderful.

Sighing deeply, she forced herself up in bed again and ran her fingers through her hair. They were supposed to meet downstairs for an early breakfast before heading back to Newton Grove. How was she supposed to face him knowing what he had done to her last night? What she had let him do? But she had no regrets. The pleasure she still felt was too intense for her to be repentant. He had wanted her and she had wanted him; yet he had maintained his control, assumed nothing and had given her pleasure while withholding his own.

As she slipped out of bed she released a long-drawn-out sigh. Aftershocks of passion surged through every part of her body. Her blood felt hot, her body hotter and more than anything she wanted him to finish what he'd started. But she'd get her chance this coming weekend to prove that although neither of them should assume anything, some things were a gimme. What Leah had said a couple of weeks ago was right: when Bas finished what he came to do he would be gone. There was nothing to hold him in Newton Grove, and she had to remember that.

But for now she wanted to enjoy whatever he was offering, and when he did leave she wouldn't have any regrets.

CHAPTER TWELVE

LEAH GLANCED UP from her book when she heard the sound of a drill outside the house. Pushing out of the chair, she crossed to the window and gasped when a man's face came into view.

Reese!

She clutched her chest, wondering what on earth he was doing outside her window. Not *her* window exactly. She had driven over to Jocelyn's house to finish doing laundry when her dad's washing machine had suddenly gone on the blink.

Reese had seen her through the window at the same time she'd seen him and through the glass she could read his expression. His frown spoke volumes. He wasn't happy at seeing her and within minutes he had made his way to the front door and was knocking hard.

She crossed the room and snatched it open. "What are you doing here, Reese?"

He narrowed his eyes at her. "I could ask you the same thing."

She decided biting each other's heads off wouldn't accomplish anything so she said as calmly as she could, "Jocelyn went away for the weekend and when Dad's washing machine broke down I decided to come over here and use hers. And I thought she mentioned that you and your brother were going to the races in Kentucky this weekend."

He leaned in the doorway, apparently annoyed. "Little Danny got sick so Daniel wanted to hang around."

"Is little Danny okay?"

He resented hearing the concern in her voice. "Yes, it's just a stomach virus but Rita almost went bonkers because he's rarely sick. Since the trip was cancelled I decided to fix that floodlight outside that's been giving Jocelyn trouble."

"Oh. Then don't let me keep you." She was about to shut the door when he stuck his foot out, halting it from closing.

"You think you can just dismiss me like that? After all these years don't you think you owe me some type of explanation, Leah?" he asked angrily.

Leah breathed in sharply. Coming face to face with Reese again a little more than a week after their first encounter wasn't good. There was nothing she could tell him, nothing she could say to make things right, so it was best not to say anything at all. "No, I don't owe you an explanation."

She made an attempt to close the door on him again, but in anger he shoved it open. She took a step back when he stormed in and slammed it shut behind him. "The hell you don't," he roared as if all the anger he'd been holding inside him had suddenly snapped.

"Have you lost your mind, Reese?"

"I lost my mind years ago since I must have been crazy to get mixed up with the likes of you in the first place," he said, anger seeping out of his every pore. "You are one ungrateful, selfish, self-centered human being."

"Get out!"

"Make me. I won't leave until I've had my say."

"I won't listen." She turned away and walked toward the kitchen.

He was right on her heels. "Oh, you'll listen. When I think of all the time and love I put into this place for you and for you to treat me like dirt and—"

She turned around, almost coming nose to nose with him. She stared at him in shock. "What are you talking about?"

"This house, damn you, was supposed to be ours. I built it for you and was going to surprise you with it on your birthday but you hauled ass. You left without looking back, letting me know I was nothing more to you than a trinket to play with. You cared nothing for me. All your words of love were nothing but lies!"

Leah went completely still, frozen in place. She blinked her dazed eyes. "What do you mean you built this house for me?"

"Look around, Leah. This house has everything you always said you wanted in a home. I built it with my own hands for you. I worked with your dad during the day and worked here late at night, sometimes past midnight, and on weekends, sometimes tired to the bone, just to give you what you wanted, or what you claimed you wanted—a place to live with me as my wife, to raise our children. But you never meant any of it."

His words were too much. She hadn't known. No

one had ever told her about the house. How could Jocelyn and her father not tell her? Just as the hold on his temper had broken earlier, so did the floodgates of pain she had held within her for five years. She wanted to scream and fisted her hand into her mouth to stop from doing so, but that didn't stop the fierce tremors that racked her body.

"What the hell's wrong with you, Leah?"

Reese's temper cleared enough for him to see that something strange was happening to Leah. It was as if all the coloring had left her face and she was shaking. He reached out and touched her and she pulled back from his touch. She resembled a creature gone wild and began backing away from him, looking at him as if she didn't know who he was. She had a crazed look in her eyes. He took a step toward her. "Leah, what's wrong?"

"No, don't touch me again. Don't come near me. No! No! Please no."

He swore and took a step toward her, concerned. "What's the matter with you, Leah? Tell me what's wrong. Why are you looking at me that way? I wouldn't hurt you, you know that."

"No! Don't come near me. Don't you dare touch me again. I belong to Reese and you can't do that to me. I won't let you. I hate you!"

Reese wasn't entirely sure what was going on here but he knew Leah had gone into some kind of shock, as if she was reliving something bad that had happened. The thought of what that could be was like a punch in his stomach.

"Who do you think I am, Leah?" he asked quietly, deciding to use another approach. "Who do you think I am?"

"I know who you are, Neil. And I won't let you hurt me again. You won't ever force yourself on me again."

Neil? Reese frowned. The only Neil he knew was Neil Grunthall, but the man was dead. In fact, come to think of it, he had died around the same time Leah had disappeared. His eyes flamed as a thought entered his mind. It was one he didn't want to consider but was forced to, knowing what a bastard Neil Grunthall had been and how the man had hated his guts. "Did Neil touch you?" he asked with deadly calm.

It was as if she hadn't heard him. She kept backing up and when he walked toward her she picked up a vase off Jocelyn's coffee table and held it high like a weapon, ready to throw it at a moment's notice. "You come near me and I'll kill you. I couldn't defend myself before but I can now."

"Oh, Leah." Her words, spoken in such a heart-wrenching and tortured tone, broke everything inside of Reese and there was no way he could not go to her at that moment.

"No! I said not to come near me!"

When he got close she made good on her threat and threw the vase at him. He ducked out of the way, and it shattered on the hardwood floor. The sound made her jerk and that was all the time Reese needed to close in and grab her.

"No, Neil, let me go!" she cried out. "I belong to

Reese. Don't do this. Don't hurt me again. I love Reese. Please let me go!"

She fought him, kicked and bit the knuckle on his left hand, but his arms wrapped around her like steel beams, refusing to let her hurt him or herself. "It's okay, baby. I'm Reese and you do belong to me," he whispered quietly against her struggles. "Neil is dead, Leah, and he won't hurt you again. He won't hurt you again."

He said the words over and over before he finally began getting through to her. When he did, she broke down and began crying in earnest. The tortured sound, similar to the sound of a wounded animal, tore at his heart and brought tears to his eyes. "It's okay, baby. It's okay."

When she went limp he picked her up and walked over to Jocelyn's spare bedroom. Shoving open the door with his shoulder, he carried her over to the bed and placed her there.

He drew back and gazed down at her. She refused to open her eyes and look at him. "Leah," he said gently, "rest and we'll talk."

She turned away from him and faced the wall. "No, please leave," she said quietly, sounding defeated, humiliated and embarrassed. "I want to be alone."

Her words tugged at his heart. There was no way in hell he would leave her alone. He remembered Jocelyn saying that she would be returning to town around noon that day and he intended to stay put until she got there. "I'm not leaving, Leah. I'll be in the living room if you need me. Try and get some rest."

He then turned and walked out of the room, quietly closing the door behind him.

WHEN THE CAR came to a traffic light Bas glanced over at Jocelyn. They were about to get on the interstate to head back to Newton Grove. She had the seat reclined to a comfortable position and was resting with her eyes closed. At least he thought they were closed but he couldn't tell beneath the dark sunglasses.

During breakfast she hadn't had a whole lot to say and had avoided discussing what they'd shared last night. But with all the memories flooding his mind, he couldn't think of anything else.

She looked different this morning. More rested and relaxed. Her hair fell in glossy curls around her shoulders and the lime green of her skirt and matching sweater made her dark coloring that much more beautiful. He remembered last night and how she'd stood there while he'd loved her with his mouth. He hadn't regretted anything about what he'd done and wondered if she had. There was only one way to find out.

"You okay?" he asked quietly.

She glanced over at him and smiled. "Yes. Is there any reason why I wouldn't be?"

He shrugged. "You've been quiet this morning."

She sighed and stared ahead. "I've been thinking."

"Oh. You want to share your thoughts?"

She glanced back over at him. "I was wondering how to convey my thanks to you for giving me something really special last night."

He felt a rush of pleasure that she didn't have any regrets about what they'd shared. "Conveying your thanks isn't necessary because you gave me something special, as well."

She raised her brow. "What?"

"A chance to savor a special part of you."

Heat sizzled her skin and a yearning erupted in the pit of her stomach when she thought of how he had done so. "Yes, but you took things a step further when you exposed me to your incredible experience and masterful skills."

He chuckled. "Did I do that?"

She angled her face toward him. "Yes, you did." Moments later she said, "And I've decided to go to your brother's party with you after all."

He smiled then, pleased with her decision. He glanced over at her when the car came to a stop at another traffic light. He wished she didn't have her sunglasses on because he wanted to look into the depths of her dark eyes, see if they held some clue as to why she'd made that decision.

"Why are you staring at me like that?"

"Mmm, I was just thinking that you have such a pretty face."

She laughed. "Thanks, and if you keep saying such nice things, I might want to keep you around."

He grinned. "That's what I'm hoping."

AN ANGRY REESE paced Jocelyn's living room, getting angrier by the second. Why hadn't anyone told him what had happened to Leah? How could they keep something like that from him? And to think that for five solid years he had hated her, despised her, tried to eradicate her from his memory…his heart.

The scene that had played out in this very living room less than an hour ago had his stomach in knots. Neil Grunthall had forced himself on Leah! The thought of her defenseless against Neil made Reese's entire body shake in rage.

He sighed, trying to recall what Jocelyn had almost let slip the other day when she'd come to Leah's defense. She was certain her sister wasn't pregnant because, according to Jocelyn, he was the last man Leah had been involved with. What she hadn't said was that someone had forced himself on her.

He doubted he would forget for as long as he lived the crazed look in Leah's eyes when he had touched her. Hell, he could just imagine what had played out in her mind. He'd watched a special episode on rape victims on CNN once and according to the reporter, some women never fully recovered from such an ordeal and were encouraged to seek some type of professional counseling. He wondered if Leah had done so.

Had that been the reason she had left town all those years ago, he wondered. Considering the timing of everything, a part of him knew that it had been. Why hadn't she come to him and told him what had happened? It would have given him sheer pleasure to kill Neil Grunthall with his bare hands. If the man wasn't already dead, there was no way he would be living now.

But hating Neil wouldn't undo what he'd done to Leah. The woman he loved was now his main concern and yes, he loved her. He had never stopped loving her and he vowed then that if her spirit was still broken from all of this, he intended to repair it.

More than anything he wanted Leah to know he would always be there for her, no matter what.

PLEASED THAT JOCELYN had no regrets about last night, Bas set his mind on getting them back to Newton Grove. She had mentioned a baby shower for a friend she wanted to attend that afternoon.

He picked up the cup of coffee and took a sip, appreciating the taste, and smiled when he thought of another taste he appreciated—the one belonging to the woman sitting beside him who had dozed off to sleep. With the windows up, her luscious scent filled the confines of the car and he couldn't stop the desire that quickly encircled his gut. It was difficult to recall the last time he'd wanted a woman so much.

He tried to rationalize his attraction to her. She was a beautiful woman but he had met beautiful women before. What was there about Jocelyn that made him feel emotions he'd never felt before? In his book she was P and P: proper and passionate.

He'd seen her proper side one evening when she hadn't been aware she was being observed. It had been a social ball a couple of weeks ago that Ms. Sadie's group of older ladies had given for some debutantes. Sadie hadn't been able to get her car started and when he'd come in from a workout at the gym, she had asked if he would drop her off. He had pulled up in front of the Civic Center in time to see a very sophisticated-looking Jocelyn meet and greet all the other guests.

She hadn't seen him, but he had seen her and what he'd called her proper side.

He smiled, knowing that beneath that proper side was a passionate side, one yet to be explored to the fullest. She was definitely a woman who could make his blood run hot. She was a distraction but a distraction that he liked.

It suddenly hit him why he felt that way, and emotions he'd tried analyzing for the past couple of weeks instantly became crystal-clear. He was falling in love with Jocelyn. And if he wasn't careful, she could become the person he loved more than anyone in his entire life.

But that thought didn't bother him and he hoped to hell it didn't bother her when she discovered how he felt. He wouldn't shock her by declaring his affections, at least not now. He wanted them to spend more time together, to have what she considered fun, before he broached such a serious subject with her. He had discovered that Jocelyn didn't handle surprises very well.

"If you've done a thorough review of the company books, then I guess you know that my dad and Noreen were having an affair."

Her words, spoken out of the blue, surprised the hell out of Bas. He jerked his head and stared at her. He thought she was sleeping. "You knew?"

She smiled. "Yes, even though they thought I didn't. Believe me, they were very discreet, but there were some things you couldn't help but notice—like the looks they gave each other when they thought no one else was around."

"Did you have a problem with it?"

Jocelyn shrugged. "I did at first. No girl wants to imagine her parent being sexually active, but then I saw how happy he was, and what a great mood he was in whenever he returned from one of his mystery trips out of town."

She chuckled. "After spending a weekend out of town with you I have an idea of just how he felt."

An hour later, after arriving back in Newton Grove, Bas was driving them through the city. "Do you want me to take you home or to your father's house?" he asked, glancing over at Jocelyn when he came to a stop at a traffic light. She looked refreshed from her nap, and the desire he'd been holding at bay suddenly kicked into high gear. Combined with the love he felt for her, the emotion completely overwhelmed him.

"You can take me on home and I—"

Before she finished whatever she was about to say, Bas leaned over and brought his mouth down on hers, effectively snatching both breath and words from her throat. She responded and when his tongue darted into her mouth, she captured it with her own, sucked on it before he could pull back.

When he straightened up in his seat, he smiled at her. "You're coming up with some pretty masterful skills yourself."

She chuckled as she raked her fingers through her hair. "Only because I have a good teacher. I was just following his lead."

Bas's pulse rate increased and he couldn't wait until he got to her place. His goodbye kiss would be one she remembered for a long time. Well, maybe not, he thought moments later when he pulled into her driveway and saw the two vehicles parked there. She had left her car for her sister to use and he recognized the truck as Reese's.

"Looks like you have company."

Jocelyn glanced up. When she saw the two vehicles, a deep frown settled on her face. "Oh, no," she said, unsnapping her seat belt before Bas brought the car to a stop. "What are the two of them doing here together?"

Her question, as well as the worried expression on her face, confused Bas. "Maybe they're trying to patch things up."

Jocelyn shook her head. "It won't be that easy."

He lifted a brow. "Why?"

"Because it won't. Please stop the car, Bas."

Upon hearing the panic in her voice, he stopped the car and the minute he did she threw open the door and raced toward her house. Not knowing what the hell was going on, he took off after her.

Before she could use her key to open the door, it was snatched open and an angry Reese came out and glared at Jocelyn. "Dammit why didn't you tell me, Joce?"

She didn't answer. Instead she tried to move past him to go into the house. "Where's Leah?"

He blocked her path. "She's asleep, but I want to know why you didn't tell me."

"Not now Reese, I have to—"

"No! I want to know why you didn't tell me."

Bas heard the anger in Reese's voice, anger that was directed at Jocelyn. He also noted that Reese was blocking the way into her own house. Bas stepped forward. "Calm down, Reese. What's going on? What has you so upset? Is something wrong with Leah?"

Reese's glare left Jocelyn and moved to Bas. "Yeah, something is wrong with her all right, something I didn't know about until today."

He then moved his gaze back to Jocelyn. The eyes that looked at her were filled with a mixture of rage and anguish. "My God, Jocelyn, why didn't you tell me that Neil Grunthall had raped her?"

CHAPTER THIRTEEN

JOCELYN'S EYES WIDENED. "Leah actually told you?"

Having his suspicions confirmed was like a kick in Reese's gut, and it took everything he had not to ram his fist into the nearest post. "She didn't tell me willingly," he said with fury lining his every word. "I confronted her about why she left and when I told her about this house she started shaking uncontrollably. I reached out to calm her down, and when I did all hell broke loose. She went berserk as if she was reliving those moments with Neil and actually thought I was him."

Reese paused long enough to rub a tortured hand down his face. The eyes that looked at Jocelyn again were hard and angrier than before. "Why didn't you or your dad tell me?"

Jocelyn inhaled deeply, hearing the hurt, pain and despair in his voice. "Dad never knew and I only found out myself a few weeks ago, Reese," she said softly. "And she made me promise not to tell you."

Reese's head fell back against the wooden post and he looked up at the sky as if the clouds held some kind of comfort for him. Then he looked back at Jocelyn. "Tell me what happened. Please. I need to know."

Jocelyn slid her gaze from Reese to Bas. He was

staring at her just as intently as Reese, although he hadn't said anything. She knew Leah was still in love with Reese just as Reese was still in love with Leah. If anyone could break through the barriers Leah had erected, it would be Reese.

"All right," she said wearily. "But I want you to promise you'll be patient and understanding and—"

"My God, Joce, of course I'll be patient and understanding. I love Leah," he said in a tortured moan. "I've never stopped loving her even when I thought she had done me wrong. If you think I'll turn my back on her now, knowing what she's been through, then you don't know me."

Jocelyn inhaled deeply. She did know him and she knew how much he loved her sister. Somehow, through it all, his heart had remained intact even when his mind had assumed the worse.

Assumed.

She shook her head. Bas had helped her to see how that one little word could cause a world of trouble. "Okay, I'll tell you what she told me."

"On that note I think I'll wait out in the car," Bas said, turning to leave, thinking he'd heard more than he should have already. This was a private matter between Jocelyn, Reese and Leah.

"No, please stay, Bas," Jocelyn said, not understanding why but knowing she needed him there.

Bas turned back around and met the silent plea in her gaze and knew at that moment he could deny her nothing.

He glanced over at Reese. "You're okay with me staying?"

Reese nodded. "Yeah, man. I'm okay with it."

MOMENTS LATER, AFTER telling the two men everything, Jocelyn shifted her gaze from Reese. It was hard not to see the tears that filled his eyes without getting misty-eyed, as well.

And then there was Bas. She had seen him ball his fist in anger several times, and although he hadn't said anything, the tightening of his jaw and the fury that lined his eyes had said it all.

"Did she get any professional help?" Reese asked, breaking the silence.

"Yes, but there are still issues she's trying to work through, hurdles she's yet to cross. It takes time recovering from an ordeal such as that."

"No matter how long it takes, I'm going to be there with her," Reese said in a firm voice. "We're going to work through this thing, Leah and I. Together."

Jocelyn smiled. "She's not going to make things easy for you, Reese. Already she's talking about returning to California in a few weeks."

Reese nodded, and although he didn't say anything, Jocelyn knew he had no intentions of letting Leah go anywhere. "She's sleeping now, but I want to be there when she wakes up, to talk to her, Jocelyn. Alone."

Jocelyn knew what he was asking of her. The mothering instinct in her demanded that she see to her sister herself, but she knew Reese was right. He was the one who needed to be there for Leah. "Okay." She then glanced over at Bas. "Do you want to go grab some lunch?"

Bas smiled. She had a feeling he agreed wholeheartedly with her decision to let Reese handle Leah in his own way. "Yes, lunch sounds good and I know just where I want to take you."

LEAH CAME AWAKE, remembering where she was. Then she recalled her argument with Reese and… "Oh my God!" She covered her face with her hands when it all came tumbling back to her. He knew. There was no way he would not have figured things out.

"Are you okay?"

She jumped then turned in the bed to face Reese, her eyes going wide. He was standing in the doorway. "What are you doing here?"

"I told you I wasn't going anywhere, Leah. Besides, I think we should talk."

No! She didn't want to talk. She wanted to be as far away from him as she could. Knowing that he knew what had happened to her was too much. She quickly slipped off the bed. "I just want to finish my laundry and leave. Jocelyn should be back any minute and—"

"Jocelyn is already back. She and Bas went somewhere for lunch. They knew I wanted to talk to you alone."

"We have nothing to talk about."

He ignored her and took a step into the room, and she automatically backed up. Her seemingly frightened retreat almost broke Reese's heart. "Why didn't you tell me what Neil had done to you? Why did you run away instead? Didn't you think I had a right to know?"

"Why? So you could kill him with your bare hands and go to jail? He wasn't worth it, Reese. He was nothing but a troublemaker and I knew I couldn't tell you or my father. Besides," she said, lowering her voice, fighting back her tears, "he wasn't your problem."

He took another step into the room. "You were mine, Leah. I loved you. I was going to marry you. Your problems were my problems. We would have worked things out."

"No, I had to leave. I felt dirty. Used. I felt unworthy. Don't you understand how difficult it is for me now, knowing that you know?"

"You should have told me. It would have changed nothing."

Leah turned away from him, trying to block whatever emotional reactions she was having to his words. Why couldn't he understand that she couldn't tell him? At the time she had felt battered, bruised and confused.

"Leah, please don't shut me out. I love you. I always have. I still do."

She turned back around, her eyes filled to capacity with tears. His admission of love was the last thing she wanted to hear, the last thing she wanted to know. Knowing he loved her and that he'd built this house for her was too much. "No, we can't go there, Reese. We can't go back. Too much has happened. After I left and went to California, I had a hard time dealing with things. If a man looked at me, I panicked. Finally, I knew I needed help and sought out professional assistance. With the aid of counselors and a very special support group, I began to see that I wasn't alone. There were other women who'd been violated like I had. And then there was Grace, the older woman who was kind enough to give me a place to stay in her home. She became the mother I had lost, the grandmother I'd never had and the friend that I needed. I've come a long way but I still have a long way to go."

"And we'll go there together. I love you too much to let you leave me a second time."

The sincerity in his words touched her and nervously she placed her lower lip between her teeth and met his gaze. He was being honest with her, leaving her no choice but to be completely honest with him, as well. "And I love you, too, Reese. Too much for you to get involved and waste your time with me. The love I knew you had for me is what helped me keep my sanity over the years. But each time I came home I knew that love was turning to hate and I had to learn how to get stronger without your love as a crutch because it wasn't there anymore and I couldn't pretend that it was."

She wiped the tears from her eyes before continuing. "I still haven't gotten over things to the point where I trust men. In fact, the thought of one ever touching me makes me ill. Even you. Knowing that, how can I even consider us picking up where we left off?"

"Like I said, we'll work through—"

"No, there's nothing to work through. In a few weeks I'm returning to California. I'm going to use the money I'm getting from Jocelyn to open a small restaurant there. My life, the one I do have, is in California. There's nothing for me here."

"I'm here, Leah," he said quietly. "The man who loves you."

She shook her head. "No, I can't take what you're offering. I can't and I won't."

Not giving him a chance to say anything else, she walked around him and out of the room.

JOCELYN REPLACED HER cell phone in her purse and glanced over at Bas when he brought the car to a stop at the traffic light. "That was Reese. Things didn't go with Leah the way he'd hoped, but he's determined to help her through this."

Bas nodded. "He loves her very much."

"Always has. At one time I actually envied what they shared, it was so special. And I've always known that if there was one person who could get Leah to change her mind about leaving Newton Grove it was going to be Reese, just like I truly believe he's the one person who can heal her hurt."

"I'm going to have to agree with you on that."

Jocelyn had been waiting to hear from Reese, and with the phone call from him out of the way, she took the time to study her surroundings out the car's window. Lifting a brow, she glanced back over at Bas. "I thought we were headed back to town for lunch. Where are we going?"

He smiled although he couldn't take his eyes off the road to look over at her. "My place. I'm treating you to lunch."

Jocelyn blinked. "Your place? I thought you were staying at Sadie's Bed and Breakfast."

"I was, until Friday. While I was out riding around with Reese a few weeks ago, I saw this cabin on the outskirts of town and thought it would be a nice piece of investment property for the Steele Corporation. All of us like to get away every once in a while and we all love the mountains. Our parents own a cabin that we use occasionally, but this one is bigger."

"So you bought it? Just like that?"

He risked glancing over at her before returning his eyes to the road. Just for that instant he felt his heart slam hard in his chest. He did love her. He was no longer falling in love with her; he had fallen—and hard.

"Yes, just like that," he said, feeling like a man on top of the world. He would feel even better if the woman who held his affections felt the same way, but he knew that she didn't. But he had time to spare, and pretty soon she would see that Reese wasn't the only man on a mission to win over the woman he loved.

"So what's for lunch?" she asked.

"I thought I'd keep it simple and fix a couple of sandwiches. I haven't had a chance to do any real grocery shopping yet, but I do have stuff to make a nice sandwich."

"What kind of sandwich?"

When he brought the car to a stop in front of his cabin, he cocked his head and shot her a smile that tilted the corners of his lips. "I hope you like peanut butter and jelly."

JOCELYN HAD TO admit that the peanut butter and jelly sandwich and glass of iced tea were good. She hadn't eaten since breakfast so her hunger might have been what had made it so delicious. But then she thought of something else that was delicious, something she liked—Bas's kisses.

"What are you thinking about?"

"Oh." A blush stained her cheeks. She'd thought he was using the restroom. She hadn't known he'd returned and had been staring at her. "I—" She paused, wondering what she could say. "I was just thinking about Reese and Leah," she lied, figuring he would believe that.

"And the thought of them is what had you smiling?"

"Er...yeah," she said, compounding her lie. "I can remember happier times."

"Don't give up on them. The happier times will return."

"You think so?"

"Yes," he said without hesitation. "When two people love each other, things will work out for them."

She lifted a brow. "You sound like someone who knows."

He shook his head. "Trust me, I'm not, but I believe it, and I've seen it happen. Take my brother Chance and his wife, Kylie. They butted heads from the start, but finally they decided to give love a try and eventually got married. And I don't know two happier people."

Jocelyn nodded, glanced around. For a place that had been moved into a mere three days ago, Bas's place looked lived in. The three-bedroom, two-bath two-story log cabin with cathedral ceilings, sat secluded on a stream with hardwood trees all around. It also had an extraordinary view of the mountains, a wood-burning fireplace and a covered porch with an outdoor hot tub.

"You still planning on going to that baby shower later?"

She turned, not knowing he had crossed the room and was standing so close. "No, I'm not in the mood," she said softly, barely realizing what she was saying. Being this close to Bas was as usual stirring her senses, all five of them.

There was the scent of him, strong and manly with a come-hither aroma that should be bottled. The sight of him, especially in his jeans, was provocative enough to make a woman's mouth water... And speaking of mouth, the taste of him from last night was still on her tongue. Even the peanut butter hadn't been able to eradicate it. Her taste buds were sensitive, tingling, anticipating kissing him again. Just thinking about it was putting another sense to work—her hearing. She could hear the pounding of her heart against her chest.

And then there was the sense of touch, something she hadn't quite explored to the fullest when it came to him. A soft sigh escaped her lungs at the thought of touching him intimately, taking him in her hands, feeling him harden beneath her fingers.

"You're smiling again," he said, resting his hip against his kitchen counter. "Still thinking about Reese and Leah?"

Jocelyn chewed the inside of her cheek, wondering

what his reaction would be if she told him what she'd really been thinking about. She swallowed, deciding not to chance it. So she told him something that wasn't a lie, but it wasn't the full truth, either. "I was thinking about this weekend."

Bas smiled. "Now isn't that a coincidence. So was I."

"And what was your favorite part?" she asked him, wondering if it was the same as hers.

He deliberately licked his lips and eased up closer to her. "I can't believe you have to ask me that, sweetheart," he said in a low voice.

Heat suddenly seemed to bubble up in Jocelyn's throat. The sight of his tongue was sending unflagging warmth all through her. "You enjoyed that, huh?"

"Most definitely," he whispered, leaning in closer to her.

Jocelyn breathed in, remembering the nights she hadn't been able to sleep because of thoughts of him, and she knew there was something she wanted to know.

Something she *had* to know.

Last night she had had an orgasm standing up. She wondered how one felt lying down in a bed. A slow burn began building between her legs at the thought of finding out. And she knew she couldn't leave this cabin until she did.

A part of her knew that she and Bas would never be a real couple. His home was in North Carolina and hers was here. There was nothing to keep him in Newton Grove when it was time for him to leave. But there was something the two of them could share while he was here. It was something she had never shared with a man before. A hot and torrid love affair. It would all be in the name of fun. In the end there would be no hard feelings and no regrets.

She could do this. She wanted to do this. She *needed* to do this.

Bas had awakened feelings and urges within her that she'd never had to deal with before. Not only had he awakened them, he had stirred them up real good and hot. She knew if she wanted to take things to the next level it would be up to her to make the move. He probably assumed that if he made them, she would accuse him of moving too fast. Hadn't he told her about the problem with assuming things?

Making the decision to take matters into her own hands, she smiled and pointed past him. "Have you used your fireplace yet?"

He glanced over his shoulder and then back at her. "No, why, are you cold?"

"No, I'm not cold." She sighed deeply. For God's sake, she told herself, don't lose your nerve now. Remember that article you read in *Today's Black Woman*? Sometimes it's up to you to let a man know what you want, Jocelyn Isabella Mason. She smiled, thinking that although she wasn't named after her father, together her initials spelled JIM.

"But I think a fire would be nice," she decided to say. She wanted this man and she intended to have him, for whatever time she could.

"Okay. Just make yourself comfortable."

"Thanks, I will," she said walking over to the sofa and taking a seat.

It didn't take Bas any time at all to get the fire started, mainly because one had already started to flame, right in his gut. He wasn't born yesterday. He could recognize seduction a mile away. But in this case it wasn't a mile away, it was right smack in his living room and sitting on his sofa.

He stood and turned around and the flame in his gut suddenly blazed. Jocelyn had her legs crossed in a way that made her skirt rise higher on her thighs. They were the same luscious thighs he had held on to tightly last night while tasting her.

He tried not to stare. He even tried to stop his body from getting hard, but it was no use. There were some things that a man couldn't control and a physical reaction to a beautiful and sexy woman was one of them. Especially when he happened to be in love with that woman.

He met her gaze, saw the heat in her eyes and saw how she suddenly took her tongue and licked her lips. At that moment all he could think about was taking that tongue, sucking it into his own mouth and having his way with it. He then watched as she switched positions and recrossed her legs, giving him a quick view of her panties. They were white.

He growled low in his throat, not even aware he'd made the sound until a pleased smile touched her lips. "You're trying to tempt me, aren't you?" he asked.

Jocelyn sat back and smiled. "You think so?"

"Yes."

She laughed. "Sounds like you're assuming things,

Mr. Steele, and what's your position on people assuming things?"

Positions. Now *that* was something he didn't want to think about at the moment. But then maybe he did…

He slowly crossed the room, not taking his eyes off her, and when he came to a stop in front of where she sat, he reached out for her arm and tugged her unresistingly to her feet, pressing her body to his and gazing deeply into her eyes. "But this time, I'm assuming right."

Jocelyn shivered, feeling the thickness of him pressed against her center. Nice. Hard. Forged of steel. "If you're assuming right, then what are you going to do about it?" she whispered.

His gaze remained locked on hers, and she was struck by passion so intense it was hard for her to swallow. She watched as his eyes darkened. "Don't ask unless you really want to know, Jocelyn."

She sucked in a deep breath when she felt him harden even more against her belly. "I really want to know, and I'm asking," she said, pushing her lower body even closer to his for a more intimate fit.

Now it was Bas who sucked in a deep breath. Bas whose arms wrapped around her tightly. Bas who leaned closer to make sure she saw the desire in his eyes. He moved in closer still and when his mouth was just inches from hers, he snaked out his tongue, slid it sensuously across her lower lip, then the upper one and watched her shudder in response.

"Well, since you really want to know…it's show time," he whispered huskily, before greedily taking her lips with his and picking her up into his arms.

CHAPTER FOURTEEN

BAS PULLED HIS mouth from Jocelyn's the moment he placed her on the king-size bed, feeling the insistent throb of desire running rampant all through him.

He hadn't intended to move this fast so soon. He had wanted to give her a chance to get used to him, to accept the place he intended to claim in her life and the intense love he had for her, before they shared ecstasy together. But now fate had stepped in and the need to stamp his claim, brand her as his, was as elemental as breathing. But first, he needed just to hold her, to feel her close to his heart, the heart she now possessed.

"Come here for a second," he said softly, opening his arms to her. And when she slid across the bed to him, into his opened arms, he held her tight, enveloped her into his warmth. She laid her head on his chest, and he knew she could hear the fast beating of his heart, but what she didn't know was that it beat at that pace just for her.

Emotions were churning through him, emotions he'd never before felt for a woman, and now he understood what Chance had meant when he'd said falling in love with Kylie had been like being hit with a ton of bricks. It had happened so fast Chance hadn't been expecting it.

It has been the same for Bas. Love was the last thing

he had been looking for when he'd arrived in Newton Grove, but the one thing he'd found with Jocelyn. There was one thing that couldn't be denied with the Steele men. When they found love they knew how to accept it and claim the woman as theirs. At least, it seemed it was that way for three of them. There was no telling how Donovan, who was slow to accept anything at face value and prone to be the most resisting of the four, would handle love once he found it.

Bas's attention was reclaimed when Jocelyn raised her head and smiled at him. Her smile triggered something deep within him. He had to touch her, feel her, taste her all over, have her naked beneath him and join her body intimately with his, make love to her until they were both out of their minds, crazy with need.

And he wanted her now.

He stripped and reached out and began removing her clothes, first her blouse and bra. When her chest was completely bare, the sight of her firm breasts quickened his pulse. He leaned forward, took them in his hands and stroked them, licked them, exhaled hot breath over the hardened dark tips.

And then his hands moved down her waist to remove her skirt while his brain could still function. And when she lay before him in nothing but a pair of white lace panties, he reached out and let his fingertips trace along the edge before touching her moist center. He heard her quick intake of breath, her quiet yet ragged moan. She caught hold of his shoulders as his fingers continued to stroke her with slow caresses. His fingers slipped beneath her panties to touch her intimately, stirring her scent, flaming her heat.

"Bas."

His name was a whispered groan. An earth-shattering moan. And when a purr of pleasure rippled from her throat, he leaned back to pull the scrap of white lace down her legs. Her scent was intense and filled the air surrounding them. A shudder passed through him, the need to mingle in her wet heat became overpowering. But first he wanted to reacquaint his tongue with her taste.

He leaned forward, reached for her hips and lifted her up gently toward his mouth. The moment his tongue entered her she screamed, but he ignored the sound as his tongue continued to push inside her, deep, and then he kissed her intimately, savoring her taste, needing to make love to her in this special and profound way again.

Jocelyn uttered an intense moan while her hips involuntarily rocked against Bas's mouth. No man had ever done this to her before him, and he was making her body crumble into a thousand pieces. She felt every bone in her body melt, and she was filled with intense heat. Her fingernails were digging into his shoulders but she couldn't help it. She was too delirious to do anything but moan in pleasure.

And then he pulled back, cupped her face into his hands and kissed her while easing her back down on the bed, covering her body with his. She felt the ridge of his erection, powerfully aroused, press against the place where his mouth had left its mark, making her thighs tremble. The sensation of his tongue inside her mouth, kissing her deeply, had her moaning incoherently.

When he pulled back she opened her eyes and looked at him, saw the deep-rooted desire in his gaze. She also saw something else in the dark depths, something she couldn't put a name to. "Now I make you mine," he whispered, nudging her legs apart. With a primal growl he eased inside her while leaning closer and trailing the dampness of his tongue around her earlobe.

Automatically her hips arched and a sizzling groan poured from her lips when he buried himself inside her to the hilt. Their connection, their joining was absolute, complete and so unerringly whole. And at that moment she thought there could not be a more perfect union between two individuals.

"You okay?" he asked, going still to glance down at her.

"Yes," she said while her feminine muscles clamped him, clutched him and claimed him. The sensations she felt were almost more than she could bear. A growing tension, one she didn't understand, begin to stir within her, right there at her center. And as if he knew exactly what she needed, he began to move, rock into her, thrust back and forth, stroke her with a rhythm that made her entire body quiver, fulfilling all her secret desires, her most wanton needs.

Her climax, more intense than any of the others, slammed into her and she screamed his name. She was aware of him driving harder into her, sending her even further over the edge. She closed her eyes and tightened her muscles around him, milking him and making him groan aloud. She wanted everything she could get from him, determined not to deny herself anything. She wrapped her legs around his waist and locked him in. She had waited too long for this. Too long for a man like him.

"Jocelyn!"

Bas screamed her name while fighting for control. Spasms of ecstasy began tearing through him, and the way her inner muscles were clutching him, draining him, was sending him over into the realms of oblivion. She had stolen his heart and now she was taking over his body, leaving him defenseless and filled with a need he could barely comprehend.

This was love, pure and unadulterated. He had never felt this way before. Nothing had been this intense, invigorating and passionate. And when she let out another scream that split the air, he felt his body explode once again as sensations ripped through him, toppled him over into another world. He lost all sense of everything, except the acceptance that the woman beneath him, to whose body he was intimately joined, was in total possession of his heart, body and soul.

JOCELYN CAME AWAKE to the sound of Bas's heartbeat. Lying with her head resting on his chest, with his arms wrapped securely around her, and their legs entwined, she felt totally exhausted. But who wouldn't after what they had shared? After making love again in the bed, they had taken the top covers off and moved to a spot in front of the fireplace where they had made love again before falling asleep in each other's arms.

It was still barely light outside and she figured she would have slept right through the night if the growling of her stomach wasn't a reminder that she hadn't eaten anything since lunch.

"Hungry?"

Jocelyn glanced up. Bas was awake and smiling down at her. The flames from the fireplace provided an austere glow to his features. The tone of his voice was sensual and in response to it, she felt a tightening in the lower part of her body. "Yes, I'm hungry," she said, trying to make her voice sound natural.

This was the first time she had awakened in a man's arms after hours of lovemaking. The last time, in college, she had asked the guy to leave her room as soon as it was over, thinking it had been a complete waste of time. But that hadn't been the case with Bas. With him nothing was wasted. They could have been like the Energizer Bunny and kept going and going and going.

"I better feed you or you'll think I'm not a very good host," he said, rising to his feet.

Jocelyn swallowed as she gazed up at him. He was stark naked, unashamedly so. He saw the way she was staring at him and flashed a teasing grin. "If you keep looking at me like that, you might not get dinner after all."

"Then what will I get?" she asked, deciding she might not be as hungry as she'd thought.

"Anything you want. I'm easy."

She moved her gaze lower to a certain part of him.

A smile tugged at her lips. "No, you're not. Right now I'd say you're extremely hard."

He chuckled. "You noticed."

"Staring me right in the face, how can I not?"

"Should I apologize?"

She shook her head. "No. What you should do is come back down here and let me take care of it."

He slowly dropped to his knees and then crawled over toward her. "And what do you have in mind?" he asked huskily.

She leaned up and pushed him on his back, then straddled him. "Oh, trust me, Mr. Steele. You're about to find out."

"I CAN'T REMEMBER the last time I ate a bowl of chicken noodle soup," Jocelyn said, taking another spoonful into her mouth.

A deep laugh vibrated from within Bas's throat. "Hey, I offered to take you into town to one of those restaurants and you turned me down."

She smiled. "Only because I'm not ready to put my clothes back on. No pun intended but I think we're on a roll."

And that, she thought, was the truth. After making love again in front of the fireplace, they had gotten into the hot tub and made love once more before deciding they needed to eat something to keep their strength up. Bas had let her borrow his robe and together they had gone into the kitchen, where, after checking his empty cabinets, they had found a couple of cans of soup amongst his fishing gear. While the soup had been warming on the stove she had taken the time to call Leah. Her sister hadn't been very talkative, and had, in fact, cut the conversation short, after assuring Jocelyn she was all right.

Satisfied that she had at least spoken to Leah, Jocelyn and Bas had sat down at his kitchen table to enjoy soup and crackers and relish the aftermath of their enjoyment of each other.

Jocelyn figured if she never made love again in her life that would be okay because within the last six hours she had made up for whatever she'd missed in the past and stocked up on what might not be coming her way in the future. But a part of her couldn't imagine sharing anything so intimate with anyone but Bas. Everything the two of them had shared had been utterly amazing. He was definitely a highly charged sexual man.

"Want some more?"

She glanced up at him and smiled. "Some more of what?"

"Jocelyn," he said warningly, "haven't you gotten enough?"

"Of what?" Her tone was innocent. "Soup or you?"

He was sitting across from her at the table wearing just a pair of jeans, and her gaze slid over his bare chest. He was as fine as fine could get and the memories of all those orgasms he'd given her had her body tingling inside out. She wanted to go to him, curl up in his lap, run her hand down his belly, inside his jeans and—

"You're staying all night?"

She moved her gaze back to his face. "Is that an invitation?"

"Yes."

She took another spoonful of soup then asked, "What about clothes?"

"We never did take your luggage out of the car."

"How convenient."

He gave her a knowing look as a smile touched the corners of his mouth. "Yeah, I think so."

LEAH FINISHED FOLDING up her laundry and decided that although it was still early she would go upstairs to bed. She heard the doorbell ring and sighed deeply, hoping and praying it wasn't Reese. They had nothing more to say to each other and she wouldn't be able to handle seeing him again that day.

Crossing the room, she wondered who it could be. At the door she asked, "Who is it?"

"Delivery for Leah Mason."

She glanced out the peephole and saw a man of about twenty standing there with a bouquet of flowers in his hands. Still, she had grown cautious over the years. "Do I need to sign for anything?" she asked through the door.

"No, ma'am."

"Please leave whatever you have on the doorstep." She watched as the man did as she requested then walked away. She moved to the window to make sure he got back in his van and drove off. Taking a deep breath, she walked back over to the door and opened it.

She couldn't help but smile upon seeing the beautiful arrangement of calla lilies, her favorite, and knew immediately who'd sent them. Couldn't Reese see what he was trying to do was useless? She would never be the woman that she used to be, a woman who'd enjoyed making love to him anytime and anywhere.

She picked up the bouquet and went back inside the house, locking the door behind her. She placed the arrangement on the table before pulling off the card.

When you hurt, I hurt. Give me a chance to take the pain away. Reese.

Leah continued to read the card, over and over. Why was Reese Singleton so stubborn? Didn't he understand what she'd told him earlier that day? Didn't he get the picture; she was incapable of allowing another man, even him, ever to touch her?

She almost jumped when the doorbell rang again. She went to the door and glanced out of the peephole and her heart began pounding. It was Reese.

A part of her wanted to ignore him, but she knew Reese refused to be ignored. Besides, he evidently hadn't comprehended what she'd been trying to tell him earlier. Maybe if she'd had the help of counselors or a support group earlier than she had, she would be a lot stronger now. But she hadn't. Instead of opening up and talking about it, she had tried to go through life without dealing with the rape, and in so doing she had erected this physical and emotional shield against all men.

Although she already knew the answer, she asked, "Who is it?"

"It's Reese, Leah. Please open the door so we can talk."

Telling him they had nothing to discuss would be useless. It was best to let him in so they could talk and then that would be the end of things.

She slowly opened the door and took a step back and Reese entered, closing the door behind him. She'd seen the look in his eyes the moment he'd gazed at her. The pity she'd expected wasn't there, but what she saw was what she remembered so many other times—desire. The thought that he still found her desirable, even after knowing about what Neil had done, was both flattering and frustrating.

"Why did you come, Reese?"

"Did you think I would stay away?"

No, she really hadn't thought that since he'd always gone after what he wanted. But she just couldn't understand why and how he could still love her after all these years. Especially now.

As if he'd read her thoughts he smiled and said, "Hey, don't even wonder about it, Leah. You knew you had my heart from the first."

She couldn't help but release a humorless laugh. "It was either me or Kristi Alford, and you deserved better."

He chuckled. "Yes, and you were definitely it. I have no regrets."

Neither had she. Still, all the good times they'd shared in the past could not wipe out everything that had happened.

"Leah, I—"

When he reached out to touch her arm, automatically she pulled back and fear jumped into her eyes as her entire body went rigid against his touch. She saw the surprise in his gaze and released a frustrated sigh. "I told you I get filled with revulsion at the thought of any man touching me, no matter how innocent. I think it will be better if you leave now."

He crossed his arms over his chest. "I'm not leaving and I'm not going to let you put distance between us. I understand the barriers you've put up, but I won't let it stop me from proving something."

"Proving what?"

"That to you I'm not a regular guy, Leah. I'm the man you loved and by your own admission, the man you still love. Somehow I'm going to remind you of that and break through those walls you've erected. I'm going to be the one man who'll make you want to be touched again."

She hugged her arms to her breasts and glared at him. "You're pretty sure of yourself, aren't you?"

He smiled. "Yes, and I'm pretty sure of you. You could never resist me when I laid things on thick."

No, she couldn't, but things weren't the same anymore. "But that was then."

"And it could be now if you let it. I want us to get back together. I want to marry you, give you babies we'll both love, and I want to be there for you until the day I die."

The sincerity in his words touched her and she couldn't help the tears that formed in her eyes. Whether he knew it or not, he was offering her a chance to re-claim her dream. But still…

"It won't work, Reese," she said quietly, again trying to make him see reason.

"How do you know if you won't give it a chance? Give us a chance. We can take things slow, start off by going out to eat, to the movies, take walks…and I promise to keep my hands to myself. In fact I will keep my hands to myself until you say you're ready for some-thing more."

She lifted a brow. "No kisses?" She remembered how much they'd liked to kiss.

He smiled softly. "And as much as it will probably drive me crazy, no kisses."

They stared at each other for a long moment and Leah thought about his words, his offer. She met his gaze, studied the expression on his face, looked into the depth of his eyes. "Why do you want to do this? There are other women in town who'd jump at the chance to—"

"You're the one I want, Leah. You're the only one I've ever wanted. You spoiled me for anyone else." He chuckled quietly. "I didn't know just how messed up I was until you left. I haven't been able to get involved with anyone else and it's been a long time."

For him it was a long time, since she knew just how passionate he was. "Why?" she asked.

"Because I couldn't imagine making love to anyone but you."

Leah wondered if he knew what that admission meant to her. But then, if he was putting all his hopes in her, he still might not be making love to anyone. "Reese, I—"

"No. Just say we can make a go of things again, Leah. We'll take thing slow but we'll still make a go. Although we enjoyed the time we were together, for us it was never just about sex anyway. Remember?"

Yes, she did remember. The sex had been good, but they had shared a special friendship, as well. "And you're sure you want to do this?" she asked, needing the reassurance.

"Yes, I'm sure. Let's start off tomorrow. Early. Invite me to breakfast. I miss your pancakes."

She couldn't help the tiny smile that touched her lips. And with the memory she recalled a time when she had prepared pancakes at his place one morning, and how they'd got sidetracked and ended up with more batter over them than in the skillet. Of course they'd had to shower together and she remembered what had happened after that....

Leah blinked. That memory had been totally unexpected. It was the first time she'd been able to recall a man touching her body and not get sick at the thought. And on that particular day Reese had touched her all over.

"So are you going to feed me pancakes in the morning?"

His question reclaimed her thoughts. "Yes, I think I can manage that."

"Good. Well, I'll leave so you can go on to bed and get your rest. See you in the morning, Leah."

After Reese left, Leah felt an inner peace for the first time in a long while.

CHAPTER FIFTEEN

JOCELYN GAZED DOWN into her coffee before taking a sip and smiled. It didn't seem possible but two weeks had passed since that night she and Bas had spent together and now they were definitely an item. They continued to do a lot of things together. Fun things.

During the day they went their separate ways with him working in the office the majority of the time and with her on the job site. Then, in the afternoons while he was at the gym, she used that time to visit with Leah, at least it had started out that way. But now Reese was dominating a lot of her sister's time and although she knew the two were taking things slowly, just the thought that Leah was spending time with a man, especially the man Leah loved, was gratifying.

Then at night Jocelyn and Bas would meet up somewhere in town, usually at some restaurant or another and enjoy a delicious meal. And since Ms. Sadie had taken Jocelyn into her confidence about Bas's health issues, she made doubly sure whatever he put in his mouth was good for him.

When night came they stayed over either at her place or his. All she had to do was close her eyes to recall any one time his hard male body had entered hers, taking her breath away, preparing her for the orgasm that he could so effortlessly give her, several times over.

At first it was awkward for her, letting a man dominate so much of her time, but pretty soon she got used to him being around. He was considerate, thoughtful and understanding and seemed to know just when she needed her space. He would give it to her, but not for long. It was as if he wanted her to know that what they were sharing was something he intended to make last until the end.

The end.

She knew they were working against a clock and soon he would be leaving to return to Charlotte. She didn't want to think about how her life would be when he left. But she had to be realistic enough to know what they were sharing wasn't forever. He had his life and she had hers. He belonged to the Steele Corporation and she belonged to Mason Construction. Her life was here and his was there. There was no middle ground.

"You're quiet this morning."

Jocelyn glanced up and met Leah's curious stare. "I was just thinking."

"About Bas?" Leah asked, leaning back against the kitchen counter.

Jocelyn opened her mouth to reply, then stopped. She looked closely at her sister. Growing up they had never shared confidences like some sisters who had close relationships. Maybe it was time they did. "Yes, I was thinking about Bas."

"The two of you have been spending a lot of time together."

Jocelyn lifted a brow. "And how do you know that?"

Leah laughed as she poured a cup of coffee. "Hey, give me a break. I wasn't born yesterday. You aren't spending the night here anymore and I doubt you're spending a lot of time at your home in your own bed, so what am I to think?"

After taking a sip of coffee she added, "And don't forget when Reese first became my boyfriend you hadn't even started showing any interest in guys. You much preferred playing the part of the builder and holding on to your virginity."

Jocelyn leaned back in her chair. "Yeah, well, I wish I had held on longer so that Bas could have been my first. I guess in a way he was."

"Yeah, I'm glad Reese was my first as well," Leah said quietly, as she came to the table to sit down.

Jocelyn waited a moment before asking, "And how are things going with you and Reese? I can't help noticing the two of you are spending more and more time together."

Jocelyn watched a tiny smile touch the corners of Leah's lips when she said, "That man is so stubborn." A frown then replaced the smile. "If it was left up to me, we wouldn't be seeing each other at all. It's so unfair to him."

"In what way?"

"Reese is everything a woman could want in a man, and I of all people should know. He's handsome, kind, considerate and understanding. He should be dating someone who can give him the things he needs, instead of someone like me, a woman who can't even think about letting him touch me."

Leah's finger caressed the handle of her cup before she continued. "We've been spending time together for a couple of weeks now and I still can't let him kiss me, although I know he wants to. And he's keeping his word by not asking. He gets here at seven every morning to share breakfast with me and before he leaves I know he's hoping that I'll open up, be responsive and let him, but I can't."

Jocelyn took another sip of her coffee and then said, "At some point you're going to have to try and put behind you that one bad time with Neil and remember all those other great times with Reese." Jocelyn's lips quirked and she added, "I remembered some of your dreams and how you would moan in your sleep. Hell, it made me wish I could have been a fly on the wall during one of those times the two of you were together."

Her comment had Leah laughing and Jocelyn felt good hearing it. When Leah's amusement finally cleared she leaned back in her chair. "Trust me, a fly would have died from too much heat. Reese was all that and then some." A sad smile then touched her lips. "God, I'd love to share some of those times with him again."

"And you can, Leah. Reese is making it possible for you to do that. All you have to do is reach out to him. Don't let what Neil did destroy the most precious thing that mattered to you—your love for Reese Singleton."

A few moments later Jocelyn said, "You know, I use to envy what you had with Reese."

Leah's brows lifted. "You did?"

"Yes."

"Why?"

"Because I knew the two of you were in love, all into each other, and I wasn't there yet with anyone. In fact, I thought the guys who tried talking to me were annoying. I was a daddy's girl who wanted to build things just like he did. I didn't have time for relationships. But that didn't mean I wouldn't occasionally wonder how things could be between a man and woman."

Leah gave her a wry smile. "And I'm sure with Bas you're making up for anything you missed out on."

Jocelyn laughed, thinking of all the things she and Bas had done over the past few weeks; some were outright scandalous, but he had assured her whatever a couple agreed to do in the bedroom was their business. "Yes, you can say that, but what I'm sharing with him isn't forever."

"It can be if you want it. I've seen the two of you together. I think he's quite taken with you. Even Reese mentioned that he was."

Jocelyn shook her head. "Bas is taken with the moment just like I am. We're mature enough to know that one day he's going to pack up and return to that life he has in Charlotte. And I have a lot to do here. This is where I belong, here in Newton Grove, keeping Dad's dream alive."

"And what about your dream? What about love?" Leah asked quietly.

Jocelyn shrugged. "I don't have any dreams and I have no desire to fall in love. I live for the moment.

That way you don't worry about what happens when things don't turn out the way you want. And as far as love is concerned, maybe the bug will hit me one day but I'm not in a hurry. What Bas and I are sharing is for today. I'm not planning on any tomorrows."

"And what if he is?"

Jocelyn chuckled. "Trust me, he's not. Bas likes the way things are just as I do."

Leah gazed at her sister a moment before saying, "I think it's all a smoke screen for you, Jocelyn. You do have dreams and you want to fall in love but you're afraid to."

"That's not true."

"I think it is. You missed Mom as much as I did but instead of withdrawing like I did, you turned your attention to Dad and began clinging to him. And then we had Aunt Susan. Now that both Dad and Aunt Susan are gone, you don't want to risk falling in love for fear of eventually losing that person, as well."

Jocelyn stared at her sister for a moment, and then shook her head. She had thought the same thing once and had dismissed the thought entirely from her mind, refusing to find a reason for her lack of interest in falling in love over the years. "I'm not afraid of falling in love or having dreams. I just have more to do with my time than indulging in either."

Leah nodded, and Jocelyn wasn't sure her sister believed what she'd said or not.

LATER THAT NIGHT Jocelyn stood at the window staring out. It was dark and cold and according to the news report a little snow might be coming their way. She wouldn't mind the snow, but bad weather wasn't good for a construction company. At least Marcella's house was finished and they had done the closing that day. To everyone's surprise it had gone off without a hitch.

"So this is where you went off to," Bas said, coming behind her and placing a hand around her waist, pulling her back against him. Her turned her into his arms and placed a kiss on her lips. "I missed you."

Jocelyn chuckled. "You didn't even notice me gone, you were so busy painting."

He took her face into his hands. "Trust me I noticed you were gone, but I am enjoying that paint-by-number set. I'm glad you talked me into getting it."

She reached up and slid her arms around his neck. "Umm, paint by numbers today and who knows, you might be asking to use my coloring books tomorrow."

"Not hardly."

She threw her head back and laughed. She and Bas had been having honest-to-goodness fun and she didn't want it to end, but she knew that one day it would. She pushed the thought away, not wanting to dwell on it. "You want to go down in the basement and play a game of pinball?" she asked.

"No, I want you to come back to bed," he whispered huskily against her ear.

Moments later, in bed, Jocelyn wondered how often a woman could come apart in a man's arms. How often could she get filled with so much intense pleasure? The thought of not being able to share this with Bas almost frightened her.

But then Bas leaned over and kissed her, and once again her mind went blank and she let herself drown in the emotions he was making her feel. And when he slid his body over hers, entered her with one long, penetrating sweep, she became totally aware of the size of him as well as his strength.

"That's it. Move with me, baby," he whispered as he began thrusting in and out of her. She moved her hips, clutched him with her thighs, locked him in with her legs and clenched him with her inner muscles, pulling everything she could out of him.

"You're getting it all," he said huskily. The dark sensuality of his voice made her clench him tighter. "Payback."

And the way he paid her back had her moaning out loud. His hands cradled her hips, he pushed deeper inside her, angling her center so he could hit a spot that built pressure near her womb, causing flames to flare to all parts of her loins.

"Bas!"

"Get ready, cause here I come," he whispered hoarsely.

And he came.

His body jerked, bucked, spilled into her, filling her with the essence of him. He threw his head back, breathed in tight before screaming her name. And Jocelyn knew this moment would be engraved in her memory forever.

THE NEXT MORNING Jocelyn was almost too tired and weak to get out of bed, so she decided to stay put just for a little while, and cuddle close to the masculine body that was spooning her naked backside.

She let out a shuddering breath when she thought of last night and all the other nights they had shared.

"You're awake?"

She smiled, wondering if he was asking her that for a particular reason. She turned over and met his drowsy gaze. "Depends on why you want to know."

He wrapped his arms tighter around her. "I need to tell you something."

He sounded serious and she wondered if he was going to tell her that he was leaving. Pretty soon his six weeks would be over and although he claimed he would hang around for at least three months, he really didn't have to. Was he needed back in Charlotte?

"What do you want to tell me?"

"First I need to get my good-morning kiss," he said, leaning over and capturing her lips with his, drinking the essence of her mouth.

When he released her lips, she smiled and said, "Keep that up and we'll never get any talking in."

He slowly pulled back and met her gaze. He reached out and traced his finger along her chin. "I feel things with you that I've never felt before with anyone, Jocelyn, and that can only mean one thing."

She lifted a brow. "What?"

"I love you."

His words, spoken simply, made her think she hadn't heard him right. But then all she had to do was stare into the clarity of his eyes and see both seriousness and sincerity in their dark depths. She felt flooded by emotions she wasn't ready for, and had to swallow a lump that suddenly formed in her throat. "No," she whispered softly. "You can't love me."

Bas reached out and touched his fingertips to her lips. "Yes, I can and you won't believe just how much I do. I want to marry you and—"

Jocelyn pulled away. "Marry me? How can you think such a thing? We can't get married."

Bas's lips tightened in a grim line as he witnessed her reaction to his words. "Yes, we can. Why would you think that we can't?"

Jocelyn pulled herself up in bed. "Because I don't expect you to move here and surely you don't expect me to just up and move to Charlotte. My life is here. The company is here. This is where I belong, Bas."

"Fine, then I'll move here."

Jocelyn lifted her chin. "And do what? You belong back at the Steele Corporation. Coming here for a while I'm sure was a nice diversion for you but you're going to leave and go back."

Bas blew out a heated breath. "Surely you knew I was falling in love with you, Jocelyn. What do you think these past few weeks have been about?"

"Fun. We were having fun."

"And that's all I've been to you?"

She glared. "I didn't say that, Bas, so don't put words into my mouth. We were indulging in a short-term affair. I'm old enough to know that. I wasn't expecting anything from you, and I most certainly didn't think you were expecting anything of me."

"Well, you assumed wrong."

"And it won't be the first time," she snapped.

The silence between them stretched, and then Jocelyn finally spoke. "Look, it's not that I'm not flattered by your offer because I am. But I can't marry you. My life here is all I know and all I want. Leah was the one who always wanted to leave and move away. I was contented to stay right here. Nothing's changed. That's what I want."

His gaze met hers and the pain she saw there almost pierced her heart. She hadn't meant to hurt him, but she had. She reached out and touched his arm. "Bas, please understand that—"

"No," he said, pulling away and getting out of bed. "There's nothing left to say. I think you've said it all."

"BREAKFAST WAS GOOD as usual, Leah," Reese said pushing the plate away.

She glanced up at him and smiled. "Thanks. I wasn't sure how you would like the mango pancakes. It's a new recipe I tried."

He chuckled. "Hey, I love all pancakes and yours are the best."

She shook her head. "It's a good thing you're as active as you are with how much you consume at breakfast. Going to the gym every day is paying off." And that was true. Reese was in the best shape he'd ever been. The proof was in his jeans. She didn't know of any man who could wear them better or could look sexier in them.

"So what are your plans today?" he asked.

This was how their day started, Leah thought. Reese

would arrive for breakfast each morning around seven and she would have everything ready. While he ate a mountain of pancakes and sipped coffee he would tell her his plans for that day and ask about hers. They would then make small talk about the weather, any happenings around town and any other topic of interest. When it was time for him to leave she would walk him to the door and tell him to have a nice day.

When it was time to walk him to the door today, she had just finished telling him about another recipe she planned to try. "Well, don't work too hard today," she said, reaching out to open the door.

"Leah?"

"Yes?" She turned around and met his gaze. He didn't say anything, but then he really didn't have to. Despite years of separation she could still read the look in his eyes.

"Nothing. Don't you work too hard, either," he finally said.

Leah nodded and stood back for him to walk out the door. But some part of her knew she had to make this morning different for them. Jocelyn was right. She couldn't let what Neil had done destroy the one thing that had been so right in her life, the one thing she had cherished the most. Reese's love.

"Reese?"

He turned around. "Yes?"

She didn't say anything at first, then she slowly leaned toward him and, without touching him, brushed a kiss across his lips. She heard his sharp intake of breath and the sound spurred her to go a little further.

So she deepened the kiss a little, and when he moaned, she closed her eyes and slipped her tongue inside his mouth.

She got just what she expected and exactly what she wanted, the tantalizing and rich taste of Reese Singleton. This is what time and distance hadn't been able to erase from her memory. Nor had Neil Grunthall.

With excruciating slowness and painstaking thoroughness, she kissed him, leaning into him but careful to keep their bodies from touching. But she needed this. After wondering for years if she'd ever be able to kiss a man again, she had her answer.

Leah slowly pulled back, or at least she tried to, but Reese's mouth followed. He gently leaned toward her, recaptured her mouth, letting her know how much he enjoyed this. So did she. So they kissed again, passionately, thoroughly. And somehow, at some point, he wrapped his arms around her and she didn't reject his touch. She was too caught up in the feel of being in his arms.

Her mind was humming that this was Reese, the man she loved, had always loved and would always love. Finally, he pulled back slightly, then began brushing kisses along her jaw. When he pulled his mouth away, their eyes met and although neither said anything, they were both aware of the importance of what had taken place.

"Thanks for making my day special," Reese said. "It was well worth the wait."

Leah nodded. She then lifted her hands to his chest. "Yes, it was, and please kiss me again."

Reese smiled and lowered his head. He was more than happy to oblige her request.

"THE BOSS IS in a bad mood," Tommy Grooms whispered to Reese when he arrived at the work site sometime later. This was their first day on a new project. The post office needed expanding and they had been awarded the job.

Considering he was in a damn good mood, Reese walked over to where Jocelyn was wielding her hammer. He waited until she was finished and tapped on her hard hat. She turned around and glared at him. "What?"

"We need to talk."

Jocelyn mentally swore as she placed her hammer aside and followed Reese into a deserted area of the room. She pulled off her safety glasses and hard hat. "What's this about?"

Reese leaned against a metal post. "You tell me. The guys think you're in a bad mood."

Jocelyn put her safety glasses back on and glared through them. "I am."

"Then you need to leave."

She blinked. "Excuse me?"

"I said you need to leave and pull yourself together. This job is no place for negative emotions right now."

Jocelyn's angered flared. "You're a fine one to talk."

"Yes, and I learned from experience. Go ahead. Take an extended lunch. Come back when you feel better."

"I feel fine."

Reese chuckled without any real amusement. "You

might feel fine but you look like hell. It's plain to see you've been crying. What's going on, Jocelyn? You and Bas have a lover's spat?"

She glared. "Don't mention his name."

Reese lifted a brow. "Wow, that sounds deep."

Jocelyn's lips twitched in anger. "Men. All of you are nuts. You want affairs then you don't want affairs. And when you do fall in love, you expect everyone to follow suit like good little soldiers. Well, not everyone wants to fall in love," she snapped.

"Then don't," Reese countered. He then smiled. "But you know what I think, Joce? Whether you want to admit it or not, you're already in love."

JOCELYN DECIDED TO have lunch at one of the local sandwich shops in town. Reese had been right. She'd needed time alone. She released a long sigh and thought about what Bas had said that morning. He loved her.

Any other woman would probably have been elated at his confession, but why was she so frightened? She sighed again as the answer came back to her. Mainly because of the unknown. To fall in love with Bas meant uprooting her life here and going someplace outside of her comfort zone. Other than her visits to Aunt Susan every summer in Florida, this was where her life had been. This was where she'd always felt she belonged.

All because of personal insecurities she'd always managed to hide.

Leah was right. The main reason she'd never formed an attachment to a man was because of the fear of eventually being left alone. That was why she'd never been involved in a serious relationship.

Before now. Before Bas.

But he wanted to take her away from here, and as much as she loved him…

Jocelyn's heart began hammering fast and furious in her chest. Reese was right. She was already in love. Suddenly the thought of not being with Bas was something she didn't want to think about and at that moment she knew to deny her love for him was a mistake. She did love him and she had to believe that things would work out and that no matter where he went or where he lived, her place was with him. He was her future as well as her present.

LATER THAT EVENING Jocelyn knocked on Bas's cabin's door as she went back and forth in her mind what she would say to him. She knew she needed to explain why she had freaked out this morning when he'd told her he loved her, and to make sure that he believed she loved him, as well.

After having lunch she had dropped by to visit Leah, only to find her sister in the best of moods. Leah shared the reason with her. Jocelyn was truly happy for her sister and proud of the progress she'd made with Reese. Now Jocelyn knew she had to get things right with her man, as well.

The door opened and she saw the surprised look on Bas's face. "Jocelyn. I didn't expect to hear from you, especially after this morning."

"I know. May I come in?"

"Sure," he said, stepping aside. She walked in and closed the door behind her.

Bas went to stand in front of the fireplace while Jocelyn remained in the center of the room. "I need to apologize about this morning, Bas."

He held her gaze. "Evidently I hit a sore spot."

Jocelyn nodded. "Yes, the thought of ever loving anyone has been a personal insecurity I've refused to acknowledge. For some reason I've equated falling with love with eventually losing that person. So, to play it safe, I never allowed myself the luxury of truly loving anyone. Until you."

He raised to his lips the glass he was holding in his hand and took a sip, never letting his eyes stray from hers. "And do you? Do you love me, Jocelyn?"

She smiled, hoping he would see the truth in her eyes. "Yes, I love you, Bas. Reese sent me away from the job site this morning so I could go someplace and rationalize things, and I did. I can't let life pass me by without having dreams, and without having love. I love you, Bas, and if your offer still stands, I want to be your wife."

Bas set his drink on the mantel and came to stand in front of Jocelyn. "The offer still stands, sweetheart," he said in a husky voice, reaching out and cradling her face in his hands.

"There's one thing you're going to discover about a Steele, Jocelyn. When we find the woman we want, that's it. We don't give up until we have her. I heard what you said this morning but there was no way I was going to give you up without a fight. What I have to offer you is my love for the rest of your days, Jocelyn. I believe in my heart there was a reason your father wanted me here and now I know what that reason is. You. All I'm asking is that you trust me enough to know that I love you, I'll take care of you and keep you safe for the rest of my life. And I meant what I said. I don't have to return to Charlotte. I'll be content living right in this town with you, as long as the two of us are together."

Tears sprang into Jocelyn's eyes. This beautiful man was willing to make sacrifices for her. "No, everything is worked out now. I've talked to Reese and Leah. They've agreed with my decision to sell the company to Cameron Cody, granted he agrees to all of the concessions I want him to make. That way Reese can use the money Dad left him to start his own business. Leah plans to stay and if things continue to work out, she will eventually open a restaurant next to Reese's shop."

She then smiled brightly. "It seems that Reese and Leah are making progress, so I'll be selling Reese back their home. That means I won't have a place to live. Any ideas?"

Bas took a step closer to her. "Baby, I have plenty. But are you sure you want to sell the company? I know how much Mason Construction means to you."

"Yes, but it was Dad's dream and not really mine. My dream is to be with you, Bas. To love you, marry you and start a family with you. I want lots of babies."

Bas laughed and pulled her into his arms. He held her for a moment before pulling back slightly and capturing her lips with his. The kiss seemed to last forever. When it ended, he pulled her closer into his arms and whispered against her hair, "You want lots of babies, do you?"

Jocelyn chuckled. "Yes, plenty of Steeles."

Bas swept her into his arms and headed for the bedroom. "That's good because I'm ready to give you everything you want, sweetheart."

EPILOGUE

"I LIKE HER, Bas."

Bas smiled at Chance over the rim of his wineglass. "Glad you do because I happen to love her."

Chance chuckled. "That doesn't surprise me."

"I figured it wouldn't."

Chance took a sip of his own drink before asking, "So, have you asked her yet?"

Bas's smile widened. "Yes, and she's said yes. We're planning to wed before the end of the year. That will give her time to wrap up a few things she has going on in Newton Grove, which includes selling the construction company to Cameron."

Chance nodded. "When are you going to tell the family?"

"Later tonight after the party."

"I wish you all the best."

"Thanks and every time I look over at Jocelyn, I know that she is just that. The best."

LATER THAT NIGHT, after Donovan's birthday party, Jocelyn snuggled closer in Bas's arms thinking how her day had gone. She had fallen in love with his family the moment she'd met them all, his brothers, cousins and parents.

Chance's wife, Kylie, was simply too nice for words, and Kylie's best friend, a Queen Latifah lookalike named Lena Spears, was also kind. Jocelyn smiled when she thought about his female cousins, Vanessa, Taylor and Cheyenne. There hadn't been a dull moment with the three of them around.

Jocelyn had noticed the heated looks Cameron Cody had given Vanessa all evening, and the same held true for the looks Morgan Steele had given Lena.

"So what do you think, Bas? Which couple will it be?"

Bas pulled her closer into his arms. He knew what she was asking since she had shared her observations with him earlier. "It will be awhile for Cameron. Vanessa is a hard one to thaw so he has his work cut out for him. My brothers and I are hoping it will be Morgan and Lena. The more she resists him, the moodier he gets. But like I told you, a Steele eventually gets what he or she wants."

Jocelyn lifted her head and gazed down at him. Her expression was suddenly serious. "And did you get what you wanted, Bas?"

He pulled her back down to him, wrapped his arms around her. "I got everything I wanted and more, Jocelyn. I love you."

"And I love you."

And when their mouths connected they knew that they were once again about to generate a little night heat.

* * * * *

PASSION

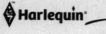
Desire

COMING NEXT MONTH
AVAILABLE MAY 8, 2012

#2155 UNDONE BY HER TENDER TOUCH
Pregnancy & Passion
Maya Banks
When one night with magnate Cam Hollingsworth results in pregnancy, no-strings-attached turns into a tangled web for caterer Pippa Laingley.

#2156 ONE DANCE WITH THE SHEIKH
Dynasties: The Kincaids
Tessa Radley

#2157 THE TIES THAT BIND
Billionaires and Babies
Emilie Rose

#2158 AN INTIMATE BARGAIN
Colorado Cattle Barons
Barbara Dunlop

#2159 RELENTLESS PURSUIT
Lone Star Legacy
Sara Orwig

#2160 READY FOR HER CLOSE-UP
Matchmakers, Inc.
Katherine Garbera

REQUEST YOUR FREE BOOKS!

2 FREE NOVELS
FROM THE ROMANCE COLLECTION
PLUS 2 FREE GIFTS!

YES! Please send me 2 FREE novels from the Romance Collection and my 2 FREE gifts (gifts are worth about $10). After receiving them, if I don't wish to receive any more books, I can return the shipping statement marked "cancel." If I don't cancel, I will receive 4 brand-new novels every month and be billed just $5.99 per book in the U.S. or $6.49 per book in Canada. That's a saving of at least 25% off the cover price. It's quite a bargain! Shipping and handling is just 50¢ per book in the U.S. and 75¢ per book in Canada.* I understand that accepting the 2 free books and gifts places me under no obligation to buy anything. I can always return a shipment and cancel at any time. Even if I never buy another book, the two free books and gifts are mine to keep forever.

194/394 MDN FELQ

Name	(PLEASE PRINT)	
Address		Apt. #
City	State/Prov.	Zip/Postal Code

Signature (if under 18, a parent or guardian must sign)

Mail to the **Reader Service**:
IN U.S.A.: P.O. Box 1867, Buffalo, NY 14240-1867
IN CANADA: P.O. Box 609, Fort Erie, Ontario L2A 5X3

Not valid for current subscribers to the Romance Collection
or the Romance/Suspense Collection.

Want to try two free books from another line?
Call 1-800-873-8635 or visit www.ReaderService.com.

* Terms and prices subject to change without notice. Prices do not include applicable taxes. Sales tax applicable in N.Y. Canadian residents will be charged applicable taxes. Offer not valid in Quebec. This offer is limited to one order per household. All orders subject to credit approval. Credit or debit balances in a customer's account(s) may be offset by any other outstanding balance owed by or to the customer. Please allow 4 to 6 weeks for delivery. Offer available while quantities last.

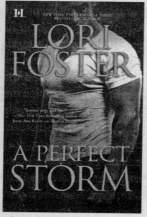

New York Times *and* USA TODAY *bestselling author*
Maya Banks presents book four in her miniseries
PREGNANCY & PASSION

UNDONE BY HER TENDER TOUCH

Available May 2012 from Harlequin® Desire!

"**W**ould you like some help?"

Pippa whirled around, still holding the bottle of champagne, and darn near tossed the contents onto the floor.

"Help?"

Cam nodded slowly. "Assistance? You look as though you could use it. How on earth did you think you'd manage to cater this event on your own?"

Pippa was horrified by his offer and then, as she processed the rest of his statement, she was irritated as hell.

"I'd hate for you to sully those pretty hands," she snapped. "And for your information, I've got this under control. The help didn't show. Not my fault. The food is impeccable, if I do say so myself. I just need to deliver it to the guests."

"I believe I just offered my assistance and you insulted me," Cam said dryly.

Her eyebrows drew together. Oh, why did the man have to be so damn delicious-looking? And why could she never perform the simplest functions around him?

"You're Ashley's guest," Pippa said firmly. "Not to mention you're used to being served, not serving others."

"How do you know what I'm used to?" he asked mildly.

She had absolutely nothing to say to that and watched in bewilderment as he hefted the tray up and walked out of the kitchen.

She sagged against the sink, her pulse racing hard enough

to make her dizzy.

Cameron Hollingsworth was gorgeous, unpolished in a rough and totally sexy way, arrogant and so wrong for her. But there was something about the man that just did it for her.

She sighed. He was a luscious specimen of a male and he couldn't be any less interested in her.

Even so, she was itching to shake his world up a little.

Realizing she was spending far too much time mooning over Cameron, she grabbed another tray, took a deep breath to compose herself and then headed toward the living room.

And Cameron Hollingsworth.

Will Pippa shake up Cameron's world?
Find out in Maya Banks's passionate new novel

UNDONE BY HER TENDER TOUCH

Available May 2012 from Harlequin® Desire!